WINTER FIRE

**Also by Elizabeth Lowell
in Large Print:**

Untamed
Forbidden
Enchanted
Autumn Lover
Forget Me Not

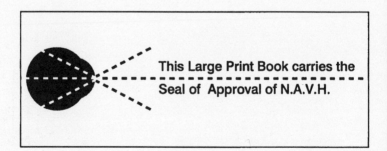

WINTER FIRE

Elizabeth Lowell

Thorndike Press • Thorndike, Maine

Published in 1997 by arrangement with
Avon Books, a division of the Hearst Corporation.

This work is a novel. Any similarity to actual persons or events
is purely coincidental.

Thorndike Large Print ® Americana Series.

The tree indicium is a trademark of Thorndike Press.

The text of this Large Print edition is unabridged.
Other aspects of the book may vary from the original edition.

Set in 16 pt. Bookman Old Style by Minnie B. Raven.

Printed in the United States on permanent paper.

Library of Congress Cataloging in Publication Data

Lowell, Elizabeth, 1944–
    Winter fire / Elizabeth Lowell.
        p.   cm.
    ISBN: 0-7862-0946-1 (lg. print : hc)
    1. Large type books.   I. Title.
[PS3562.O8847W56   1997]
813'.54—dc21   96-46334

For my editor, Carrie Feron,
and for her lovely little Charlotte.

1

Winter 1868
Utah Territory

"Don't move. Don't even breathe."

The man's low, emotionless voice was enough to freeze Sarah Kennedy in place. But even if his voice hadn't stilled her, the rest of him would have.

Moving and breathing just weren't possible.

Sarah was stretched out full-length on her stomach, pinned to cold slick-rock at the edge of a drop-off, flattened beneath a stranger's overwhelming weight. The man covered her from head to heels.

Lord, but that's a lot of man, she thought fearfully. *Not fat. Just big.*

Too big.

Even if the stranger gave her an opening, she wouldn't have a chance in a fight against him. Despite his size, he was quick and quiet as a hawk.

Sarah had never even suspected that she was no longer alone beneath the stone overhang of the shallow cave.

The stranger's body was as hard as the cold rock that was squashing her breasts and gouging her hipbones even through her winter clothing. The man's leather-gloved right hand was across her mouth with a grip that meant to stay there no matter how she twisted or tried to bite him.

She didn't waste her strength in useless fighting. An unhappy marriage had taught her that even a young, healthy girl didn't have much chance against an old man her own size and weight.

The man pinning her down right now was neither old nor her size and weight.

And that wasn't the worst of it.

Despite the dry winter chill, the stranger's left hand was bare. It held a six-gun that looked entirely too well used.

As though Sarah's captor understood that she wasn't going to fight him, his grip eased enough for her to breathe.

But not enough for her to cry out.

"I won't hurt you," the man said very quietly against her ear.

Like hell you won't, she thought.

That's all most men are good for. Hurting women.

Silently she swallowed against the fear and nausea roiling in her stomach.

"Easy now, little one," the man murmured. "I don't mistreat women, horses, or dogs."

She hadn't heard that saying since her father's death. It startled her even as it gave her a flicker of hope.

"But if those Culpeppers gathering at the bottom of the cliff get their hands on you," the stranger continued, "they'll make you pray for death. Your prayers will be answered, but not nearly quick enough to suit you."

A chill washed over Sarah that had nothing to do with the winter night or the icy rock she was lying on.

"Nod if you understand me," the man said.

Despite his educated accents and the hint of a drawl, his voice was low, soft, deadly.

She nodded.

"Now, nod if you believe me," he added dryly.

An absurd desire to laugh shot through her.

Hysteria, she thought. *Get hold of*

yourself. You've been through worse and come out right side up.

Again, Sarah nodded.

"Girl, I hope you're not lying to me."

She shook her head vigorously.

"Good," he murmured. "Because sure as God made little green apples, as soon as you scream we're going to be up to our butts in hot lead."

Once again she felt a crazy desire to laugh. She controlled it.

Barely.

Slowly the stranger's hand came away from her mouth.

Sarah took a long, deep, silent breath. The air she drew into her body tasted of leather and was spiced with an intriguing scent.

Apple, she realized. *He's just eaten an apple.* A bit more of the aching tension left her body.

Her husband had demanded sex only when he was drinking, not when he was eating.

Even more reassuring to her, there wasn't the faintest trace of liquor on the stranger's breath. Nor was there any hint of liquor on his skin or clothes. All she could smell was a trace of soap, leather, heat, and . . . apple.

That's why I'm not as scared as I should be, she realized. *He may be an outlaw, but he's sober, smells clean, and likes apples.*

Maybe he's no meaner than he has to be.

The slow easing of her painful tension communicated itself to the man whose body was covering hers like a heavy, living blanket.

"That's better," the man murmured. "I'm going to take some of my weight off you. But don't you move at all. Not a bit. Hear me?"

Sarah nodded.

With a silence and speed that left her feeling a bit dizzy, the man shifted to one side.

Rock no longer dug into her breasts and belly. Now the weight and strength of the man lay lightly along her right side.

He was still there, still poised. If he wanted to, he could cover her again as swiftly and silently as he had before.

"You all right?" the man asked softly.

She nodded.

Then she wondered if the man would understand her silent communication now that he wasn't close enough to feel her every heartbeat. It was as dark as the inside of a boot beneath the over-hang of rock.

"Good girl," he murmured.

He must have eyes like an eagle, Sarah thought. *Lord, if only I had the wings of an eagle I would fly away.*

The thought sent a shudder of pure longing through her.

"Now don't go all contrary on me," the stranger said softly. "We're not out of this mess by a long sight."

We? she asked silently. *Last time I looked, I was alone and there wasn't any mess at all!*

Men's voices, the creaking of saddle leather, and a horse's impatient snort drifted up from the blackness at the base of the cliff.

In the night stillness of the red rock desert, sound carried a long, long way.

All right, she amended silently. *I was alone and a mess was gathering around me.*

Now I'm not alone. Danger is right within reach.

And it smells of apples.

Sarah struggled against a smile.

She lost.

Case Maxwell saw the flash of her smile. He wondered what the girl found worth smiling about in this unholy mess.

And despite the darkness, despite the heavy men's clothes she wore, Case had no doubt that it was a female he was lying halfway across. She was soft, slender, and smelled of summer roses.

Must be Sarah Kennedy, he decided. *Either that or Big Lola. They're the only white women for several days' ride.*

Somehow he doubted that the girl he had discovered in the shallow cave was Big Lola. Word had it that Lola was man-sized, man-hard, and tough as any sporting gal who had ever ventured west of the Mississippi.

The slender waif who was trying not to smile didn't have the attitude — or the smell — of a sporting gal.

Sarah Kennedy, he said to himself. *Has to be.*

As it had during the Civil War, his mind worked quickly, assembling the information he had on the subject of a girl called Sarah Kennedy.

Widow. Young. Avoids men, quiet as a shadow, and even harder to lasso.

A kid brother called Conner, an old

outlaw known as Ute, and Big Lola live with her on Lost River Canyon ranch.

Wonder why nobody mentioned that Sarah smells of summer roses and has a smile quick as lightning?

Just what the hell is she smiling about, anyway?

He was opening his lips to ask when the sound of approaching horses came up to him from the black and silver land below. The horsemen were headed toward the foot of the cliff, which was barely thirty feet below the cavelike overhang Case was hiding in while he spied on Ab Culpepper and his savage kin.

Then Case had discovered that he wasn't the only one who wanted to listen in on the uneasy negotiations between the Culpepper boys and the outfit known as Moody's Breeds.

Hell of a place to find a girl who dresses like a man and smells like summer rain and roses, he thought.

Hell of a place for a girl, period.

Only a few inches beyond his head was the outer edge of a shallow cave that water had eaten from a solid stone cliff. The far end of the cave was barely ten feet behind his boots.

A tiny stream of water from the seep at the back of the overhang wound along the downward slanting rock just a few inches from his gun. From there the water spun over the lip of stone and out of sight into the night.

That little trickle wouldn't cover the sound of a bird fart, Case thought grimly. *Hope Sarah has as much sense and grit as she seems to.*

Any rash move by either of them would give away their presence to the outlaws below.

At least she had sense enough not to scream, he consoled himself. *We might get out of this yet with our hides intact.*

On the other hand, he wasn't counting on a happy outcome. War and its brutal aftermath had taught him not to expect any kind of luck but the kind that killed you and destroyed whatever you held dear.

Very slowly he lifted his right hand. He touched his index finger against Sarah's lips in a command for silence. Though the touch was light, he felt her flinch away.

Sarah nodded to show she understood that she must be very quiet.

As she nodded, the brushing of her

mouth against his supple glove disturbed Case. He would have sworn that he could feel the warmth of her living breath even through the leather.

It was like touching fire.

An elemental masculine heat shot through him, shocking him.

Bloody hell, as Elyssa would say, he thought. *Of all the damned inconvenient times to get randy.*

Never knew I liked the smell of roses so much.

"— dammit, doesn't have a damned thing to do with it and you damned well know it, dammit."

The voice from below floated up, taking his mind off his unexpected response to the female who lay lightly against him.

"That's Joe Moody," Case breathed against Sarah's ear. "His men call him Dammit, but not to his face."

Again, her smile gleamed swiftly.

"Too ugly to look at?" she suggested in a voice as low as his.

To Case the faint huskiness of her voice was like sipping whiskey. He took a slow, careful, very thorough breath. He told himself that he wasn't doing it to savor the scent of roses and womanly warmth in the midst of desert winter.

The urgent quickening of his body told him that he lied.

"Dammit, that old buzzard found silver, dammit!" Moody said.

"Then why is his widow living no better than an Injun?" came the cold retort.

The tension that went through Case at the sound of the voice lasted only an instant, but Sarah felt it.

Just as she had felt the other change in his body.

"Ab Culpepper," Case said against Sarah's ear.

The quality of his voice sent a queasy chill through her. It was the same unemotional voice he had used when he first overwhelmed her. It was the voice of a man to whom nothing mattered — not heat, not chill, not pain, not pleasure.

Not even death.

"Dammit, how should I know why she ain't living high on the hog on all that silver?" Moody asked in a high voice. "She's a female, dammit!"

"Even the devil don't know a female's mind," Ab agreed calmly. "Worthless sluts, all of them."

Without realizing it Sarah made a low sound of protest and tensed even more. Her husband had sounded a lot like Moody. Half-drunk. All irritable. Unreasonable. Woman hater, except when lust was riding him.

Case felt the subtle return of tension to her body.

"Quiet," he breathed.

She didn't so much as nod her head, but he knew that she understood. She made no more sounds.

"Like I say, dammit!" Moody said triumphantly. "She could be a settin' on all that silver like a broody hen."

"Not with Ute and Big Lola around," Ab said. "Parnell tells me the two of them used to rob banks. Ute won't let no slip of a girl stand between him and a heap of Spanish silver."

"Dammit, maybe he don't know, dammit!"

A horse stamped impatiently. Or a mule.

Sarah couldn't be certain. She only knew that the Culpeppers rode big sorrel mules that were faster than lightning and lean as mustangs.

"Moody," Ab said impatiently, "a man can't eat no silver."

"Dammit, we ain't gone hungry. My boys —"

"— rustle too close to home," Ab interrupted. "Them beeves two of your boys just butchered back of camp are Circle A stock."

"So?" Moody challenged.

"That's only two days' ride from Spring Canyon," Ab said flatly. "I told you three days and no less."

" 'Twas three days, dammit!"

"What y'all riding?" a third voice asked sarcastically. "Two-legged possums?"

That comment was followed by loud voices and swearing between the Culpeppers and Moody's men about the speed of horses versus mules.

Case listened intently, trying to sort out the voices.

Parnell Culpepper was easy to recognize. His voice was thin and grating. His cousin Quincy had a fuller voice, but no easier on the ears. Reginald Culpepper, who was both cousin and brother to the other two, hardly ever said anything.

Kester Culpepper wasn't much more talkative, unless he was drunk. Then he didn't shut up until he passed out

19

or someone got sick of his rambling and knocked him senseless.

Moody's men were harder for Case to sort out, because he had spent less time stalking them. There was one called Crip, whose left arm was withered. Word had it that he made up for the injury with the strength of his right arm and a sawed-off, lever-action rifle.

Another man was called Whiskey Jim. He drank. When he was sober, he was a good hand with dynamite, a useful skill for former bank robbers.

There were at least five others in the gang known as Moody's Breeds, but Case hadn't put names with the faces or voices yet. He had been too busy keeping track of Culpeppers.

This time he was going to be certain that not one of them escaped. The Culpeppers' long history of raiding, rape, and murder was going to end here, in the wilderness of red stone.

No more men coming home to find their ranches ruined and their women tortured and killed, he thought.

No more broken children thrown away like whiskey bottles along the trail.

Case was going to see to it.

Personally.

Yet it wasn't a hot, passionate need for vengeance that drove him. War had burned all emotion out of him, except for the bond with his older brother, Hunter — the brother Case had dragged off to join a futile war.

After the war the brothers went home to Texas, expecting to create a better life. They found nothing left of their home but the sickening wreckage of a Culpepper raid.

If Case felt anything at all these days, it was in his dreams, and he was careful not to remember them.

All that moved him was a cold sense of justice. The way he saw it, God had been too busy to take care of all His children during the war. The devil, however, had looked after his own.

Now Case was going to balance the scales.

"Shut up, all of you!"

Ab's cold voice cut through the heckling like a knife, gutting the argument, leaving silence welling up as thick as blood.

Sarah fought against an urge to flee. At his very worst, Hal had sounded just like Ab. That was when she had grabbed Conner and escaped into the

21

maze of red stone pillars and dry canyons. Only the birds of prey could find their way through the stone wilderness.

She had watched the wild birds, and she had learned. She and her younger brother had survived the grim times when her husband went crazy with drink.

But running right now will get you killed, she reminded herself fiercely. *Then who would take care of Conner? Ute is loyal only to me and Lola is loyal only to Ute.*

Conner would be on his own.

Just as Sarah had been on her own after her parents died in the flood. That was what had driven her at fourteen to marry a stranger three times her age.

Thank God Hal is dead, she thought, not for the first time.

Once she had felt guilty for being glad to be rid of her cruel husband. Once, but no more. She was simply grateful that she and her younger brother had survived Hal Kennedy.

"We agreed on no raiding close to Spring Canyon," Ab said loudly. "Remember, Moody?"

"Dammit, I —"

"You remember or not?" Ab snarled.

Case saw the hints of movement below as members of the Moody bunch squared off against the Culpeppers.

Good, he thought. *Maybe Moody will just kill the lot of them and spare me the trouble. Then I can get on with looking for a place to build a ranch of my own.*

But Case didn't really think he would get that lucky. Ab Culpepper was too wily to be killed by the likes of Moody.

"Dammit!" Moody said.

He repeated himself several times. There was more bluster than conviction in his voice.

"The Circle A is too close," Ab said. "You want beef, you go farther. You want game, you hunt anywhere you please. Savvy?"

"Dammit, I still think —"

"You don't think nothin'," Ab interrupted impatiently. "That's my job. If you was any good at thinking, you wouldn't be dead broke in winter, chasing your own tail in this red hell."

"You're doin' the same thing, dammit."

"I got twenty Yankee dollars, saddlebags full of bullets, and I ain't chasing nothing."

"Dammit! We go all the way to New

Mexico Territory for our beef and, dammit, we don't have no time to look for Spanish silver, dammit."

"You can look after we get the meat we need so we ain't eating roots like Injuns come spring."

"What about women, dammit?"

"What about them, dammit?" Ab mocked.

"A man can't go all winter without a woman to warm his jeans and cook his beans."

"Steal or buy some down in Mexico. Or get a Injun."

"Dam—"

"Just be damned sure she ain't no chief's wife or daughter, savvy?" Ab said, talking right over Moody. "Some of them redskins are pure poison when they're on the prod."

If Case had been a smiling kind of man, the words would have made him smile. He knew just why Ab was so touchy on the subject of stealing the wrong Indian girl.

Over in the Ruby Mountains of Nevada, Ab and some of his kin had tangled with Indians over a stolen girl. Ab and Kester were the only Culpeppers who survived. They had faded out of the losing fight, mounted up, and gone to join their remaining kin in Utah Territory.

"What about them two white women over to Lost River Canyon?" asked a new voice. "They's close. All they got guarding them is a kid and that old outlaw. Them's good odds."

"That girl is supposed to be right tasty, dammit," Moody said eagerly.

Other men joined in with a chorus of rough comments about the girl they had seen only through their spyglasses.

Hearing the voices, Sarah fought against the nausea that was trying to wring her stomach like a washrag.

"Shut up," Ab said flatly. "Get it through your noggins. Ain't no raiding close to camp."

"But —"

"*Shut up.*"

For a moment there was only the faint sound of water trickling down stone into darkness.

"Nothin' riles the army like a white woman gettin' raped by half-breeds," Ab said coldly. "If I decide the Kennedy widow needs taking care of, I'll do it personally and legally. I'll marry it."

There were faint grumblings from Moody and his men, but no real protest. When they first met, one of Moody's gang had tested Ab's temper. The man had died before his gun was even partway out of the holster.

Ab was as fast with a six-shooter as any man Moody's Breeds had ever seen, and they thought they had seen them all.

Until Ab Culpepper.

"Be easier to winter at Lost River ranch, dammit," Moody said.

"Easy ain't always best. Time you learned that. We're gonna do just what we planned."

"Stay in Spring Canyon?" asked another voice. "*Por Dios*, the wind there, she is very cold."

"If you and the rest of the breeds got the lead out of your butts," Ab said, "camp would be snug as a tick in a hound's ear."

Someone swore in disgust but no one spoke up.

"I'll kill the next man I see rustling Circle A beef," Ab said.

No one said a word.

"Same for any man who messes with them white women," he added.

"Even Big Lola?" Moody asked in disbelief.

"I hear she done give up the sporting life."

"Sure, but dammit, she's just an old whore, dammit!"

"Leave her be. We're gonna do what them 'Paches do. Live quiet at home and raid far off."

There were restless movements but no voice spoke against Ab Culpepper's calm, ruthless orders.

"In a year or so," Ab said, "we'll have ourselves a thousand head of stock and enough women for a sultan's palace. Anyone got trouble with that?"

Silence.

"All right. Get your tails back to camp. Kester and me will ride the back trail and see if any Circle A folks take a notion to come calling. You got any questions, talk to Parnell."

Shod hooves clicked on stones. The unshod hooves of the mustangs Moody's men rode made less noise.

The smell of dust rose up to the shallow cave where Sarah and Case lay motionless.

After it had been silent for several minutes, she started to get up. In-

27

stantly he was over her again, flattening her, silencing her with a hand across her mouth.

"Ab," was all Case whispered.

It was all he had to say. She became utterly still.

Long minutes went by.

"Told you," Kester said.

"An' I'm telling you," Ab said, "that someone is out there."

"Ghost."

"Ghost," Ab mocked. "Ain't no ghosts, boy. How many times I have to tell you?"

"Seen 'em."

"Only at the bottom of a bottle."

"Seen 'em," Kester repeated.

"Ain't you the baby. Pa woulda kicked your sorry ass all the way round the holler."

"Seen 'em."

"Shee-it. Next you'll be whining about them Texicans following us."

"Ain't seen 'em."

"Shee-it."

With that, Ab reined his mule around and trotted off into the darkness. Kester's mule followed.

Case didn't move.

Neither did Sarah, for the simple reason that she was still pinned beneath him.

Finally, slowly, he rolled aside. Before she could move to get up, he pressed a hand firmly between her shoulder blades.

Together, motionless, they listened to the immense silence of the land.

If she hadn't been accustomed to hunting or simply watching wild animals, she would have grown impatient long before Case gave her any signal that it was all right to move.

But she had spent many years with a rifle or shotgun, providing food for her younger brother and her worthless, treasure-hunting husband. She endured the discomfort because there was no other sensible thing to do.

Her patience impressed Case as much as her absolute stillness. He had known few men and no women who could be motionless for long periods of time. Sooner or later, most men fidgeted.

Sooner or later, most men died.

Lord, but this girl smells good, he thought. *Feels good, too. Soft, but not pudding soft. Like a rosebud, all springy and alive.*

Wonder if she tastes like rain and heat and roses all mixed together?

With a silent curse at his unruly thoughts — and body — Case lifted his hand from Sarah's back, freeing her.

"Keep your voice down," he said softly. "Sound carries a long way down these stone draws."

"I know."

"You have a horse?"

"No."

What she didn't say was that a horse would have made too much noise, alerting Conner that she was going off alone into the night. She had done that more and more often lately, driven by a restlessness she didn't understand. She only knew that she found peace in the clean, moonlit silence of the land.

"Can you ride, Mrs. Kennedy?" Case asked.

"Yes."

"I'll see you safely home."

"That's not necessary, Mr., er . . ."

"Just call me Case. My horse is in a grassy draw off to the south," he said. "You know the place?"

"Yes."

"Good. I'll follow you."

Sarah started to speak, shrugged,

and turned away. There was no point in arguing. If he wanted to see her home, then he would do so whether she liked it or not.

Yet if he indeed was following her, he didn't make any noise about it. After a few minutes her curiosity won out. She stopped and turned around to look for him.

He was right there.

The startled sound she made at seeing him looming so close behind her brought an even more startling reaction from him. One instant his hands were empty. The next instant a six-gun was gleaming in the moonlight, cocked and ready to fire.

Case took a gliding step, then another, not stopping until he was close enough to breathe a soft question into Sarah's ear.

"What's wrong?" he asked.

"I didn't hear you, so I turned and you were right on my heels," she whispered. "It surprised me, that's all."

The gun vanished into its holster with as little warning as it had appeared.

"Being noisy can get a man killed," he said matter-of-factly. "Especially in a war."

Sarah took a shaky breath, turned around, and started walking again.

His horse was waiting at the narrow end of the draw. The only noise the big animal made was the quiet ripping of grass as he grazed in the little oasis. When the horse scented her, his head came up fast, ears pricked.

The shape of the horse's head against the moonlight told her that this was no ordinary animal. The clean lines, straight nose, flaring nostrils, and widely spaced eyes shouted of good breeding.

"Stay back," Case said to Sarah. Then, "Easy, Cricket. It's just me."

When he brushed past her, she realized why he was so soft on his feet. He was wearing knee-high fringed moccasins rather than the boots most white men wore.

With smooth, efficient motions, Case tightened the saddle cinch, picked up the reins, and led Cricket toward her.

The horse was huge.

"Biggest cricket I've ever seen," she muttered. "Seventeen hands if he's an inch."

"He was cricket-sized when I named him."

She doubted it, but kept her mouth shut.

"Let him get your scent," Case said. "Don't be afraid. He's a stallion, but he's a gentleman as long as I'm around."

"Afraid of a horse?" she retorted. "Not on your life."

Then her voice changed. It became low, soothing, almost singsong, as clear and unthreatening as the murmur of water in a creek.

Cricket was as pleased by the musical sounds as Case was. The stallion's surprisingly delicate velvet muzzle snuffled over her hat, lipped at her long braids, and whuffled over her wool jacket. Then Cricket lowered his head and butted her chest in a naked request to be petted.

Sarah's soft laughter licked over Case like fire. He watched without a word while she slipped off her gloves and rubbed Cricket's head and ears. She slid her fingers under the bridle to the spots where leather itched on horsehide and only human hands could scratch.

Cricket sighed, nudged again, then leaned his head against her chest, as relaxed as a dog.

Case couldn't help wondering how it

would feel to have such sweetly knowing hands in his hair, on his body, and
to hear her pleased laughter at his
response.

Damnation, he swore silently. *What's
wrong with me? I keep thinking like that
and it's going to be a long, uncomfortable
ride.*

"Need any help getting on?" he asked
curtly.

"He's your horse. Do I?"

Case moved so quickly that Sarah
never knew what happened. One moment she was petting Cricket. The next
instant she was in the saddle with the
memory of Case lifting her as though
she weighed no more than moonlight.

Before she could adjust to the
change, he made another lightning
move. Suddenly he was behind her,
surrounding her.

She went rigid as old terror exploded
in her.

Cricket sensed her fear and shied
wildly.

"Easy," Case said in a soft voice.
Then, less gently, "I thought you said
you could ride."

"I can," she said through her teeth.

"Then take the ramrod out of your

spine. You're making Cricket nervous."

Sarah let out a long breath as she realized that he had been reaching for the reins, not for her.

"You're a sudden sort of man," she muttered

"So I'm told."

He reined the stallion around and headed out of the ravine.

Slowly she relaxed. Cricket's walk was an easy, swinging sort of gait that covered a lot of ground without any fuss at all.

"Good horse," she said after a time. "Really good."

"He and Bugle Boy are the last of them."

"Of what?"

"The horses my brother and I bred. War and raiders got the rest, including my brother's family."

His voice was calm, emotionless, as though he were describing something that had happened to a stranger.

"At least you had something left," Sarah said. "All I had was a ragged dress, a young brother, and enough hunger to eat grass."

"War?"

"Hurricane. Six years ago."

Subtly Case shifted position, trying to get more comfortable. The fragrance and warmth and closeness of Sarah Kennedy were giving his body pure hell.

"Louisiana?" he asked, forcing himself to speak normally.

"East Texas."

He took a breath. The scent of female warmth and roses made him wish he hadn't.

"Six years?" he said. "You must have been a kid."

"Thirteen going on fourteen. Old enough."

"For what?"

"Marriage."

The tone of her voice didn't encourage any more questions.

That was all right with Case. The faintly husky, wholly feminine sound of her voice was doing nothing to settle the heavy running of his blood.

Cricket's big strides ate up the few miles to Sarah's home. She never gave directions. Case never asked.

He knew exactly where to go.

The realization sank into her as slowly and completely as the scent of apples, horse, and leather. Yet instead of being frightened that a stranger knew

36

the precise location of her isolated home, she was intrigued.

Wonder what he's doing here? She asked herself.

She didn't voice her curiosity aloud. Even if she had been rude enough to ask Case what he was doing in the wilderness, she wasn't a fool. Only outlaws, Indians, prospectors, cowboys, and crazy artists came to the remote stone desert that was her home.

She doubted that he was a cowhand. Cricket certainly wasn't an ordinary cow pony. Nor was there any sign of prospecting gear tied on behind the saddle.

From what she could see of him, he didn't look Indian. That left outlaw or crazy artist.

Whatever else Case was, he wasn't crazy.

He reined in at the head of the steep trail that led down to Lost River Canyon's wide, cottonwood-lined valley. Because the moon shone brilliantly between the flying clouds, he was careful to stay in shadows.

A few hundred feet below the lip of the plateau, a lantern shone through the cracks of an awkwardly built cabin.

A pole corral with a woven willow shelter at one end served as a barn. There was an orderly kitchen garden, fruit trees bare-branched in winter, and meadow hay stacked behind the willow shelter. A wickiup and a small, low hut stood well off to one side.

"Who's on guard?" Case asked.

"No one."

His eyes narrowed. Instinct told him two things. The first was that she wasn't lying.

The second was that someone was on guard.

With a swift movement he dismounted, keeping the bulk of Cricket between himself and the small ranch.

"No point in alarming your menfolk," he said. "I'll watch you to safety from here."

Sarah wasn't surprised to find herself lifted off the big stallion and lowered to the ground. What surprised her was that she was beginning to like the feel of Case's strength as much as she liked the scent of apples on his breath.

I wonder what he looks like beneath that wide-brimmed hat, she thought. *His eyes seem light and his hair is dark, he hasn't shaved in a week or two, but he's clean otherwise.*

Would he taste like apples warmed by the sun?

The idle thought shocked her more than anything else that had happened that night.

Case heard the broken breath she drew and saw the sudden widening of her eyes. He knew with primitive certainty that the same fire burning in him had touched her as well.

"Don't go out alone again," he said flatly. "Next time I might not be around to get you out of trouble."

"I wasn't *in* trouble until you flattened me beneath you like a shirt for ironing," she retorted.

"I'm sorry. I didn't mean to hurt you."

"You didn't. You're just . . . a lot of man."

Again, the husky edge to her voice touched him like a whip of fire.

"Stop looking at me like that," he said.

"Like what?"

"Like a girl with love on her mind. There's no love left in me. All I have is *this.*"

He bent and caught her mouth beneath his. He meant the kiss to be hard and swift, a warning not to spin dreams around him.

Yet as he bent down, he drew in the scent of roses.

He found he could no more ravage her mouth than he would have shredded a rosebud. The tip of his tongue glided over her lips in a tender, searing caress.

Then Case was gone, leaving Sarah alone in the night with the taste of a stranger on her lips and the wonder of her first kiss shivering through her body.

2

The next morning Case was awake well before dawn. The desert night had been cold as a mountain creek, but that wasn't why he was up and about early.

He hadn't slept much. The taste of Sarah kept coming to him just as he drifted off to sleep. Then he would come awake in a rush that guaranteed he would stay awake until his blood cooled.

That was why he was up before the sun, sitting on his heels, talking to his horse.

"Well, Cricket. I was right. She tasted of roses and heat and just enough salt to tell a man that she's all woman."

The big bay stallion flicked an ear in Case's direction, but didn't otherwise interrupt his grazing.

"And I'm a damned fool for finding out."

Cricket snorted, swept his muzzle across his foreleg, and resumed grazing.

"No need to rub it in."

The horse ignored him.

"What Sarah doesn't know is that Ab isn't a patient man. Along about the first real snow, he'll get tired of living in a brush wickiup. He'll start thinking about that crooked little cabin and the warm girl inside it."

Cricket lifted his head, pricked his ears, and looked beyond Case.

Even as he spun around and came to his feet, a six-gun appeared in his left hand. Calmly he waited for whatever the horse had already discovered.

From the crest of the ravine, a coyote's yapping howl rose into a sky that was slowly being bleached of stars by a lemon-colored dawn.

After a moment Cricket returned to grazing.

"Just a lonely song dog, huh?"

He holstered his six-gun and went back to sitting on his heels. Since he wasn't planning on stalking anyone at the moment, he was wearing riding boots instead of moccasins.

There was no fire to give warmth and comfort to the cold dawn. His breakfast was as spare as his camp — jerky, hard biscuits, and water from the seep where he had found Sarah Kennedy hiding.

Ab knows about her, Case thought uneasily. *He knows where she is. He knows all she has to defend her is an old outlaw, a whore, and a boy.*

"Maybe I should stop dogging Ab's trail and waiting for a chance to get the Culpeppers all at once," he said to Cricket.

Grass ripped off by strong white teeth was Cricket's only comment.

"Maybe I should hang out in that rawhide little settlement over to the river. That's where the boys let off steam. What do you think, Cricket?"

Whatever the stallion thought, he kept on grazing.

"I could take cards in another poker game," Case said. "Sooner or later one of the Culpeppers will call me out, just like their kin Jeremiah and Ichabod did down near the Spanish Bottoms."

He didn't talk about the fact that Ichabod had been almost as fast on the draw as Case himself. He had come very close to dying that night.

It hadn't mattered too much then.

Now it bothered him a bit. Not the thought of dying. The war had burned that emotion out of him along with the others.

But he couldn't help feeling responsible for Sarah.

He knew with gut-wrenching certainty just how cruel Ab could be to women. Case had seen the results of Ab's work, and that of his kin, scattered from Texas to Nevada. The more helpless the victim, the better the Culpeppers liked it.

Even children weren't safe.

Ted and little Em, Case thought. *They would still be alive if I hadn't talked Hunter into going off to war to fight for honor and nobility and Rebel pride.*

At fifteen I was all hellfire and brimstone, ready to kill Yankees from dawn to sundown to dawn.

At fifteen I was a real horse's butt.

There was no heat in his thoughts, simply acceptance. He had taken Hunter away from family and off to war, leaving the little children in the hands of their mother, a woman who wasn't fit to raise a pup, much less a child.

No one had been there when the Culpeppers descended on Ted and little Emily.

Water under the bridge, he told himself. *Or it will be when I shovel dirt on the last Culpepper grave.*

"Sooner I start, sooner I finish," he said aloud. "Then I can stop burying garbage and get on with what's important — finding the right place for a ranch."

He swallowed the last of the water from his tin cup, hooked it onto his belt, and stood.

Dawn spilled over the land in a silent golden wave. Pillars, buttes, pinnacles, mesas, and plateaus of solid stone condensed out of the dawn in every shade of red and darkness.

As though summoned by daybreak, a long wind stirred. Clean, cold air curled around Case like a lover, ruffling his black hair and caressing his face. The air was scented with time and distance, stone and ancient sunrises.

The song dog called again.

The wind answered.

"I'll build my ranch in a place like this," he said softly. "These stone battlements were here long before Adam. They'll be here long after the last man is nothing but the taste of ashes in God's mouth."

For a few moments longer he stood and watched the land being born from the womb of the night. Something close to peace softened the hard line of his mouth.

"The land abides," he said. "No matter how foolish or evil men are, the land is born clean again each day."

The coyote sang once more, then was silent.

"Amen, brother. Amen."

His mind made up, he turned away from the haunting beauty of the dawn. With an economy of motion that spoke of long practice living out of saddlebags, he rolled his bedding in a tarpaulin, tied it, and set it aside.

The saddle was upside down over a rock so that the sheepskin lining could dry out. So was the saddle blanket, which doubled as extra bedding for Case when the weather was bitter.

As soon as he reached for the saddle, Cricket started grazing faster. The stallion knew they would be on the trail soon. Grass in the stone desert wasn't easy to come by.

The horse didn't pause in his eating while Case gave him a quick grooming, cleaned his hooves, and cinched the saddle up tight.

As always, Case checked his repeating rifle and shotgun before he mounted. As always, he found them in battle-ready condition. He slid them into their individual saddle sheaths.

He didn't need to check his six-gun. He had done that the instant he awakened.

Quickly he tied on the saddlebags and the bedroll, picked up Cricket's bridle, and looked around for anything that he might have forgotten.

The ground was bare of everything except tracks. Case wasn't a forgetting kind of man.

As he approached Cricket, bridle in hand, the stallion ripped grass, chewed, and swallowed with impressive speed.

"You just love slobbering up that bit with green stuff, don't you?"

The stallion lifted his head to receive the bit. Ropes of green drool hung down either side of his elegant muzzle.

Case made a disgusted sound. "I know you're laughing at me, you spoiled devil."

Despite his words, he was gentle as he bridled Cricket. He had been raised to value good horseflesh in the same way a smart man valued a good weapon. Take care of them and they would take care of you in turn.

Too bad people aren't like horses and guns, he thought. *Be fewer wars that way.*

And no Culpeppers at all.

He swung into the saddle with a swift, easy movement. Cricket didn't flatten his ears or hump his back like many Western horses first thing in the morning. He accepted being ridden the same way he accepted dawn, just a normal part of life.

"C'mon, Cricket. Let's you and me check out that raggedy-ass wickiup saloon. We'll see if that one-eyed padre is marking the cards any smarter this time."

It was late afternoon before Case reached the place that was mockingly referred to by one and all as Spanish Church.

The name partly came from the fact that the huge rock formation that was the rear wall of the building looked like a Spanish church if the man doing the looking was too drunk to focus very well. The rest of the name owed its origins to the original owner of the saloon, Pader Gunther. Pader was quickly corrupted into "padre." Since then, whoever ran the bar was called the padre.

The nickname Spanish Church stuck to the place like a bad reputation. The bad reputation, at least, was earned.

The settlement was hardly more than a handful of rough shacks strewn along Cottonwood River. Most of the time the "river" was a creek small enough to spit across, but it ran year-round, which was rare in this part of the West. The creek's source was in a cluster of distant mountains, where spring runoff raced down from snowy peaks through dry slickrock country, and from there into a maze of stone canyons no white man had penetrated.

Spanish Church had no real street, no building worthy of the name, and no stable. The watering trough was the same muddy pool that supplied drinking water for the humans whose thirst wasn't quenched by the local rotgut.

From the top of the nearby rise, Case watched Spanish Church through his spyglass. He could see eight riding animals tied or hobbled along the creek.

Two of them were sorrel mules.

No matter how carefully he studied the mules, he couldn't tell which

49

Culpepper was inside the brush and canvas structure that passed for a saloon.

"Good thing you spent most of the night filling your belly," he said to Cricket. "It's mighty thin pickings down there for man and beast alike."

Too many animals had been left along the creek to forage for themselves while their riders drank away the days and nights until their money or their stomachs gave out.

"Maybe Ab rode one of those mules," Case said softly. "Maybe I'll just cut off the snake's head and let the rest of the body thrash around until it dies of its own accord."

Maybe . . .

His mouth flattened into a grim line beneath his black beard stubble.

But not damned likely, he thought. *Ab might have been the one who personally savaged Ted and Em before he sold them to the Comancheros, but the rest of his kith and kin didn't raise a finger to stop him.*

For a few minutes longer Case weighed the advantages and dangers of riding into the settlement.

If Ab was there, Case would be recognized, but not as one of the "Texicans" who was following the Culpeppers with a saddlebag full of "Wanted Dead or Alive" posters.

Ab would see him as a gunhand hired in Nevada's Ruby Mountains by the recently deceased Gaylord Culpepper. The Culpeppers had tried to get a good hideout the easy way — an outright grab of the B Bar and Ladder S ranches from their legal owners.

The grab had failed, but it had been touch and go for a while.

What Case didn't know was whether anyone had figured out that he had been working against the Culpeppers in Nevada.

If Ab knew, he would shoot Case on sight.

Only one way to find out, he decided.

Absently he drew his six-gun, spun the cylinder to check the load once more, holstered the gun, and secured the revolver with a rawhide thong. He pulled a second cylinder from his jacket pocket, saw that it was fully loaded, and put it away once more.

It would be nice to have Hunter at my back when I ride down there, he thought.

Then he thought of Elyssa, who loved Hunter as few men were ever privileged to be loved by a woman.

Better for Hunter to stay in the Rubys. If I don't come back, no woman will hang crêpe and no kids will go hungry.

He mounted Cricket with the same economy of movement that he did everything. Until people saw Case standing next to other men, his size wasn't noticeable. He was just another quiet, easy-moving man who was thoroughly at home on a horse.

As always, he inspected the enemy territory close up in addition to his earlier study at a distance. He chose a path down the long rise that would circle the settlement.

He wasn't particularly expecting guards or an ambush. On the other hand, it wouldn't have surprised him. Spanish Church was no place for choirboys.

The first man he saw was facedown near a huge clump of rabbit brush. He was either dead drunk or dead, period. It was hard to say from a hundred feet away, and that was as close as Case planned on coming.

Cricket cocked an ear in the man's

direction, snorted, and chose a wide path around him.

"Don't blame you, boy," Case said. "I've smelled sweeter skunks left out in the sun to dry."

Before he went into the saloon, he reined Cricket in a circle around the other grazing animals, checking brands.

Circle A. Rocking M.

He recognized the brands instantly. Both were from ranches that were close to Sarah Kennedy's home. Not very close, however. Calling them neighbors would be stretching the truth thin enough to read newsprint through.

The owners of the Circle A and Rocking M had settled in the water-rich high country. It was a hard two days' ride from the stone desert where Hal Kennedy had staked his claim.

The remaining horses wore brands that were either botched too badly to read or had been deliberately doctored to change the original brand.

The mules' shiny sorrel hides weren't branded at all.

There were three more horses back up a shady draw, standing three-legged and swatting flies with their long tails.

One horse was saddled. The others wore packs full of supplies. The packs were tied off with neat diamond hitches.

The horses were mustangs, but they had good clean legs, reasonably deep chests, and muscular rumps. Though obviously well cared for, the animals weren't shod. They didn't need to be. Any mustang that got sore feet from running over stony ground didn't last long enough to grow up in the first place.

Pick of the litter, Case thought, looking at the three mustangs. *Somebody around here knows horseflesh.*

When he went closer, he saw that all of the mustangs wore the same brand: S-C.

S-C Connected, he thought. *Sarah Kennedy's brand.*

Wonder if she knows that three of her horses have wandered off to this outlaw's nest?

When he closed in on the three horses, he saw that there was a small seep at the head of the ravine. There had been enough rain in autumn and early winter so that the seep was running even after summer's natural drought.

Though the hooves of the other horses had cut deeply into the red soil around the seep, the water was still clear. He let Cricket drink, but not enough to make the stallion logy if they had to leave the settlement at a hard run.

"Sorry, boy," he said as he reined Cricket away from the water. "You're going to stay on duty for a time."

True to his word, Case left the saddle cinched up tight when he tied Cricket to a bush on the sunny side of the "church." The spot he chose was close to the front door of the saloon — if a stained, tattered canvas flap could be called a front door.

He knew that his greatest moment of danger would come when he ducked under the tarp and went from bright sun to smoke-filled gloom in the space of a breath. He didn't hesitate. He simply slipped the thong that secured his six-gun in its holster as he bent and entered the saloon.

A fast glance told him there were fewer men in the room than there were horses outside. He didn't like that, but there was nothing he could do about it.

Maybe they're sleeping off their toot

somewhere in the brush, he told himself.

But he didn't count on it. He chose a place at the bar that would give him a clear view of the dingy room and the only door.

No one came to wait on him.

No one was asleep in the narrow room that had been dug out of rock behind the bar.

He turned his back on the empty bar and looked over the rest of the saloon.

Four men were playing cards. Two were Culpeppers, but Ab wasn't one of them. Though there was little physical difference between Culpeppers — they ran to lean, squinty, straw-blond, and mean — Case had been chasing his enemies long enough to tell them apart.

Quincy, Reginald, and no Ab, he thought in disgust. *Damnation. That old boy never is around when dying time comes.*

He cooled the flick of irritation by reminding himself that Quincy and Reginald weren't exactly wide-eyed virgins. Their names were on most of the "Wanted" posters in Cricket's saddlebags. They were reputed to be gun handy and ready to draw at a sideways look. Though they were fast with their belt guns, it was whispered both men preferred to ambush their prey.

Reginald and Quincy were infamous for gut-shooting anyone who displeased them and then betting on how long the unlucky man would live. One of their victims had lasted three weeks. At the end, the bets were on how often he would scream before he finally packed it in.

A fifth man was sprawled near the fire, snoring. A thin, mangy dog was stretched out next to him.

Case began sizing up the room itself. It was little more than a natural overhang walled off on three sides by brush and covered by canvas that had been old about the time Lazarus was raised from the dead.

There was no chimney for the fire that burned inside a ragged circle of red rocks. Smoke just drifted through the room, joined by streams curling up from cigarettes and cheroots. If the wind blew hard enough, the air cleared a bit. It also got cold enough to hang meat.

Spanish Church wasn't a lounging around kind of place with a cherrywood bar, brass foot rails, mirrors, and fancy spittoons. The bar was made of whiskey barrels with planks stretched across their tops. The tables were the same, except for the one that had come from the bottom of Pader Gunther's original wagon.

Whiskey barrels cut in half and turned upside down served as chairs. Other chairs were made of mismatched cottonwood branches with cowhide stretched across for a seat. Wherever men hadn't sat, hair in shades of red and brindle and white still clung to the stiff hides.

There were many brands on the cowhides. Spanish Church had been a trading place for outlaws and rustlers for as long as the settlement had been crouched along a source of good water in a dry wilderness.

"Anyone seen the padre?" Case asked easily.

"Don't boil your kettle," Quincy said without looking up from his tattered cards. "He's a-getting his beauty sleep."

Case glanced at the bartender and the dog. "That his wife?"

One of the men snickered. He wore his gray-streaked hair Indian style, cut off at the shoulders with a knife and held away from his eyes by a band across his forehead. The headband wasn't made of a rag or a length of rawhide. It was woven with a bold design that was neither Indian nor European.

Though the man was a half-breed, he wasn't a member of Moody's gang.

That's the old outlaw they call Ute, Case thought. *He must be here to get supplies for Sarah.*

Or himself. He wouldn't be the first man to steal from a widow and kid.

Ute looked at the sleeping man and dog, snickered again, and glanced at Case. Abruptly the old outlaw's eyes narrowed, as though he somehow recognized Case.

If so, Ute neither said nor did anything to draw attention to him.

"Old man, ya gonna ante up or pass gas?" Reginald snarled at Ute.

The tone of his voice said that he was on the losing end of the card game.

Ute scooped a handful of silver coins from the table and dropped them in his pocket. Then he gave Reginald a gap-toothed smile and said in Spanish that his mother was a whore and his sister walked on all fours.

The man to Reginald's left smiled thinly, but neither Culpepper knew enough Spanish to realize the insult.

"Hey, you ain't gonna take my money without giving me no chance to win it back!" Reginald said.

"Come here at the new moon," Ute said.

"But —"

Whatever else Reginald wanted to say was cut off when Ute kicked over the table and shot to his feet with a speed surprising in a man his age.

By the time the other players recovered, Ute was standing up, waiting for whatever came. A double-barreled shotgun was in his hands. Both hammers were eared back and ready to go. One of his thick, scarred fingers was across the triggers.

"New moon," Ute said.

Case was careful not to move. He also kept both hands in sight, a courtesy that didn't pass unnoticed.

Ute gave him a gap-toothed grin and backed out of the room before either Culpepper could stop him.

"I'm gonna gut-shoot that son of a bitch," Reginald said bitterly.

"Not today you ain't," Quincy said. "Today we're playing cards. Deal, Beaver."

The man called Beaver picked up the cards and dealt.

The padre snored.

Case sauntered over to the fire and gave the padre's rump a brisk nudge with the toe of his boot.

The padre kept right on snoring.

"Man enjoys his own bug juice," Case said to no one in particular.

"I'm flat as a flea," Reginald said. "Gimme the ante, Quincy."

"You ain't paid me from the last time."

"Shee-it. I'm your brother!"

"Half-brother."

"Shee-*it*."

Reginald turned his back on the table in disgust. He focused on the first thing that came into view.

Case.

"Ain't I seen you?" Reginald asked.

"I've been here and there."

"Where you been lately?" he demanded.

Beaver cast a worried look over his cards. Asking a man where he was from was not only rude, it could be dangerous. Reginald might be too irritable to miss the stranger's quiet self-confidence, but Beaver wasn't.

Instinctively Beaver began looking for a place to go when the lead started flying. He had no intention of helping Reginald out. As far as he was concerned, there were too many Culpeppers hanging around as it was. One more or less wouldn't be missed.

"There," Case said.

"Huh?" Reginald asked.

"You asked me where I've been," he said calmly. "I told you."

Reginald came to his feet in a rush. "There?" he repeated. "Shee-it, what kinda answer is that?"

"The only kind you're going to get."

Quincy leaped to his feet.

Beaver dove for what he hoped would be a quiet corner of the saloon.

"You're outnumbered, boy," Quincy said, "or can't you count that high?"

"I can count, but I don't count fleas."

"Are you calling us fleas?" Reginald demanded.

"Not me," Case said. "I have no call to insult fleas."

With the speed of striking snakes, the Culpeppers went for their belt guns.

Damn, those boys are fast!

Even as the thought flashed through

His hands were frighteningly clumsy.

Got to get home, he thought dizzily.

But he had no home.

With the last of his strength, he sent Cricket toward the stone wilderness at a dead run.

his mind, Case drew and fired in a relentless roll of thunder that didn't stop until there were no more bullets in his six-gun. Without a wasted motion he swapped the empty cylinder for the full one in his pocket.

When he walked forward, there was a hesitation in his gait that hadn't been there before.

"I ain't part of this," Beaver said from the corner.

"Keep it that way."

"Yessir."

The padre sat up, blinked, and looked around.

"What's that racket?" he said hoarsely.

"Go back to sleep," Case said.

"Smells like gunfire," the padre said. "Anyone kilt?"

"Fleas, that's all. Just fleas."

"Hell. Waste of good powder, shootin' fleas. Just crunch 'em 'tween your thumbnails."

With that, the padre flopped back again. His second breath was a deep snore.

Ignoring the blood running down his leg, Case circled the fallen Culpeppers. He kicked the guns away from their limp fingers before he bent over to check on the men.

Both Culpeppers were still alive, but not very happy about it. As time wore on they would be less happy. All of their wounds were below the belt.

"Sorry, boys," he said. "If you hadn't been so damned fast on the draw, I'd have made a clean end of it for you. Those first bullets I took knocked me off my stride."

Slowly he stood. He stripped off his bandanna, wrapped it around his right thigh, and tied it tight.

Blood welled up relentlessly. More blood welled from a wound on his right arm.

"You're in a bad way, hombre," Beaver said.

Ignoring him, Case dug inside his shirt, pulled out a "Wanted Dead or Alive" poster, and unrolled it against his body. Using his own blood as ink, he drew lines through the names of Quincy and Reginald Culpepper. There were other, older lines drawn. Other dead Culpeppers.

There were names that had no line through them.

Too many.

"Better get a move on," Beaver sa[id]. "Them boys have kin. They'll track y[ou] down and toast your brains over a sl[ow] fire same as 'Paches do."

Case dropped the poster between th[e] two Culpeppers. Then he threw down [a] handful of coins.

"Here's the ante," he said to Reginald. "Now you and Quincy can bet on who dies first."

Slowly Case backed toward the door. He watched Beaver every step of the way. Case might have been wounded, but the six-gun in his left hand never wavered from the other man's chest.

Beaver was very careful not to so much as blink.

Once Case reached the door, he gave a high, oddly musical whistle, like the sound of a hawk calling from an empty sky.

Hurry, he silently urged his horse. *I've got to go to ground before I pass out.*

Brush rattled and canvas flapped as Cricket tore free and trotted toward his rider. Case reached for the saddle horn and hauled himself aboard.

With each heartbeat, waves of pain and nausea washed over him. He set his teeth and tied himself to the saddle.

3

"Brung something for you," Ute said.

Sarah looked up from the hawk she was tending. One of the outlaws camped at Spring Canyon had decided to use the bird for target practice. Fortunately the hawk's wing wasn't broken. It would heal. But until then, the bird had to be fed or it would starve to death.

"Books?" she asked eagerly.

Mouth agape, the hawk struggled to be free. She held it against her body and murmured soothingly.

"Some of them, too," Ute said.

"What else?"

He jerked his head toward the front of the cabin. "Best hurry. It won't keep."

She gave him an odd glance but didn't argue. She fitted a soft leather hood to the hawk's head, tied its leg to a perch, and hurried outside.

At first glance all Sarah really saw was the rider's blood — dried, fresh, caked, oozing, blood everywhere on the man who was slumped over an equally bloody saddle.

Then she recognized the stallion.

"Dear God," she said. *Case.*

"Found him like this, so I brung him to you like all the other hurt critters."

"Get him down," she said curtly.

Then she began shouting orders.

"Conner! *Conner!* Come help Ute right now! Lola, bring your healing herbs!"

Ute pulled out a knife that was as long as his forearm and went to work on the bindings that held Case in the saddle.

As the last thongs were cut, Conner came running up from the creek. He was a big-boned, lean fifteen-year-old who hadn't yet grown into his own body.

"What's wrong, sis?" he demanded.

"Take a look," she said, waving her hand at the bloody rider. "The Culpeppers must have found him."

Case started sliding out of the saddle. Conner grunted as he helped Ute catch the dead weight.

"Hell, he's a big 'un," Conner muttered.

"Don't swear," she said automatically.

"And the word is pronounced *one,* not *'un.*"

"Are you going to lecture me on grammar or help this man?"

"I can do both at once," she snapped. "Bring Case inside and put him on my bed."

"Case, huh?" Conner asked.

He grabbed the big, blood-streaked boots and straightened under the weight. Ute did the same with Case's shoulders. Together they carried him toward the cabin.

"Is this the hombre who walked you home night before last?" Conner asked.

"Yes," she said absently. Then, startled, "How did you know?"

"I saw him."

"What were you doing up at that time of night?"

"When Ute is gone, I sleep real light," Conner said simply.

Sarah turned aside to hide her suddenly bright cheeks.

Did Conner see Case kiss me? she wondered.

"Lola!" she called loudly. "Where in blazes are you?"

"I'm coming, gal. Some of us ain't as spry as others."

The words came from the direction of the wickiup where Ute and Lola made their home.

"Put him on my bed," Sarah said.

Conner looked doubtfully from the bloody man to his sister's spotless bedding.

"Do it!" she snapped.

"Shoot," he muttered. "Who put a weasel in your henhouse?"

They lowered Case to the bedding, which lay on a pallet of woven reeds.

"Draw fresh water from the creek," Sarah said to Conner. "Ute, bring those clean rags in from the laundry line."

Both males hurried to obey her. When she got that fierce gleam in her eyes, it was easier just to take orders than to argue.

She knelt next to Case. As carefully as she could, she dragged off his boots and socks. Though he made no sound, she knew he was still alive, because blood was still oozing from his wounds. When a man's heartbeat stopped, so did any bleeding.

Too much blood, she thought fearfully, feeling the slipperiness of the boots. *Too damned much!*

She untangled the chin strap of his

hat and tossed it onto a nearby chest made of woven willow branches. With quick motions she unbuttoned his shirt, peeled it from his limp body, and went to work on his undershirt.

When she was finished, she had a clear view of the wedge of black hair that spread from his collarbone to his belt. Blood matted the hair along his right side.

Delicately she ran her fingers over his chest, seeking any wounds beneath the blood. She found none except the one she had already noticed on the inside of his right arm.

Shallow wound, she thought, relieved. *Bloody but otherwise not much damage.*

She undid his belt. Then she eased his pants and underwear down his torso, fearing every bit of the way what she would discover.

Please, God, not a gut wound, she prayed silently.

The only blood on his abdomen had dripped down from the wound on his arm.

She let out a rush of pent-up breath. With great care she peeled his pants down his legs.

The wounds on his thigh made her stomach clench.

"Lordy, but that's a prime lot of male flesh," Lola said from behind Sarah.

"Lordy, but he looks more like stew meat than steak at the moment," she shot back. "Get my uncle's medical bag, please."

Laughing, Lola went to the willow-branch chest, opened it, and pulled out an old black leather bag.

"What do you need?" she asked.

"A miracle," Sarah said.

"Didn't know you stored 'em in this bag."

"Neither did I."

After that there was silence except for the splash of water while Sarah gently cleaned Case's wounds. She started with his arm. As she had hoped, the wound was more bloody than serious.

"That's not worth stitching," Lola commented.

All Sarah said was, "Hot water, please. Soap. And more rags. He's a mess."

"Ute!" Lola called.

"I hear you," he answered gruffly. "But why you bother with all that scrubbing when —"

"Quit grousing," Lola interrupted. "She saved your sorry hide once, didn't she?"

Muttering, Ute stoked up the fire and checked the pot hanging on the trivet over the flames.

"Getting there," he said.

"Thank you," Sarah answered without looking up.

He watched her work with reverent black eyes. At some wordless level of his being he was convinced that she was a cinnamon-haired angel put on earth to help creatures that couldn't help themselves.

It was something he rarely spoke about, but it was more real to him than any words he knew.

While water heated, Sarah gently cleaned blood from Case's body. When she was finished, she looked down at her handiwork.

Lola is right, she decided in a distracted way. *This is a prime piece of man.*

The idle thought surprised her. Since her harsh initiation into a wife's duties in the marriage bed, men hadn't appealed to her physically.

Hastily she draped a clean cloth over

Case, preserving at least the shreds of modesty.

But she would be a long time forgetting what she had seen.

He's bigger than Hal was.

All over.

The thought made Sarah shudder. She had endured enough pain from her slightly built husband. Lying with teeth clenched while a man Case's size rutted between her legs was unthinkable.

"Here you be," Ute said.

"Thank you."

She took the pan of hot water. Then she looked up into Ute's narrow, black eyes.

"Uncle William," she said quietly, "told me that a clean wound heals better than a dirty one, and any woman knows that hot water and soap cleans things better than cold water alone."

Ute's nod was almost a bow.

"I didn't mean no belittling of you," he said uncomfortably.

She touched one of his blunt, scarred hands.

"I know," she said. "I just wanted you to understand, so if I get hurt someday you'll know what to do."

"God won't never let you get hurt."

"God is very busy."

"Not too busy for His angels."

With a sad kind of smile, Sarah turned back to Case. She had no illusions about holding a special place in anyone's eyes, much less God's.

Gently, thoroughly, she cleaned wounds until she could see nothing but raw flesh and fresh blood. One of the leg wounds was high on the inside of his thigh. She probed delicately and felt no lump of lead. The bullet had simply taken out a furrow of flesh and gone on its way.

The second leg wound was deeper, more serious. It bled steadily, but not with the spurting that her uncle had warned her often meant death.

"Still carrying lead?" Lola asked.

"Yes," Sarah said unhappily. "From the angle the bullet went in, it's lodged in the back of his thigh, if it missed the bone . . ."

Matter-of-factly Lola slid her hand beneath his thigh. She prodded intact skin and muscle with her fingertips, seeking the bullet. When Case groaned, she didn't flinch.

Sarah did.

"Lucky," the older woman said. "Just got the meat."

"Are you sure?"

"Yep. Clean missed the bone. Ute, hand me over your knife. I'll cut that there lead out quick as a snake licking its lips."

"Wait!" Sarah said.

Lola gave her an odd look. "Heals better without lead."

"I know. It's just . . ."

Sarah's voice dried up. She didn't know how to tell Lola that the thought of cutting into Case's smooth, muscular flesh made her feel anxious and sad and angry at the same time.

"You all right, sis?" Conner asked. "You look kind of pale. Maybe you better leave this to us."

"I'm fine," she said curtly. "Ute was shot up a lot worse than this when we found him. I cut and stitched him like a wedding quilt, remember?"

"I remember that you threw up afterward," her brother muttered.

"So?" Lola retorted before Sarah could. "She got the job done first, and that's all that counts. You done your share of puking, boy, and don't you be forgetting it."

Conner narrowed his green eyes and swallowed a word that he knew would get him a lecture from his older sister.

"Ute," Sarah said quickly. "Roll Case onto his side. I'll take the bullet out with a scalpel."

"I'll turn him," Conner said.

She looked up, surprised. She kept thinking of him as a nine-year-old child sobbing at the graveside of his parents. But today her younger brother was a big, rawboned man-child, already taller than she was by a head and easily twice as strong.

He's growing up too fast, she realized with sudden fear.

If I don't find that Spanish treasure soon, it will be too late. Conner will ride out of here and vanish like any other drifter, wandering toward whatever dead end awaits him.

He deserves better than that. He has a fine mind. He could be a doctor or a judge or a scholar like our father was.

Case groaned again as Conner turned him.

"Careful!" Sarah said instantly.

"He's out cold."

"Do you think he's singing hymns to you?" she retorted. "Case is hurting, even if he isn't wide awake."

"You bet," Ute said. "If he was awake, he wouldn't make nary a sound."

"How do you know?" Conner asked.

"I seen him in Spanish Church. Calm and steady like. Hate to get on his bad side."

Conner finished turning Case. Gently.

A bullet bulged just beneath the skin of his muscular thigh.

"Told ya," Lola said.

Sarah didn't say anything. She simply picked up the clean scalpel, took a hidden breath, and told herself that it was a haunch of venison she was slicing.

One swift cut was all it took. The bullet popped free and rolled onto the hard-packed dirt that was the cabin's only floor.

Conner retrieved the lead with a casual motion that was both quick and oddly coltish. He was still getting used to his own rapidly changing body.

"Here you go," he said, tossing the bullet toward Ute. "One more round for the melting pot."

Ute caught the lead, grunted, and stuffed it into his pocket.

"Too bad he didn't pick up the brass,

too," Conner added. "We're short on cases."

"For heaven's sake," Sarah said. "Only an idiot would bleed to death picking up brass."

"Only an idiot would get shot up in the first place," her brother retorted.

"Boy," Ute said, "you ain't no damned fool so don't go to acting like one. This here hombre drew on two Culpeppers. He walked away. They didn't."

Sarah's hands stilled.

"What?" she said.

"Culpeppers," Ute repeated. "Reginald and Quincy."

"Well, the devil will have two more souls for supper," Lola said. "Can't say as I'm sorry."

Ute grunted.

"We better be ready for visitors," the old outlaw said calmly. "Beaver won't last two breaths once Ab starts questioning him."

Sarah turned quickly and stared at Ute.

He shrugged. "I tried to brush out the tracks, but Case was bleeding real bad. I hear them Culpeppers are right fine sign cutters. They'll know he's here."

Lola muttered something under her breath that Sarah hoped her brother didn't overhear.

"Sufficient unto the day are the troubles thereof," she said briskly. "Do we have bullets?"

"Yes'm," Ute said.

"Enough?"

"More than we have guns to shoot 'em."

"You take the first watch on the rim."

Ute was gone before the words left her mouth.

"Conner," Sarah said, "you take the next. I'll —"

"You'll stay put and tend this here hombre," Lola interrupted. "I don't have your soft touch, and he needs it. I'll do your turn up on the rim."

"But your hip —"

"It's just fine," Lola interrupted again. "Start patching this boy up 'fore he bleeds to death."

Sarah didn't argue any longer. She threaded a special needle with fine silk and went to work stitching up the cut she had made in Case's skin.

The hair on his thighs was as black and silky as the thread she used. His skin was warm, surprisingly smooth, supple as fine leather.

"Turn him onto his back," she said.

Her voice was husky, almost breathless. Hastily she cleared her throat.

Conner gave her an odd look before he bent and rolled Case over onto his back.

"Your sheets are bloody now," he said.

"Ain't the first time," Lola muttered.

"What?" he asked.

"A woman's monthlies, boy. Use your head for something more than a hatrack."

Spots of red burned on Conner's cheeks but he bit his tongue. He had learned not to get into slanging matches with Big Lola. She knew the kind of words that could singe stone.

And when provoked, she used them.

Sarah ducked her head to hide her smile at her brother's chagrin. Lola was as hard and blunt as a stone ax, but she wasn't cruel. She simply had no patience for thick-skulled male foolishness.

Nor did Sarah.

Quickly she folded clean cloth into a pad and pressed it over the wound. When she applied more force, Case groaned. She bit her lower lip and kept on pressing down.

After a time she cautiously lifted a corner of the cloth. Blood still flowed, but slowly.

"More," Lola said. "Ain't stopped yet."

Sarah repeated the process with a new cloth. Her teeth sank into her lower lip when he twitched and moaned.

"Don't fret," Lola said. "He ain't really feeling it."

"I hope you're right."

"Hell, gal, he's an outlaw, not some fine, fainting lady."

"That doesn't mean he can't feel pain."

"I'll mix the poultice," was all Lola said.

Finally the bleeding slowed enough for Sarah to finish dressing the wound. Lola handed her a jar of strong-smelling poultice.

Holding her breath, Sarah smeared the blend of herbs, oils, and moldy bread onto a clean bandage, placed it over both wounds, and waited while Lola did the same to the wound on the back of Case's thigh. Quickly Sarah wrapped his leg with clean ribbons of cloth that still smelled of the sunny winter day.

"That's it," Lola said. "Cover him, put some warming bricks in the bed, and leave him be."

She was still talking when Sarah started pulling the top layer of bricks from the fire ring. They were hot. Breath hissed between her teeth as she wrapped the bricks in old flour sacks. She tucked the bricks at Case's feet and added a few more along his legs for good measure.

"Feverish?" Lola asked.

"Not yet."

She grunted. "It'll come."

Sarah bit her lower lip, but didn't argue. Lola's experience with gunshot wounds was greater than her own.

"Will he make it?" Sarah asked.

"Hope so. Shame to waste prime males. Ain't enough of them as it is."

Sarah pulled up the covers and tucked them around Case's shoulders. Like everything else in the cabin, the bedclothes were as clean as hard work, hot water, and soap could make them.

Lola grunted, heaved herself to her feet, and walked to the door. With each step the folds of her flour-sack skirt swung briskly over her knee-high moccasins. Her homespun blouse was the color of unbleached muslin. The headband she wore to hold back her thick gray braids was finely woven, colorful, and spun from the hair of goats she kept for their milk, meat, and silky wool.

"Check the rifles and shotguns," Sarah said to her brother without looking away from Case. "Is there more fresh water?"

"I'll get it," he said. Then, almost reluctantly, "What do you think? Will he be all right?"

For an instant she closed her eyes. "I don't know. If his wounds don't infect . . ."

"You pulled Ute through."

"I was lucky. So was he."

"Maybe this one will be lucky, too."

"I hope so."

She stood and looked around the cabin, listing things that had to be done.

"More water from the creek," she said, "more firewood, a place for me to sleep next to Case, Lola will probably need help with her medicinal herbs . . ."

"I'm gone," Conner said.

Sarah smiled as her brother hurried out of the cabin. He was a good boy, despite a wide streak of wildness in him that kept her awake nights worrying.

Conner needs something more to look up to than outlaws, she thought. *I've got to find that treasure. I've simply got to.*

Case moaned softly and tried to sit up.

Instantly she was on her knees beside him, holding his shoulders down.

He swept her aside as though she was no more than straw floating on the wind. Sitting up, he shook his head, trying to clear it.

She put her hand on his thick hair and soothed him like a wounded hawk.

"Case," she said distinctly. "Case, can you hear me?"

Slowly his eyes opened and focused on her.

An odd kind of gray-blue-green, she thought. *Not really hazel. More a pale green.*

Clear as winter and twice as deep. Colder, too.

"Sarah?" he asked hoarsely. "Sarah Kennedy?"

"That's me," she agreed. "Lie down, Case."

She pressed on his shoulders again. This time she noticed the resilience of his muscles beneath her palms, the male power coiled under his naked skin.

And the heat. Not fever. Just . . . life.

"What happened?" he asked thickly.

"You were shot. Ute found you and brought you here."

"Culpeppers?"

"Reginald and Quincy."

"Got to get up," he muttered. "Coming after me."

"I doubt it. From what Ute said, the only place those two are going is straight to hell."

Case blinked and rubbed one hand across his eyes.

"Other Culpeppers," he said.

His left hand moved as though reaching for a gun. His fingers found nothing but bare skin.

"Gun," he said hoarsely. "Where?"

"Lie down. You couldn't fight a baby chick in your condition."

Case shook off Sarah and tried to stand. A wave of pain slammed through him. Stifling a groan, he sank back down onto the bed.

"Got to — get up," he said.

"I'll bring you a gun if you'll just lie down," she said quickly. "Please, Case.

If you move around you'll start bleeding again and then you'll die!"

The urgency of Sarah's tone got through to him. He stopped struggling and allowed himself to be tucked in again. Then he watched with pain-hazed eyes while she stood and went to get his gun.

As was her custom, Sarah was dressed in men's clothes. Skirts and petticoats were worse than useless when she was climbing the stone canyons searching for treasure, or tending sick animals, or riding one of the skittish mustangs Conner and Ute had caught to provide mounts.

"Men's clothes," Case said in a blurred voice.

"What?"

"Pants."

She flushed brightly. "I, er, that is . . ."

Her voice faded as she remembered the picture Case had made when she undressed him. Even bloody and half-dead, he had been enough to make her heartbeat quicken.

Ninny, she told herself. *Just because he kissed you sweetly as a butterfly doesn't mean he wouldn't hurt you for his own pleasure.*

He is, after all, a man.

A big one.

"I'll bring your shirt as soon as I get the blood off it," she said. "But you shouldn't wear it or pants for a time. All the rubbing would just make it harder for your wounds to heal."

He looked confused.

"I was talking about your clothes, not mine," he said carefully.

"Good thing," she retorted, "because you're not wearing any to speak of at the moment."

He tried to answer, but dizziness was breaking over him like a long winter storm. He closed his eyes, clenched his teeth, and fought to keep a clear head.

But it was one battle Case knew he would lose.

"Here," she said. "I emptied the first chamber."

He felt the cold, familiar weight of his six-gun pressed into his left hand.

"Now lie down again," she ordered.

He allowed himself to be pushed back onto the pallet. When she bent to tuck the bedcovers around his shoulders, one of her braids fell forward. It brushed across his cheek like a silken rope.

"Roses," he said.

"What?"

He opened his eyes. He found himself staring into eyes that were the color of mist and silver intermixed, compassionate and wary and admiring all at once.

"Roses and sunshine," he said thickly. "I kissed you."

"Yes," she whispered. "You kissed me."

"Dumbest thing I ever did."

"What?"

There was no answer. Case was unconscious.

4

Sarah sat cross-legged next to the pallet where Case slept restlessly, gripped by pain and fever. Except to care for the wounded hawk, she had barely moved from Case's side for the past three days.

"Em . . ." he said hoarsely. *"Emily."*

The agony in his voice made Sarah's throat ache with tears she had forgotten how to shed.

She didn't know who Emily was. She knew only that Case loved her. He called out other names, too — Ted and Belinda, Hunter and Morgan — but it was Emily's name that was torn from him in naked anguish.

"Case," she said, using the voice she reserved for frightened animals. "You're safe, Case. Here, drink this. It will help the fever and pain."

As she spoke soothingly, she propped up his head and held a cup to his lips.

He swallowed without a fight. He knew with a gut-deep certainty that the murmurous voice and cool hands would help rather than hurt him.

"Roses," he said hoarsely, sighing.

Sarah's smile was as sad as the mist-gray eyes that watched his flushed face. She had taken care of many hurt creatures in her life, but never had she shared their pain in quite this way.

"Sleep," she murmured. "Sleep. And don't dream, Case. Your dreams . . . hurt too much."

After a few more minutes he sighed and slid back into the twilight world that was neither sleeping nor waking. But he was calmer now.

She barely dared to breathe deeply for fear of disturbing him. His fever was less than yesterday or the day before, and the infection in his wounds was subsiding, but he was far from well.

Moving slowly, noiselessly, she trimmed the wick of the lantern, lit it, and checked the hawk's wing. The bird protested at being touched, but like Case, the hawk no longer fought her when she rubbed in salve. Her gentle hands and voice had calmed the wild bird to the point that she no longer had to hood it to keep it from panicking.

"Healing nicely," she murmured. "You'll be soaring winter skies again, my fierce friend. Soon."

She set the lantern near the pallet where Case lay. Settling close by, she picked up a small bundle of wool and began twisting it onto a wooden spindle. Her fingers flew, spinning a shapeless mass of goat hair into soft yarn. As though by magic, yarn grew fat around the spindle as the pile of wool shrank.

The cabin door opened and shut quickly. Without looking up, Sarah could tell from the footsteps that it was her brother.

"How's he doing?" Conner asked.

"Better. Less fever."

"Told you he'd make it."

She smiled wanly.

"You look tired," he said. "Why don't you sleep? I'll watch him."

She shook her head.

Her brother started to argue, then shrugged and held his tongue. Lola was right — no one had Sarah's touch. Somehow she could reassure everything from hawks to mustangs that they were safe in her hands.

"Anything happening up on the rim?" she asked.

"No sign of Culpeppers, if that's what you mean."

"Ute must have done a better job of wiping out Case's trail than he thought."

"Maybe. And maybe they're just waiting."

"For what?" she asked.

"How should I know? I'm not a Culpepper. Any beans left?"

"You just ate."

"That was hours ago," he said.

"One hour."

"I'm hungry."

"Finish the beans, wash the pot, and put more —"

"— beans in to soak," he interrupted, reciting the familiar instructions. "Shoot, you'd think I was still in diapers or something. I know how to make beans."

"Really? Do you think they grow in dirty pots? Is that why I had to wash out the pot and start today's supper in the middle of last night?"

Conner's mouth flattened.

Sarah regretted her sharp words the instant they were out of her mouth. Sighing, she wondered how parents managed to keep their tempers at all. One moment Conner acted as responsibly as any fully grown man. The next moment he was worse than a two-year-old.

Yet she desperately needed to be able to count on him.

That's hardly fair to Conner, Sarah reminded herself. *He's only a boy.*

"Sorry," she said. "You were up half the night on watch."

Saying nothing, he scraped the last of the beans onto a plate. He knew he was in the wrong. He should have started the beans even if he was cross-eyed from lack of sleep. He had just plain forgotten.

"I won't forget again," he muttered.

"It's all right."

"No, it ain't."

"Isn't," she said automatically.

"*Isn't.* Hell's fire, what difference does it make? I'm not going to no — *any* — fancy Eastern school!"

"Yes, you are. Just as soon as I find that treasure."

"We'll all be dead as last year's flowers before that happens. Besides, I don't want to go."

"I'll find the silver," she said. "You'll go."

Conner heard the stubbornness in his sister's voice and changed the subject. Every time they talked about his lack of formal schooling, they argued. The older he got, the fiercer the arguments became.

He didn't want to hurt his sister, but he had no intention of going back East and leaving her to fend for herself. She would never admit that she needed him, but she did.

He stalked out into the night to wash the pot in the creek.

The vague whisper of goat hair being spun into yarn filled the silence. Sarah worked quickly and deftly, and tried not to think about the future.

It was impossible.

Conner is growing up too fast.

Though she would have died sooner than admit it, she was frightened that she wouldn't find the Spanish silver in time to save her young brother from the rootless life lived by too many Western men.

And now I have those Culpeppers and Moody's gang to worry about.

She bit her bottom lip and kept on spinning without a pause.

I'll spend so much time looking over my shoulder that my only chance of finding the silver will be to trip over it on my way to the privy.

Next time I'm out I'll try the land north and west of the ranch. The outlaws don't go there much. No reason to. In most of the canyons there's no water, no forage, no hunting.

No silver, either. Not yet.

But there will be.

There has to be.

Despite her bleak thoughts, her fingers never stopped working. Conner's wrists were hanging out of the last jacket Lola had woven for him. There was no money to buy another.

Spinning and weaving, spinning and weaving, she thought. *Lord, I wish all of life was so simple.*

She knew it wasn't. On the other hand, spinning and weaving at least accomplished something. All that treasure hunting had done was to wear out her moccasins as fast as Ute could make them.

Conner came back inside, bringing a gust of cold air with him. Though there was no snow yet, the land itself was icy at night.

Without a word, he put some beans to soak. Then he curled up on his pallet near the fire. He was asleep between one breath and the next.

With a small sigh, Sarah stretched her back and ran her fingers through her freshly washed hair. The scent of wild roses drifted up from her fingers. She had taken advantage of her brother's absence earlier to have a thorough bath, something she did so often that Ute swore she was going to sprout scales and fins.

Her waist-length hair was cool and still faintly damp to the touch.

Not dry enough to braid yet, she decided. *I might as well just stay awake until it's time to change the bandages and coax Case into drinking some more water.*

She picked up her spinning again and settled in for more quiet hours of spinning, caring for Case, and fretting about Conner's future.

When fever released Case from its grip, a rhythmic kind of whispering was the first thing he heard. Most men in his situation would have opened their eyes to find out where they were, or moved, or made a sound.

He gave not one sign that he had awakened.

His senses told him that he wasn't

alone. Since the only person he trusted was clear over in the Ruby Mountains of Nevada, the fact that there was someone nearby meant danger.

Hidden beneath blankets, his left hand moved, searching for the weapon that was never far from him even while he slept.

The six-gun was there.

And he was naked.

Very carefully his fingers closed around the gun. Secretly he gathered himself to fight.

Despite his iron self-control, the sudden stab of pain in his right leg when he moved it almost tore a cry from him. Memories followed the lightning stroke of agony. Some were as sharp as the pain itself. Some were dreamlike in their softness.

The fight at Spanish Church was one of the sharp memories.

Did Ab Culpepper track me down?

As soon as the thought came, Case dismissed it.

If Ab had found me, I wouldn't be waking up at all, and I sure as sin wouldn't have a gun in my hand.

I was wounded, he remembered painfully. *I tied myself to Cricket, spurred him into a run, and . . .*

Memory ended in a swirl of agony and darkness.

He listened intently, but heard no sound that told him Cricket was grazing nearby. All he could hear was a soft, somehow reassuring sound, like whispering breaths.

But it wasn't breathing. Not quite.

Spinning, he realized suddenly. *Someone is sitting close to me and spinning yarn.*

Other memories came, the scent of roses and warmth, gentle hands soothing him, water easing between his lips to cool the fiery thirst that was consuming him, a woman's long hair outlined by lantern light.

Sarah?

Fragments of the past cascaded over Case like colored glass, sharp-edged and beautiful at once.

Gray eyes and hair the color of cinnamon.

She tastes even sweeter than she smells.

I never should have kissed her.

Dumbest thing I ever did.

Really dumb.

Cautiously he opened his eyes just

enough to see without revealing that he was awake.

Sarah was sitting within arm's reach. Her hands moved in deft, soothing rhythms as she spun yarn from a pile of black wool. Her hair fell over her shoulders in silky, cinnamon waves that cried out to be stroked by a man's hand. Her eyes reflected the luminous gold of lantern light.

She was watching him.

"How do you feel?" she asked softly.

"Dumb."

She didn't ask why. She was afraid she already knew.

The kiss.

Even the memory of that sweet, searing caress was enough to make her fingers tremble.

"No need to berate yourself," she said matter-of-factly. "You're not the first man to get shot."

Or the first one to kiss a girl, Case thought.

Well, at least she's a widow. She won't mistake a man's hunger for a promise of now and ever after.

"How bad is it?" he asked.

"Your wounds?"

He nodded.

"One bullet went between the inside of your right arm and your chest."

As she spoke, she bent over and touched his right shoulder gently.

"You were shot twice in the right thigh," she continued.

"Infection?" he asked, his voice emotionless.

She set aside her spinning. "You can see for yourself. It's time to change the dressings."

He watched intently while she went about the simple tasks of gathering clean rags, warm water, and a jar of something pungent he couldn't identify.

"Do you want anything for pain?" Sarah asked. "Ute has some homemade whiskey that —"

"No," Case said. "I want a clear head."

She wasn't surprised. Though pale, obviously in pain, and not able to stand, he had an animal alertness that was unmistakable.

He was a man used to living with danger.

Ute had been the same way when he first came to Lost River ranch.

Often, he still was.

"How did I end up here?" Case asked.

"Ute found you."

Calmly she peeled the bedcovers down to his waist. As she bent forward and began unwrapping the bandage on his arm, her hair slid in a soft cascade across his chest.

Cool, yet it burned him like naked flame. His breath hissed in and his heartbeat doubled.

"Sorry," Sarah said, lifting her hands instantly. "Are you sure you don't want something for the pain?"

"Yes," he said through set teeth.

Her eyelids flinched but she said nothing. She simply got on with the task of unwrapping the rest of the bandage on his arm. Delicately her fingertips brushed the area around the furrow left by the bullet.

Again his breath hissed in.

She frowned. "Is it that tender?"

"No."

"Are you certain?"

"Yes," he said, jaw clenched.

She gave him a wary look. Then she went back to her tender tracing of the skin around the shallow wound.

This time Case didn't make a sound, despite the heat in his blood that had been summoned by a simple, impersonal touch.

Never should have kissed her, he told himself savagely. *Dumb. I haven't wanted a woman like this since . . .*

His thoughts scattered.

He hadn't ever wanted a woman the way he wanted Sarah Kennedy.

For a few more seconds the gentle, delicious torment of her touch continued. Then she withdrew.

"The skin around the wound is cool," she said. "No infection, but you'll have a scar."

"It won't be the first."

"Or the last," she said, thinking of the wounds on his thigh. "Since you're awake now, I won't wrap your arm again. It will heal faster in the air."

Case watched her face while she pulled the blankets up over his bare chest. Then she shocked him by flipping the covers off his legs all the way to his navel.

"Judas priest!"

One-handed, he raked the covers back over himself.

Sarah was too surprised to stop him.

"Sis?" Conner called drowsily.

"Go back to sleep," she said. "It's just Case thrashing around."

"You need me to hold him while you

change the bandages again?"

She raised her cinnamon eyebrows at Case in silent question.

"Do I?" she mouthed.

His eyes widened. He had just figured out that there wasn't one inch of him that Sarah Kennedy hadn't already seen.

Dead naked.

Red burned on his cheekbones above his weeks'-old beard. He took his hands away from the covers.

"I can handle it, Conner," Sarah said neutrally. "Go back to sleep. You have to relieve Ute in a few hours."

Her brother made a muffled sound, rolled over, and slid back into the sleep his growing body craved.

"Get me a loincloth," Case said flatly.

Without a word she stood up, went to a basket in the corner, and shook out the last shirt that Conner had outgrown and worn to shreds in the process. The remaining fabric had been destined for the rag rug she was making. If it took a detour on the way, no harm would be done.

"Will this do?" she asked.

"Yes."

He held out his right hand. Plainly he intended to put the cloth on himself.

"If you move around," she said, "you could open the wounds again. Let me wrap —"

"No," he interrupted curtly.

One look at his face was enough to tell Sarah that he meant it. She could hand over the cloth or she could fight him.

"Don't be foolish," she said crisply. "I raised Conner, I was married, and I nursed Ute back to health when he was in worse shape than you. I'm not going to faint at the sight of — of your — that is —"

To Sarah's horror, a blush climbed her cheeks. Abruptly she threw the cloth at him and turned her back.

"Go ahead," she said through her teeth. "But if you open up those wounds, don't come crying to me about how it hurts."

"The day I cry is the day the sun will set in the east."

She didn't doubt it. He wasn't an emotional kind of man. While she took a rawhide thong from around her wrist and tied back her long hair, she thought about the grim set of his face.

"What about laughing?" Sarah asked without thinking.

"What about it?"

"Do you?"

"Laugh?" Case asked.

"Yes."

"When I find something funny."

"When was the last time?" she retorted.

He grunted in pain when he lifted his hips to finish wrapping the loincloth around himself.

"Well?" she persisted.

"Can't remember. Why?"

"How about smiling?"

"What is this, a catechism?" he asked. "You expected to find Robin Goodfellow shot full of holes and making jokes to entertain you?"

Sarah laughed softly.

"Robin Goodfellow," she said. "Lord, I haven't thought of Shakespeare for a long time. Did you like *A Midsummer Night's Dream*?"

"Once."

"But not now?"

"Since the war, *Hamlet* is more to my taste."

There was something in Case's tone that made chills course over Sarah's skin.

"Vengeance," she said.

"I'm ready," he said, tying the cloth in place. "You can do whatever you've been doing to my leg."

As she turned around, he lay back on the pallet. She saw immediately that he had started undoing the bandage on his thigh but hadn't finished the job.

Clearly, the simple act of wrapping the loincloth around himself had almost been beyond his strength. His face was pale above his black beard. A sheen of sweat stood on his forehead. His mouth was drawn into a line so narrow it was almost invisible.

"You should have let me do it," Sarah said. "You need your strength for healing."

"Either change the damned bandage or don't. It's all the same to me."

If his voice hadn't been thinned by pain, she would have kept on scolding him as though he were her younger brother.

"We don't laugh," she muttered as she knelt by his side, "we don't cry, we don't smile. But we do have a temper, don't we?"

With difficulty, he bit back a scalding reply.

He was surprised by the effort it took

simply to hold his tongue. He, who had vowed to feel nothing at all after Ted and Emily's death.

Not even anger.

Must be the fever, Case thought grimly.

But he was afraid it was the rose-scented, sharp-tongued angel of mercy who was kneeling by his side.

He gritted his teeth and endured the gentle, searing touch of Sarah's hands while she unwrapped the bandage on his thigh. More than once he felt the brush of her shirt against his naked legs as she worked.

Twice he was certain that he felt the satin weight of her breasts.

Pain should have kept him from becoming aroused. It didn't. The loincloth he had just tied around himself was rapidly losing the contest between modesty and blunt male hunger.

"Hell's fire," he hissed.

Sarah flinched. Every time she unwrapped the bandage one turn, she was forced to brush against his crotch. The bulge that had grown beneath the loincloth was intimidating.

"I'm sorry," she said. "I'm trying to be careful."

"Stop being so fairy-fingered. Just get it over with."

She bit her tongue and finished unwrapping the bandage. She didn't even protest when he levered himself up on his elbows to look at the wounds.

One wound was scabbed over and healing well. The other was a red, puckered hole in his upper thigh. Poultice glistened on his skin like dark rain.

"Am I carrying lead?" he asked.

She gave a sideways, hidden look at the loincloth.

Fully loaded in all chambers, from what I can see.

Her thought came with a combination of alarm and something else, something odd that she couldn't put a name to.

"Er, no," she said. "I cut out the bullet on the other side. It missed the bone."

"Thought so. It didn't knock me down. Threw off my aim, though."

"Not by much. Ute said you were the only one to walk away."

"There's plenty more Culpeppers where those two came from."

Case sat up enough to feel the back of his thigh. Neatly knotted stitches greeted his fingertips. He bent over the open wound on top of his thigh and breathed in deeply.

Waves of pain slammed through him with each heartbeat, but he didn't straighten until he was satisfied. There was no sign of infection in the wound. No smell of it, either.

Thank God, he thought.

While death itself held no particular terror for him, there were some ways of dying he would just as soon avoid. From what he had seen in the Civil War, gangrene was a worse way to die than being gut-shot.

With a rough sound he lay back, breathing hard.

"Good doctoring," he said hoarsely. "Thank you."

"You can thank me by not pulling out the stitches or reopening wounds by thrashing around."

"I'll work on it."

"You do that," she muttered.

Despite her tart tone, her hands were very gentle as she spread the healing poultice on a fresh bandage and wrapped it around the open wound. The pallor of his skin worried her, as did the raggedness of his breathing.

"Are you all right?" she whispered.

"Fine as frog hair."

"I've always wondered just how fine that was."

"Finer than silk," Case said through his teeth, "but not so fine as your hair."

Sarah gave him a startled look. His eyes were closed. Obviously he was fighting not to reveal the pain he was in.

He probably doesn't even know what he said, she thought.

"There's some broth warming by the fire," she said in a brisk tone. "You should drink some if your stomach is steady enough to hold on to it."

Case didn't answer.

He was asleep.

Very gently she brushed his thick hair away from his eyes, pulled the covers more securely around him, and rested the inside of her wrist against his forehead.

There was a faint sheen of sweat caused by pain, but no sign of fever. She smiled and trailed her fingertips down his broad, bearded cheek.

"Good night, sweet prince," she murmured, thinking of his liking for *Hamlet.*

Then she remembered more of the play and felt chilled.

The sweet prince had died.

Sarah wrapped a blanket around herself and curled up next to Case. Even when she slept, her fingertips rested on his wrist where his pulse beat, as though she needed reassurance that he was still alive.

5

Standing outside in the yard, Sarah fished bandages from a kettle of boiling water and draped them over a wash line that was strung between clumps of big sage.

Several bandages steamed slightly into the fresh, early-morning air. The sun was a golden benediction over the land, heightening the red of the cliffs that lined the valley on both sides.

High overhead a golden eagle soared on transparent currents of wind. The bird's rippling, keening cry was so beautiful it brought goose bumps to Sarah's arms.

Stay away from Spring Canyon, she warned the bird silently. *Sure as sin, those no-good outlaws would shoot you just because they can.*

"You keep boiling them rags and there won't be nothing left but threads," Lola said.

Sarah flipped the last bandage over

the line and turned with a smile. "Good morning."

"Ain't you the cheerful one. I take it your pet outlaw is getting better."

"You don't know that Case is an outlaw."

"Huh," Lola said. "Gal, ain't no other kind of man out here but damned fools, and that hombre in there sure as hell ain't nobody's damned fool."

"He could be a marshal."

"No badge," Lola said succinctly.

"How do you know?"

"I went through his gear."

"Lola! You had no right to do that."

The older woman's black eyes looked upward as though the answer to Sarah's foolishness was to be found in the sky.

"He has a fistful of 'Wanted' posters from Texas," Lola said, "a spare belt gun, two long guns — good 'uns — enough bullets for a grand dust-up, a change of clothes, soap, razor, spyglass, and maybe three hundred in gold. From the cut of his overcoat, he was a Johnny Reb. And he was carrying a little cup and saucer, like for a doll, all wrapped up careful like."

"None of that makes him an outlaw."

Lola snorted. "Difference between an outlaw and a bounty hunter ain't a great stretch."

"Was Ute mentioned on any of those posters?" Sarah asked bluntly.

"Nary a one. Culpeppers was featured."

Suddenly she remembered the conversation she had overheard between Ab and Kester Culpepper.

Shee-it. Next you'll be whining about them Texicans dogging our trail.

Ain't seen 'em.

Sarah suspected that she had seen at least one of the "Texicans" who were following the Culpeppers.

"Don't look so down in the mouth," Lola said. "Ain't no reason to shed tears over the likes of them Culpeppers. If even half what them 'Wanted' posters say is true, they're as sorry an excuse for men as any woman ever whelped. And Ab is the worst of a bad lot."

"I don't doubt it," Sarah said, remembering bits of what she had overheard Ab Culpepper say.

Even the devil don't know a female's mind. Worthless sluts, all of them.

Steal or buy a female down in Mexico. Or get a Injun.

If I decide the Kennedy gal needs taking care of, I'll do it personally.

"What did the Culpeppers do in Texas?" Sarah asked uneasily.

"Robbed banks, raped, and murdered mostly."

She winced.

"And they sold kids to the Comancheros," Lola added, "after doing things to the young'uns that would shame Satan."

Sarah didn't ask for any more details. She simply swallowed hard and began wringing out the now-cool rags. The ferocity of her motions said more than words.

"Sounds like Case might have a personal reason for hunting Culpeppers," Sarah said after a few moments.

"Likely," Lola agreed. "Hope he gets on his feet right quick."

"Why?"

"Cuz we're going to need him, that's why."

"What do you mean?"

"Them Culpeppers been sniffing around."

Sarah's stomach clenched.

"Are you certain?" she asked.

"Ute saw their sign alongside his and

Case's back trail."

Silently Sarah wrung out another bandage and spread it on the line to dry. She didn't ask if Ute was certain who had made the tracks he saw. Before he turned outlaw, he had been the best army scout west of the Rocky Mountains.

"Does Conner know?" Sarah asked.

"Told him myself."

For an instant she closed her eyes. She couldn't help wondering how long five people — one of them badly wounded — would last if the Culpepper and Moody gangs descended on the little ranch. The only shred of hope she had was Ab's blunt orders not to cause a fuss within three days' ride of Spring Canyon.

"What about the army?" Sarah asked.

"Oh, they might take a notion and come over this way, but not in time to do us any good. Them soldier boys have their plates plumb overflowing with redskins."

"Well," she said, shaking out a bandage with a brisk snap, "we'll just have to do the best we can. I'll start taking a turn on watch at the rim."

"No."

"Why not?"

"You wouldn't shoot them outlaws on sight," Lola said.

"Neither would Conner."

Lola tilted her head and looked at the younger woman with narrowed black eyes.

"You don't know that boy real good, do you?" Lola asked. "He'll do whatever it takes to keep you safe."

"I'd do the same for him."

Lola smiled with surprising gentleness. "Hell, I know that. You sold yourself to a crazy old man for your brother."

"Hush," Sarah said, looking around quickly. "Don't ever say a thing like that in front of Conner!"

"You think he don't already know it?" the other woman asked sarcastically.

"There's no need to talk about it. I mean that."

Sighing, Lola crossed her thick arms. Though she was just under six feet tall and nearly three feet wide, there wasn't a whole lot of fat on her thick body. As always, she wore a revolver on her right hip.

"Talking won't change what was and what is," Lola said bluntly. "Conner and Ute and me had a palaver. You're staying here. We'll take the watches on the rim."

"That's ridiculous."

"No it ain't. You're too soft-hearted to shoot a man from ambush. Even a Culpepper. Sure as hell you'd get buck fever and freeze on the trigger."

"I —"

A long, shrill whistle from the rimrock overlooking the ranch cut off whatever argument Sarah had in mind.

As one the women turned and ran to the place where they had left their shotguns leaning against the outside of the cabin.

Three short whistles followed the first warning.

"Just three men coming," Sarah said, grabbing her shotgun.

"That means they want to palaver."

Lola whipped the sling of one shotgun over her head and left shoulder. Then she picked up a second shotgun and cocked both barrels. Her six-gun hung in its holster, right at hand if needed.

Looking at her, Sarah could believe that Ute and Big Lola used to rob banks together.

"Why would the outlaws waste time talking to us?" she asked.

"Would you rather take on a bear blind, or have a look-see around his den first?" Lola retorted.

"I don't think Moody is that smart."

"He ain't. But Ab Culpepper is clever as a he-coon and twice as mean."

A low whistle from the cottonwoods lining the creek told the women that Conner was in place, covering their flank.

"Ute will be coming down the rim on the short trail," Lola said. "He'll be here right quick."

Sarah didn't say anything. With the cabin at their backs, Conner at their left side and Ute at their right, they were ready to fight if they had to.

She hoped it wouldn't come to that.

"No," Lola said, squinting against the sun. "It sure as sin ain't no shooting party."

"What makes you so certain?"

"Ute wouldn't wait for no engraved invite to open the ball. He'd shoot fast as he could load and fire. If he ain't shooting by now, it ain't a shooting occasion."

Despite Lola's words, Sarah's hands tightened around the shotgun until they ached.

Since Ute had come more dead than alive to the little valley and given his devotion to her, there had been no problem from the bands of Indians that occasionally came and went through Lost River ranch on their way to traditional hunting grounds. The three men riding down off the rim right now were as close to raiders as Sarah had faced in years.

Oh God, I hope Conner doesn't get hurt, she thought helplessly.

None of her fear showed on her face. Motionless, she and Lola watched two long, thin men ride into the ranch yard on sorrel mules that were lean and hard as jackrabbits.

"There are only two of them," Sarah said.

Lola grunted. "I can count."

"Where's the third?"

"Hanging back, most likely." She gave Sarah a quick, gap-toothed smile. "A man can get hisself shot that way."

Sarah smiled rather wanly. The idea of someone sneaking up behind her wasn't comforting.

As Ute had taught her to do, she angled herself slightly away from Lola so that their fields of fire didn't overlap. The other woman did the same.

At least the cabin is at our backs, Sarah thought grimly.

The sun-dried, ill-cut boards weren't much as protection went, but they were better than nothing.

"Well, they be Culpeppers," Lola said after a moment.

"How do you know?"

"Them boys favor big sorrel mules."

Both women watched as the red mules separated themselves from the equally red rock of the cliffs that lined the valley. At a quarter-mile away, the riders looked as dusty and faded as rabbit bush in high summer.

"Wonder which Culpeppers they are?" Sarah asked.

"Can't tell from here. Ute says there are five of the devils living in Spring Canyon."

Sarah's breath came in sharply. She leaned forward, staring intently at the base of the cliffs.

She still saw only two riders.

"Do you see the third one any-wheres?" Lola asked.

"No."

"Wish you didn't hate chewing tobacco so much. A good chaw would be right comforting now."

"Then chew. This is no time for parlor manners."

Lola dug a plug of tobacco out of her shirt pocket, ground off a chunk between her back molars, and stuffed the plug back in her pocket.

"I'm obliged," Lola said.

"You're welcome. Just don't spit on the laundry."

Lola laughed past the tobacco bulging in her cheek, but her eyes never left the approaching riders.

Sarah just kept watching the two riders, praying that they had somehow missed seeing the third one.

Maybe Ab is the one who stayed behind to cover their backs, she thought hopefully.

She really didn't want to be any closer to Ab Culpepper than she had been in the shallow cave overlooking the outlaw rendezvous. The promise of violence in his voice when he ordered Moody to stop raiding close to home could chill her even in memory.

"Good thing the Culpeppers don't trust Moody," she said. "I'll bet Ab stayed behind to keep an eye on him."

Lola chuckled. It wasn't a warm sound.

"No critter with half a brain would trust Moody," the old woman said. "He'd steal his toothless granny's egg money and dance on his ma's grave."

"You sound like you know him."

"He diddled me out of a night's pay down to New Mexico. Course, I was a lot younger then. No more notion than a flea about the cheating ways of men."

Sarah smiled slightly. She couldn't imagine anyone cheating Lola now — man or woman.

The two sorrel mules were barely a hundred yards away. Their long-legged strides looked lazy but covered a lot of ground very fast.

"You do the talking," Lola said. "If it comes to shooting, you dive for the cabin and leave 'em to me."

"I'm not going to —"

"The hell you ain't!" she interrupted fiercely. "Ute and me know how it's done. We won't go to shooting each other by mistake."

There was no time for Sarah to argue. The Culpeppers were only thirty feet away. Dust from the mules' hooves hung in the air for an instant before being chased away by the shifting wind.

From the empty blue sky, the eagle's call came again. The sound was high and free and beautiful.

Sarah envied the eagle as she had envied few things in her life.

"I be Ab Culpepper," the first rider said. "That's Kester, my kin. He don't say much."

Neither Culpepper looked at the women right away. Instead, the men looked everywhere else, taking stock of the homestead.

"Good morning to both of you," Sarah said tightly. "I'm Mrs. Kennedy."

Kester shifted in the saddle but still didn't turn toward the women. His faded blue eyes looked around ceaselessly, missing nothing.

Lola is right, Sarah thought with a combination of relief and anger. *They're just checking out our defenses.*

Bastards.

She straightened. Though neither her shotgun nor Lola's was pointing at the riders, the guns weren't far off the mark, either.

"Howdy," Kester said absently.

Almost as an afterthought he touched the brim of his worn, chewed-looking hat.

"Company manners," Lola said softly out of the side of her mouth. "Been so

125

long since he used 'em they creak in the joints."

Sarah smiled rather grimly.

Through the gap in her teeth, Lola spit a brown stream just to the side of the mule's feet. The distance was over six feet.

Kester looked at her with admiration.

"Can you spare some hot java?" Ab asked bluntly.

So you can look around inside, too? Sarah thought. *No, Ab. I won't make it that easy for you to count our guns.*

"Sorry," she said. "We don't have coffee. Too costly."

"Mormon tea, then," Ab said. "Something hot."

"We put the cabin fire out at dawn and worked outside," she said. "Wash day, you know."

Ab's expression said he didn't believe her.

Looking at the condition of the Culpeppers' clothes, Sarah understood his distrust. His pants looked as if they hadn't been washed in a month of Sundays. He probably had forgotten what a lot of work wash day was.

Or maybe he had never known.

"No biscuits," Sarah continued in a

126

calm voice, "no beans, no bacon, not even venison jerky. Hate to seem inhospitable, but I wasn't expecting callers."

Turning in the saddle slightly, Ab tilted back his hat and looked directly at her.

It was all she could do not to take a step away from him. There was something in his eyes that made her stomach churn.

Then she remembered what Lola had said about Ab and his kin.

They sold kids to the Comancheros, after doing things to the young'uns that would shame Satan.

"If your mules are thirsty," Sarah said grudgingly, "you can water them at the creek."

"Ain't thirsty," Ab said.

Not even the eagle's cry came to relieve the silence that descended.

"You ain't real friendly like, are you?" he asked finally.

"I have friends."

Her tone said she didn't want any more — especially Culpeppers.

"Gal alone like you can't have too many friends," he said.

"I'm not alone."

127

Ab glanced at Lola, then back at Sarah.

"I meant gentlemen friends," he said.

"I have no interest in men, Mr. Culpepper. None whatsoever."

"Well, little lady, then I guess you won't mind giving me back my man, will you?"

"If I had one of your men, you could have him instantly," she said. "I don't, so you had best look for your lost man elsewhere. Now."

Ab's face seemed to flatten. His watery blue eyes took on an odd sheen.

"Not so fast, missy," he said. "I ain't no trash to be sent packing by the likes of you and an old whore."

All pretense at civility was gone. Ab was using the cold tone Sarah remembered, the tone that said all females were worthless sluts.

But it was his eyes that shocked her. She had never seen such naked hatred.

"I don't care for your language, Mr. Culpepper," she said evenly. "Please remove yourself from Lost River ranch."

"I come for the polecat what murdered my kin," he snarled. "Give him over."

"I don't know what you're talking

about," she said coolly. "There is no murderer on Lost River ranch."

Kester's mule took a few steps to the left.

Lola's shotgun came up in blunt warning. She brought both hammers back and watched Kester like the rattlesnake he was.

"He's here," Ab said. "We done tracked the murdering devil from Spanish Church."

"Were your kin wearing guns?" Sarah asked.

"Of course they was. They're Culpeppers!"

"Were they shot from the front?"

"Culpeppers ain't no cowards," he said. "They was facing him."

"Then there was no murder, was there?" she pointed out reasonably. "Your kin simply drew on the wrong man. They paid for their misjudgment with their lives."

Ab's face flushed, then went pale.

"The man what killed my kin is in that there cabin," he said coldly. "Get him."

"No," she said. "He's near dead himself."

"Who cares? Get him!"

"If he survives, you may pursue your vendetta elsewhere," Sarah said. "Until then, the man is my guest."

Ab stared down at her as though he couldn't believe what he was hearing.

Despite the cold sweat on her ribs, she stared right back at him. Then she leveled the shotgun at his belt.

"Don't take your eyes off him," Lola said. "No matter what happens elsewhere."

"I won't." Sarah's voice was thin but steady. "Good-bye, Mr. Culpepper. Please don't hurry back. We don't take kindly to unexpected visitors."

A stream of tobacco juice landed wetly on the ground as Lola cleared her mouth.

"What she means," Lola said bluntly, "is that we shoot 'em on sight and plant 'em where they lay. Savvy?"

Ab understood. He didn't like it any better than he liked the shotgun pointing at his brisket.

A shot rang out from inside the cabin. It was followed quickly by two more.

Sarah flinched but kept her attention — and her shotgun — on Ab.

Lola didn't even flinch.

There was no return fire from beyond the cabin.

"Sounds like planting time," Lola said. "You boys either grab iron or git."

Neither Culpepper moved toward his gun. Each man was looking straight down both barrels of a shotgun that was loaded, cocked, and ready to fire. The fact that women were holding the guns wasn't a comfort.

It took no particular strength to pull a trigger.

"Parnell!" Ab yelled.

No one answered.

"More kin?" Lola asked blandly. "You boys sure are careless of yourselves."

Not once did Ab look away from Sarah. He memorized her face, her body, and her hands on the gun.

"Your turn be coming," he said. "And I be the man to lay it to you. Same for that hotheaded young pup lying back in the cottonwoods. Keep him leashed, else he won't have no fancies to strut in front of the gals."

Ab's hand jerked on the reins. His mule spun on its hocks and trotted off. Kester's mule followed.

Neither rider looked back.

6

"Keep watching them," Sarah said tightly.

Lola spat another juicy stream. "I weren't born yesterday."

Without answering, Sarah uncocked her shotgun and ran into the cabin. She spared a quick glance for the injured hawk on its perch in a corner. The bird was ruffled and skittish from the noise, but otherwise unhurt.

Not as much could be said of the man.

Case was slumped on the floor at the back of the cabin, naked but for the loincloth. His forehead was propped against the wall. His six-gun was in his hands. The barrel was rammed through an opening in the planks where the chinking had fallen out.

The bitter smell of gun smoke hung in the still air.

"Case?" she asked.

His only answer was an indistinct sound. He didn't turn toward her.

She rushed across the room and sank to her knees beside him. Hastily she propped her shotgun against the wall and began running her hands over his back and legs, searching for new injury.

The gentle touches went through him like lightning. His breath hissed in on a muffled curse. He lifted his shaggy head and turned glittering gray-green eyes on her.

"Are you all right?" she whispered.

"No."

She made a small sound and stroked his back as if he were a frightened hawk.

"Where do you hurt?" she asked. "Were you shot again? Your back looks all right. Roll over and let me check your front."

The thought of having Sarah's gentle, quick hands exploring every inch of him sent another jolt of sensual lightning through Case.

"Don't tempt me," he said.

"What?"

He said something rough under his breath. Her touch had transformed the fear he felt for her when the Culpeppers rode up into raw, reckless desire.

"Nothing is wrong with me," he said,

"except that I missed the son of a bitch."

"Who?"

"Parnell, from what Ab called out," Case said. "Hellfire and damnation!"

"Where was he?"

"See that pile of rocks yonder?"

Sarah bent and peered through the broad crack. The only pile of rocks she could see was a lot more than a hundred yards away. She glanced at Case's revolver.

"Good Lord," she said. "Of course you missed him. All you had was a six-gun."

"That's all I should have needed."

She started to argue.

The look in his eyes changed her mind.

"Let me help you back to bed," she said.

"You go watch those Culpeppers. I'm fine where I am."

"Lola's watching them, Ute is trailing them, and Conner is lying back in the shadows to send up a shout if anyone else appears."

Case looked out through the crack in the chinking for a long time before he answered.

Nothing moved on the landscape, not even the shadow of a high flying bird.

In the silence, the metallic sounds of Case uncocking his six-gun seemed almost as loud as the shooting had.

"I guess you've done this a time or two before," he said.

"Ute figures it's better to plan ahead than to die regretting your carelessness."

Case grunted. "Sounds like Hunter."

"Hunter?"

"My brother. He was a colonel back when the South had uniforms of its own and fools dying to wear them. Not that Hunter was a fool. I was the only fool in the family."

"I doubt that."

"I don't."

The emptiness in his voice brought an unexpected ache to Sarah's throat. Without realizing it, she stroked his back again with long, gentle sweeps of her hand.

"Let me help you back to bed," she said after a time.

"I can get back the same way I got here."

"But you're hurt."

Case felt the glide of her hand down his spine and fought to keep from lashing out at her.

Or grabbing her.

"Case?"

"If you don't stop petting me like a tabby cat," he said in a level voice, "I'm going to grab you and show you just how healthy I'm feeling right now."

"Tabby cat?" She laughed. "You're more like a cougar than a housecat."

He started to roll over on his good side and reveal just what was bothering him. But even beginning the movement brought a searing agony, pinning him in place.

Well, that should cure me, he thought.

But it didn't. Not completely.

Another dose should take care of it, he told himself.

With grim determination, he rolled over onto his good leg. Ignoring Sarah's protests, he half-crawled, half-dragged himself back across the cabin.

"There," he said, stretching out on the pallet. "Satisfied?"

She looked at the ashen color of his skin, the sweat standing on his forehead, and his pale, changeable-green eyes slitted against pain.

"You could teach stubborn to those Culpepper mules," she said angrily.

"No doubt."

"Do you like making extra work for me?"

He blinked. "I beg your pardon?"

"Look at you. Dirt from head to toe. You'll have to be washed right along with your bandages and loincloth."

Case wanted to argue, but exhaustion opened beneath him like a whirlpool, sucking him down. The extent of his own weakness shocked him.

"Too . . . tired," he managed.

"I'm not. You'll be clean before you know it."

He tried to object, but the whirlpool pulled him under. His words came out a meaningless mumble.

For a few moments Sarah watched his eyelids flicker and finally close. When they stayed shut, she sighed with relief. Even when he was so obviously spent from pain, she doubted that she could wrestle him into doing anything he didn't want to do.

"Stubborn, stubborn man," she muttered.

His eyes remained closed.

She couldn't help noticing that his black lashes were thick, long fans that curled slightly at the end. They made him look oddly vulnerable.

"Eyelashes any girl would envy," she said in a low voice, "and God gives them to a man who's tough enough to eat steel and spit razors."

If he heard, he gave no sign.

"Thank you, Case, whoever you are, wherever you came from," Sarah said softly.

He didn't move.

"We've always known the back of the cabin was our weak spot," she continued, walking over to where he lay. "Conner can't see it from the cottonwoods and Ute can't see it once he comes down off the rim to cover our other flank."

Case's breathing deepened as exhaustion pulled him into a healing sleep.

She knelt next to him and put the inside of her wrist on his forehead.

Cool. Smooth. Damp with sweat that was drying even as she touched him.

"Well, let's see how bad you hurt yourself defending our backs," she said quietly.

With quick motions she undid the bandage on his thigh.

No new blood showed, even on the deep wound.

"Thank God," she whispered. "You're

as tough physically as you are thick-skulled."

A long whistle came from beyond the cabin.

All clear.

Relief hit Sarah in a wave that left her light-headed.

After a few moments she took a deep breath, gathered herself, and went to work preparing a bath.

Despite what she had told the Culpeppers, there was still a small fire in the cabin. It was just enough to take the bite out of the winter air and keep a bucket of water warm.

"Everything all right in there?" Lola called.

"Case didn't open up his wounds, if that's what you mean," she answered. "Are the Culpeppers gone?"

"Nothing but dust hanging in the air."

"Where's Conner?"

"Watching the back of the cabin. Ute's tracking the third son of a bitch."

"I'll take care of Case and be out as soon as I can."

"No need. As it is, I'm about as useless as teats on a bull standing around out here. You want a hand at nursing?"

"No," Sarah said quickly. "I can handle it alone."

Only after she had spoken did she realize that she was reluctant to have anyone else see Case naked.

It had been one thing when he was desperately ill. It was quite another when he was healthy enough to crawl around the cabin. Somehow it was more . . . personal.

You're being addlepated, she scolded herself. *Lola has seen more men naked than I've seen clothed.*

Even so, Sarah rebelled at the thought of the other woman handling Case's sleek, muscular body now.

"When you can," she called out, "get some more water from the creek."

"Lordy, gal. What are you going to do with it all, wash them stone cliffs and hang them out on the clouds to dry?"

Sarah laughed softly. No one approved of all the soap and water she lavished on everything that didn't run away.

"No cliffs," she murmured. "Just a man. A big one."

When she thought of Case as a man instead of a wounded creature needing her care, her stomach did a funny little flip. It wasn't fear or even nervousness, although it felt a bit like both.

"What's wrong with you, Sarah Jane Lawson?" she asked herself softly, mimicking the rhythm and words of her long-dead grandmother. "A person would think you have taken leave of what smidgen of sense God gave you."

Unexpectedly, her throat closed around a grief she had never given way to.

She hadn't thought of her dead family in a long time. At first she simply hadn't been able to bear it. Finally it had become a habit.

"The future, not the past," she reminded herself. "Conner is the future for me."

The only future.

She would never again allow herself to be put at a man's mercy through marriage. All her hopes and longings for a family were bound up in her younger brother, the brother Ab had threatened just a few minutes ago.

Keep him leashed, else he won't have no fancies to strut in front of the gals.

Case stirred, then settled deeper into sleep.

Putting everything else out of her mind, Sarah bent over him and began the familiar ritual of unwrapping his wound, inspecting it, putting on salve, and wrapping the injury again with clean bandages.

As she worked on him, she talked softly, describing what she was doing. She spoke aloud because experience had taught her that wild creatures were less likely to startle if she let them know exactly where she was by keeping up a constant, gentle flow of words.

In some ways, Case reminded Sarah of a wild creature — strong, solitary, self-sufficient until man and his guns interrupted the natural order.

The only change in the normal routine of caring for him came after she moved his leg enough to look at the stitches on the back of his thigh. The skin around them was puckered and pulling against the thread.

"Goodness, you heal quickly," she said in her soft, crooning voice. "Healthy as a horse, as Uncle William would say."

Again, an unexpected grief gripped her. She rarely allowed herself to think of the bachelor doctor whose only legacy to the world was the black bag of his profession.

"I've taken good care of it for you," she whispered. "I've kept the instruments clean and bright . . . Do you know that, wherever you are? Does it make up for all the times I followed you around and pestered you until you taught me what you could before you died?"

No answer came from the silence.

She didn't expect one. She had grown used to asking questions that had no answers.

With shiny, oddly shaped little scissors, she snipped the stitches on the back of Case's leg. When she pulled them out with tweezers, he stirred slightly.

"It's all right," she murmured soothingly. "I'm just taking out stitches you don't need. Nothing to wake up over."

She didn't expect an answer from him any more than she had expected an answer from her dead uncle or the wild creatures she tended. Because Case wasn't resisting her in any way, she assumed he was still deeply asleep.

"There," she murmured. "That's the last stitch. Now I'll just bandage you up again. It won't hurt a bit."

His eyelashes lifted for an instant, revealing slivers of pale green. He started to tell Sarah that she wasn't hurting him, but it was too much effort.

It was easier just to lie quietly and let her soothe him with words and touches.

"Lola swears this smelly salve keeps infection out of wounds better than soap," she murmured. "I don't know what my uncle would say, but it certainly worked on Ute and you and the rest of the wild creatures."

She set down the jar of salve. It thumped gently onto the floor near her patient's shoulder.

The mixed scents of juniper, sage, and other herbs Case couldn't identify flowed over him each time he breathed in. He preferred the sunshine and rose-petal smell of Sarah's skin, but he lacked the energy to tell her.

"That's it," she encouraged. "Just keep sleeping. I'll have a clean bandage back on in two shakes of a lamb's tail."

The sensation of her hands on his skin was familiar to him by now, as was the faint brushing of her breasts against him while she wrapped the bandage all the way around his thigh.

His body's reaction was familiar, too.

He didn't bother trying to fight the arousal that came whether he willed it or not. He simply hoped the loincloth covered him.

"Now we'll just stretch out this leg," she murmured. "It shouldn't hurt for but a moment."

Her hands slid under the knee and heel of his wounded leg. Gently she guided his leg into a more natural position.

"It's a good thing I only have to move part of you at a time," she said softly. "You're big even lying down."

Her hand smoothed gently down his uninjured leg, enjoying the warmth and resilience of his flesh.

"Such strength," she said. "It must be wonderful to be that strong."

Case didn't speak for the simple reason that he didn't want the soft petting to stop. He hadn't experienced anything as sweet in too many years to count.

"You're dusty, too," she added with a soft laugh. "How do people raise a family on a dirt floor and keep the little ones clean?"

While she spoke, her hand repeated its calming sweep down his leg.

He knew the motion was meant to be soothing. He had watched her pet and murmur over her wounded hawk in just the same slow, gentle way, easing the bird's restlessness when she put medicine on its wound.

"I wish Conner and Ute could take a week to go to the mountains and saw some planks for the floor," she murmured. "But that isn't likely. So much work, so little time . . ."

She picked up the jar of salve, covered Case with a flannel sheet, and moved away from his side.

He gave a silent sigh that was part disappointment and part relief. Being petted like that was both arousing and oddly poignant.

She would be a good mother, he thought. *But first she'll have to find a man young or brave or stupid enough to ask God for children he can't protect.*

Case wasn't that young anymore. He hadn't been since he came home from the war and found the bloody remains of his brother's family.

Five Culpeppers left, he told himself. *Then it will be over.*

He didn't linger over what had been done or what remained to be done. No

146

man enjoyed digging out a privy, but no man worth his salt ignored the duty when he drew the short straw.

The Culpeppers had to be stopped.

Case had drawn the short straw.

A slight rush of air and the faint scent of roses told him that Sarah had returned.

"I hope this doesn't wake you," she murmured. "Just a warm wet rag and some soap. Nothing to worry a strong man like you."

Slim fingers combed through his hair, moving it back from his forehead. He enjoyed the caresses in a suspended kind of way, like a fever dream.

Rose-scented and soapy, the rag moved over his face. It reminded him of a big, warm, slightly rough tongue.

"I'll wash your hair tomorrow, when you're less tired," she crooned. "I could tell from the feel of it the first time I touched your hair that you're used to keeping it clean. I like that in a man."

The murmuring voice washed over Case as gently as the cloth. He floated in a place that was neither sleep nor waking, absorbing the gentle words and touches like desert ground soaking up water after a long drought.

"Your hair is all black and cool and sleek, like a horse's mane, only much silkier. It's as pretty as your eyelashes."

Being described as pretty in any way at all amused him, but nothing of his reaction showed. Like youth, laughter had fled from him after the war.

The delicate, musical sounds of Sarah rinsing and wringing out the washcloth were like her voice. Soothing and arousing. Real and unreal. Close and far beyond reach.

"Maybe I'll shave you in a few days, too," she continued in a low voice. "But not your mustache. It's longer than the new beard, so you must have it all the time."

Warm cloth and gentle words flowed over Case. He drifted closer and closer to real sleep with a trust that would have shocked him if he had noticed.

But he didn't. He was as bemused by Sarah's care as every other wary, wild creature that had fallen into her hands.

The flannel sheet slid down to his hips, disturbing him. He made an indistinct sound of protest. His right hand moved slightly, as though seeking to pull up the cover again.

"Hush," she murmured. "It's all right,

Case. I'm just cleaning the dirt off of you. Then I'll let you be."

His hand relaxed. He let out a long breath.

"That's it," she crooned. "That's just right. Keep sleeping and heal up until you're strong enough to fly again. Though you won't fly, will you? You'll just get on Cricket and ride out . . ."

The murmur of water and Sarah's voice blended in Case's mind. He drifted again toward the half-world that was neither sleeping nor waking.

Warm, wet, sweetly abrasive, the washrag licked over his arms and chest, removing evidence of his painful journey across the cabin's dirt floor.

"Culpepper . . . sneaking up . . . behind."

Case didn't know he had spoken aloud until Sarah answered him with words and gentling motions of the washrag on his chest.

"You're safe at Lost River ranch," she murmured. "You're safe with me. Sleep, Case. I won't let anyone harm you."

Distantly he realized that he had heard variations of those words when pain and fever had gripped him in a vise that he thought would end only with his death.

Safe at Lost River ranch.

Sleep, Case.

You're safe with me.

His breathing deepened and slowed to match the easy movement of the hands that cared for him so sweetly. Relaxed despite his hungry sexuality, he let the rose-scented dream of peace close around him.

He made no protest when he sensed the loincloth loosen. All he cared was that sweetness continue. Soothed, aroused, nearly asleep, wholly alive, he knew only that a moist warmth stroked him. He gave himself to it, for it was what he needed more than breath itself.

Pleasure tingled over him, pulsed like a slowly beating heart, and set him adrift again.

With a sigh that was almost a groan, Case fell headlong into sleep, leaving a wide-eyed Sarah behind.

"What in heaven's name . . . ?" she asked.

Such a thing had never happened when she nursed Ute back to his feet, and he had been shot up even worse than Case.

"Infection?" she whispered.

She bent over his torso and breathed in an indefinable mixture of salt and rain and man and rose soap.

"Thank God," she said in a low voice.

Whatever had happened to him, it hadn't been the result of infection.

Then she saw that his arousal was slowly subsiding. Her husband had looked like that when he finally got satisfaction from his silent, rigid wife.

Realization stained her cheeks in a wave of heat that was both embarrassment and something else, something that made her stomach give that funny little dip again.

"Well, you're definitely healing," she muttered.

Then she laughed softly, unexpectedly, and continued bathing him.

"You *do* learn something new every day," she murmured. "I never knew a man could get pleasure unless he hurt a woman."

Suddenly she remembered the tender, searing kiss that Case had given her. Her stomach quivered. Nerve endings she didn't know existed shimmered briefly deep inside her, startling her with a tingling rush of pleasure.

"Where did that come from?" she muttered. "Do you suppose it's catching?"

The idea that a man's pleasure could be contagious was more unsettling to Sarah than her first kiss had been.

Working quickly, she finished the bath and covered Case up again. To her relief, neither her patient nor her own stomach did anything unexpected during the process.

7

"What do you think you're doing?" Sarah demanded as she stepped into the cabin.

"What does it look like?" Case asked curtly.

The door closed hard behind her, shutting out a rectangle of winter-bright sun.

"From here," she said, "it looks like a darn fool hopping around on one leg using a rifle for a crutch and a bullet for a brain."

"You're right about the rifle."

Despite her irritation, she smiled. Case's quick mind livened up her days.

Not that Conner didn't have a quick mind, too. But that wasn't the same. She didn't take much sass from her little brother.

Case was a different matter entirely.

Through narrowed eyes, she watched his awkward progress. The first time she had found him fully dressed and hobbling around the cabin, she had

153

hidden his clothes while he slept.

But if she had thought having only a loincloth to cover him would keep Case in bed, she had been wrong. The proof was in front of her eyes.

And it was impressive.

"What's the hurry?" she asked reasonably, trying a different approach.

"Ten days lying here on my back have left me weak as a kitten."

Sarah looked at the muscular length of his body and laughed out loud.

"A kitten?" she asked. "Case, even lions don't have cubs like you."

His only answer was a muttered word.

"Would you care to repeat that?" she asked innocently.

"I'd care to, but you wouldn't care to hear it."

The rifle butt slipped on the dirt. He lurched and probably would have fallen if she hadn't leaped forward and offered her shoulder for balance.

"Easy there," she murmured, steadying him.

"Save that sugar and satin voice for your hawk. He's blind enough to believe it."

"He's wearing a hood at the moment."

"Like I said. Blind."

She smiled at Case.

He didn't smile in return.

She was neither surprised nor upset. She had learned that he didn't laugh or smile, though he had a sense of humor that obviously had been honed by living with a loving, mischievous family.

At first she had assumed that the pain of his wounds kept him from smiling. But as he healed, she realized that nothing as simple as bullet wounds had taken his laughter.

She didn't know what had happened to kill all joy in him. She suspected it had something to do with the names he called out in his fever — Emily and Ted, Belinda and Hunter.

But Emily most of all. Case called her name with a rage and grief and despair that tore at Sarah.

She knew only too well how it felt to lose everything, to be torn from warmth and love, to be left shivering and stunned and alone but for a child who depended on her for sheer survival.

"If I hood you, will you stay where you belong?" she asked lightly.

"You get anywhere near me with a

blindfold and Ute better have a gun on me."

She looked up at Case's eyes. Their corners weren't crinkled even the littlest bit, which told her that he wasn't teasing.

She sighed.

"Conner carved you a crutch," she said after a moment. "I'll get it."

"Get my clothes, too."

"No."

Case's mouth narrowed. He stared down into her determined face. As happened all too often, he was distracted by the mysterious color of her eyes, a gray that could dance with blue lights, shimmer with silver fire, or darken into storm clouds, depending on her mood.

"You want me running around in front of you naked," he said evenly, "then so be it."

But his voice wasn't as hard as he wanted it be. The idea of being naked with the quick-tongued, courageous little widow appealed to him entirely too much.

"You're not naked," she countered.

"You sure about that?" he drawled. "Maybe you better check below my neck. Never know what might have come undone while I was lurching around."

Pink flared on Sarah's cheekbones, but she kept her eyes above his chin.

"The point is," she said gamely, "that you're still too weak to be hopping around, whether buck naked or dressed like a lord on Easter Day."

"The point is, pretty widow, that you won't be safe from Ab Culpepper until I'm gone from here."

"I'm not pretty and I won't be safer with you gone."

"I heard what Ab said. He came to Lost River ranch for me, not for you."

"You didn't hear all of it," she said bluntly. "He threatened to castrate Conner."

Case drew a quick breath. "Judas priest. Why?"

"I don't know, but I can guess."

"I'm listening," he said.

"My brother is . . . impulsive."

Case waited.

"I think Conner tiptoed into the raiders' Spring Canyon camp," she said, "mixed up salt with the sugar, stirred fresh cow manure into the breakfast beans, and turned their horses loose to cover his own tracks."

"Would have been a damned sight more useful if he had slit some throats while he was at it."

Sarah's breath came in sharply. "No! I don't want Conner to have to live like that!"

"Then you're living in the wrong place."

"I'm not. He is. That's why I'm going to send him East to school."

Saying nothing, Case looked around the cabin. Its sparse furnishings and dirt floor told him that money was rare on Lost River ranch.

"Conner is close to man-sized," he said neutrally. "He might want a say in where he goes or doesn't go."

"There's more to the world than a river running through a red stone wilderness," she said, her voice tight.

"Is that you talking, or your brother?"

"Lost River ranch is all I want of the world. Being here suits me all the way to my soul."

The intensity in her voice was matched by her eyes. They fairly burned with silver fire.

"But Conner is different," she said fiercely. "He could be a doctor or a lawyer or a teacher. He could travel across the sea and meet kings. He could be anything!"

"Is that what he wants?"

"How can Conner know what he wants?" she countered in a rising voice. "All he really knows is this narrow canyon. If he takes a look around the world and wants to come back here, fine. But so help me God, *my brother will have the chance to look.*"

Because Sarah was still against Case's side, supporting him, he felt the tension vibrating through her body. She was like a wire much too tightly drawn, humming with strain.

Wires stretched that tight had a habit of breaking.

"Easy, little one," he murmured, turning her toward him. "These last ten days have been a trial for you."

"Hang the last ten days! I just want — I just —"

Her final, fragmented words were spoken against his chest. With a tenderness surprising in a man so powerful, he stroked her hair and back, gentling her rigid body.

Slowly she became less stiff.

"How old were you when your parents

died?" he asked quietly.

"Thirteen."

His eyes closed. He had seen young girls orphaned during the war. Some, the lucky ones, had kin nearby who took them in. Other orphans survived however they could, fighting with dogs for scraps of food. Too many of the children died.

Somehow he doubted that Sarah had been one of the lucky orphans who found shelter with kin.

"How old was Conner?" Case asked.

"Nine."

"Youngest in the family?" he guessed.

"Yes."

"Spoiled in the bargain, too, I'll bet."

"He isn't spoiled," she said instantly.

"Huh. He has a smile that could get around Satan, much less a doting older sister."

Sarah looked up, meeting Case's clear glance. Though she was pale, there were no tears shimmering in her eyes.

"I was the second oldest of five," she said. "And the only girl. Mother was a long time healing from Conner's birth. I rocked him, fed him, sang to him, kissed his hurts . . ."

The clarity of Case's glance became unbearable to her. It was as though he was seeing past her words right into her soul.

She looked away.

With great care he nestled her cheek against his chest. After a brief hesitation, she accepted the comfort.

She couldn't remember the last time she had felt like she could lean on someone. Since her parents' death, she always had been the strong one, the one who saw what had to be done and did it, come hell or high water.

"You were Conner's mother in all but name," Case said after a time.

She nodded.

"The flood got the others," she said after a moment, "but when the house started coming apart around us, I grabbed Conner and hung on until I found a tree big enough to hold us above the water."

"Your brother is a lucky young man," Case said. "Spoiled enough to know he's loved and not so spoiled that he's worthless."

"He's not spoiled," she insisted.

"Uh-huh. That's why you tore a strip off him yesterday for tracking deer and forgetting to get more firewood."

She tried to lean her head back and glare at Case, only to discover that she couldn't. The hand that was stroking her hair so soothingly was as firm as a rock wall. She could fight the gentleness or she could simply give in and enjoy it the way she enjoyed an unexpected summer rain.

Drawing in a deep breath, she sighed and relaxed against him. The scent of soap and man filled her nostrils. The heat of him, and the cushion of curly black hair beneath her cheek, reminded her that he was nearly naked.

The masculine textures intrigued her. She had never been so close to a bare-chested man. When Hal had demanded his rights as a husband, he always wore his long, scratchy underwear and he smelled of alcohol and old sweat.

"You smell like roses," she said after a moment. "Only different."

Case's big hand hesitated, then resumed stroking her hair.

"Blame your soap," he said.

"Blame it?"

She shook her head vigorously, sending her long braids slapping softly against his skin.

"I like the way you smell," she said. "Do you mind?"

"Cricket might wonder what happened to me, but, no, I don't mind."

"Good. The only other soap we have is lye. It would take the bark off a tree."

She sighed again and snuggled against his chest, as trusting as a kitten.

Heat shot through Case, even though he knew there was nothing flirtatious in her actions. Sarah was simply accepting the comfort he was offering.

Yet ever since he had first seen the cinnamon glory of her unbound hair, he had wanted to touch it.

Maybe she won't mind, he thought. *It's not like I'm trying to seduce her. I just want to stroke that beautiful hair.*

Comfort, that's all.

For both of us.

Bracing himself with one hand on the rifle, Case untied the thongs that kept her braids from unraveling. Using his fingertips he carefully combed the long strands until they were free from any restraint.

Cool hair spilled over his skin. His fingers clenched in the rose-scented cascade. He brought a fistful of her hair to his face, inhaled deeply, and slowly released the silky mass.

"I like the way you smell, too, Sarah Kennedy."

The huskiness of his voice pleased her. It was as tender and yet as masculine as the hand that had resumed stroking her hair.

"Now I know how my hawks feel," she said.

He made a rumbling, questioning kind of sound in his chest.

"Cosseted," she said, sighing. "It's very nice."

Moved without knowing why, Case brushed his lips over her hair so lightly that she didn't feel it. He couldn't explain the almost painful tenderness he felt toward her at that moment. He knew only that he had seen too many women and children destroyed by the war.

He hadn't been able to do anything about easing their pain, no matter how hard he tried.

Just as he hadn't been able to save his niece and nephew.

"Conner is lucky to have a sister like you," Case said.

"I need an older brother like you,"

Sarah said, smiling slightly. "Want to adopt me?"

Something like pain passed over his face, but the gentle stroking of his hand over her hair never hesitated.

"Kids need love," he said calmly. "I don't have any left in me."

"Of course you do. You're gentle and kind."

"That would come as a surprise to the Culpeppers."

"A lot of things would come as a surprise to them. They have less education than their mules."

Case put his finger beneath her chin and lifted her head until she couldn't avoid looking into his eyes.

"Don't fool yourself, Sarah Kennedy," he said quietly. "I don't have love left in me. I don't want it. I'll never again love anything that can die."

She wanted to look away from the calm certainty in his eyes, but she didn't. Instead, she let the truth of him sink into her like invisible steel talons.

The depth of the silent, tearing hurt surprised her. She hadn't known until that instant how much of herself she had given to Case.

Case, a man who wanted nothing from her.

He was like the wild birds of prey that hadn't wanted to be her captives, even long enough to heal.

But that's the nature of hawks, she reminded herself. *Case didn't start out that way.*

What drove him to shunning love?

She didn't ask the question aloud. There was no point. It would only bring him pain.

"You believe me," he said.

It wasn't a question. He could see her belief in the quenching of light in her eyes and the utter stillness of her body, as though her heart had stopped beating.

"I believe you," Sarah whispered.

He nodded. "Good. I don't want any falsehood between us."

"Why does it matter?" she asked with faint anger. "You're just one more wild creature that came over my doorstep wounded and will leave as soon as it can."

"Ute didn't leave."

"You sound like that worries you."

"It should. Healing is a kind of . . . magic."

166

For the space of several heartbeats Sarah stared into Case's eyes, eyes that now were color of the first, fragile green of spring. But it was a spring that would never come for him.

He didn't want it.

He shunned life the way most men shunned death.

The smile she gave him then was as painful as her thoughts.

"Don't let it worry you," she said. "I'm not a witch cackling over a cauldron of toads. I'm just a widow who learned the hard way how to deal with cuts, breaks, and bullet wounds."

The tension in his face changed. Few people would have noticed it. Fewer still would have guessed that it was his way of smiling.

"No toads, huh?" he asked.

"Not a one."

"Takes a load off my mind."

With a reluctance he didn't show, he stopped stroking her hair, turned away, and gathered himself to resume the painful circuits of the cabin.

Sarah turned with Case, acting as a second crutch.

He hesitated, then accepted her help.

"I'm not speaking for Lola's salves,

mind you," she said with determined lightness. "There might be an occasional snake in her medicines. Or in her stews, for that matter."

"Big Lola." He shook his head. "How did you end up with that old wh— er, sporting lady?"

"She came down the bluff about a month after I found Ute nearly shot to death in the Fingers of Dawn."

"Never heard of them."

She shrugged. "They're not on any army map. I named them. There are so many stone shapes out there, I have to name them to keep track of where I've looked for treasure and where I haven't."

Awkwardly Case moved around the cabin, forcing himself to listen to what Sarah was saying. It helped to take his mind off the heat surging through his blood.

"I think you've had enough," she said. "You look strained."

He simply shook his head. It wasn't pain that was thinning his lips. It was raw hunger.

Her right arm was around his waist. Her fingers were flexed against the naked skin above his loincloth. Her right side — breast, hip, and thigh — pressed against him with each step as she helped him keep his balance.

Every motion of his body reminded Case of the surprisingly soft curves hidden beneath Sarah's rough clothing.

Is she doing it on purpose? he asked silently, savagely.

A swift look at her face told him that she had no idea of what her closeness was doing to him.

For a widow she's damned naive.

Or maybe she meant just what she said. She wants a big brother, not a lover.

"Careful," she said.

"How did Lola know Ute was here?" Case asked, determined to keep his mind on something else.

"She followed rumors of his death back to here. Then she found out he wasn't dead. She has stayed ever since."

"Because Ute stayed?"

Sarah nodded. Her loose hair slid over his bare skin like a lover's caress.

His breath came in hard.

"Do you know Ute's reputation?" he muttered.

"I can guess," she said. "Chances are

he wasn't a church deacon."

"You can go to the bank with that."

"Are you hunting him?" she asked bluntly.

"Why would I?"

"Bounty money."

"Is that what you think?" Case asked in a cold tone. "That I came here hunting bounties?"

"On Ute? No."

Case grunted. "That's another truth you can go to the bank on."

"But the Culpeppers have a lot of bounty money on their narrow heads," Sarah said.

"I would hunt them for free."

"Why?"

He didn't answer.

She didn't ask again.

Silently they made a few more turns around the cabin. His skin seemed very warm beneath her hand.

"Don't you think you should rest now?" she asked anxiously. "You're getting overheated."

Overheated, he thought grimly. *That's one way of putting it. Downright hot and bothered would be another.*

Randy as an elk in rut would be closest to the truth.

Case didn't like it. At all. If his sexuality had indeed come back to stay, it would be damned inconvenient for him.

Especially with the gentle, sharp-tongued widow so close by.

"Let go of me," he said through his teeth. "I can walk alone."

"Don't talk nonsense."

"I'm not."

"Of course you are," she retorted. "If you fall, I'll have to wash you all over again. You could take a chill or — or something."

Case give Sarah a sideways look. Her cheeks were pink with more than the effort of helping him lurch around the cabin.

The dream of sweet release that had haunted him at odd times during the past week returned in a rush.

Maybe it wasn't a dream.

"Watch it!" she said, bracing herself.

Swearing, he dropped the rifle and caught himself with both hands against the cabin wall. She ended up between him and the rough planks.

"Oof," she said. "You're heavy."

"You're soft. Too soft. Damnation, I didn't want this!"

He made a rough, hungry sound as

he lowered his mouth. Her lips were deep rose, glistening. They were parted with the same surprise that widened her eyes.

If Sarah's first kiss had been tender and searing, her second was deep, hot, and overwhelming. She couldn't breathe for the weight of Case pressed against her body. She couldn't speak for the thrusting of his tongue against hers, filling her mouth.

She couldn't even move to push him away.

Grimly she set herself to endure him as she had learned to endure her husband.

If only Case weren't so big that way, she thought, *it wouldn't be so bad.*

And if he were gentle . . .

With a muffled sound, Case curbed his violent, unexpected hunger. When he lifted his head, he saw that her skin was pale and her lips were rubbed red from the force of his kiss. Her pupils had dilated until there was little left but darkness rimmed with silver.

She looked like a frightened girl rather than a woman interested in passion.

"I'm sorry," he said, thoroughly disgusted with himself. "You took me by surprise."

"I t-took you!" she asked in disbelief. "I didn't do one darned thing!"

He closed his eyes so that he wouldn't have to see the shadows and accusation in hers.

"I bruised your mouth," he said in a low voice. "That's never happened before. I've never been rough with a woman, even back when I wanted them."

His eyes opened, but they were no longer glittering with passion. Slowly he lowered his head again.

Sarah drew a startled, half-fearful breath. It came out in a ragged sigh of surprise when the tip of his tongue began tracing a warm, tender path around her lips. This was the gentle kiss she remembered, the one that made her stomach dip and her nerve endings shimmer.

"Case?" she whispered.

"It's all right. Just an apology. Nothing more . . ."

His teeth nibbled gently around the same path his tongue had taken.

"Does that hurt?" he asked.

She shook her head. The motion

173

brushed her lips over his. When she felt his whole body clench in response, she drew back so quickly that her head knocked against the cabin wall.

"Easy," he said. "I'm not going to hurt you."

"But I —" she began, only to be stopped by the turmoil in his brilliant eyes. "Case? I — I don't —"

"Hell, I know you don't want me. Can't say as I blame you. I wouldn't want a lover who had no more manners than a grizzly."

With that, he pushed away from her.

Dazed, uncertain, caught between tenderness and fear, Sarah watched him as he balanced one-handed against the wall. Awkwardly he retrieved the rifle he had been using as a crutch. He turned to face her, leaning against the rifle butt.

When she moved to help him back to the bed, he stopped her with a look.

The gentleness and regret and hunger in his eyes was gone. Clear ice would have had more emotion.

"I haven't even wanted a woman since the end of the war," he said flatly. "But I want you, Sarah Kennedy."

"I — I —"

"Don't worry that I'll force myself on you. I won't. You have my word on that."

After a moment, she nodded. If he had been that kind of man, he would have done it already.

"I believe you," she said softly.

"Then believe this," he said, his voice as distant as his eyes. "I hate wanting you. It means not as much of me died as I'd hoped."

8

"The sweat lodge will do him good," Ute said. "Sweating is good for what ails a man."

Without answering, Sarah threw more grain to the chickens that were squawking and squabbling around her feet.

The fowl ignored a plate of supper scraps she had placed in a nearby willow thicket. Ghost, a half-wild herding dog that had adopted the chickens when he wasn't watching goats for Lola, lurked in the willows.

Like most of the creatures on Lost River ranch, Ghost had arrived more dead than alive. Like Ute, the dog had decided to stay.

"Sarah?" Conner asked.

"I'm thinking."

But she wasn't. Not really. She was looking a few feet beyond the chickens, where Lost River ran clear and clean over a bed that was made of solid stone and gravel bars whose dominant color was rust-red.

The chickens' preferred roosting area was in the cottonwoods and willows lining the water course. Every year she lost a few chicks or full-grown birds to coyotes and hawks. She would have lost a lot more if it weren't for Ghost.

Someday I'll have enough money to build a proper coop for the chickens, she thought.

She fished in the bucket for a bit more corn. The kernels were smooth and hard and cold, like small river pebbles. In the rich, slanting sunlight the corn glowed in shades of red and blue, white and gold.

Indian corn, grown on the fertile floodplain of the creek. Squash and beans grew there as well, but corn had been especially abundant this year. She was using it to fatten the chickens against the winter chill.

"What about it?" Conner asked again.

She tossed out more corn without answering.

"You can't keep Case cooped up forever," her brother insisted. "The chickens have more freedom than he does."

"More clothes, too," Ute muttered.

"There's frost on the ground," she said with exaggerated patience.

"Usually is, this time of year," Ute said.

"It's been barely three weeks since you brought Case here more dead than alive," she said pointedly.

"Damned sure looks lively now," Ute said. "Jumpy as a flea. Man's got cabin fever, sure enough."

"C'mon, sis. Lola is up on the rim and the Culpeppers haven't been sniffing around since Case shot Parnell in the a— er, rump."

"Fine shootin'," Ute said to no one in particular. "Really fine. Could have used that boy in my younger days."

Sarah grimaced.

His answering grin revealed strong, tobacco-stained teeth.

"Don't worry that pretty head none about them Spring Canyon trash coming back to bother you," Ute said. "They're scared of leaving camp."

"I doubt that," she said.

"Every time they leave, something happens," Conner said, looking at the sky.

"Even when they don't, bad luck comes calling anywise," Ute added. "Hear them boys lost a passel of bullets. Them cartridges just up and hit

178

the trail all by theirselves."

Conner snickered.

Sarah gave Ute a sideways look. His straight gray hair, narrow dark eyes, and high cheekbones should have belonged to a prophet or a priest.

Instead they belonged to an old outlaw who would kick over a beehive just to enjoy the hullabaloo that followed.

"If you must bait the Culpeppers," she said to him, "don't take Conner with you."

Ute looked down at his dusty moccasins. Only Sarah had the ability to make him feel sheepish. He was convinced that she was a gray-eyed angel of mercy put on earth to remind sinners like himself of what goodness was.

As far as he was concerned, there could have been no other reason that she would have saved his worthless life.

"Yes'm," he said.

"I mean that, Ute."

"Yes'm."

"But sis, they're —" Conner began.

"Hush," she interrupted. "You listen to me, both of you. Stay away from Spring Canyon."

"But they're hunting Hal's treasure," Conner said. "Really hunting it, quartering the canyons the way you do."

A chill of anxiety went through Sarah. *That Spanish silver is Conner's future,* she thought. *I have to find it first.*

Abruptly she scattered the rest of the corn on the ground. Then she turned away from the bustling, pecking chickens and headed back for the cabin with long strides.

The men followed at a quickstep.

"Sis?"

"Let the outlaws hunt," she said. "They won't find the treasure. They don't know the canyons like I do."

There was more hope than certainty in her voice. Since the Culpeppers and Moody's Breeds had come to the wilderness of stone buttes and mazelike canyons, her treasure hunting time had been reduced to a few stolen hours.

Since Case had come into her care, she hadn't found time to look for treasure at all. Between nursing him, keeping an eye on Conner and Ute, and taking care of her normal chores, she had enough work for three women.

"Any eggs?" she asked Conner.

"Six fresh. Some others that will be chicks."

"They won't make it through the winter. You should have been gathering eggs for us to eat instead of playing pranks on outlaws."

"Ghost will watch out for those chicks better than any mother hen," Conner said.

Sarah gave her brother a look that he ignored. In silence they approached the cabin.

"What about it?" he asked her after a moment.

"What about what?" she asked.

"Case," Conner said, disgusted. "It will do him good."

"No."

"Oh, c'mon, don't be a —"

"No," she interrupted flatly.

"Why don't you ask me?" Case said. "I'm of age."

She made a startled sound and spun toward the cabin.

Case was standing in the doorway, fully clothed from hat to boots. A six-gun was holstered around his lean hips. There wasn't a crutch in sight.

He looked dangerous.

"You found your clothes," she said weakly.

It was the only thing she could think of to say.

"Thank you for cleaning and mending them," he said. "I can barely find where the bullet holes were."

"You're welcome. But if you do what Conner and Ute want, you won't need them."

"No man needs bullet holes," Case said dryly.

Conner laughed, then coughed to conceal it.

She flushed. Since that tangled moment when Case had plastered her against the cabin wall and frightened her with his blunt male hunger — and then apologized in a way that made her tingle just to remember it — he had treated her as if he were the blood kin she had asked for.

I need an older brother like you. Want to adopt me?

Sometimes she was grateful for his casual manner. Most often, she was irritated without knowing why.

Yet, when he thought she was too busy changing his bandages to notice, he had a way of giving her a veiled look that made her cheeks burn.

Just as they were burning now.

What's wrong with me? she asked herself angrily. *I asked for an older brother and I got it. Teasing and all.*

Hallelujah.

Yet somehow she didn't feeling like rejoicing.

"I was referring to your clothes," she said remotely, "not bullet holes."

"Are you planning on stealing them again?" Case asked, his face expressionless. "If so, I have to warn you I wouldn't take kindly to it."

"Where's your crutch?" she asked.

"In the fire."

"For the love of God," she said, throwing up her hands. "Fine. Go to the sweat lodge with Conner and Ute. Turn the color of a lobster and keel over on your furry face!"

Thoughtfully Case ran a big hand over his cheeks and tried to remember the last time he had shaved.

Must have been Hunter and Elyssa's wedding, he decided.

"I broke my shaving mirror," he said.

Case looked from Ute to Conner.

No help there. Neither one of them had enough chin fur to be worth a razor. Nor were there any windows in the cabin to use as a makeshift mirror.

He looked at Sarah.

"I don't have a mirror," she said.

183

"Neither does Lola."

"How do you get your hair braided so neatly?"

"Practice."

He didn't ask about Lola. As far as he could tell, Lola braided her hair when she washed it, which wasn't very often.

"What did your husband do?" Case asked.

"She used to shave him," Conner said.

Speculatively Sarah looked at Case's thick pelt.

"I'd wear out a razor on you," she said.

"I'll hone it," he said.

She shrugged. "It's your hide."

"I'm not worried. You'll patch up whatever you cut and fuss over me like a mother hen in the bargain."

Something in his tone suggested that he liked having her fussing over him.

She looked away from him, afraid that her cheeks were warming again.

First he says that he hates wanting me, she thought. *Then he acts like he can't wait to have my hands on him again.*

Or is he just being a teasing big brother again?

Men are such annoying, unpredictable creatures. It's a wonder mothers don't just drown all of them at birth.

"Let me by, please," Sarah said in a tight voice. "I have a hawk that's overdue to be set free."

When she went through the doorway, Case moved aside, but more slowly than she expected. She bumped solidly into him.

"I'm sorry," she said, trying to step aside.

Her shoulders thumped against the door frame. There was barely room for her to breathe.

"Heavens, there's a lot of you," she muttered.

The corners of his eyes crinkled a bit.

An instant later Case startled Sarah by lifting her casually and setting her inside the cabin. Instinctively she braced her hands against his shoulders as he lifted. The flexed power of his muscles did odd things to her stomach and nerve endings.

It wasn't fear. Sarah was sure of it.

She knew what fearing a man felt like.

"There's just enough of you," he said too softly for anyone else to overhear.

He released her with a slow move-

185

ment of his hands that was just short of a caress. Then he turned to the other males.

"Sarah's right," he said. "I'm not up to a sweat lodge and a dip in a cold creek just yet."

Conner opened his mouth to argue.

Ute was faster.

"Good," he said. "Stand guard on Sarah. She's got less sense than a chicken when she's watching a hawk fly."

"A whole troop of soldiers and a brass band could march up behind her and she wouldn't notice," Conner agreed.

"That's not true," she said.

"Huh," Ute said.

Her brother laughed.

"I rode a green-broke mustang bucking and pawing toward her, making enough noise to raise the dead," Conner said to Case, "and when she looked away from the hawk, she jumped like I'd popped up out of the ground under her feet."

"You're lucky she didn't shoot you," Case said.

"That was before those sons of —" Conner began.

Sarah stiffened.

"— er, that trash moved into Spring Canyon," he amended. "We weren't toting guns all the time."

Case looked at the younger man. He was wearing a holster filled with a big old Colt Dragoon percussion model six-shooter. Case noticed the gun had been altered to take metal cartridges. He had little doubt that Ute was the gunsmith who made the change.

I hope Conner is half as good with that belt gun as he thinks he is, Case thought. *Otherwise he'll bite off a bigger chunk of Culpepper than he and Ute can chew.*

"I'll take care of your sister for you," he said, looking over Sarah's head.

Oddly unwilling, Conner looked at her.

"Sis?"

"Go sweat yourself foolish," she said. "I'll be fine."

Still her brother hesitated. He gave Case a look that was surprisingly adult in its measuring quality.

"She'll be safe," Case said evenly. "You have my word on that."

Conner looked at him again, then nodded. He and Ute headed toward the sweat lodge, which was about two hundred yards away. The small building was close to a deep pool that had been gouged out of bedrock during seasonal floods.

Several times on the way to the sweat lodge, Conner looked back over his shoulder.

Each time Sarah waved.

Finally her brother vanished around a bend in the creek.

"He's very protective of you," Case said.

Her expression changed. She didn't like to think about why Conner had such an adult concern for his sister. Twice he had found her huddled around herself after one of Hal's drunken sprees.

There hadn't been a third time.

"He's a good boy," she said.

"He's man-sized."

"He's fifteen."

"Old enough to kill," Case said.

She looked at him. What she saw in his eyes made her wish that she had kept on watching her brother.

"Is that how old you were when you went to war?" she asked against her better judgment.

"Yes."

Nothing about his manner encouraged pursuing the subject, yet she couldn't let it drop.

"Alone?" she asked.

"No. I dragged my older brother Hunter along with me."

"Did he — is he —"

"Hunter survived," Case said curtly. "His family didn't."

"You sound like you blame yourself."

"I do."

"You were just a boy."

He looked at her with eyes that were older than winter and much less inviting.

"Should I saddle Cricket for this expedition," he asked, "or do you just release the hawk around here?"

"I usually climb up to the south rim and walk back in about a mile. That way my chickens aren't the first thing to catch the hawk's interest."

"I'll saddle up."

"You don't have to go. I'm sure it's safe enough. We haven't seen any sign of Moody's men or the Culpeppers in —"

Sarah sighed and shut up. She was talking to herself.

Case was headed toward the brush lean-to where bridles, saddles, and what small equipment they had for the ranch was stored.

Conner is just like that when he doesn't want to listen to reason, she thought. *Irritating, irritating creatures!*

"Men," she said under her breath as she closed the cabin door being her. "What was God thinking of?"

Then she began crooning gently to the hawk as she approached it.

The bird's wings flared and flapped strongly. Because it was leashed to the perch by rawhide thongs, the hawk made no real attempt to fly. It simply exercised its wings and its temper on whatever came close enough.

"Hello, my fierce feathered beast," she murmured. "You've been working those wings so often, I bet you'll jump toward the sky and just keep on going."

The hawk moved sharply, as though it sensed freedom.

"Yes, yes," she said soothingly. "The next mouse or snake you eat will be one you catch. No more having chunks stuffed down your throat willy-nilly."

While she talked, she slipped a leather hood over the hawk's head. Immediately the fierce bird stilled, for it could no longer see.

Before Sarah managed to get on her

jacket, hat, and the leather gauntlet Ute had sewn for her, Cricket had trotted up to the front of the cabin.

"Sarah?" Case called. "Better hurry, or it will be sunset before we get to the top."

"I'm hurrying."

But there was no impatience in her voice or hands when she reached for the hawk. She had learned that birds of prey were uncanny in their sensitivity to her mood.

Gently she coaxed the hawk off the perch and onto her arm.

"There, there, no need to get all ruffled," she murmured. "You've been on my arm before."

Alertly the hawk rode her arm to the cabin door. Even hooded, the bird sensed the difference between the interior of the cabin and the open sky beyond. The yellow beak gaped wide as the hawk gave a high, wild cry.

Cricket snorted and shied.

"Easy, you puddinghead," his rider said soothingly. "You're too big to be a hawk's supper."

Sarah looked up at the tall stallion. Doubt was clear on her face.

Case dismounted. Other than a brief

hesitation when he took weight on his injured leg, he showed little sign that he had been fighting for his life three weeks before.

"You ride up front," he said. "Ready?"

"For what?"

"A hand up. Two hands, actually. Put your left hand on the saddle horn and your left foot in my hands."

"But what about your wound?" she objected, even as she followed his directions.

"Up you go."

He boosted Sarah into the saddle so smoothly that the hawk didn't even flare its wings.

"Keep your foot out of the stirrup for now," he said, his voice low and mellow as candlelight. "I'm going to reach around you and get up behind the saddle. Ready?"

By the time she realized that the crooning, velvet voice belonged to Case, he was settling onto Cricket behind her.

"Can you ride without stirrups?" he asked, still using the soothing voice.

"I usually ride without the whole saddle."

"Good," he murmured. "Stirrups make it easier on my leg."

"Where did you learn to talk like that?"

"Like what?"

"Butter and honey and lamplight."

"Training horses," he said. "Seemed to soothe them."

"Soothes birds, too."

"How about people?"

"I'm still awake," she retorted in a deliberately velvety voice, "but only barely."

The corners of his eyes shifted slightly upward.

When he breathed in, the scent of roses and sunshine and fresh air lifted from her in a perfume more subtle and fascinating than anything that he had ever smelled from a fancy crystal bottle.

She wants a big brother, not a lover, he reminded himself. *That's what I want to be to her, too.*

Then, irritably, *Wish to hell I could convince my dumb handle of that. I haven't been this randy since I first discovered I could do more than piss with it.*

He rearranged his weight behind the saddle to accommodate his increasing arousal. As he shifted, he tried to forget just how yielding and yet resilient

Sarah's flesh had felt beneath his hands when he lifted her past him in the cabin doorway.

She's just the right size, he thought again. *Not so little that a man would lose her in the bedding, and not the size of a barn door, like Lola.*

Lola would make two of Ute.

Must make for some interesting nights in the old wickiup.

"See that notch in the rim off to the right?" Sarah asked.

"Yes."

"Head for it. There's a trail up and over the rim."

He reined Cricket toward the notch.

The land began to slant upward slowly. The farther the horse got from the river, the drier the underlying ground became. Instead of the musical murmurings of the creek and songbirds hidden in the willows, there was only the occasional rasp of the stirrups against underbrush.

Massive cottonwoods quickly gave way to ragged, narrow-leafed bushes. Prickly pear and other cactus appeared from time to time where the land was too dry or poor for grass. In the deeply slanting rays of the sun, cactus spines outlined their plants in shimmering gold.

Colder air from the mesa top sighed past the riders on the way down to the valley. The breeze brought with it the scent of the coming night, cool and crisp and mysterious.

The creak of leather and the steady breathing of the stallion became the only sounds in the stillness of the late afternoon.

As always, Case's eyes roved the landscape, probing for danger. This time he saw nothing but the stark, impossible beauty of a landscape where stones took on the color of earthbound rainbows and the shape of man's wildest fancies.

Beyond the rim the path became more level, but only for a mile or so. Then the land pitched up again into a wall of rusty cliffs and dizzying red spires. Dry watercourses showed as lighter bands against the ground and darker bands on the cliffs.

"How much farther?" Case asked.

"See that rocky knoll off to the left? The wind gives a nice lift at the top."

Cricket wound among boulders and scrambled across sheets of rubble-strewn bedrock. Though the stallion was carrying double, he didn't raise a sweat or breathe hard.

"This is far enough," Sarah said.

Case swung down off Cricket. As he reached up to help her, slanting sunlight turned her eyes to a luminous golden-gray, like twin candles burning in mist. The same light transformed the cinnamon of her hair into fire, sleek and radiant and inviting.

It was all he could do to keep from pulling off her battered slouch hat, untying her braids, and plunging his fingers into the silky flames.

Hunger pulsed, angering Case with its urgency. He lifted Sarah out of the saddle, set her on the ground, and quickly stepped away from her.

The fact that he limped when he moved didn't improve his temper at all.

"You know that hawk is going to get some of your chickens," he said, his voice carefully neutral.

She gave him a sideways glance. Although he appeared controlled to the point of coldness, she sensed that there was more to his feelings at the moment than he was showing.

"The hit-or-miss way Conner collects

eggs," she said, "there should be plenty of chicks to go around."

Case shrugged.

"Stay here until I free the hawk," she said. "I'll need room to swing my arm."

Crooning gently to the bird of prey, she walked to a point where a level slab of bedrock jutted out from the steeply sloping knoll that Cricket had just climbed.

Despite cool air flowing down from distant heights, the land far below kept enough heat to send currents of warm air rising along the knoll. Like an invisible wave, the breeze lifting up from the canyon floor broke across the ledge where she stood. Once past the ledge, the warm air rose up into the sky.

The hawk flapped its wings and leaned eagerly into the warm wind.

Crooning softly, Sarah stroked the bird, calming it.

"Hush now," she murmured. "Your craw is full of food. Your wing is healed. There are a lot of safe roosts nearby. All you need is a good boost to be on your way."

After a time the bird stopped trying to fly. But eager shudders still ran though the hawk's body, as though it knew freedom was finally at hand.

What followed happened so fast that Case could barely separate the motions Sarah made. She pulled off the hood with a quick movement of her left hand and at the same time launched the hawk into the air with an upward sweep of her right arm.

Wings flared blackly against the golden-orange light of the setting sun. The hawk dropped below the lip of the rock and vanished.

For a heartbeat Case was afraid that the hawk had been unable to fly. Then a shape burst above the ledge of rock like a black comet. The hawk shot higher and higher with each powerful wing beat until it was invisible against the colorful radiance of the sky.

A sweet, wild cry fell down to the earthbound man and woman watching from below.

Limping slightly, he went to the ledge. He ignored the ache in his wounds. He had endured much worse before. He had no doubt that worse was probably in store for him in the future.

But at the moment, all that mattered to him was the silvery flash of sorrow he had seen in Sarah's eyes.

Silently he came and stood next to her.

"The hawk will be all right," he said. "It's flying beautifully."

"I know," she said huskily. "It's just . . ."

"What?"

"I would give my soul to fly with it."

The yearning in her stitched through him like a golden needle. He felt a kinship with her so intense it was painful.

More dangerous than any physical desire, the sense of being joined to Sarah pierced the armor Case had built against all feeling. She touched him in an elemental, frightening way.

Abruptly he turned away from her and stared out over the deserted, mysterious land.

To the northwest the snowy heights of a distant cluster of mountains peeked above the high plateaus that lay between and desert. The mountaintops reflected a rich, creamy yellow light. All but the highest part of the peaks was hidden by the series of ragged, eroded plateaus that swept out and down in all directions.

The sun descended swiftly until it

was only a handspan from the horizon. Darkness gathered.

In the vast landscape, the knoll where Case and Sarah stood was no more significant than a grain of sand.

Time to be going, he thought reluctantly.

As he turned back toward the lip of the ledge, shimmering orange light spilled over mesas and buttes, making them glow with crimson fire. Tongues of midnight licked out from the deep canyons and creases. Darkness pooled and rose in a silent, unstoppable tide. Pinnacles of stone became columns of fire burning against the coming night.

No sign of man showed in all the land. No roads. No fixed trails. No lantern glow. Not even smoke rising into the flawless sky.

A man could live here, Case thought. *Really live.*

No crowding from neighbors. No townspeople reaching into your pockets with both hands and a false smile on their lips.

No memories.

No other place like this, anywhere.

Let other men take the rolling green hills and wide green valleys. This is for me. Clean and wild and free of the past.

An unfamiliar feeling of belonging stole over him. He took a deep, slow breath, then another, then another, filling himself with the stark, unflinching beauty of the land.

Down below, along the bottom of the biggest canyon, there were two curving, haphazard lines where cottonwood and willows stood out against the darker land.

Lost River, he thought. *Lost River Canyon.*

Water.

He reached into the pocket of what had started as a Confederate overcoat but had long since been stripped of all bright buttons and braid. The spyglass was a familiar, cool weight in his hand. He put the viewing end to his left eye and began quartering the land below.

No matter how carefully he looked, he found few signs of water. There were solitary cottonwoods in some rocky creases, but there was only one winding ribbon of trees and brush to mark the presence of a reliable river.

Lost River ranch is the only good water

for a long, long way in all directions, he realized.

Without water, a ranch just isn't possible.

And the reliable water was already taken.

Yet Case knew he belonged to this land. He was more certain of it than he had been of anything in his life.

There is something waiting for me after I'm finished with the Culpeppers, he thought. *This land.*

Land that can't be maimed or murdered by men.

Land where there's room to breathe, to stretch, to build a ranch. New land, clean of memories.

Land, but not water.

Only Lost River ranch has any water worth mentioning.

And Sarah Kennedy owned Lost River ranch.

Absently he collapsed the spyglass and stored it once more in the pocket of his overcoat.

I suppose I could marry her for it.

No sooner did the idea come than an icy blackness burst through his soul, freezing the fragile tendril of hope for the future he had just felt.

Marriage meant children.

Children meant a nightmare of helpless, maimed bodies.

No, he thought savagely. *Never again. Never!*

There had to be another way to win Lost River ranch.

A safe way.

A way without any feeling at all.

Case was silent all the way back to the ranch. Not even the tilted, silvery smile of the moon penetrated the night that filled his soul.

9

The next day Case awakened long before dawn. As always, he lay motionless, orienting himself.

What woke me up?

The answer came in a butterfly-soft brush of fabric against his shoulders as someone tucked the covers around him.

Sarah, he thought.

Still watching over me.

A warmth that was only partly sexual radiated through him. Even as he slid back toward sleep, he decided that he would move on in the morning.

He had to.

Otherwise his relentless male hunger would overcome his common sense.

Wouldn't be the first time a man got led down the wrong road by his dumb handle, he thought sleepily. *It happened to Hunter the first time around. His blood got so hot he married the wrong girl.*

Soft, sweet breath flowed over Case.

He tried to ignore the rose-scented heat of Sarah.

He couldn't, any more than he could ignore his insistent, pulsing hunger for her.

A hunger she didn't share.

She wants me as a big brother, he reminded himself, amused and nettled and relieved all at once.

He hadn't thought of a gentle way to tell Sarah that he didn't want any kinship with her. Not brother, not cousin, not uncle.

Especially not uncle.

What the war hadn't destroyed in Case, finding the bodies of his nephew and niece did.

After that, he had been a long time learning how to sleep again, how to eat, how to live without feeling anything at all.

Even rage.

Sarah was more dangerous to his hard-won lack of emotion than a loaded, cocked gun pointed right at his face.

Air shifted and stirred lightly, disturbed by her silent withdrawal from his side. A moment later small sounds came as she curled up a few feet away. Soon her breathing slowed and deepened.

Wonder how many times she has got-

ten up all through the night to check on some hurt creature? he thought.

The thought of her padding barefoot across the cold dirt floor to check on him bothered Case.

No need for that. I'm fine. Hasn't she ever heard of letting sleeping dogs lie?

An owl called from behind the cabin.

Case came out from under the blankets in a single, silent rush. One hand closed around his shotgun, which was propped against the wall. The weight of the weapon told him that it was fully loaded.

When he cocked the shotgun, both Sarah and Conner woke up.

"What's go—" Conner asked.

"Quiet," Case interrupted.

Though his voice was very low, Conner shut up instantly.

"An owl called out back," Case said softly.

"So?" Conner whispered. "We have lots of owls around here."

"Never heard one sound like that. Do you have your shotgun?"

"Right in my hands."

"Good. Guard Sarah."

"I can guard myself," she said in a low voice.

As though to prove her point, she cocked the shotgun she was holding.

"Stay here anyway," Case said.

"But —" Conner began.

"Less people moving around out there," he said over the boy's objection, "less chance we'll shoot one another by mistake. Stay put."

"Do as he says," Sarah said to her brother.

"Who's on the rim now?" Case asked.

"Ute," Conner said.

"Good. None of the Culpeppers are built like Lola. Even in the dark, I'd know not to shoot her."

Conner laughed quietly.

Case knelt and looked out the back of the cabin through one of the many chinks between the ill-fitting planks. The light outside was as thin as the moon itself. A river of stars cascaded silently overhead, throwing off an eerie radiance.

No shadows moved. No brush stirred. No pebbles rattled in the stillness. No birds called sleepily, disturbed by the passage of man. Not even a coyote sang to the darkness.

Quickly Case dressed. The black wool pants and shirt he put on made him dissolve into the darkness. Instead of boots, he wore knee-high moccasins. In addition to his belt gun, he strapped on a knife whose blade was eight inches long. He hung the shotgun by its leather sling across his left shoulder and down his right side, handy but not in the way.

"Don't shoot unless you know who it is," Case said. "I'll call like a hawk before I come in."

"Case," Sarah whispered.

Unerringly he turned toward her, though she was no more than a faint blur in the darkness.

"Yes?" he asked softly.

"I . . . Be careful."

"Don't worry. I did a lot of this sort of thing during the war. If I were a careless kind of man, I'd be dead."

"Let me guard your back," Conner said.

Case turned toward the darkness where the boy waited, a shotgun in his hands.

Sarah hasn't spoiled her brother too much, Case thought. *He's man-sized in more than his rawboned body.*

"You can help me most by not talking or moving around in here," he said. "I'm going to be listening outside. If there's shooting, keep your sister in the cabin if you have to sit on her. Hear me?"

"I don't like it, but I hear you."

Sarah muttered something neither male bothered to acknowledge.

The door creaked as Case opened it and slipped out into the darkness. He closed the door behind him and stood motionless with his back to the cabin, listening to the night with his ears and other, far more subtle senses.

The lack of sound was overwhelming, silent eternity flowing overhead like the stars, but in darkness rather than light. There was an icy stillness to the air that told of time and distance and the slowly deepening grip of winter.

The quiet was absolute.

Somebody is out there, he thought. *No night is this quiet unless men are sneaking around.*

Crouching, he went to the corner of the cabin and peered around it. There were no human shadows prowling about on that side. He ghosted down the side of the cabin, crouched again, and listened.

Silence.

Counting seconds in his mind, Case waited.

More than four minutes went by.

While he waited, tiny sounds began to sift through the darkness once more. The night creatures were picking up their normal business of finding food, spurred on by the chill and the coming winter.

A pack rat hurried across an opening between a man-high sagebrush plant and the smaller shrubs that grew ten feet away. Instants later an owl swept by on noiseless wings. There was a tiny, frantic squeal and the beat of wings on dirt.

The owl lifted into the night. Outlined against the stars, a pack rat hung limply from the bird's talons.

An owl called from the brush at the back of the cabin. Another owl answered.

Silence returned, as deep as the night itself.

The critters are no more fooled by those hoots than I am, Case thought dryly.

He judged that the calls were about ten yards closer to the cabin than the first round of false hooting he had heard.

Suddenly the silhouette of a man moved against the stars. It was just for an instant, but it was more than enough for Case to see and note the man's location.

A hundred feet away, another shadow moved.

At least two, Case decided. *Not Culpeppers, unless those boys have started wearing Mexican-style head-gear.*

Wonder where they left their horses?

Within a thousand yards of the cabin there were only a few places that had enough cover to hide horses.

Bet they came down that ravine a few hundred feet beyond the privy, he thought. *They're too damned lazy to walk a step farther than they have to.*

Crouched over, he went quickly and silently across the cleared area around the cabin. He eeled through the brush and grass until he was past the privy.

Keeping the outhouse between himself and the area where he had seen the men, he straightened and moved swiftly toward the ravine that opened out onto the flats just beyond the cabin.

Three horses waited in the ravine, tied to the skeleton of a dead juniper.

Hell's fire, he thought. *Horses.*

He had been hoping to see mules. It would be easier to take the Culpeppers on one at a time in the dark than head-on in a gunfight the way he had at Spanish Church.

Less risky, too.

Ab must be more patient than he used to be. Too bad. It makes him more dangerous.

A quick, careful circuit of the mouth of the ravine told Case that no one had been left behind to guard the animals.

An empty whiskey bottle gleamed in the starlight just beyond the juniper's twisted, dead branches. Gnawed bones from a rabbit had been tossed near the bottle.

Guess those boys waited here awhile, he thought. *Hope it was long enough to get impatient.*

Impatient men made mistakes.

A few minutes of soft talking and slow moving assured the horses that Case, despite his strange scent, meant them no harm.

The animals stood quietly while he cut their reins free of the bridle. He used the braided leather to hobble the horses. Then he loosened the cinches and removed the bridles entirely.

If any raider made it back to his horse, he would have the devil's own time getting away.

Now, Case thought, *it's time to see how drunk those boys really are.*

He made no more noise on the way back toward the cabin than he had on the way out. In fact, he was so quiet he nearly tripped over the first raider.

"Rusty?" whispered the man. "What 'n hell you doin' over here? You'll get your turn on that gal after I break her to —"

The words ended an instant after Case's knife slid out of its sheath. He caught the dead man and lowered him to the ground.

Then he crouched, listening.

The night was far too quiet.

There were too many memories welling up, darker than any night.

Air is too dry, he thought distantly. *No trees rustling softly. No lush green. No campfires burning a hundred feet away.*

But one thing hadn't changed. Death still smelled the same as it had during the War Between the States.

A hooting sound came from his left.

Nothing moved to his right.

Case kept quiet. The last time he had heard two men calling, that had been the pattern — one hoot, one answer.

He was hoping that the dead man wasn't one of the outlaws who had been calling back and forth.

The hooting came again from the left.

Damn, he thought. *I'd better answer.*

It was hard, but he tried to mangle the hooting call of an owl as badly as Moody's men had.

A faint stirring sound came from the left.

Brush rubbing over buckskin, he thought. *The raider must be in that clump of big sage off to the left.*

Slowly, relentlessly, Case closed in on the area where the false owl call had come from.

A shape that only a seasoned night fighter would recognize as a man slipped through the clump of tall sagebrush and paused at its edge.

Case recognized the human outline instantly.

Can you see him, Conner? he asked silently. *He'll be at the back of the cabin if I miss him.*

But Case didn't plan on missing the

raider. He kept hearing what the other man had said just before he died.

You'll get your turn on that gal after I break her.

Case was certain the man hadn't been talking about Big Lola.

Wonder where that third man is? he asked silently. *And why he's so quiet.*

At the moment, there was nothing he could do about the missing raider.

The man in the big sage was moving again.

Silently Case inched closer to the outlaw who was even now heading for the cabin.

Hope to hell Conner follows orders. If he unloads his shotgun at the raider, he'll get me in the bargain.

Case was eight feet from the outlaw before the man sensed that something was wrong. The raider spun around, drawing his gun.

A shotgun butt hit the outlaw like a falling mountain. With a hoarse sound the man folded up and dropped to the ground.

As quickly as Case had come out of the darkness into the cleared area, he vanished back into the clump of tall sagebrush.

The outlaw stayed where he fell.

Silence came.

Breathing deeply yet very quietly, Case strained to hear any sign of the third man.

He heard nothing but the unnatural silence of the night.

Guess the third man isn't as impatient to get his hands on Sarah as the others were, he decided.

After five minutes the normal night sounds slowly resumed. Case settled in for a long wait. He had played this deadly game many, many times before. The first man to lose patience was usually the one who died.

Behind him the night sounds abruptly stopped. Silence descended.

The hair on the back of his neck stirred. He threw himself to the side just before a six-gun shattered the silence with two rapid shots, then one more for good measure.

Lead whined through the thicket where his head had been. Even as he dove for cover, he turned and brought the shotgun to bear on the muzzle flash of the raider's six-gun.

Case triggered the first round of buckshot so quickly that its deeper sound masked that of the outlaw's fourth bullet. Lead pellets shredded through the sagebrush, then went ripping through the night in a deadly metal hail.

The raider grunted twice.

If he made any other noises, they were lost beneath the sounds Case made as he rolled swiftly to a new position. He knew his own muzzle flash had given away his location.

Yet even as he rolled, he realized there wasn't any place to hide. The outlaw was too close to fool for long.

The fifth bullet tugged at Case's sleeve. Another sprayed dirt and pieces of bark over his face even as he scrambled for better cover.

From the darkness came the distinctive sound of a second six-gun being cocked.

Case triggered the second barrel of the shotgun toward the sound and threw himself in the opposite direction. Before he hit the ground, his six-gun was in his left hand.

Forcing himself to breathe quietly, he waited.

No more tongues of fire leaped toward him out of the darkness.

There was a groan, a thrashing noise as though a large animal was staggering through the brush, a thud . . .

And then nothing.

He waited.

Cold sweat ran down his forehead and his ribs. His lungs ached for deep, sweet gulps of air rather than the stingy, shallow breaths that were all he permitted himself.

No more sounds came from the darkness.

He kept on waiting.

And waiting.

Long after other men would have moved, Case lay absolutely still, eyes closed but for the narrowest of slits. Six-gun in hand, he waited with all the skill he had learned during the war.

He waited as death waited. Patiently. Relentlessly.

The brush stirred and crackled. Uneven steps came toward his hiding place.

He didn't move.

The outlaw wasn't trying to be especially quiet. He simply wanted to make sure Case was dead.

The instant the raider saw the dark, motionless form against the lighter brush, he brought his six-gun to bear and started to pull the trigger.

Three shots split the night.

All of them went into the raider.

This time when the man fell, there was no theatrical thrashing and groaning. The outlaw simply slumped facedown on the ground and lay there.

Six-gun pointed and cocked, Case came to his feet, walked a few steps, and turned the man over with his foot.

He was wearing a sombrero rather than an old Confederate cap, but even in the wan light, the raider's long, lanky body, narrow face, and straw-colored hair were unmistakable.

Be damned, Case thought, startled. *Why didn't he ride his mule?*

Then, *Wonder which Culpepper it is?*

There was no ready answer.

Doesn't matter, I suppose. One varmint is pretty much like another.

Except for Ab, he amended. *That old boy could teach evil to the devil himself.*

Once more Case blended his silhouette with that of the tall sagebrush. By touch alone he reloaded his six-gun and shotgun. The cartridges went in smoothly, almost silently.

Once more he waited.

This time nothing stirred, no matter how long he listened to the small sounds of the night.

Slowly he let out a long breath. For the first time he noticed that he was cold, his wounded leg throbbed, and his forehead stung where bullets had kicked bits of bark across his skin.

He had to lick his lips twice before they were wet enough to send a hawk's fluting call through the darkness.

A hawk answered from inside the cabin.

Limping, he set out for the ragged black rectangle that was all that showed of the cabin. Though he didn't expect to encounter any more outlaws sneaking around the underbrush, he wasn't careless. He used every bit of cover to break up his silhouette.

As a precaution, he whistled again before he touched the front door.

A hawk cried sweetly from just beyond the rough planks. The door opened. The pale moonlight showed Conner standing just inside.

His shotgun was leveled at Case's belt buckle.

"See?" Conner said, uncocking the gun and stepping aside. "I told you he would be all right."

Sarah hurried around her brother.

"Case?" she asked huskily. "Are you hurt?"

Her voice trembled. So did the hands that went lightly over him, searching for injuries.

"Tired, dirty, and scuffed up a bit," he said, closing the door behind him. "Nothing to worry about."

"Light the lamp," she said to her brother.

Conner looked at Case, who nodded.

"What happened?" Conner asked.

"Come dawn, we'll have some shovel work."

A match scraped on the iron trivet. A tongue of orange-red light flared, followed by the more mellow light from the wick of an oil lamp. The glass chimney clinked softly against the metal holder as Conner replaced it.

"Shovel work, huh?" he asked, looking at Case.

"Any trouble up on the rim?" Case asked.

"How many did you kill?" the boy persisted. "How did you find them before they found you? Where —"

"That's enough," Sarah interrupted

curtly. "Case is barely three weeks away from dying, he's been out in the dark fighting for our lives, and now you're pestering him to death."

"But —"

A glittering silver glance shut Conner up.

"Hell's fire," he muttered. "You'd think I was still wearing rompers."

She ignored her brother.

"Sit down," she said to Case. "You're bleeding."

"Nothing to —" he began.

Sarah exploded.

"Will you just shut up and sit down!" she snarled. "I'm sick unto death of being ordered around by males who are too damned big for their damned britches!"

Case gave her a wary look. Then he sat down in one of the two chairs the cabin had. The chair's cottonwood frame creaked when it took his weight.

She gave her brother a measuring glance, obviously seeking another target for her anger.

"Uh," Conner said, "I think it's time for me to spell Ute up on the rim."

"Go ahead," Case said. "But keep your eyes peeled."

"Are there more raiders?" Conner asked with subdued eagerness.

"Not unless they rode double, and I doubt that those little mustangs could carry that much freight."

"Ute will wonder about the gunfire. What shall I tell him?"

"To bring a shovel," Sarah said sharply.

Conner opened the door and left without another word.

"Thank you for keeping your sister in the cabin," Case called.

"My pleasure," the boy called back.

Then his laugher rippled through the night.

"You should have heard her when I sat on her," Conner called through the wall. "I didn't know she knew so many cuss words. Hell, I bet even Big Lola couldn't —"

"*Conner Lawson,*" Sarah said in a threatening tone.

Laughter floated back, further outraging his sister.

"Must have been something to hear," Case said neutrally.

Red burned brightly on her otherwise pale face. Then she saw the faint upward tilt at one corner of his mouth.

Suddenly she was laughing too, almost dizzy with relief that Case was all right, Conner was all right, everything was all right.

For tonight, at least, they were safe.

"I didn't know I knew that many words, either," she admitted.

The corners of his eyes crinkled.

She smiled wryly.

"I must have been a sight to behold," she said, "cussing a blue streak while that overgrown boy sat squarely on top of me."

"When you do a man's job, you aren't a boy anymore."

Her smile faded as she thought what it must have been like for Case at fifteen during the war — and for him tonight, fighting a different kind of war in the dark.

Come dawn, we'll have some shovel work.

But his eyes said more. They said that death took a price even from the victorious.

Sarah turned aside, dipped water from the bucket with a tin cup, and poured it into a battered tin bowl. Silently she took a clean rag from a reed basket. When the rag was thoroughly wet, she squeezed water from it and walked back to Case.

He watched her with eyes turned to shadowed gold-green gemstones by the lantern light.

Blood slowly welled from a shallow cut on his forehead. Small, bright drops gathered in his left eyebrow, curved around his eye, and ran down his cheek like scarlet tears.

"There's no need —" he began.

"There's every need," she countered instantly.

It would have been easy for him to turn aside, to refuse the small service she offered.

He did not. He sat and let her care for him as though it was his right.

And hers.

Silently she bathed his face with cool water, washing away the dirt and the red tears.

The shadows in his eyes remained.

I wonder if anything could wash them away, she thought unhappily.

"Are you sure you aren't hurt?" she whispered.

"Yes."

"I was so afraid for you when I heard the second round of shots. And the third. And then the silence. The silence went on forever. Like death."

"Sarah . . ."

But no words came to Case that would erase the memory of stark fear in her eyes.

She had been afraid for him, as though he were family instead of a wounded stranger passing through.

Gently he pulled her into his lap.

"Your wound," she protested.

He settled her so that she was sitting on his right thigh. Then he held her and stroked her unbound hair.

She gave a broken sigh and leaned against him. For a time she fought the emotions welling up within her, making her throat tight and her eyes burn.

Then suddenly, silently, she wept, releasing emotions that had been dammed up for too many years.

He caught her tears on his fingertips and wiped them away. Dust he had picked up fighting for his life in the clump of big sage turned dark red on her face, marking the passage of his hand.

Tenderly he took the rag she had been using on him, shook it out, and found a clean corner to wipe the red dust from her face.

Tears welled up faster than he could wash them away.

"I'm sorry," she said finally.

"What for?"

"I — can't stop — crying."

"Nobody's asking you to."

"But — but I don't — don't cry — ever."

"I won't tell anyone if you won't."

She made a sound that could have been a laugh or a sob or both together.

And then she simply wept.

"It's not fair," she said after a time.

"What isn't?"

"That you had to go out there and — and —"

"Better me than Conner," Case said. "He doesn't have the patience yet."

"P-patience?"

"That's what all the silence was about. One of the Culpeppers was trying to wear out my patience."

"Was it Ab?" Sarah tried to keep the hope out of her voice, but couldn't.

"No. But he was canny. Those Culpeppers might not be much when it comes to kindness or decency, but they're pure blazing hell at fighting."

A tremor went through Sarah.

"Conner," she whispered. "Ab will kill him. My God, what can I do?"

"Take your brother and leave Lost River Canyon," Case said succinctly.

"I don't have any —" Her breath broke.

It was a moment before she could speak.

"I don't have any money to send Conner off," she said painfully.

"He's big enough to earn his own way."

Tears ran down her face. She shook her head with a combination of weariness and acceptance. When she spoke, her voice was as steady as the flow of her tears.

"Conner won't go and leave me on my own," she said. "I've tried."

"Then go with him."

"And do what? Take Lola's path?"

His eyelids flinched. "There are other kinds of work."

She laughed bleakly. "Not for a girl who has only the clothes on her back."

"You could marry a —"

"No," she interrupted savagely. "I'll never suffer a husband again. *Never.*"

Case started to point out that all men

weren't as hard to live with as her dead husband obviously had been, but decided there was no purpose.

It was like telling himself to go ahead and marry and have kids, because all children didn't end up maimed and killed by raiders.

That was true as far as it went. But he had lived the rest of the truth.

Some children died.

"All right, then," he said. "Just kick Conner off your ranch."

"I can't do that."

"You mean you don't want to."

Wearily she rubbed her forehead. She didn't feel up to explaining that she had given half of Lost River ranch to Conner when he was thirteen.

Case would wonder why.

And that was something she never had talked about, ever, with anyone.

Dear God, she thought. *What a tangle. Why did those damned raiders have to settle around here?*

There was no answer.

She didn't expect one, any more than she expected to know why she and Conner had survived the flood that killed the rest of their family.

Whys don't matter, she told herself as

she had so many times before. *All that matters is here and now, not then and might-have-been.*

"I love Lost River ranch more than anything on God's earth except my brother," Sarah said calmly. "As soon as I find the Spanish silver and send Conner off to an Eastern school, everything will be fine."

Case hesitated. He had a hard time seeing the hot-headed, rawboned boy in an Eastern schoolroom conjugating Latin verbs and memorizing multiplication tables.

"What does Conner think about that?" he asked.

"It doesn't matter. He's going."

Case opened his mouth to point out that her brother was of an age to make his own decisions, then shrugged. Sarah would figure that out just as soon as she tried to push Conner into doing something he really didn't want to do.

"What if you don't find the silver?" Case asked instead.

"I will."

The stubborn set of her chin told him that the subject could be argued from sunrise to sunrise and nothing would change.

Shaking his head slightly, he sighed and smoothed his hand over the cinnamon silk of her hair.

"If only Conner and Ute hadn't baited the raiders," she said after a moment. "Maybe they would have left us alone."

"Maybe, but I doubt it."

"Why?"

"Moody's boys are too bone-lazy to raid very far from camp."

"What about the Culpeppers?" she asked.

"They used to be that lazy, but it looks like most of those boys finally learned not to dig their outhouse too close to their drinking water."

"Damn those raiders."

"Amen."

Closing her eyes, Sarah sat very still for a time.

Then she opened her eyes and started talking about an idea that had been growing in her mind. She talked fast, for she really didn't want to ask.

Yet she had no other choice except to wring her hands while Conner was killed by raiders who were older and far more cunning than her impulsive younger brother.

"If you keep the raiders off my back

while I hunt silver I'll give you half what I find," she said in a rush.

It took Case a few moments to figure out what she was talking about. When he did, he shook his head.

"No," he said simply.

"You don't think I'll find the silver."

"Even if you did, it wouldn't matter. Silver, gold, paper money — none of it is worth dying for."

"What is?" she asked bitterly.

"Half of Lost River ranch."

Sarah felt her blood drain away, leaving her as pale as salt.

Half of Lost River ranch.

Then she thought of her brother lying dead somewhere, ambushed by raiders.

She tried to speak, but couldn't. She swallowed painfully.

"Half the ranch," she agreed, her voice hoarse. "But you must promise you won't tell Conner. *Promise me.*"

"Done."

She sat very still, listening to the echoes of the bargain she had made. She was glad that she had finally cried all her tears.

Only she would know how much the loss of her beloved ranch grieved her.

10

Breath from the horses hung in the air like silver smoke. Though the sky was every color of peach and pale blue known to man, daybreak hadn't come yet.

"Are you still fussing over your horse?" Sarah asked impatiently.

Case looked up from the cinch he was tightening around Cricket's sleek barrel. Sarah was sitting astride one of the mustangs he had first seen in Spanish Church, wearing a pack saddle.

Normally she rode bareback. This morning he had insisted that the little horse she called Shaker wear one of the saddles the dead raiders no longer needed. As far as Case was concerned, riding bareback in rough country was too dangerous.

The mustangs that had belonged to the outlaws were now scattered along the creek close to the ranch, mixed with Sarah's stock. The new animals had quickly decided that the graze at Lost

River ranch was better than Spring Canyon's sparse feed.

"Well?" she persisted.

"The silver has been lost for centuries," he said reasonably. "It will keep another minute while I take up the cinch."

Visibly she bit back impatient words.

Lips compressed, she looked off toward the rim. She couldn't see Lola, but knew the older woman was sitting somewhere up there, a loaded shotgun across her ample lap.

Ute and Conner were still abed, worn out from long nights of broken sleep. Someone was always up on the rim, even though the raiders hadn't come back since four nights ago, when Case had taught them that sneaking up in back of the little cabin was a good way to die.

With an easy motion he stepped into the stirrup and swung onto Cricket.

"You're sure you feel good enough to ride and hike?" she asked for the third time. "Sometimes it's really a scramble."

"I'm sure," he said for the third time. "And I'm damned sure we should be scouting firewood instead of wasting time looking for dead men's treasure."

"Scout all the firewood you like," she shot back. "I'm looking for silver."

With that she reined her little brown mustang around and sent the mare at a lope toward the distant mouth of Lost River Canyon.

"Easy, Cricket," Case muttered, reining in the stallion. "No need to rush off into a cold dawn."

He settled his hat firmly in place. Then he checked the shotgun and rifle in their separate saddle sheaths. He didn't really need to look over the weapons, but it gave him an excuse to get a better grip on his temper.

Sarah has been going her own way too long, he told himself. *Real good at giving orders and no damned good at taking them.*

It's a blazing wonder Conner didn't sit on his sister sooner. And harder.

With a quick motion, Case returned the shotgun to its sheath. The instant he lifted the reins, Cricket shot forward, eager to overtake the little mare.

"Easy, you puddinghead," he muttered. "She's not going anywhere you can't go faster."

The stallion shortened his stride, but

not by much. He hated having any horse in front of him.

The small brown mustang loped along Lost River. The horse was following a vague trail left by game and Indian hunters long before Hal Kennedy built his rough cabin and started hunting for Spanish silver.

Sometimes a low cottonwood branch forced Sarah to flatten out against Shaker's neck. At other times fallen logs lay across the way. The little horse leaped the logs with a lack of fuss that meant the nearly invisible trail was a familiar one to the mustang.

And so was the speed.

Often Sarah checked the position of the sun. It hadn't peeked over the rim of the canyon yet, but it would very quickly.

I should have been on the trail an hour ago, she thought in irritation.

But Case had refused to let her ride off in the dark, even if he was with her. She had tried to argue, cajole, and reason her way to an agreement to leave earlier. Nothing had worked.

When Case refused, he meant it.

Stubborn, disagreeable creature, she thought.

One mile blurred beneath Shaker's hard little feet, then two, then three. The wiry mare didn't even breathe hard. She could lope at that pace all day long.

Occasionally Sarah looked over her shoulder to check on Case's progress. Each time she did, Cricket was in the same place, about a hundred feet back. The stallion showed no sign of tiring, even though he was carrying easily twice the weight the mustang was.

Irritating males, she thought uncharitably. *Thick of limb and thin of brain.*

But it was hard for her to sustain her bad mood in the face of the golden light that came washing over the land. Between rosy clouds, the sky was a blue so pale it shone like clear glass in the dawn.

How can I leave this land? she asked silently.

It was a question that had come often to her in the days since she had made her bargain with Case. The only answer she had was the same one that had gotten her through the months after her parents had died.

I will do what I must. For Conner, who deserves better than life gave him.

She had never regretted the choices

forced on her by circumstance. She was simply grateful that she and Conner had survived when too many others had not.

After the sun peeked over the canyon rim, the land slid by in countless shades of ochre and rust, red and gold. She slowed only when one of Lost River Canyon's many side canyons opened onto the river's edge. Then she let the mustang pick a careful way through the slickrock, boulders, and dry creek beds that marked the mouth of each smaller canyon.

Case's pale green eyes roved the countryside constantly. He wasn't just looking for danger. He was memorizing landmarks from every angle so that he would be able to find his way back over the trail without a guide.

As he learned the land, he marked the flight of eagles and hawks, the bursting speed and sudden stillness of rabbits, and the abundant sign of deer. Once he was certain he saw cougar tracks hardened in a patch of dry mud at the mouth of a side canyon.

Half of this is mine.

That fact kept echoing through him with every new sign of life, every wild new vista. Each time the realization came, he felt a measure of calm touch parts of his soul that had known only turmoil since the war.

The certainty that he belonged to the land grew greater with every moment, every breath.

He would die, but the land would not.

The land would go through eternity untouched by the hell that lived within the worst of men.

For Case, the land's unchanging reality offered the possibility of a calm that was more than skin deep. Through his bond with the land, he was part of something greater than the sum of all evil caused by men.

The thought was balm for an agony that had known no ease for so long that he had stopped noticing it; he simply accepted agony as men who had lost limbs learned to live without them.

When Sarah finally reined in her mustang to a walk, he let Cricket come alongside the little mare.

"Nothing like a little run to work off your temper," he said casually.

She gave him a narrow look and said nothing.

"Need a few more miles?" he asked.

"This time you carry the saddle."

As always, her sense of humor won out over her irritation. She laughed and shook her head.

"You and Conner," she said.

"What about us?"

"You both can get around me in no time at all."

"That's because you're not hard enough for this world," Case said.

She groaned. "Not you, too."

"What?"

"Ute believes I'm an angel," she said.

Case didn't look at all surprised.

"I mean it," she said. "He truly does."

"A man wakes up sick and hurting and sees lantern light shining around your hair and feels your hands all cool and gentle on his skin . . ."

His voice died. Then he shrugged.

"Ute can hardly be blamed for seeing you as a sweet angel of mercy bending down to touch him," Case said.

Sarah flushed.

"I'm no angel," she said. "Ask my brother."

"Oh, I'm not doubting you. It's Ute who needs convincing."

"I've tried. It's like trying to talk Shakespeare to a rock."

"You have to remember that Ute is comparing you to the other women he has known," Case said dryly.

She winced.

"Lola is a good woman," she said. "Hard, but decent."

"You've got that half-right," he muttered.

"What?"

"Big Lola is a legend in some parts."

"That was then," Sarah said firmly. "Since she came to Lost River ranch, she hasn't done anything that needs apology. Except cursing, and that doesn't count. Not really."

The corners of his eyes crinkled.

"Cussing doesn't count?" he asked neutrally. "Well, that explains it."

"What?"

"An angel of mercy with a vocabulary that could scorch hell. Of course, I only heard that at secondhand. Could be an outright falsehood."

Her cheekbones burned with more than the crisp winter air.

"I said I wasn't an angel," she pointed out.

The suggestion of a smile deepened around his eyes.

Sarah kept glancing at him, but no

matter how often she tried, she couldn't see if Case was actually smiling.

"I should have shaved you," she said.

"Why?" he asked, surprised by the change of subject.

"I swear you're smiling underneath all that chin fur, but I can't tell for certain."

"It's too cold to go without fur," was all he said.

"It wouldn't be too cold if you slept in the cabin."

She didn't know why it still rankled her that he had moved out of the cabin, but it surely did.

"I spent too long in your bed as it was," he said bluntly.

What he didn't say was that her rose-scented bedcovers haunted his dreams even when he slept outside. He woke up as hard as the cliffs. When the savage ache finally subsided, it was never for long. It ambushed him at the most inconvenient moments.

Such as now.

Cursing silently, he shifted in the saddle.

It was useless. In his condition there just wasn't any comfortable way to ride.

"Why don't you sleep next to Conner?" she asked. "There's plenty of room near the stove."

"Your brother thrashes around like a young bull."

"But what are you going to do when it snows?"

"What I always have."

"Which is?" she asked.

"Survive."

The single bleak word went into Sarah like a blade of ice.

"There's more to life than survival," she said.

"Yes. There's the land."

"I meant hope and laughter and love."

"They die with people. The land doesn't. It endures."

His look and his tone said that the subject was closed.

For a time she was silent. In the end, her curiosity about his past was too great.

"What happened?" she asked baldly.

"When?"

"Why don't you have hope and laughter and love?"

Case didn't answer.

"Is it something to do with Emily?" Sarah asked. "Did she run off with another man and break your heart?"

His head whipped around toward her. The look in his eyes would have frozen flame.

"What did you say?" he asked softly.

Her mouth went dry. She wished she had never let curiosity get the better of common sense. She swallowed, tried to speak, and swallowed again.

"You called her name," Sarah said. "When you were out of your mind with fever. Over and over. Emily, Emily, Em—"

"Don't ever say that name to me again," he interrupted savagely.

Silence expanded like the wind, filling the land.

"Is she dead?" Sarah asked finally.

There was no answer. Case didn't even so much as look her way.

The pain she felt surprised her.

Well, she thought, *I guess that answers one of my questions. Case loved Emily and she betrayed him.*

"All women aren't like that," Sarah said.

The silence kept expanding.

Suddenly she was glad that she hadn't shaved Case. She didn't want any better idea of what he was thinking than she already had.

"Fine," she said. "Close up like a bear trap. But hasn't anyone ever told you that talking about something can ease the pain?"

He gave her a sideways look.

"So tell me about your marriage, Mrs. Kennedy," he said, his tone sardonic. "What was so awful that you decided never to 'suffer' a man again?"

"That's none of —" Abruptly her mouth snapped shut.

"— my business?" he finished smoothly. "Then why is what did or didn't happen to me *your* business?"

Again silence competed with the wind.

In the end, silence won.

When Sarah finally reined her little mare up into a side canyon, she hoped that Case's thoughts were happier than hers.

But she doubted it.

"I suppose there's a reason you chose this canyon out of all the others we've passed," he said, breaking the long silence.

"Yes."

"Mind telling me why, or is that another thing that's none of my business?"

245

She looked sideways at Case. Her eyes were the color of hammered silver. Her voice wasn't any warmer.

"There are ruins halfway up on the south side," she said distinctly. "There are also fingers of red rock where the canyon branches up toward the rim."

"What kind of ruins?"

"Like castles, only different."

"Well, that tells me a whole lot. Now I know exactly what I'm looking for."

"What you're looking for is a good dressing-down," she muttered.

He simply turned and watched her with eyes that were far too wintry for a man who otherwise looked only a few years older than Sarah herself.

Suddenly she felt weary all the way to her soul. Her thoughtless questions had transformed Case into a cold stranger rather than the intriguing man she had brought back from death with her hands and her prayers and sleepless nights. A man whose dry humor and gentleness hinted at possibilities she didn't even name.

But she knew they existed.

She had sensed them as clearly as she sensed his male hunger for her.

Never mind that, she told herself.

Never mind who Emily was or what she did to Case. It doesn't matter.

Nothing matters but finding the silver for Conner. He knows how to laugh and love and hope.

"Hal had an old map," Sarah said.

"How old?"

She shrugged. "He didn't say. I didn't ask."

"Was it just a drawing or were there words?"

"A few here and there. And a letter."

"What did it say?" Case asked, curious despite himself.

"That a pack train of silver crosses, coins, bars, cups, plates, candle holders, and rosaries was lost during a flood."

"A whole pack train?"

She nodded.

"Most of the worked silver was recovered by the Spanish," she said, "but ten bags of silver coins weren't found. About three hundred pounds of silver bars were never seen again either."

He whistled softly. Then he ran a speculative eye over the immense, rugged land around him and called himself a fool for even being interested.

Three hundred pounds of silver bullion could vanish into any one of the thousands of nameless little canyons and never cause a ripple. The land was built on the scale of eternity rather than man.

"Were the words in Spanish or English or French or Latin?" he asked, curious despite himself.

"Latin mostly," she said. "Some Spanish."

"Are you certain?"

"The man who wrote the letter was a Jesuit priest," she said distinctly. "Latin was the preferred language for church documents, although some correspondence was in an ancient form of Spanish."

His dark eyebrows rose. "Your husband must have been quite a scholar to figure out that letter."

"Hal couldn't read or write English, much less anything else."

"Who translated the letter?"

"I did."

Case made a satisfied sound, as though he finally had run some prey to ground.

"You know Latin," he said.

"Yes."

"Greek?"

"Yes." She looked over at him. "Surprised?"

"Only that you're still at Lost River ranch."

"What do you mean?"

"With your education, you could get a job teaching school in Denver or Santa Fe or San Francisco."

Sarah felt her throat contract and her face stiffen.

She didn't want to live in the cities where her learning would be valued. All she wanted was to live on her ranch with the wild canyons and the sweet water and the timeless wind singing to her soul.

But it's my land only until I find the silver, she reminded herself. *Then my half of the ranch belongs to Case.*

"I could," she agreed.

Her tone said that she would rather be in chains.

"Where is the map now?" he asked.

"I don't know."

"A secret, huh?"

"No. I simply don't know," she said evenly. "The last time I saw it — and Hal — was years ago in autumn when he went looking for silver."

"He never came back?"

"No."

"How did he die?" Case asked.

"I don't know."

"But you're certain he's dead?"

"Yes."

"How?"

"My brother backtracked Hal and found him dying. Conner buried him where he lay."

"Seems kind of strange that a man in his prime would just up and die," Case said neutrally.

"Hal was more than three times my age."

He gave Sarah a swift sideways look. He tried to imagine someone with her quick tongue and gift of laughter being married to a man old enough to be her grandfather.

No wonder she doesn't want to talk about it, he thought uneasily. *I doubt that a man that old had much patience with girlish ways.*

"I'm surprised your brother didn't bring back the map," he said after a time.

"He brought back what we needed to survive — the horse, the overcoat, the supplies, and the weapons."

Case pictured the Kennedy cabin in his mind. Ten feet by fourteen. Ill-made.

No window glass. No floor but dirt that Sarah drew whimsical designs on when she wasn't too tired from spinning and cooking and washing and nursing various creatures.

Without the touches that she brought to the cabin — the herbs drying in one corner, the scented sprigs of juniper tucked in the mattresses, the smell of cornbread and fresh laundry — without them the cabin would have been about as welcoming as a grave.

"Must have been pretty tough for you with a young boy to raise and no man to help out," Case said.

"Conner learned to be a fine hunter. I'm a fair shot myself."

"What about your husband?"

"Hal was gone treasure hunting a lot of the time. He expected food on the table when he came back."

That wasn't all her husband had expected. She didn't think about the rest of it anymore, except sometimes in the middle of the night, when she would wake up cold and sweating with fear.

"How long did Hal look for silver before he died?" Case asked.

She shrugged. "All the time I knew

him and some years before that, I suppose."

"That map must have been worth less than a hill of beans."

"Why?"

"He didn't find anything."

"Hal drank."

The stark words told Case more than anything else Sarah had said about her husband.

"When he sobered up," she said, "he didn't remember anything that had happened."

"Are you telling me that you think he found the treasure and then forgot it?"

"Yes."

"A man would have to be pretty damned drunk to forget finding a treasure."

"When Hal was drinking, he was blind, deaf, and dumb as a rock," she said grimly.

Case watched her out of the corner of his eye. From what he had gathered in the past weeks, she was no older than twenty, and maybe younger.

Yet when she talked about her husband, she looked as worn as a widow twice her age.

"If Hal found the treasure," he said

after a while, "then lost it again, the map won't do you much good, will it?"

"There's no 'if' about it. I know Hal found the treasure."

The certainty in Sarah's voice stopped Case. He turned in the saddle and stared at her.

"How do you know?" he asked bluntly.

She took off one of her deerskin gloves and dug into the pocket of her pants. After a moment she held out her hand to him.

Two crudely cut silver *reales* lay against her palm. Despite the tarnish brought on by age, silver gleamed through the black where someone had polished a part of each coin.

"Do you want to change your mind about taking half the treasure instead of half the ranch?" she asked.

He looked from the ancient coins to the wild, untouched land surrounding him.

"No," he said. "This country has something that money can't buy. You can have the silver."

I don't want it, Sarah thought bleakly. *Like you, I only want the land.*

Yet half of the ranch she loved belonged to Conner.

And all too soon the other half would belong to a man who didn't believe in laughter, hope, or love.

11

A cold, clean wind blew down the canyon. The river-bed Sarah and Case were using as a trail lacked water except for occasional shallow pools. Despite that, grass and shrubs flourished at the margins of the dry wash and on up the steep slope to the point where the sheer stone cliffs began.

"That's good graze for cattle," he said. "Surprising, without running water."

She smiled slightly.

"The land is full of surprises like that," she said. "There are a handful of springs and countless seeps where water trickles out of cracks in the stone."

Through narrowed eyes, he scanned the rugged sides of the canyon. There were indeed places where the brush grew thickly. In fact, isolated pine trees were tucked into some of the most protected and well-watered creases.

Like money in the bank, he thought.

Little caches of water and feed hidden away.

No wonder there's so much sign of game.

"In West Texas," he said, "when it was dry, it was generally dry all the way to the bone."

"That's the way it is farther down Lost River Canyon," she said. "The mouth of the canyon opens onto a wide valley. The river flows for a while, the land drops down, and finally it all unravels into a maze of slickrock and barren red canyons."

"Where does Lost River go?"

"According to Ute, it doesn't go anywhere. It just gets smaller and smaller until it dries up completely."

Case looked thoughtful, as though he were rearranging the land in his mind.

"Lost River doesn't flow into other water?" he asked.

"No."

"Does it end in a lake?"

Sarah shook her head. Her next words confirmed what he already suspected.

"During the dry season," she said, "Lost River is the only sizable water for a long way in all directions."

"Has the river ever dried up before it gets to the ranch?"

"Not in the six seasons I've been here."

"What does Ute say?"

"He's never heard of it going dry in Lost River Canyon," she said.

"Chancy thing, just the same."

"I'd feel better if I had the time and skill to build a few simple spreader dams and maybe a pond for the worst times," she admitted. "A well would be nice, too."

"We'll work on that after you get the silver out of your system."

Her eyelids flickered.

She wouldn't be on the ranch after she found the silver.

Saying nothing, she turned away from him and watched the flight of an eagle. The bird was first black against the sky, then a radiant bronze as it turned and caught the sun at a different angle.

Case waited, but Sarah still didn't say anything about the time when he would own half of Lost River ranch.

"Or did you plan on dividing the land and have me take one side of the river and you the other?" he asked.

It was a moment before she answered.

And even then, she looked at the eagle's flight instead of him.

"No," she said huskily. "I think it would be better to keep the ranch intact. Unless you want it divided . . . ?"

He shook his head, but she didn't see.

"I'm not much of a hand with gardens and spinning and weaving," he said, "but I know ranching. I think we all would do better if we kept on pooling our talents the way you and Ute and Lola have."

For Sarah, speaking was impossible without revealing the sorrow that was strangling her. She simply nodded and longed with all her soul for the freedom of an eagle riding the wind.

Silently Case looked from one side of the rapidly narrowing canyon to the other. The land was pitching up more and more steeply beneath his stallion's hooves. Timber that had been washed down from higher up the canyon was lodged in crevices six feet above his head.

"I'd hate to be here when a flood comes," he said after a time.

"It's . . . frightening."

Caught by the raw edge of terror in her voice, he turned and looked at her. Only then did he remember how her family had died.

"Sorry," he said. "I didn't mean to bring back bad memories."

"I'm used to them."

"Sometimes that doesn't make them any easier."

"No, sometimes it doesn't," she said matter-of-factly, meeting his glance. "Those are the bad times."

His breath caught. Looking into her eyes right now was like looking into a mirror — beneath the surface there were shadows of horror and grief, rage and pain.

Yet on the surface, nothing.

Nothing at all.

It told Case that Sarah had been as deeply hurt by life as he had. Yet she hadn't turned her back on emotion in order to survive.

How did she learn to laugh again? he wondered.

Then came a question he had never asked himself.

Why?

Why did she open herself up to more grief?

Laughter and hope and love . . . The road to hell is paved with them.

He had vowed never to return to that agonizing hell. He nearly hadn't survived the first time through.

Sarah isn't stupid. Surely she knows the pain that feelings cause as well as I do.

And yet she smiles, she laughs, she cries.

She even loves.

That's why Ute thinks she's an angel. Despite everything, she allows herself to care.

Her reckless courage was breathtaking.

"When did you first see those coins?" Case asked abruptly, uneasy with his own thoughts.

She accepted the change of subject with a relief that didn't show in her expression.

"After Hal died," she said.

"Where did you find them?"

"In a tobacco pouch in his jacket pocket."

"Do you think he found the silver just before he died?"

For a time Sarah didn't answer. The rhythmic noise of the horses' hooves, the cry of a startled bird, and the restless wind were the only sounds.

"No," she said finally.

"Why?"

"He was on his way out to prospect rather than coming back to the ranch."

Case looked thoughtful.

"Where did your husband die?"

"I don't know."

"You said Conner tracked him."

"My brother was twelve years old and on foot," she said. "He had never been away from the cabin without me. If Hal's horse hadn't known the way home . . ."

Her voice faded. She shook her head without finishing the sentence.

Case started to ask what Conner had been doing out on foot alone, but the look on Sarah's face stopped him like a wall.

"I backtracked the horse as far as I could," she said. "But it was raining like the sea turned upside down. Every ravine was full of water. Lost River was a muddy flood too wide and deep and dangerous to ride alongside, much less cross."

"So the tracks washed away."

"Yes."

"Then what's the point of continuing the search?" he asked. "What are you looking for now?"

"Just what I said I was. Ruins and red pillars and a narrow canyon. That's all Conner remembers."

"How many places within a day's ride fit that description?"

"I don't know."

"Guess."

"Hundreds."

He grunted. "How many have you searched?"

"How many did we pass on the way here?" she asked sardonically.

What she didn't say was that there was one canyon she was dreading searching, but she didn't know just which one it was.

She hoped she never would. The thought of stumbling over her husband's bones made her cold.

Conner, she thought helplessly. *How can I ever repay you? How can I ever make it up to you?*

"No wonder you don't have enough firewood, much less a tight cabin," Case said. "You've been too busy chasing foolish hopes of silver."

"That's my business."

"Not when I have to watch you shiver with cold every morning," he said flatly.

When she ignored him, he went back to searching the sides of the canyon. Silver skeletons of piñon, big sage, and juniper stood against the rusty cliffs. Pine logs washed down by past floods lay scattered about. A lot of the wood was still solid enough to make a hot fire.

"Next time we'll bring packhorses," he said. "We can collect firewood while we look for dead men's silver."

"Next time I'll bring Conner. He doesn't complain every step of the way."

"Like hell you will."

She turned sharply and faced Case with narrowed eyes.

"I'm a widow and fully grown. If I want to come out here alone, I will."

"You're not that much of a fool."

She didn't bother answering.

"You know as well as I do that Ab has someone watching the ranch," Case pointed out.

"I haven't seen anyone."

"You haven't been up on the rim."

"But —"

"If you don't believe me," he interrupted impatiently, "ask your brother."

"Why would he know better than I do?"

"Hell of a question."

"What does that mean?"

"It means," he said in a flat voice, "that you have Conner tied so tight to you with those apron strings it's a blazing wonder he can breathe."

For a moment she was too angry to answer. By the time she found her tongue, she also had a better grip on her temper.

"Conner is my business," she said coldly. "Keep out of it."

Case gave her a sideways look.

"What are you going to do when your brother wants to marry and move on?" he asked bluntly.

The startled look on her face told him that she hadn't thought of her brother in that way.

"He's just a boy," she protested.

"Horse apples," Case said in disgust. "When will Conner be sixteen?"

"In a few months."

"I've known *men* that age with a wife and a baby."

"No. I want Conner to have an education."

"Put what you want in one hand and

spit in the other and see which hand fills up first," he suggested sardonically.

"I'd rather spit in your hand."

The corners of his eyes crinkled.

"I don't doubt that one bit," he said.

Pointedly she looked away from him and up the canyon where it branched around a jutting nose of rock.

"The ruins are up on the south side, not too far from here," she said.

Her tone said even more. It told Case that she was finished talking about Conner.

"I spotted the ruins the last time I came here," she said, "but it was too late in the day. I had to go back."

She urged her mustang forward. The little mare obliged with a trot that nearly shook the *reales* out of Sarah's pockets. Cricket kept up with a fast, fancy kind of walking gait that was smooth as satin.

Sarah tried not to notice the difference between the two mounts, but it was impossible. The shovel tied on behind her saddle kept bouncing up and banging her in the rear every few steps.

Shaker had been well-named.

The dry creek wound around a nose of solid rock. A few hundred feet farther up, another piece of cliff came in from the other side. The bottom of the canyon narrowed and became steeper as it climbed higher. Finally there was little more than thirty feet between the base of the cliffs that formed the canyon sides.

Huge blocks of sandstone rose out of the dirt and brush, silent testimony to fact that even the massive canyon cliffs were slowly being brought down by rain, ice, and wind.

The horses scrambled through the obstacle course of rocks and thick brush. The mustang had an easier time of it than the stallion, but both horses were sweating by the time Sarah reined in.

"There," she said, pointing to the south rim of the canyon. "See the castle?"

It took Case a moment to notice the ruined walls poking out from a deep alcove near the base of the canyon wall. Though half-tumbled down and screened by brush, the walls were definitely made by man.

The ruins appeared to be little more than four or five small rooms with a few stone storage cribs off to one side.

"Castle?" he asked. "Looks more like stables."

"Whoever stayed here lived better than we do at Lost River ranch," she said dryly.

"Try chinking the logs instead of looking for treasure."

"Chinking won't make the cabin any bigger."

"Be a damned sight warmer, though. Another room to sleep in wouldn't be amiss, either."

"Conner won't need it. He'll be away at school."

"I was thinking of you," Case said, "not your brother."

"What about me?"

"A girl shouldn't have to share her bedroom with every wounded drifter who turns up. Wouldn't that kind of privacy be a treasure worth working for?"

Sarah didn't answer.

He looked at the determined set of her jaw, swore under his breath, and tilted his hat back on his head.

"Now that we're at the so-called castle," he said, "what do we do next?"

"We look for silver."

"Didn't you tell me that the silver was

buried at the base of a tall pillar of red rock?"

"It was supposed to be. I can't say where it might be now."

"If the treasure weighed in at a few hundred pounds, and your husband was too drunk to remember finding it, chances are he didn't pack it out on his back."

Sarah had thought about that. A lot. On the other hand . . .

"I've dug around all the pillars in this canyon," she said firmly. "Now it's time to go over the ruins."

"If there's nothing there, then what?"

"I'll try the next canyon."

"And then?"

"I'll go on to the next canyon and the next and the next until I run out of canyons or find that damned silver."

Case looked at the worn, hard-used shovel that was tied behind her saddle.

"Well, it beats digging graves," he said.

He dismounted and pulled the shotgun sling over his head. Then he tied the reins around Cricket's neck, took the rifle out of its sheath, and turned toward Sarah.

"After you," he invited.

268

"Planning on starting a war?" she asked, dismounting.

"I'd hate to disappoint any Culpepper who came around looking for a ration of lead."

His tone was dry but there was nothing amusing about the look in his eyes. He had looked like that when he came back to the cabin after the raiders attacked.

Without a word Sarah hobbled Shaker, grabbed her own shotgun and shovel, and set off toward the ruins at a brisk pace. As she took each step, she tried not to remember how frightening it had been to wait with Conner inside the cabin and not know if Case was alive, dead, or dying alone in the cold darkness.

Twice she had headed for the door. The first time Conner had stopped her simply by putting his hand on her arm. The second time he had been forced to wrestle her to the floor and sit on her to keep her inside the cabin.

Her brother might have found the minutes that followed entertaining, but she still felt both furious and chilled when she thought of Case lying helpless in the dark, perhaps dying when she could have saved his life.

Shovel and shotgun over her shoulder, she scrambled up the slope. Thanks to Ute, her moccasins were new. Unfortunately, the sharp rocks would soon wear through the deer hide.

Just before she went up the last, steep slope of the rubble mound that led to the ruins, she stopped to catch her breath.

"Give me the shovel," Case said.

"You shouldn't be carrying —" she began as she turned toward him.

Her protest ended. He wasn't winded at all.

She handed over the heavy shovel, keeping only the shotgun for herself.

Without the shovel, the rest of the scramble to the ruins was a lot easier for her. If the long-handled shovel or his recently wounded leg bothered Case, it didn't show in his speed. He was right behind her when she came up over the lip of the debris slope and onto the flat area where the ruins were.

With speculative gray eyes, she looked over the ragged walls and piles of fallen stone.

"Where do you want me to dig?" he asked.

"First let's just look around. We might get lucky."

"Mounds of silver shining in the sun?"

"More like rotten hide bags of bullion and coins tarnished by a few centuries of neglect," she retorted.

She turned on her heel and walked toward the first ragged room.

"Stay away from the walls," he said.

"I've done this before."

"Just stay clear of the walls. Looks like a sneeze would bring them down."

Her mouth flattened, but the memory of how easy it had been for her younger brother to restrain her was still vivid.

Irritating, bullying creatures, she thought. *Why can't they just let a woman get on with her work? Why do they have to keep interfering?*

Pointedly she kept well away from the walls while she looked into and around each ruined room.

Once Case was certain that Sarah was going to be sensible about exploring the ruins, he divided his attention between watching her and watching for raiders.

Watching her was much more interesting. She had a female way of moving

271

that made him think of how good her breasts had felt against his leg when she changed his bandage. The thought of enjoying that sensation again, without his wound and her clothes to distract him, had a predictable effect on the fit of his pants.

Damn, he thought. *I better keep her mad at me. It's easy enough to do. She's so damned independent.*

But what he really wanted to do was kiss her curving, female body until she melted and ran like honey on his tongue.

Think about something else, he told himself.

It was hard, even when she was out of sight.

By the time Sarah scrambled out from behind the last wall of the ruins, her jacket was unbuttoned, her hat was pushed back on her head, and her doeskin shirt was unlaced to let air run over her hot skin.

Beneath the loose laces, Case was sure he could see the velvet shadow between her breasts. He wanted nothing more than to bury his face in that sweet, warm flesh.

"Well?" he asked roughly.

"No silver."

"I figured that out. Any sign that someone has been here since the Indians left?"

"There are a few places that show recent fires," she said. "But Ute and Conner hunt game in this canyon, and Hal surely searched here"

She shrugged as her voice faded.

"Show me where to dig," Case said.

"You shouldn't do that. You leg is hardly healed."

"My leg stood up just fine to the last shovel work I did," he said evenly.

She grimaced. She had lost that argument, too. He had taken his turn burying raiders right along with Ute and Conner.

"Fine," she said tightly. "Dig down to China for all I care."

"I doubt the padres hid the silver that deep. They believed they would find hell long before they found new heathens to save."

A smile tugged at her mouth. Determined not to let him see it, she turned away.

"I'll show you where to dig," she muttered.

The digging went more slowly than the original search had. The ground was either packed hard or heaped up with rubble from the walls, or both.

Soon Case discarded his hat and jacket. Then he unbuttoned his black wool shirt to the waist, started to pull out the tails, and stopped. He looked toward Sarah.

"Go ahead," she said. "I won't faint."

What she didn't say was that she had seen him without anything at all, even a bandage. She didn't have to say it.

The knowledge quivered in the air between them like a bell recently struck.

He took off his shirt, hung it over a dead piñon branch, and picked up the shovel again. He wore nothing but a wedge of curly black hair that narrowed as it approached his belt buckle.

Sarah knew what was beneath that, too.

Her breath shortened and she looked hastily away. Her stomach gave an odd little lurch as a tingling sensation rippled through her body.

What's wrong with me? she thought frantically. *It's not like I'm some wide-eyed girl to get all flustered at the sight of a man's bare chest.*

But widow or not, she was unsettled

by his half-naked body. She was also too fascinated to look away for long.

He filled her eyes.

His deceptively easy movements were a combination of strength and grace that reminded her of an eagle circling overhead, utterly at home within his strength in ways that she could only envy.

Someday Conner will be like that, she thought. *Strong, quick, supple.*

Fully grown.

Fully male.

The thought brought both pain and pleasure to her. Pain because Conner was growing up too quickly. Pleasure because he was growing up so well.

But no man can be as beautiful as Case, she thought. *Not to me. Case is . . . special.*

That thought was even more unsettling to her than the idea of her younger brother teetering on the brink of manhood.

"Nothing here but more rubble," Case said.

"Try over there."

The husky note in her voice brought his head up sharply. She was looking off down the canyon, checking on the horses.

"Don't worry," he said. "Cricket won't wander even though he isn't hobbled."

She nodded without looking back toward him. Then she raised her hot cheeks to the breeze. She wasn't aware that the motion lifted her breasts against her shirt.

Case stared at the gentle, unmistakably female curves pressed against the clinging doeskin. His blood surged and his body leaped with an urgency that he was becoming used to.

That didn't mean he liked it. He didn't.

If he had felt that way about women in general, it would have been one thing.

But only Sarah had this instant effect on his body.

With a soundless curse, he walked fifteen feet along the wall and began digging again.

More rubble.

He kept digging, grateful for the physical work. It helped to take the edge off his prowling, relentless sexual hunger for the young widow who watched him with shadowed, mist-gray eyes.

The blade of the shovel hit something that was neither stone nor dirt. Ignoring the ache in his thigh, he knelt and began pulling away rectangular blocks of rubble that were about the size of adobe bricks. Shards of pottery appeared. He looked at each one, then set it aside.

"What is it?" Sarah asked eagerly.

"Don't know yet."

She hurried over and stood near him as he dug.

"Stay back," he said. "I don't want you near the wall."

"You're near it."

"That's different."

She didn't bother to argue with such an illogical creature. She simply stayed where she was and watched.

Yet instead of keeping her eyes on where he was digging, she was distracted by the flex and play of his body as he worked over the stubborn rubble. Like swift water flowing over boulders, he had both power and elegance. The sleek texture of his skin had an allure that made her palms itch to smooth down his back.

Her hand was halfway to his shoulder when she realized what she was doing. She snatched back her fingers as though they had been burned.

What am I thinking of? she asked herself. *I've never wanted to pet a man in my life.*

Except Case.

She didn't know why he drew her so strongly. She knew only that he did. There was something deep inside him that called to her as surely as the flight of a wild hawk.

Just as she called to him in turn, no matter how he tried to ignore it.

I hate wanting you. It means not as much of me died as I'd hoped.

She couldn't help wondering if the ability to love was one of the things that the war hadn't quite been able to kill in him.

The thought was like the man himself — unnerving and alluring at the same time.

Pushing away more rubble, Case reached carefully into the shoulder-deep hole.

"Got it," he said triumphantly.

"Silver?"

He didn't answer.

"What is it?" she asked.

"Keep your shirt on."

"Why? You didn't."

His head snapped up. He saw imme-

278

diately that she wasn't looking at his hands. Instead, she was looking at him the way a kid looked at a half-unwrapped Christmas present.

At that instant, he wanted nothing more than to do a little unwrapping himself.

Don't be more stupid than God made you, he told himself savagely. *You seduce her and next thing you know she'll be building dreams of hearth and home and kids around you.*

Kids.

A chill rippled through Case, freezing him.

Sarah had been hard used by life as it was. He didn't want to hurt her any more. But if he gave in to the raw hunger coursing through him, sooner or later he would hurt her as surely as the sun rose in the east.

He simply didn't have what she needed. All he had was a hunger that was dangerous to both of them.

Maybe she's right, he thought. *Maybe I should take half of the silver and run.*

Maybe I should just run, period.

Yet even before the idea was fully formed, he rejected it with a finality that went all the way to his soul.

It was bad enough to have to keep his hands in his pockets around the most desirable female he had ever met.

Giving up the land, too, was unthinkable.

"Watch it!" Sarah said.

Hoping to stop one side of the hole from collapsing, she threw herself on her knees and made a wall of her hands. In the process, she thumped solidly into Case. He took her sudden weight without giving way an inch.

Some of the hole collapsed despite her efforts.

"Sorry," she said. "I thought you were going to be buried up to your armpits."

"Instead, we're both in up to our elbows," he said dryly.

She looked down at her forearms, which had vanished into the loose rubble. So had his. For some reason the sight struck her as so ridiculous that she laughed out loud.

The unexpected sound heightened his senses almost painfully, as though he had just seen a particularly beautiful dawn.

He turned toward Sarah, who was still leaning against him to keep from tumbling headfirst into the hole he had been digging. Only a few inches away from him, silver-gray eyes looked back at him, gleaming with amusement over life in general and the present situation in particular.

How can she still laugh? he asked silently. *She saw her family die. Her husband died. She's poor as a wooden plate. Raiders are all around, just waiting to get their hands on her.*

And she laughs!

"Are you all right?" she asked, breathless from laughter.

"Of course I am."

"For a moment you looked like you were in pain."

"For a moment you acted like you were crazy," he retorted. "Laughing like a song dog."

"We look silly buried up to our elbows like kids in a sandbox."

He couldn't bear the dancing humor in her eyes. He glanced down at her mouth.

Her lips were parted with the laughter that still quivered through her.

The next thing Case knew he was so close to Sarah that he could feel the warmth of her breath on his lips.

I shouldn't do this, he thought.

But he did it anyway.

Her laughter died when she felt the sudden heat of his breath against her lips. Then his mouth was over hers, enveloping her in a kiss. Instinctively she stiffened, expecting to be overwhelmed by his much greater strength.

Instead, he tasted her with a restraint that was astonishing in its leashed intensity.

An odd sound came from the back of her throat. With the tip of her tongue, she returned the delicate, questing touch.

The tremor that went through him was felt by both of them. He pulled away with a sharp movement.

"Sorry," he said curtly. "I shouldn't have done that."

Puzzled, she simply looked at him with luminous gray eyes.

"Don't get the wrong idea," he said. "I just — *hell.* I just wanted to know what laughter tasted like."

Sarah took a quick, soft breath. Something shivered in the pit of her stomach, a response to his words as much as his kiss.

"So, what does it taste like?" she asked in a husky voice.

"Like you, what else?" he said roughly.

"I thought it tasted like you."

He muttered something under his breath. When he looked at her again, his eyes were as distant as his voice.

"Are you stuck in there or can you pull out your hands?" he asked.

She looked at him and flinched.

I hate wanting you. It means not as much of me died as I'd hoped.

But this time Case didn't have to say the words aloud. They were in every cold line of his face.

Her mouth twisted in a curve that was more resigned than humorous. Without saying a word she straightened and pulled her hands free of the rubble, wincing when one chunk of rock scrubbed roughly over her wrist.

"Are you all right?" he asked grudgingly.

With brisk motions she dusted off her gloves.

"Sure. What about you?"

Without saying anything he yanked out his hands. But he held them together in a peculiar, sheltering way, as though they were painful.

"You're hurt!" she cried.

He shook his head. Holding his hands side by side to form a bowl, he slowly opened his fingers.

Nestled on his rough leather gloves was an odd, miniature piece of pottery consisting of two mugs joined at the handles. But the cups were too small to have been of any real use.

"It looks like part of a little girl's tea set," Sarah said.

Case went white.

"Take it away," he said harshly.

A single look at his face killed any protest she might have made. She lifted the ancient pottery from his hands.

He stood abruptly and stalked off with long strides.

"Where are you going?" she asked.

"To check on Cricket."

"He's grazing more toward the north side, down near that thick patch of brush."

If Case heard, he didn't change direction. Soon he was out of sight.

Sarah looked at the tiny double mug and wondered why it had made a grown man flee.

12

"It's a toy," Conner said, as delighted as a child. "Look. My fingertip fills one mug."

Sarah smiled.

"Careful," she said. "It's very old."

Lola chuckled and admired the joined, tiny black and white mugs resting on Sarah's palm.

"I haven't seen anything that cunning since my cousin made me a doll small enough to fit in a duck-egg cradle," Lola said. "Lordy, lordy, that was a long time ago."

Ute looked at the odd mug from all sides, grunted, and said one word.

"Wedding."

"What?" Sarah asked.

"It's like a . . ." Ute searched for a word.

"Ceremonial mug?" she suggested. "Only used on special occasions?"

He nodded vigorously.

"My mother's brother's people used them when a couple got hitched," Ute said. "Some 'Paches do, too, so I hear. Shaped different, though."

"As small as this?" Sarah asked.

"Hell, no," he said in disgust. "Man couldn't wet even half of his whistle with them thimbles."

"Have you ever heard of anything like this?" Conner asked, turning toward Case.

Case shrugged without bothering to turn around.

Disappointed by the other man's lack of interest, Conner shifted his attention back to Sarah.

"Was there any more?" he asked his sister eagerly.

"Listen to you," she said, laughing. "They way you're acting, you'd think it was Spanish silver."

"It's as good as," Conner said.

Ute snorted. "Boy, you try spending that trash and you'll find out right quick the difference twixt mud and metal."

Conner shot Ute a disgusted look.

"What I meant," Conner said, "was that the mug and Spanish silver are both valuable because they're . . . well, history, I guess. It's like touching a piece of something or someone who lived a long, long time ago."

"Yes," Sarah agreed. "Kind of ghostly, but in a good way."

Her brother stared at the miniature pottery, obviously fascinated.

"If you found enough things like this," he said finally, "maybe you could understand what the people who made it were like, what they thought and felt and dreamed."

"You sound like Father," she whispered. "He loved the ancient things best of all."

"What do you need a bunch of junk for?" Lola asked. "You already know what them folks was like."

"Why do you say that?" Conner asked. "Because Ute came from people like these?"

"Hell, boy. Ute's more a mongrel than that dog slinking around trying to herd chickens."

Ute chuckled.

"They was people," Lola said, pointing to the double mug. "Good, bad, greedy, giving, smart, stupid, and everything betwixt and between. Just people like us."

"We don't make mugs like that," Conner said.

"But we get thirsty and we drink out of more than our hands," she retorted.

"We make toys for our children that are miniatures of things we use every day," Sarah added.

"Little wagons instead of big?" Conner asked.

"Dolls instead of babies," she agreed, smiling. "And tea sets instead of —"

The cabin door shut behind Case. Hard.

"Whew," Lola said. "Glad to see the back of that boy heading out. Like having a grizzly with a sore tooth in to supper."

"Some folks don't like ghost things," Ute said.

"Huh," Conner said. "You think he's scared of a little —"

"Afraid of," Sarah corrected.

"*Afraid of* a girl's toy?"

"Not liking something ain't the same as being scared of it," Ute said. "I don't like fish worth a tinker's damn, but I sure ain't scared of 'em."

"You eat snakes," Conner said.

"They ain't slimy. Fish is slimy as snot."

Sarah cleared her throat.

" 'Scuse me," Ute muttered. "Got to

288

get some firewood."

"Good idea," she said, looking directly at her brother. "Take the piebald mustang. She's used to awkward loads."

"Hell, I know that," Conner said, disgusted. "Who do you think taught her to pack loads like a burro?"

She bit back an impatient retort. He was right. He had been the one to coax the mustang into accepting double duty as a pack animal.

But the habit of giving orders to her little brother was hard to break.

You have Conner tied so tight to you with those apron strings it's a blazing wonder he can breathe.

"I'm sorry," Sarah said quietly.

Surprised, Conner turned back and stared at his sister.

"I shouldn't be telling you things you already know," she explained. "I'll try to do better."

He smiled with a gentleness that made her eyes burn.

"That's all right," he said. "Sometimes I need reminding, even though I shouldn't."

She smiled, went to her brother, and gave him a quick hug. Though he lacked the muscle he would carry when fully grown, her head fit easily beneath his chin.

"I keep forgetting how big you are," she said.

"So does he," Lola said. "Keeps tripping over things with them outsized hooves of his."

"See if I hold any more yarn for you to wind," Conner threatened.

"I'll just find you where you fall and use your big feet," she retorted.

Laughing, Conner left the cabin to help scrounge firewood.

"What's for dinner?" he called from just beyond the door.

"Beans," Lola and Sarah yelled at the same time.

"Lord, what a treat!" he called. "I haven't had beans for, oh, two, three hours."

"There are sage hens, too," Sarah added.

The front door opened suddenly.

"Sage hens?" Conner asked.

"Case shot them," she said.

"Well, at least we won't have to look for lead," her brother said in a resigned voice. "We'll just pick it out of our teeth."

"He didn't use a shotgun."

Conner's eyes widened. "How did he get them?"

"Six-gun," she said succinctly.

"Waste of lead," Lola muttered.

"One shot each," Sarah said. "Three birds. Three bullets. Fastest thing I ever saw."

Lola's eyebrows rose.

Conner whistled.

"That's mighty fine shootin'. Mighty fine," Lola said. "No wonder he survived a showdown with them Culpeppers."

"He nearly didn't," Sarah said tightly.

"Gal, I ain't never heard of no one walkin' away from a Culpepper shootin' at all, and you can go to church with that."

"Huh," Conner said. "And here I was thinking that he mustn't be much good with that six-gun of his."

"Why?" Sarah asked, startled. "Just because he was shot?"

"No. Because he doesn't file off the sight, he hasn't shortened the barrel, and he hasn't honed the firing pin or changed the trigger to make it shoot faster."

"Parlor tricks," Lola said.

"Maybe, but those tricks make the

Culpeppers lightning on the draw," he retorted.

"Is that what Ute is teaching you when you're supposed to be doing chores?" Sarah demanded.

"*Adios,*" her brother said, closing the door firmly behind him. "We'll be back before dark with more wood."

"Conner Lawson!" she called. "Answer me!"

Silence answered, which told her as much as words. She turned on Lola.

"I don't want Ute teaching Conner gunfighter tricks," Sarah said flatly.

"Don't jaw at me. Jaw at your brother. He's the one doing the pestering about six-guns and such."

Sarah bit her lip and turned away. With great care she put the tiny joined mugs in a natural niche in the logs.

I've got to find that treasure, she thought again. *I've got to find it.*

But no real progress had been made today.

Case had dug several more holes. He found only broken pottery and the remains of old campfires for his trouble. Other than pottery, a burned can that had been used to warm beans over a campfire, and a broken, dried-up leather hobble, the area around the ruins hadn't yielded any sign of man.

"You listening to me?" Lola asked impatiently.

Startled out of her unhappy thoughts, Sarah turned.

"Were you saying something?" she asked.

"Damned straight I was."

"Sorry. I was . . . thinking."

"Then set your mind to this," Lola said. "You best be glad your little brother has a keen eye, fast hands, and the grit to use 'em in a fight. Them Culpepper boys ain't the church-going, prayer-shouting sort. They're poison mean clear to the bone. Every last damned one of them."

Sarah looked up. The certainty in the older woman's voice was reinforced by the harsh lines of her face.

"You once knew the Culpeppers, didn't you?" Sarah asked. "Not just Ab, but the whole clan."

"I was raised near 'em. My ma shot one of Ab's uncles from ambush for forcing hisself on me when I was twelve. Didn't kill him, sorry to say."

Sarah looked as shocked as she felt.

"He weren't the first," Lola said, "or

the last. Ma brung me into the business as a young'un."

The older woman shrugged and gave a gap-toothed smile.

"I only mention it," she said, "so's you won't go to nagging Conner for him doing what's got to be done to protect his own."

"I don't want that for my brother," she said with quiet desperation.

"Man does what he's going to do, and women take the hindmost."

Sarah's mouth flattened. She wanted to argue but knew it was herself she was fighting with, not Lola.

To hell with firewood, Sarah thought harshly. *I'm looking for Spanish silver tomorrow and the day after and the day after that.*

I'll find it.

I have to.

"Speakin' of man doing and women taking," Lola said, "you looking to get big from more than you et?"

"Excuse me?" Sarah said, confused.

"You do know where babes come from, don't you?"

"Of course I do."

"Then do you want a young'un or do you have something to keep you from catching?"

"It's not a problem. Half of what I need to get pregnant is missing."

"Hell it is," Lola retorted. "Case has just what you need, an it's by God loaded for bear every time he looks at you."

Sarah felt her cheeks getting hot as she remembered bathing Case when he was asleep.

He was indeed quite capable of getting her pregnant.

"He wouldn't force me," Sarah said tightly.

"He wouldn't have to. Or ain't you figured that out yet?"

"What?"

The older woman threw up her hands.

"Long on book learning and short on female learning," Lola said, disgusted.

Sarah didn't say a word.

"You want Case," Lola said flatly. "It's plain as the nose on your face."

"Whether I do or not," she said in an even voice, "Case doesn't want me."

"Horseshit."

"Please, don't use —"

"Don't go to chewing on me for speaking plain," Lola interrupted curtly. "Plain speaking is downright needful unless you want to be breeding Case's babe. Do you?"

"It doesn't matter. He won't touch me that way."

"Hell, gal, they all say that whilst they put their pecker up your skirt."

"Case hates wanting me," Sarah said bluntly. "He told me so."

Lola blinked. "How come?"

"He doesn't want to feel anything."

"Only critter that don't feel nothing is a dead critter."

Sarah's smile was weary but real.

"Case doesn't mind feeling something toward the land," she said. "It's people he doesn't want to care about."

"Huh."

Lola pursed her weathered, wrinkled lips, reached into her pocket for a plug of chewing tobacco, and remembered where she was. She sighed.

"Well, makes no nevermind what a man's two-eyed head wants," the old woman said. "His one-eyed head gets the last word."

When Sarah figured out what Lola was saying, she couldn't help laughing.

"Ain't you never heard it called that?" the older woman asked, grinning.

Sarah simply shook her head.

"For a widow woman, you sure are green," Lola said. "How did you keep from gettin' a big belly when your husband was alive? Or was he just too old?"

"Partly. Usually he was too drunk to run me to ground."

Lola's big shoulders moved in silent laughter. Then she reached into a pants pocket, pulled out a small leather bag, and threw it.

Instinctively Sarah caught the bag. It weighed hardly anything.

"What is it?" she asked.

"Bits of sponge. Case ain't no drinker and he ain't too old to plant kids in your belly."

Sarah looked at the bag. "So?"

"So when you get to feeling randy, soak one of them bits in vinegar and put it where your monthlies come from. Poke it up as far as you can. Then go do what you got to."

"I won't get pregnant, is that what you're saying?"

"Oh, you might catch now an' again, depending on how often you spread your legs."

Sarah looked at the small bag and hoped that her cheeks weren't as red as they felt.

"Nothin' to be shamed over," Lola said. "I'm told some women like it."

A shudder of distaste went through Sarah.

"I didn't," she said, her voice flat.

"Never much cared for it myself, until Ute. Liking a man makes it tolerable. More you like him, more tolerable it gets."

Blindly Sarah held the bag out.

"Take it," she said. "I won't need it."

"That's what Conner said when you told him to wear a jacket a few weeks back. And what happened?"

"He didn't take it," Sarah retorted.

"And then he come back home with his tail tucked between his legs, half-froze solid."

"I'm not Conner."

"Hell, gal, course you ain't. He can't carry a kid in his belly."

Sarah grabbed Lola's hand, slapped the small leather pouch into it, and let go.

The older woman shrugged and tucked the small leather pouch into her pants.

"You change your mind, just holler," she said.

Sarah nodded, but as she did, she

couldn't help thinking that there were worse things than having Case's baby.

A lot worse.

"Sarah, you awake?"

Ute's soft call brought her awake in a rush that left her heart pounding.

"What is it?" she whispered. "Raiders?"

"No. It's Case."

"What's wrong?"

"He tossing and groaning in his sleep fit to wake the dead."

She thought quickly. She hadn't seen Case since yesterday afternoon, when he had walked out of the cabin while the rest of them were admiring the ancient pottery.

"Is he sick?" she asked.

"No, ma'am. Just real restless like. Calling out names and such."

Just like the fever dreams, she thought. *Is he calling for his precious Emily again?*

"Wake him up," she said.

"No, ma'am," Ute said emphatically.

"Why not?"

"Last time I woke a fighting man up when he was a tossing and a groaning, he durn near killed me 'fore he come to

299

his senses. But Case wouldn't harm nary a hair on your head, no matter what."

"All right," she said, throwing aside the covers. "Is Conner up on the rim?"

"Yes'm. That's how I come to hear Case. I was passing his camp on my way back in."

"Go get some sleep. I'll see to Case."

"Uh, ma'am?"

"What?"

"You might talk to him first, real quiet like, 'fore you go grabbing his shoulder."

"I've worked with wild animals before," she said dryly.

Ute's laugh sounded like two handfuls of gravel being rubbed together.

Sarah pulled on her clothes, grabbed a jacket, and hurried out into the night.

Overhead the sky was an explosion of silver and black. The beauty of it held her spellbound for several heartbeats. Her breath came out in a wondering sigh that turned to silver and rose toward the glittering vault of the night.

Then the cold bit through her jacket, doeskin shirt, and doeskin pants. Shivering, she set off toward the clump of big sage where Case had set up his "camp."

Ute was right.

Case was thrashing and turning and muttering words. The incoherent sounds were barely louder than the crackle and creak of the tarpaulin he slept on.

Yet Sarah was certain that Emily's name was the one most often spoken.

Cautiously she approached him. She longed to gather him in her arms and soothe away whatever was causing his wild sleep. She had done the same thing many times for Conner in the years after the flood killed their family.

But instead of touching Case, she sat on her heels just beyond his reach. He was a fighting man who had fallen asleep alone, outside the cabin. If anything grabbed him, he wouldn't expect it to be a friend.

"Case," she said gently. "It's Sarah. You're all right. I'm here. You're safe, Case. It's all right."

She repeated the words many times, using her most soothing voice, the one Case had described as sunlight and honey.

After a time he stopped twisting and

turning in the covers. He was still restless, but he no longer twitched and jerked like a wild animal caught in a trap.

"That's it," she murmured. "You're all right. No one is going to hurt you. I won't let them."

She eased closer to him, talking softly the whole time. What she said was a mixture of sense and nonsense, a soothing flow of sound that reassured him on a deeper level than words alone could.

When she stroked his hand, he sighed raggedly. His arm closed around her and he pulled her toward him.

"Emily," he said in a blurred voice. "Thought you were gone. Snuggle in here and go to sleep. Uncle Case will keep the ghosts away."

Sarah was too surprised to pull back when he smoothed his hand tenderly over her hair, tucked her head against his chest, and pulled the bedroll covers up over both of them.

There was nothing sexual in his manner. It was as though she were a child rather than a woman.

Uncle Case? she thought, stunned. *Is his beloved, lost Emily his niece?*

302

Sarah started to wake him and tell him that she wasn't Emily. The utter relaxation of his body stopped her. No longer was he restless, mumbling, struggling against something only he could see. His body was relaxed, supple.

He sighed deep and long, cuddling her to his side. Then the rhythms of his breathing slowed, telling her that he was fully asleep.

For a time she listened to his heartbeat beneath her cheek and watched the glory of the stars where a corner of the blanket had slipped down. The cold of the night was held at bay by Case's sheer warmth. It was like curling up next to a fire that never had to be fed.

A deep breath brought the scent of sage and wool and man into her nostrils. She sighed and snuggled even closer, loving the feeling of his arm around her, his hand cradling her cheek, and his breath warm in her hair.

The heat of him seeped all the way to her core, relaxing her so completely that she felt almost dizzy. Not since the hurricane destroyed her family had she felt so much at peace with life.

I should go back to the cabin, she

thought sleepily. *Case is fine now.*

Reluctantly she began to withdraw from the tranquillity and warmth of the shared nest.

His arm tightened around her, holding her in place.

"Case?" she whispered. "Are you awake?"

He didn't answer. Nor did the rhythm of his heartbeat or breathing change.

She waited until his arm relaxed. Then she tried again to leave.

His arm tightened again. He murmured something and moved restlessly.

"Hush," she said soothingly. "It's all right. I won't leave."

For a while, she amended silently.

Sighing, Sarah settled in to watch the splendor of the stars wheel slowly through the opening in the blanket.

She didn't try to leave a third time. She fell as deeply asleep as Case.

13

Case awoke before dawn. It was an odd sort of waking for him, slow and lazy rather than quick and dangerous. A feeling of calm, of rightness, was inside him as deeply as his heartbeat.

Lord, he thought sleepily. *It's been a long time since I felt Emily's little body putting my arm to sleep.*

Wonder what she does for nightmares when Uncle Case isn't around?

Abruptly he realized that, while his arm was asleep, it wasn't from a child's weight.

There was a woman's resilient softness pressed against his side. There was a woman's long, thick hair lying silky against his neck. Each breath he took was infused with a woman's warmth.

And roses.

Sarah.

His eyes came fully open. The inky outline of sage boughs was overhead. In the openings between branches, stars glittered. The moon had set. Dawn was a faint whisper of pink in the east.

What the hell is she doing out in the brush with me? he thought.

The quickest way to find out was to wake her up and ask her. He started to do just that. He got as far as pulling the blanket down to her shoulders, and then he forgot why he was in such a blazing hurry to disturb her.

Starlight washed gently over Sarah's face. Lack of sunlight quenched the gold and red in her hair, but the silkiness of it shone like black water. Her eyelashes were so long they rested against her cheeks. Her mouth was full, relaxed, slightly curved, almost smiling.

Thoroughly tempting.

I shouldn't, he thought as he bent down.

He stopped.

At least, he thought he had stopped. Then he found that he could no more resist her than a moth could turn away from the incandescent lure of flames.

She's a fire in the middle of winter, Case thought. *God, I've been cold so long . . .*

His lips brushed over hers, sipping at the gentle curve of her sleeping smile.

His fingers eased carefully, completely into her hair, seeking the warmth beneath the cool strands. When he could get no closer to the heat of her, he held her head cupped in his hands, warming himself.

Sarah sighed and moved her head slightly, as though savoring the feel of his hands.

A shiver that had nothing to do with cold went through his body. It was desire and something more, something frightening stirring beneath the years of bleak denial.

But desire was the only thing Case admitted to feeling.

Desire was something he understood all too well since coming to Lost River ranch.

Slowly, gently, he shifted until Sarah was lying half beneath him. When the blanket started to slide away, he caught it with his teeth and dragged it back over both of them so that she wouldn't get cold and wake up.

There was no danger that he would notice the bite of the winter dawn. The scent and feel and taste of her were burning him alive.

His fingers went to the laces of her

buckskin shirt. He pulled first one lace through a hole, then the other.

I shouldn't, he thought despite the hard, heavy running of his blood.

Yet even as he told himself not to, he eased each lace through one more hole.

Her skin gleamed like a pearl in the mixture of starlight and softly growing dawn.

The hell with should or shouldn't, he thought. *If she didn't want this as much as I do, she wouldn't be here.*

Surely a widow knows how a man wakes up in the morning.

That's why she came crawling under my covers while I was asleep. She knew I wouldn't make the first move, so she came up on my blind side.

All I'm doing is returning the favor.

Case was surprised to find that the lacing on the shirt went down all the way to Sarah's navel, but he wasn't complaining. He smoothed the flaps of doeskin aside and pulled back to see her better.

I'll just look at her. That's all. There's no harm in seeing her.

She was silver and dusk and softly gleaming curves. A satin shadow lay between her breasts. Velvet darkness gathered at their tips, responding to the cold air flowing beneath the blanket.

He stifled a groan of raw desire.

My God. I could spend myself just looking at her.

But he couldn't stop looking at her any more than he could stop wanting to feel and taste and explore the softness he had just uncovered.

He lowered his face between her breasts and took a deep, deep breath.

It was like breathing a silky kind of fire.

He stroked his forehead against the firm slope of one breast, then the other. When he discovered a velvety nipple, he lifted his head. His lips opened and his breath sighed out around her.

With a hunger that was all the greater for his restraint, he drew the tip of her breast into his mouth. Licking, sucking, savoring, he shaped her into a velvety hardness that rubbed against his tongue, begging for more.

I've got to stop this, he thought. *I can't give her what she wants along with the sex.*

Hearth, home, children.

He lifted his head and saw her breast taut and pouting in the starlight.

But God knows I can give her body what it hungers for.

And God knows I'm a fool to even think about it.

He didn't know how much of a fool he was until he tasted the velvet texture of her nipple again, warming the sweet female flesh, shaping it with his mouth, drawing it even tighter.

Hunger raced through him like thunder, shaking him. Even as he bent his head to her other breast, he wondered if he could stop at all. There was even sweeter, hotter flesh waiting to be discovered, touched, cherished.

He needed that. He needed it more than he needed to breathe.

Sarah made a sleepy, throaty sound. She moved beneath Case, back arching slightly, both giving herself to him and demanding more of his loving.

The motion was elemental, sensual, provocative, but she didn't know any of that. All she knew was that she was lying beneath a beautiful, hot sun while liquid rays of warmth caressed her lazily, wonderfully.

It made no sense, but then, dreams weren't supposed to.

All that mattered to her was that she

was safe within the sensuous embrace of the dream. She knew it with a certainty that was greater than anything else, even the pleasure spreading through her body in slowly expanding rings.

Without warning a hot rain of delight coursed through her. She arched slightly in primitive reflex, giving herself to the beauty of the sun's penetrating, caressing heat.

Distantly she realized that her shoulders were cold and her breasts were bare and wet and someone was breathing in tiny, ragged whimpers. She tried to stay within the dream

And then she sat bolt upright.

She had just realized that it wasn't the sun between her legs. It was a hand.

A man's hand.

Case muffled Sarah's attempt to scream the fastest way he could. His mouth covered hers so thoroughly that only a small cry escaped.

He assumed that she would stop struggling when she realized where she was, and who was kissing her, and why. After all, she had been the one to come to him.

But she went after him like a wildcat,

kicking and clawing with every bit of her strength.

He twisted until he lay heavily on her, pinning her legs to the ground. Then he caught her hands and dragged them together. Holding both of her wrists with one hand, he lifted his head just long enough to cover her mouth with his other hand.

"Sarah, it's me, Case," he said softly.

Her narrowed, glittering eyes told him that she didn't care who the hell he was.

"Sarah!" Conner called from thirty feet away. "What's going on?"

She jerked beneath Case, but he didn't give an inch. He covered her the way he had when they were in a rocky alcove and the Culpeppers were right below.

"Are you all right?" her brother called. "Sarah!"

"Just a bad dream," Case called softly. "She's fine. No need to wake the dead."

"What's she doing out here?" Conner asked, his voice low.

Sarah and Case looked at one another.

"If you start screaming," he said in a low voice, "there's going to be a lot of explaining to do — starting with why you crawled into my bed if you didn't want just what I was giving to you!"

She went still. Belatedly she remembered where she was, and why.

"Sis?" Conner called quietly. "Are you sure you're all right?"

Case lifted his hand.

"Nothing is wrong," she whispered.

"What?" her brother asked.

"I'm fine," Sarah said more loudly.

"What are you doing out here? Is Case sick?"

Case's black eyebrow lifted in sardonic query.

"Am I sick?" he mouthed silently.

"When Ute came in from his watch, he said Case was thrashing and groaning," she said. "I came out to check on him."

Surprise showed for an instant on Case's face. Then his expression became as hard as the cliffs rising out of the dawn.

"That was hours ago," Conner said. "I'm coming in from watch myself."

"I fell asleep," she said.

"Oh." Conner hesitated. "Are you going back to the cabin now?"

She had a stark vision of what she

must look like at the moment, with her shirt undone and her pants around her knees.

"Go on without me," she said through her teeth.

"Are you sure?"

"Conner, for heaven's sake! Do you want to walk me to the privy personally, or can I have just a wee bit of privacy?"

"Oh, sure. Sorry. I just . . ."

"I know," Sarah said, her voice gentle. "I shouldn't have snapped. You know how quick off the mark I am when I first wake up."

"Especially after a nightmare," Conner said.

She didn't correct her brother's idea of who had been the one with bad dreams.

"Go on," she said. "I'll be along in a minute."

"Should I start the fire?"

"No need. Just go to sleep. I'll take care of the morning chores."

There was a moment of silence. Then Conner withdrew toward the cabin.

When she could no longer hear any trace of her younger brother's presence, she looked directly into Case's eyes.

"Get off me," she said through her teeth.

Without a word he rolled aside. He watched her warily, as though uncertain of what she might do next.

Blood welled from a nick just beneath his eye.

"Have the decency to turn your back while I dress," she said bitterly.

"Climb down from your high horse," Case said, his voice even. "I'm not the one who came crawling into your bed."

But even as he spoke, he rolled over and turned his back on her.

"I didn't come 'crawling into your bed,' " she said angrily. "You were having a nightmare."

"I don't remember any dreams."

"You were twitching and jerking and thrashing like a wolf in a trap."

"Doesn't sound real inviting to me," he drawled.

"Ute didn't think so, either."

"But you crawled right in."

"No," Sarah said, yanking the last lace tight. "You dragged me in."

"I suppose Ute saw that, too."

She started pulling her underwear and pants up. At first she thought the slick heat between her legs meant that her monthly had come early. But there was no dark stain of blood. Simply a steamy, scented moisture.

"What did you do to me?" she asked, startled.

Case looked over his shoulder. There was a vision of dense auburn curls and pearly skin vanishing rapidly into worn doeskin pants.

Hunger hit him like a fist, making it hard to breathe.

"You were married," he said roughly. "What do you think I did to you?"

"If I knew, I wouldn't be asking, would I?" she snapped.

For a moment he thought she was joking.

Then he saw the wariness in her eyes. She was fastening her pants as though her body belonged to a stranger.

Case didn't know what to say.

"Oh, never mind," she muttered. "I shouldn't have let you tuck me in next to you like a child. Then I went and fell asleep. I suppose I had it coming, whatever you did to me."

He opened his mouth. Nothing came out but silence.

She jumped to her feet, grabbed her jacket, and pulled it on. As she did, she flinched slightly. Her nipples were still hard, still very sensitive.

She looked puzzled by that, too.

So did Case.

Absently he brushed the stinging skin near his eye. The drops of blood that came away on his fingertip testified to Sarah's speed and aim with her nails.

The corners of his eyes crinkled slightly.

"You're a hellcat with those finger-nails." he said.

"Practice makes perfect," she said, her voice icy.

His eyes narrowed.

"The next time you have nightmares about your niece," she said in a clipped voice, "you can damned well have them by yourself."

"My niece?" Case asked, startled. "What are you talking about?"

"It will be tough telling you," she drawled sarcastically, "seeing as how you told me never to say her name again."

"Emily?"

"That's the one."

She started for the privy.

"How do you know I was dreaming about her?" he asked.

Pausing, Sarah looked over her shoulder.

"Do I take that as permission to say the sacred name?" she asked sweetly.

"Hell, say whatever you want."

"My, you do know how to tempt a woman."

"Just spit it out."

She almost gave in to temptation. The icy clarity of his eyes stopped her.

"You were thrashing —" she began.

"— around and muttering," he interrupted curtly. "I know that part."

"Who's telling the story, you or me?"

"Neither one, near as I can tell."

She bit back a searing word.

Normally it wasn't difficult to keep her temper. But this one man got under her skin worse than nettles.

"I talked to you for a time," she said tightly. "Soothing you."

"With that honey and sunshine voice," he suggested, his face expressionless.

She shrugged.

"When you settled down some," she said, "I got close enough to touch you. I wanted to wake you up gently."

"You sure you weren't dreaming? I don't remember any of this."

"You were asleep," she shot back.

"Uh huh."

"When I touched you, you didn't wake up, not all the way," she said, biting off each word. "You just mumbled Emily's name, and then something about how you thought she had gone."

Case didn't move, yet he closed up completely.

"Keep talking," he said.

"You put your arm around me, pulled me under the covers, and told me not to worry, Uncle Case would chase the ghosts away."

His eyelids flinched. It was the only sign that he heard Sarah's words.

"Then you tucked me along your side," she said, "cradled my face with your hand, and went back to sleep. It was a good sleep, clean and gentle."

She waited, but all he said was, "Anything else?"

"When I tried to ease out of your bed, your arm tightened and you started to wake up. I waited, and tried again. Same thing."

Case looked away from Sarah, but she sensed that she still had his full attention.

"I fell asleep," she said simply. "It was

319

so warm and peaceful to be held like that. No wonder Emily came to you when her dreams troubled her."

A flash of stark pain went over his face like black lightning.

Sarah's breath caught. Despite everything, she wanted to go to him, to hold him and be held in turn.

There were times when life simply hurt too much to bear alone.

"Emily is dead, isn't she?" Sarah whispered.

Only silence answered the question.

"Is that why you're hunting Culpeppers?" she asked.

"I will see every last one of them in hell."

His voice was like winter itself — quiet, cold, unstoppable.

She shivered and rubbed her hands over her arms.

"I don't doubt it," she said. "Unless you get yourself killed first."

"No one will hang crêpe if I die."

"I would."

Slowly Case looked back to her.

"Don't," he said simply.

"Don't what?"

"Care about me. It will only hurt you."

Sarah's smile was bittersweet.

"That's how you know you're alive, Case. You hurt."

After that, nothing disturbed the morning silence but the sound of her footsteps moving away.

Case dumped an armload of wood in the cabin. Sitting on his heels, he sorted and stacked the wood neatly near the fire.

Sarah looked up from her spinning. Though she was tired enough to fall on her face after a day of grinding corn with Lola, boiling laundry, and making soap, the spinning still had to be done. The cloth not only made their own clothes, it was one of the few sources of cash she had.

Unfortunately she wasn't too tired to blush every time she thought of what had happened that morning, with the sun barely up, her pants down around her knees, and a wild singing in her body.

Hastily she looked away from Case. The firewood he had brought in was obviously from the higher country beyond Lost River Canyon. There was even some pine wood among the piñon and juniper.

"Thank you," she said. "You're very

handy with that ax Ute, uh, found."

She suspected Ute had "found" the ax — and more besides — at the raiders' camp in Spring Canyon.

"No thanks necessary," Case said. "I eat food cooked over that fire just like Conner does."

The cabin door opened. Conner stuck his head in.

"If you're finished with that wood," he said to Case, "I could use a hand."

Sarah looked up quickly from her spinning.

"What is it?" she asked.

"Nothing you need to worry about," her brother said.

"Then Case doesn't need to worry about it, either," she said. "He worked like a donkey getting firewood today."

"It won't take long," Conner said.

Case glanced at the rawboned boy and stood up smoothly. He had been expecting something like this ever since Conner had reluctantly walked off this morning, leaving his sister in Case's bed.

"Be right with you," he said.

Conner withdrew. Rather pointedly he left the door open behind him.

"That boy," Sarah muttered, setting aside her spinning. "You would think

322

he was born in a barn."

"I'll get the door on my way out."

When Case closed the door behind him, Conner was standing off toward one of the clumps of big sage. In the waning light, the boy cast a long, thin shadow. The six-gun he wore was a blunt black bulge on his hip.

He put the sun behind him, Case realized. *Right in my eyes. The boy has promise.*

Hope he lives long enough to grow into it.

"What happened this morning?" Conner demanded as soon as the other man was within speaking range.

"You heard your sister."

"How did you nick your eye?"

"What's on your mind? Something special eating on you?"

"Sarah. Leave her alone."

Deliberately Case hooked his thumbs through his belt and took a relaxed stance.

"You do recall whose bed is out in the brush and whose is in the cabin?" he asked quietly. "Have you considered that you might be lecturing the wrong person?"

Conner's mouth thinned. The look in

his dark green eyes was far too adult for a boy of fifteen.

"Sarah wouldn't turn away from a creature in need," he said. "Ute said you needed her. She went to you and you grabbed her."

"Your sister came to me. I didn't grab her. That's all you need to know. If you don't believe me, ask her. She won't tell you any different."

Conner gave Case a level, measuring look.

"My sister wouldn't tell me different even if you had raped her," he said flatly. "She would be worried about me calling you on it and getting killed."

"But you aren't worried."

"I'm not that stupid. I can no more beat you in a fair fight than Sarah could outwrestle you in the dark."

Case nodded, but he wasn't as relaxed as he looked. He half-expected to have to jump Conner when the boy went for his out-sized belt gun.

"So I wouldn't fight fair," Conner said coolly. "I'd come at you with a shotgun from ambush. This is the only warning you'll get. *Leave Sarah alone.*"

For a moment Case looked thoughtful.

"What if she comes to me again?" he asked.

"If she does, it wouldn't be for sex."

Case's left eyebrow rose in a dark arc.

"Just because Sarah is your sister doesn't mean that she lacks womanly needs," he said evenly.

"Sex?" Conner asked derisively.

"Sex," Case agreed.

"Anything that leaves a woman bloody and whimpering isn't something she would seek out. Sarah sure didn't. She ran like hell every chance she got."

Case went still. "What?"

"You heard me."

"You think that's what sex is?"

"Isn't it?"

"No."

"Then why do men have to pay women to get it?" Conner asked sardonically.

"Not all men do."

The boy shrugged. "So they marry for it. Same thing in the end. The husband pays room and board and the wife suffers his attentions in exchange."

Case took a deep breath and blew it out soundlessly. He had no idea where to begin fixing Conner's sour view of what sex between a man and a woman was all about.

"Big Lola may not be the best example of womanhood to judge sex by," Case said after a moment.

"She sure as hell has a lot of experience."

"Of a kind, yes. But there's another kind."

"Marriage?"

Case thought of Hunter and Elyssa. Their love for each other haunted him even as he avoided any possibility of such emotion for himself.

"Love makes it different," he said finally.

"Uh huh," Conner said, not convinced.

"It's true. When a woman loves a man, she wants him. Physically. There's no bribery, no threat, no force. Just the kind of loving that makes the sun shine brighter."

"I haven't seen anything like that."

"I haven't seen Paris but that doesn't mean it doesn't exist."

"Are you saying that my sister *loves* you?"

The blunt question made Case wish he had never started the conversation.

"I'm not saying anything of the sort," he muttered.

"Sounded like it."

Case blew out another breath and tried again.

"A lot of people never know the special kind of love that makes the sun brighter," he said. "But that doesn't mean they don't enjoy sex with someone they like."

For a long time Conner looked at the older man without speaking. Then slowly, subtly, the boy relaxed.

"You didn't force Sarah?" he asked.

"No. And the next time you even hint at such a thing, I will personally whale the living tar out of you."

Surprisingly, Conner laughed.

"I'll bet you would," the boy agreed. "I'm sorry if I insulted you. I just had to know that Sarah wasn't being forced by a man again."

"You were pretty young when she was married. You might have misunderstood what all the, er, grunting and groaning was about."

"Even a baby knows the difference between a pat and a fist."

Case tried to think of a tactful way to ask his next question.

He came up empty-handed.

"Wasn't there any tenderness between Sarah and her husband?" he asked bluntly.

"Tenderness?"

"Like kissing and such."

"Far as I know, my sister got her first kiss the night she came back riding double with you."

"Judas priest," Case whispered. "Why did she marry the old — never mind. None of my business."

Conner's face seemed to flatten and tighten. It was a flash of the man he would become in time, honesty and strength and force in equal parts.

"Why do you think my sister married him?" he asked coldly.

"Necessity."

"Damned straight. She was barely fourteen and I was nine. No relatives survived the flood. We were starving. She answered an advertisement in the newspaper."

"And married Hal?"

Conner nodded. "The old son of a bitch couldn't even get a squaw to put up with him."

"How did you kill Hal?"

The easy question caught Conner off-guard. He looked around quickly.

No one else was in sight.

"How did you know?" he asked.

"I didn't, until now."

"Don't tell my sister," he said urgently. "I want your word on that."

I'm supposed to keep my half of the ranch secret from Conner, Case thought wryly, *and now here's a second secret I'm supposed to keep from Sarah.*

"Are you sure she doesn't already know?" he asked.

"Yes!"

"What happened?"

Conner made a hard, chopping motion with his hand.

"What does it matter? He's dead."

"Shotgun from ambush?" Case asked casually.

"No. Hell's fire, I didn't even mean to kill the old bastard."

Case lifted an eyebrow and waited.

Sighing, Conner ran a hand through his hair, settled his hat with a jerk, and started to talk.

"He'd been after her the night before. It was one of the few times he caught her."

Case's eyelids flinched once, then again. He didn't like thinking about

Sarah and an old man so cruel he couldn't even get an outcast Indian woman to live with him.

Far as I know, my sister got her first kiss the night she came back riding double with you.

"He was on a real toot," Conner said. "He was still drinking when he rode out prospecting the next morning. I followed him."

"On foot?"

"Hal's horse was as old as he was. But he was a real walking fool. It was afternoon by the time I caught up."

Case watched the boy through narrowed eyes.

"I told Hal to quit mistreating my sister," Conner said. "He started to pistol whip me. It wasn't the first time, but it sure was the last."

"You shot him?"

"We fought over the gun, it went off, and Hal just sort of folded up."

Despite Conner's matter-of-fact words, Case could see the shadows of old anger and horror in the boy's green eyes and thinned mouth.

"I tried to feel bad about it afterward," Conner said softly. "But I felt worse when I had to shoot a mustang that had a broken leg."

"How old were you when Hal died?"

"Twelve."

"Hard way to grow up."

"I grew up when I was nine," Conner said. "After that, all that mattered was Sarah."

"And you're all that matters to her."

"Me and the land. And now you."

Case ducked the veiled question.

"What about Ute and Lola?" he asked.

"It's not the same. Oh, we all get along real well, and Ute would fight to the death for Sarah, but . . ." Conner shrugged. "My sister doesn't fret about them the way she does about me or you."

"I think she values your hide one hell of a lot more than she values mine."

Conner hesitated, then shrugged. "Maybe."

Yet the boy's steady green eyes said that he thought the older man was wrong.

I should have run when the running was good, Case told himself.

Then he thought of the land calling to him and knew he couldn't run. At that instant he understood what it felt like to be a wolf in a trap.

Nowhere to run.

Nothing to fight but himself.

A lot of wolves died that way, bleeding to death when they gnawed off their own legs in a desperate try for freedom.

14

Disgusted, Case leaned on the shovel and stared down at the cold hole he had dug at the base of a finger of red rock. It looked a lot like the other holes he had dug in the past two weeks.

Empty.

Before he had started digging, there were signs that the ground had been a camping spot. But it was impossible to tell whether the rock had been blackened by a campfire three years ago, or thirty, or three hundred.

Or three thousand. The dry air of the stone desert preserved everything from wood to bones to broken pottery.

I'm a damned fool to be digging holes when I could be building a cabin of my own to live in, he thought.

A cold wind wailing up the nameless canyon seemed to agree with him.

He was a fool.

Sweaty and naked to the waist despite the wind, he picked up the shovel and went back to work. The steel edge grated against a combination of dirt, sand, and rubble that was anywhere from the size of a penny to that of a pony.

I could be catching a few mustangs of my own, he thought. *There's some promising horseflesh running loose out there.*

With Cricket as a stud, and a few good mares from California or Virginia, a man could breed some fine animals.

The sound of something heavy being dragged toward Case scattered his thoughts. He straightened from digging and looked up the canyon.

"Damnation, Sarah!" he yelled, "I told you to leave the big stuff for me."

"You should see — what I left — up there," she panted.

Despite the wind and the frost that still sparkled in the shadow of north-facing rocks, she wore only doeskin pants and a shirt with a thin camisole beneath. Her pants were scarred by brush and stained from plain hard work.

Her jacket was hanging over a low bush about a hundred yards down the canyon, near the first hole he had dug. Her hat was on top of the jacket. From certain angles, the bush looked enough like a hunched-over man that Case had reached for his belt gun twice.

Even knowing what was really there didn't keep him from starting when he caught a glimpse of the man-shape from the corner of his eye.

Sarah dragged her prize another few yards and dropped it with the wood she had gathered while he was digging. For a minute she just breathed hard and looked at the mound of firewood.

"There should be enough for both packhorses, plus my own little mustang," she said.

"Shaker is a better packhorse than a mount. Her trot would jolt teeth loose."

"How do you think she got her name?"

He looked at the mound of firewood. The last piece she had added wasn't a branch — it was the whole trunk.

"You should have left that log for me with the rest of the big stuff up the canyon," he said.

She ignored him.

He wasn't surprised. He had discovered in the past two weeks that Sarah was very good at ignoring what she didn't want to discuss.

Sex was number one on her list of things to ignore.

Maybe I should just trip her, sit on her, and force her to listen, he thought. *If I do it now, I sure wouldn't have to worry about getting her clothes dirty.*

In all, she was almost as dusty as he was. When she wasn't pawing through a pile of rubble from whatever hole he was digging, she was dragging downed wood back to where the horses grazed.

Sarah stretched her back, sighed, and reached for the cross-cut saw that Ute had "found" along with the ax.

"I'll saw that last one up," Case said.

"You dig. I'll saw what I can."

His mouth flattened. As far as he was concerned, she worked as hard as two men.

"What about resting?" he asked mildly.

"What about it?"

"I'm tired."

Immediately she was contrite. She set aside the saw and hurried toward him.

"I'm sorry," she said. "I keep forgetting about your wounds."

So did he, but he saw no reason to mention it. He liked the concern in her expressive eyes as she came toward him. He liked the willowy strength of her body and the unconscious swing of her hips when she walked.

He liked every bit of her too much.

He kept remembering how she had felt and tasted at dawn, hot silk in his hands and honey on his tongue.

All that woman going to waste.

No sooner did the thought come to him than he pushed it aside. What the hardworking widow did or didn't do about men and sex was none of his business.

Now, if only I can convince my dumb handle of that, he thought dryly.

But he doubted he could. He came to a point like a bird dog whenever Sarah walked by. The only thing that made the situation bearable was that she didn't notice her effect on him.

Or if she did, she didn't let on.

"Case? Are you feeling all right?"

He looked down into her beautiful misty gray eyes and realized that she had been talking to him while his mind had been somewhere else entirely.

Below his belt.

"Put the shovel down," she said firmly. "It's time to rest. We'll have an early lunch. You sit there under the —"

The scream of bullets ricocheting through the canyon cut off the rest of her words.

Case grabbed Sarah and rolled between two pillars of rock before the echoes came back.

"My shotgun is —" she began.

His hand covered her mouth.

Here I am, facedown in the dirt again, chewing on his gritty leather glove, she thought. *How come I always end up on the bottom?*

But there was a difference this time, and she knew it to the marrow of her bones. He was using his body to shield her rather than to overwhelm her.

Motionless, together, they listened.

The distant sound of shod hooves somewhere on the canyon rim came back on the wind.

"Maybe five hundred yards off," he murmured into her ear. "One mule. Maybe another horse. Can't tell."

"How can you — oh, that's right," she muttered. "Moody doesn't shoe his mustangs."

In his mind Case constructed a picture of the lower part of the canyon. They were at the head of a treelike, branching network of dry canyons. Lost River Canyon was the main trunk. About where the little side canyon they were in bent south to merge with another, larger branch canyon, there were several places up on the rim where a man could lie in ambush.

No more sounds came to Case or Sarah on the wind. When she would have spoken again, he muffled her mouth with his hand.

She bit the base of his thumb.

Gently.

Heat went through him like a firestorm.

Judas priest, he thought. *Of all the times for her to get playful.*

Jaw clenched, he concentrated on listening for distant sounds rather than on the nearby soft breaths of the woman lying beneath him.

Case heard exactly what he didn't want to hear. Hoofbeats and the rattle of rock as mustangs or mules scrambled down a steep slope.

He rolled aside.

"Stay here and stay low no matter what happens," he said softly.

"Where are you going?" she asked in an equally soft voice.

"After my rifle."

"Where is it?"

"At the base of that pillar," he said, pointing.

"I'll belly crawl to it."

A hard, strong hand clamped over the back of her right thigh, pinning her in place.

"What the hell do you think you're doing?" he asked in a low, furious voice.

"Just what I said — getting your rifle."

"Stay here."

"My leg isn't wounded," she objected. "Yours is."

Case gave Sarah a look that would have etched steel.

"Stay here," he said softly.

Her mouth flattened, but she stayed where she was.

"Whatever happens, don't show yourself," he said. "The first one who sticks up his head gets a bullet between the eyes. Patience is the game."

"I understand," she said very quietly. "I won't move from here."

"Promise me."

"Yes."

A cold steel weight pressed against her right hand. A glance told her that it was his six-gun.

"If you see something you don't like, shoot it," he said. "Beyond a hundred feet, the gun pulls a bit to the left. Over two hundred feet, shift the barrel one inch to the right. Anything farther away than that, ignore. Understand?"

Sarah nodded.

"There's a round in the chamber," Case added very quietly. "Try not to shoot me by mistake."

"I don't shoot what I can't see."

"That would be a comfort if you weren't angry enough at me to skin me out for a rug."

Her teeth flashed against her dusty skin.

"A mighty fine rug you would make, too," she murmured. "I'm sure tired of that dirt floor."

"If you don't shoot me, I'll cut you some flooring planks up in the mountains."

"It's a deal."

She couldn't see his face, but she sensed the amusement buried inside him.

Someday I'm going to sneak up on that man's blind side and catch him smiling, she vowed.

He left the cover of the red pillars like

a hunting cat — on his belly. Using the insides of his feet, his elbows, and the sheer power of his body, he wriggled forward.

Never once did he raise his head above the level of the brush and rubble surrounding him. His dusty clothes and skin blended perfectly with the landscape.

Sarah had to squint to be certain that it was Case she was watching, rather than shadows cast by wind-stirred brush.

No wonder he's such a good hunter, she thought. *He can sneak close enough to reach out and grab the game by the throat.*

Case vanished.

A chill went over her. She blinked and blinked again. She saw nothing.

He was gone as completely as a flame blown out.

At that instant she understood with chilling certainty how he had survived the night when three attackers hadn't.

Yet despite his unnerving skill on the stalk, he had come very close to dying out there in the night. Some of the men he was stalking were as expert as he was.

Sweat gathered coldly in the small of her back. Part of her fear was for Case. Part of it was for herself. She didn't like the idea of a shadow creeping up on her and killing her before she even had a chance to scream.

Very slowly she inched the six-gun up along her side until she could sight over its barrel. The gun was too heavy for her to hold in place for long. Blindly she felt around for pieces of stone. When she had enough, she built a small mound for the barrel of the pistol to rest on. Sighting over it, she watched the land.

And she waited.

A rifle shot split the silence. Instantly there was return fire from the direction in which Case had vanished. Bullets screamed off rock and ricocheted through the narrow canyon.

Even as Sarah flinched, she lined up the barrel of the six-gun with the lower part of the canyon and prayed that Case wasn't hurt.

The sound of a running horse came up the canyon. The stone walls of the canyon caused each hoofbeat to echo and reecho, overlapping the sounds, making it impossible for her to be certain where the horse was.

Abruptly Case's head and rifle showed for an instant over the brush. He fired, levered in another bullet, fired and levered and fired again. The bullets were so closely spaced they sounded like a single burst of thunder.

The sound of the running horse slowed and then faded into silence.

Bullets screamed from a different direction.

She waited, but Case didn't return the fire.

It was the same as the night the raiders had attacked. Waiting and listening with her heart beating like a captive bird and terror lying cold in her belly.

Is he hurt? she thought fearfully.

Lying there waiting and worrying and wondering was against her nature. She itched to go out and check on Case. There was no Conner to sit on her and make her endure not knowing.

Yet she didn't move.

She had given Case her word that she would stay where she was.

He wouldn't be expecting to find her crawling around out there. If he was alive, she didn't want to distract him.

If he was dead, she didn't want to give away her position. If he was hurt . . .

The thought was unbearable.

Holding the six-gun steady, she bit her lip and prayed that Case would come back to her.

After a time, a hawk called softly.

Lips trembling, she gave an answering whistle.

Moments later Case snaked through the brush and into the shelter of the pillars. He was sweaty, dirty, and scratched.

The rifle he held was clean and ready to fire.

"How many?" Sarah asked very quietly.

"Three."

"Where?"

"Two of them are coming up the canyon," he said.

"Where's the third?"

"On his way to hell."

She made a low sound.

"Don't feel bad for him," Case said quietly. "When I got him, he was shooting holes in your jacket as fast as he could."

Suddenly her mouth was very dry. "Did he think it was me?"

"He didn't care whether it was you, me, or Conner."

The thought of her brother being murdered between one heartbeat and the next changed Sarah's expression.

"I hope the raider enjoys hell," she said in a low voice.

"I hope he doesn't."

The cool finality of Case's tone sent another chill over her.

"Now what?" she whispered.

"We wait."

"For what?"

"Whatever comes," he said.

"What if Ute or Conner heard the shots? Sometimes sound carries for a long way in these canyons."

"Ute knows better than to ride blind into a gunfight."

"Conner," was all she said.

Case didn't answer. Instead, he sighted down the rifle barrel, let out his breath, and squeezed the trigger very gently. The rifle kicked.

The report knifed through Sarah's head.

Down the canyon, halfway up the opposite side, a man pitched forward. He slid down the debris slope until a boulder stopped him.

The boneless lines of the man's body said that he had been knocked sense- less or was dead.

"Culpepper?" she whispered hope- fully.

"No. Too short. Too dark."

The canyon was quiet again except for the cold wind searching through every crease and crevice.

After fifteen minutes, shivers began to run through her body. Her doeskin shirt and pants had been enough to keep her warm as long as she was dragging dead wood up and down the canyon. But lying against the ground on the north side of a winter canyon was draining heat from her body with every heartbeat.

From the corner of her eye, she looked at Case, who was naked to the waist. He was watching the land within reach of his rifle fire. His eyes were narrowed, intent. If he noticed the cold, he didn't show it.

She tried to stop the shivers that kept rippling through her, but couldn't. She clenched her teeth so that they wouldn't chatter and distract him.

After ten more minutes, her hands were shaking so much that it was impossible to hold the six-gun steady. Case took the gun from her fingers and holstered it.

"Lie against me," he said quietly. "I'm warmer than stone."

She eased closer until she was alongside him. He moved onto his side and tucked her against his body, then rolled partway over again, sheltering her.

"Now cuddle in like a cold tabby cat," he murmured.

"I'll g-get in your w-way."

"If I move suddenly, cover your ears."

They waited.

After a time the noise of retreating hoofbeats drifted back up the canyon. It was a single animal, moving fast. Each strike of hoof against stone was clear. In fact, sometimes it sounded like a hammer hitting rock.

"Shod," Case said.

"I don't care if it's winged," Sarah said against his collarbone, "as long as the raider is gone."

"Quit wiggling."

She sighed hard enough to stir the hair on his chest and lay still.

Ignoring her head tucked below his, he waited and watched, every sense alert.

348

For a long time the wind was all that moved, all that spoke, all that showed any sign of life.

They're gone, he decided.

Case was certain of it. The back of his neck no longer felt tight.

He took a slow, deep breath. Along with air, he inhaled the presence of Sarah. Right now she smelled more like rock dust than roses, but it didn't matter. His body hardened in a rush that made him feel as heavy as the cliff at his back.

"Case?" she whispered.

"What?"

"Are they gone?"

"I think so."

She started to get up.

Before he could think better of it, he found himself holding her where she was.

Close.

The memory of her jacket leaping while bullets tore it apart made him cold all the way to his soul. It so easily could have been her flesh rather than cloth.

He didn't know what he would have done then. He didn't even want to think about it. All he knew was that he wasn't ready to let go of Sarah yet.

"Just to be sure it's safe," he said, "we'll wait right here a while longer."

"It was worth a try," she muttered.

Her words were so muffled that he couldn't understand any of them.

"What?" he asked.

She sighed. "Nothing. I just love being the slice of cold meat in a stone sandwich."

"I'm not stone."

"Could have fooled me. You're hard as a rock."

The left corner of his mouth lifted enough to show even beneath the beard he hadn't yet let her shave.

"A lady isn't supposed to notice," he whispered against her ear.

"How hard your body is? I'd have to be frozen like an icicle not to — ulp."

She had just realized that there was hard, and then there was hard.

At the moment, his body suited both meanings of the word.

"I'll bet that blush warmed you right up," he said dryly.

"Watch it. I'll bite you again."

A shudder of pure hunger went through Case.

"You keep talking like that," he said

against her ear, "and I'm going to forget all about the Culpeppers' nasty habit of leaving a man behind to finish off the wounded."

"Talking like what?"

"About biting me."

While he spoke, his teeth closed delicately over the rim of her ear.

She shivered and made a small sound.

"Cold?" he whispered.

"N-no."

"You're trembling."

"Nobody ever bit me like that," she said.

"Like what?"

Sarah's teeth scraped gently over a pad of muscle on his chest.

His heartbeat doubled.

"Like that," she whispered. "Gentle and teasing."

"I did. You just don't remember it."

"When?"

"A few weeks back, when you crawled into my bed."

Her body stiffened.

"I didn't mean *that*," she said.

"Sex?"

"Yes."

"Sarah . . ." He searched for words.

"Honey, sex can be tender and teasing and hot and wild and everything in between."

"For a man, maybe. Not for a woman."

"You didn't like my gentle bite?"

She rubbed her nose against the thatch of hair on his chest.

"I liked it," she admitted.

"You didn't like having your breasts petted and kissed two weeks ago?"

"Case!"

"Did you or didn't you?" he asked.

"How would I know? I was asleep!"

"What were you dreaming?"

A shiver went through Sarah as she remembered.

"I was lying in the sun," she whispered. "I was warm all over, as though . . . as though . . . I don't know. I never felt that way before."

"You liked it."

"How do you know?" she retorted. "You weren't in my dream."

"No, but I was in your body. I could feel how much you liked my mouth and my hands all over you."

A wild, hot thrill went through her.

I was in your body.

No other man had been that close to her except her husband. Her only memories of Hal were fear and pain and a throttled kind of rage that she should have to endure being bruised and ill-used in exchange for a roof over her head and food on Conner's plate.

"In my body?" she asked thinly.

"Not the way you mean. Just . . ."

His voice died.

How do I explain to an experienced innocent that men tease women with their fingers? he wondered.

"I was petting you," he said. "That's all."

"Inside?" she asked, shocked.

The corners of his eyes crinkled.

"Inside," he agreed. "It didn't hurt you, did it?"

"I don't know," she said through her teeth.

"Sure you do. You were awake at the last."

"I don't want to talk about it."

"Why?"

"I just don't!"

"You'll face off raiders over a shotgun and you won't talk about whether or not something hurt you?" he asked. "They're just words, not bullets."

She didn't say anything.

"Your husband was a piss-poor man,"

Case said matter-of-factly. "Most men are more decent to their women."

"Sure," she said sarcastically. "That's why men pay women to put up with them. Well, there's not enough silver in all of creation to make me put up with *that* again."

"What about your dream of lying naked in the sun, with heat caressing you all over?"

"What about it?"

"It was me."

"What?"

"I was the sun. I was touching you all over. And you liked it, Sarah. I know you did. You ran like warm honey over my fingers."

She went very still, barely breathing.

"When you asked me that morning what I had done to you," Case said, "I thought you were joking."

She shook her head slowly. "I wasn't. I . . . hadn't ever . . . didn't know . . . there was never anything like . . . ."

She gave up trying to talk and buried her hot face against his chest.

"I feel like such a fool," she whispered.

"Your husband was the fool."

"Why?"

"You have real passion in you," Case said. "He never bothered to find it."

Sarah's head came up so quickly she almost clipped his chin.

"Passion?" she asked in disbelief. "You mean I *like* sex?"

"You liked what you had of it with me."

"But I didn't have, er, all of you. I ran away before you could hurt me."

His left eyebrow went up in a black arc.

"What makes you think I would have hurt you?" he asked mildly. "I hadn't hurt you up to then, had I?"

Despite the heat sweeping up her cheeks again, she spoke as plainly as Case had. She was determined that he understand how mistaken he was.

She didn't like sex.

Period.

"I've seen you naked," she said bluntly. "You're big. Hal wasn't nearly as big and he hurt me."

Case's black eyelashes lowered for an instant. He hoped he wasn't blushing as much as she had, but he wouldn't have bet a lot of money on it.

Talking about sex was a lot harder than simply doing it.

"It hurt because you weren't ready for him," Case said finally.

She frowned in confusion.

"Ready?" she asked. "What does that mean?"

"A woman's body . . . changes when she's ready for her man."

"Lola never said anything about a woman being ready. When the man is ready he has sex, that's all."

"Lola was a prostitute," he said bluntly. "The men who came to her wanted sex and they wanted it fast. They paid to get it that way."

"So?"

Case opened his mouth, then closed it.

"Did you and Lola ever talk about seduction?" he asked after a time.

"Sure. That's where women are fooled into believing it won't hurt."

"It doesn't!"

"Not for the man," she retorted.

Carefully he put down his rifle. He cupped both hands over her face.

"Will you let me kiss you?" he asked.

"Just kissing?"

"Just kissing."

"That's all?"

"That's all," he whispered against her lips.

Then he lifted his head and watched her troubled gray eyes while she thought it over.

Suddenly she smiled at him almost shyly.

"All right," she whispered. "I liked being kissed by you."

Case came very close to smiling in return when he thought of the depth of her sensual ignorance.

Just kissing covered a lot of very sweet territory.

15

Sarah watched Case's head lower to hers and his black eyelashes close. She felt the brushing warmth of his lips over hers all the way to her toes. She sighed and shivered at the same time.

"You're still cold," he said huskily. "I should get your jacket."

"I'm not cold."

"You're shivering."

"Not that way. I just felt quivery and good all over when you kissed me."

She both felt and heard the quick breath he took.

"Then I'll do it some more," he said.

His lips moved over hers again, and again she trembled slightly in response. He nuzzled the corners of her mouth, the edge of her jaw, the delicate lobe of one ear. Then he sipped at the pulse beating quickly in her neck.

With each motion of his head, his beard stroked her skin like a soft brush, bringing her nerve endings to wild, shimmering life.

"You sure you're not cold?" he asked.

Nodding her head, she made a murmuring, purring kind of sound.

"Like it?" he asked.

"Yes," she whispered.

"Good. Slide your arms around me and come in real close."

"I'm not cold. Really."

"I am," he lied.

"Oh," she said, contrite. "I didn't think of that. You always feel so warm to me."

Sarah slid her arms around Case and nestled in close. Her breasts pressed against him. She was surprised to find that her nipples were sensitive again. Not hurting, just . . . alive.

And when she moved subtly against his chest, the odd, shivery feeling rippled through her from her breasts to her knees. It felt so good that she arched her back slightly and rubbed against him again, more slowly.

"Is there a rock under your hip?" he teased.

"No. I just like . . ."

Her voice frayed into silence.

"What do you like?" he asked.

She licked suddenly dry lips.

"From the color of your cheeks," he

said, "I think I know what you're trying to say. Let me help."

She gave him a startled look.

"First I'll just get rid of my gloves and put my hand here," he said.

His long fingers spread wide between Sarah's shoulder blades. As he arched her back, he dragged his chest slowly against her breasts.

Heat shot through her.

"Oh!" she said, startled.

"Too hard?" he asked.

Only then did she understand that his movements had been anything but accidental. Curious, she stared at him.

"Honey?" he said. "Was I too rough?"

She shook her head, watching him.

"Lord," he whispered. "You have the most beautiful eyes."

"I do?" she asked, startled again.

He knew that she wasn't being coy. There simply wasn't a coy bone in her body.

"You do," he said. "Sometimes they're like mist and sometimes they're like a storm and sometimes they're a silver as deep as the sea."

The look in his eyes made Sarah's mouth go dry. She licked her lips.

He watched her tongue.

"You're right," he said. "It's time for more."

"What?"

"Nothing to worry about. Just another kiss."

"Oh. Good."

"For me, too," he said.

"What —"

The heated glide of his tongue over her mouth scattered her thoughts. She forgot the question she had been going to ask. All her attention was focused on her lips. They were vividly alive, hot where his tongue was touching and cool where it had passed on.

Her arms tightened around Case until she was pressed hard against him. He helped by arching her back and rubbing her breasts over his chest again, bringing her even closer.

Her breath came in brokenly, opening her mouth. His tongue dipped beneath her upper lip, gliding, probing, circling. His teeth caught her lower lip. He tugged gently.

She didn't know that she made a ragged sound and opened her lips wider. She knew only that his tongue was hot inside her mouth and the taste of his kiss was sweet beyond bearing.

She wanted to tell him how good it felt, but she didn't want to end the sweetness. So she gave him back the kiss, sliding her tongue over his, probing the sultry corners of his mouth, then catching his tongue delicately between her teeth.

His breath came out with a hoarse sound.

Instantly she released him.

"I'm sorry," she said quickly. "I don't know anything about this. You're the only one I've ever kissed besides blood family, and that's different."

Conner was right, Case thought grimly. *She was married for years and never even kissed.*

An odd kind of pain twisted through him, sadness and hunger combined, and a need to cherish Sarah that was greater than any other emotion.

"Are you all right?" she asked unhappily. "I didn't mean to hurt you."

"You didn't."

His voice was husky and his eyes were a smoldering silver-green between his nearly closed lashes.

"You groaned," she said.

"So did you, two weeks ago."

"I don't remember."

"You will this time."

Sarah stiffened subtly. All she remembered was how she had ended up that morning — her pants around her knees and his hand between her legs.

"We weren't just kissing then," she said.

"You weren't kissing me at all. I was kissing you."

"But —"

"Hush," Case said, lowering his mouth over hers again. "It's just kissing."

"Mmmph."

After a few moments she forgot all about what was and wasn't kissing. The feelings cascading through her were delicious. So was the taste of Case, his heat, the textures of beard and lips, tongue and teeth.

The softening of her body told him that she was no longer anxious about what might happen. Instead, she was returning the intimate kiss with a shy, hesitant, yet passionate thoroughness that made his head spin.

He forgot about the rock digging into his side and the cold wind blowing over his naked back. He forgot about everything except the hot secrets of Sarah's mouth.

At the back of his mind Case knew he should stop before he got in over his head. He had been a long, long time without a woman. And this particular woman appealed to him far too much for his hard-won peace of mind.

She healed my wounds, he thought. *It's only fair that I heal hers in return.*

If I can.

If she'll even let me try.

He merged his mouth with hers the same way he hungered to merge their bodies. Slowly. Tenderly.

Completely.

Sarah matched him breath for breath, touch for touch, hunger for hunger, until Case felt everything sliding away, leaving only her. He didn't know he had undone the laces on her doeskin shirt until she tore her mouth free from his.

"You said just kissing," she accused.

"It's hard to kiss through doeskin."

When she understood what he was saying, her eyes widened. Her flushed lips and cheeks made the color of her eyes a radiant, clear silver.

"I'm not wearing doeskin over my mouth," she said, breathing unevenly.

"I'm not talking about kissing your mouth."

She stared at him. His eyes were pale green fire against the heightened color of his skin. Each time his head moved, light shimmered over his short black beard like stars against midnight. His lips were red from the pressure of their shared kisses.

"You want to stop kissing, is that it?" she asked.

"No," he said. "I want to keep on kissing you and kissing you until the honey flows and you're as soft as I am hard and we . . ."

With a sharp breath Case reined in his runaway tongue.

Sarah waited, watching him with wide eyes. Both passion and wariness were in her expression. Passion was stronger. She was watching his mouth rather than his eyes.

"That's the idea," he said huskily. "Watch me. Watch us . . . kissing."

His lips and beard were silky against her ear, her neck, the pulse beating just beneath her skin. When his tongue probed the hollow at the base of her throat, her breath broke. He sucked on her skin, bit her tenderly, and shared the ripple of response that went through her.

By the time her shirt was fully un-laced, she had no idea how it had happened. She knew only that the shirt was undone and her nipples were firm rosy crowns standing up against the thin muslin of her chemise.

He bent down. His lips parted over one veiled nipple.

"Case?" she asked uncertainly.

"Just kissing," he said, his voice deep.

"But I'm not kissing you."

"There's more than one way to kiss each other. Watch."

The sight of him nibbling gently on her breast made an odd, breathless feeling twist through Sarah. The stark contrast of masculine beard and fragile muslin somehow heightened the inten-sity of the caress.

Slowly, deliberately, he licked the thin cloth that separated his tongue from her taut nipple.

Sensations glittered through her like hidden lightning. Embarrassed, fasci-nated, held in a delicious net of plea-sure, she watched the muslin darken beneath his tongue.

Before she quite knew what was hap-pening, the tip of her breast vanished into his mouth. As he had once seduced her lips, now he seduced her breast, stroking it with tongue and teeth.

Her back arched instinctively, rubbing her nipple even more firmly over his tongue. He responded by increasing the sucking pressure until she whimpered and held him to her breast.

When Case finally lifted his head, her chemise looked as though the muslin had dissolved away, leaving her breast naked to his caressing tongue. She knew she should be embarrassed to see herself so clearly, and to know that he was seeing her in the same way, but her flushed cheeks came from rising passion rather than shame.

She loved watching him caress her.

Delicately, repeatedly, he sipped at the tight pink crown. When his teeth closed tenderly around the nipple, she shivered and cried out sharply.

He lifted his head.

"Did I hurt you?" he asked, concerned.

She shook her head.

"Your eyes are as big as silver dollars," he whispered.

Sarah looked down at her breast.

"What did you do?" she asked. "I've never looked like that, even on the coldest mornings."

"This?" he asked.

He touched her nipple with the tip of his tongue.

"Yes," she whispered.

"It's your body's way of saying it likes being kissed. It's kissing me in return."

"Just . . . kissing?"

He made a rumbling sound of agreement.

"Of course," he said deeply, "if you wouldn't mind, I would love to pet those pretty breasts while I'm kissing them."

She shivered at the look in his eyes — half-open, heavy-lidded, he was watching her breasts the way a starving man watched a banquet.

"Just petting?" she asked in a small voice.

"Just petting."

"Will it leave marks?"

His head lifted sharply. "Did he bruise you?"

"Only when I wouldn't hold still. Then he . . ."

Sarah's voice died.

"What did he do?" Case asked gently, wondering if she had mistaken passion for ill use. "I don't want to scare you."

"He just grabbed my breasts and dug

in with his fingernails until I quit fighting."

For a moment Case couldn't even
speak.

*It's a good thing Conner killed Hal
accidentally,* he thought. *I sure as hell
would have done it deliberately, and
hanged for it.*

"I would never hurt you that way,"
Case said simply.

She hesitated, then let out a ragged
little breath.

"All right," she said in a rush. "You
can do what — what you said you
wanted to."

"It will feel better without your chemise. For both of us."

"Nothing covering me?" she asked in
a high voice.

"My mouth. My hands."

She shivered at the thought of wearing him as intimately as her own under-
clothes.

"All right," she whispered, for her
mouth was too dry to speak any other
way.

He took off her shirt and shifted her
until she was lying on her back with
the doeskin beneath her. His hands slid
up along her ribs beneath her chemise.

He lifted his thumbs to ease the muslin up over her aroused breasts.

And then he simply looked at her.

"Lord, woman," he breathed. "You put the sun and moon to shame."

Sarah blushed from her breasts to her forehead.

He bent and smoothed his face against her, from her collarbone down over each breast and back again, kissing and stroking every bit of the way. The thought of such delicate beauty being savaged by any man, even her lawful husband, made Case want to lick and kiss and pet away every last memory of pain.

Bracing himself on his elbows, he dipped his face between her breasts, stroking her, aching for the ill treatment she had known. If he could have, he would have taken her pain inside himself, all of it, leaving her with only the pleasure.

The thought that such a healing might be possible was almost agonizing to him. He shuddered and redoubled his caresses, tenderly devouring her.

For Sarah, it was like her dream all over again, with the sun worshipping her naked skin. The rough silk of his beard brought her breasts to aching peaks that were soothed by his tongue and caressed by his fingertips and palms. Her breasts were flushed and taut, fully alive for the first time in her life.

She made a hoarse sound and jerked when his mouth closed over a nipple.

"I've never done this with a woman," Case whispered, lifting his head. "You'll have to tell me if I do something you don't like."

At first she didn't really hear the words, for she was too caught up in the pleasure that rippled and shimmered through her to understand anything else.

"Never done this?" she managed finally.

"Not like this."

"How is it different?"

"I want to take all the pain and leave sweetness in its place. Before now, all I wanted was . . ."

His voice died as he kissed the inner curve of Sarah's breasts, then raked his teeth with exquisite care over each nipple. The jerk of her response and her fingers clenching suddenly in his hair told him just how much she enjoyed his caresses.

"Hell," he said huskily. "I can't even remember how it was before. I just know it wasn't like this."

He lowered his head and delicately consumed her breasts, lingering over the hard pink tips.

"There's more of you I want to pet and pleasure," he said. "Will you let me?"

Her only answer was a dazed sound and her fingers silently urging his head back to her hungry breasts.

"You'll like it even more than what I've done so far," he said. "Let me touch all of you, honey. Let me."

"It won't . . . hurt?" she asked raggedly.

"Have you ever felt something so good it almost hurt?" he whispered.

"You mean, like the song of the first meadowlark in spring?"

Her words made him clench with pain and pleasure combined. He had never guessed that anyone else felt like that about hearing a meadowlark for the first time after winter's long, icy silence.

Until this instant, Case had forgotten what it was to feel like that himself.

"Yes," he said unevenly. "Like a silver needle stitching through your soul.

That's not a real hurt, is it?"

"No. It's beautiful. Like you, so strong and yet so careful of me."

Case kissed Sarah very gently.

"I'd give my soul to take back what that savage old man did to you," he whispered.

Tears came suddenly to her eyes. She touched his mouth tenderly with her fingertips.

"You can't go back," she whispered. "You can only go forward."

With a hoarse sound, he put his forehead against her heart and let the steady beat of her life sink into him. Slowly, very slowly, his mouth slid down to her navel. He probed the sensitive hollow with his tongue.

She gasped in surprise at the sensations radiating through her with each movement of his tongue. His hands circled her breasts and plucked the aching peaks. At the same time he repeated his velvet probing of her navel. Her back arched and she cried out in a low voice.

An answering wave of passion swept through him, shaking him. Knowing that he was bringing her pleasure for the first time in her life was like a drug to him. He repeated the caresses again and again and again, tenderly, recklessly.

He didn't want to stop. He didn't even want to try.

With trembling hands he unfastened her pants and eased them down her hips. Beneath doeskin and muslin, the scent of roses and feminine arousal combined in a heady perfume. He inhaled deeply, dizzy with the sensual possibilities of her body.

"Case?" she asked, her voice uncertain.

"The sun, the moon, the stars," he said thickly, looking at her. "Nothing is more beautiful than you."

The pale fire of his eyes devoured her, yet his hands and mouth on her body were as gentle as the golden shadow of flame.

Torn between embarrassment and a heat she had felt only once before, in a dream of sunlight, she watched him caressing her. She didn't object when he slid her pants completely off her legs and tucked the clothing under her. She didn't object when he laid his cheek on her body and stroked her belly as he had once stroked her breasts, teeth and tongue and hands combined.

Then he began smoothing his forehead and bearded cheeks over the top of her thighs. His silky mouth and sensuously hard hands followed. The sweetly conflicting textures were heightened by the tender raking of his teeth.

Gently he seduced her legs as completely as he had seduced the rest of her body. She forgot that she was vulnerable to his much greater strength. She forgot the cold wind and the hard rock. She forgot everything but the pleasure gathering deep inside her with each kiss he gave her, each caress, each husky word telling her how much he cherished her body.

The stiffness of her legs melted away before his tender assault. Distantly she realized that he was kissing and stroking the inside of her knees, her thighs, her —

"Case."

He made a hungry, questioning, oddly soothing sound.

"You're inside me," she said in a high voice.

"God, yes. You're pure honey."

He moved his hand again, slowly.

Satin heat flowed once more.

"Honey and fire enough to melt winter itself," he whispered.

She tried to speak. She couldn't. A wave of intense pleasure was bursting through her, arching her back like a drawn bow.

With heavy-lidded eyes, Case watched shock and surprise and sensuality overwhelm Sarah. She no longer protested his hand moving so intimately between her legs. Instead, she gave herself to his caresses with a trust that humbled and savagely aroused him at the same time.

Slowly, steadily, he doubled his presence inside her body, testing and stretching her in the same sensuous motions.

She made a ragged, throaty sound.

"Does it hurt?" he asked.

She couldn't answer, but her body could.

Her sultry response was even more irresistible to him than the call of the first meadowlark after winter's silence. He shifted until he was kneeling between her legs. Then he repeated the caress slowly, deeply.

In that instant Sarah realized she was

completely vulnerable to him. She started to protest her helplessness, but words became a husky cry of pleasure as his hand moved again. When he was deep inside her once more, his thumb rubbed over the sleek bud that rising passion had revealed.

Intense, shocking pleasure burst inside her, drenching her with heat.

He shifted again, moving over her in a gentle, overwhelming wave. He was everywhere, hot and powerful, tender and caressing, surrounding her.

"Tell me if I hurt you," he said huskily.

She barely heard the words. She knew only a sense of heat between her legs, and a stretching that went on and on, delicious, frightening, endless, sensuous beyond belief.

Case made a throttled sound as he felt the sultry resistance of her body both pushing against him and at the same time inviting him to penetrate more deeply.

"Sarah?" he asked hoarsely. "Am I hurting you?"

"I feel so . . . strange."

She shivered rhythmically. The fragile movements were like a mouth moving over his aroused flesh, kissing him intimately.

"It doesn't hurt," she said. "Not exactly."

He rolled over, taking her with him.

She made a surprised sound when she found herself on top of his hips.

"What are you doing?" she asked.

"You're so sweet and tight," he said, his voice thick. "This way you can decide how much of me you want."

"I don't understand."

The corner of his mouth lifted.

"Look down," he said.

Sarah did. Her eyes widened when she saw that their bodies were joined in the most elemental way possible.

"We're . . ." Her voice dried up.

"We sure are. Well," he amended, "we're halfway there. The rest is up to you."

"How?"

"If you want more, settle down on me a little, then lift up a little, then come back down."

Hesitantly she moved her hips.

Sultry silk tugged at him.

He clenched his jaw against the temptation to spend himself right then and there.

"How does it feel?" Case asked through his teeth.

"I think I . . . like it."

She moved again, then again.

He made a hoarse sound.

Sarah froze.

"Does it hurt you?" she asked.

"Like a meadowlark singing."

She hesitated, then smiled, understanding.

"You like it, too," she murmured.

"I'm not sure," he said, lying through his teeth. "Try it a few more times."

Slowly she slid up and then down, then up again.

His hand moved. Fingertips searched through her slick auburn thatch until he found the swollen knot of passion. He circled it, retreated, circled, retreated, spreading the liquid heat of her response between them.

Eyes closed, shivering, whimpering with each breath, Sarah tried to get closer to his maddening, wildly arousing fingertips. Her hips rocked less tentatively over the aroused male flesh between her legs. He was a hard, full presence that wasn't hurting her at all, not any longer.

He felt incredibly good.

Eyes smoldering, watching her, Case teased Sarah until her pleasure drenched both of them. Then he retreated.

Her hips moved sharply, sinking him so far into her that his hand was pinned between their bodies. Only then did he give her what she needed, teasing and teaching her with every driving motion of his hips.

Something both wild and beautiful spread up from their hot, joined bodies. Sarah's eyes widened. There was no color in them, only dark centers dilated with pleasure. She shuddered and rocked hungrily, wanting more of Case, wanting to feel every bit of him as deep into her as he could get.

Suddenly his whole body corded. With repeated, throttled shouts he spent himself inside her sleek heat.

When the sounds and throbbing pulses went on and on, she became still, afraid that she had somehow hurt him. Anxiously she looked down at his face.

It was drawn as though in pain. Sweat glistened on his forehead.

"Is it your wound?" Sarah asked.

He didn't understand the words. All

he knew was that her weight was lifting from him. He didn't want that. He wanted to stay a while longer inside the tight, welcoming heat of her body.

"Don't move," he said thickly.

"It *is* your wound," she said, lifting herself away from him.

With a hoarse sound he slid his hands across her thighs and buried himself inside her once more. Then he rolled his hips against her.

Hard.

Pleasure burst through her. She couldn't move her hips in response, but she discovered she could move secretly, measuring and caressing him even while he pulsed deeply inside her.

The shivering sweetness doubled. She clenched her body around him again and again, and gasped at the expanding pleasure. It was like talons of fire sliding into her, pulsing, releasing, pulsing again.

She groaned and moved against him, trying to get even closer, desperate for something she couldn't name. But like a hooded hawk, she knew it was there, the freedom of the sky calling wildly, just beyond her reach.

She wept with need of it.

Case put his hands on her hips, jerked forward and drove into her.

A wild heat pulsed through Sarah, beating like the wings of a newly freed hawk.

And then she, too, was free.

Each broken breath she took was a cry of ecstasy that was also his name.

He heard her pleasure, probed deeply the pulsing of her body, and felt the hot rush of her release. He could no more resist her flight than he could stop breathing. A shocking pleasure raked through him, cording his body again. He thrust deep and hard and let go of everything but Sarah and the shattering, endless pulses of ecstasy she had brought him once again.

Only when the last drops of passion were utterly spent did Case realize what he had done.

What if I got her pregnant?

The thought was like being dumped naked into a snowbank.

Abruptly he lifted her off his body.

Talk about locking the barn door after the horse is stolen, he thought savagely, but he set her aside just the same.

"Case?" she asked, startled.

"Get dressed before you catch a chill."

She shivered, but not from the wind. His eyes were as cold as the winter moon.

16

"Wonder what changed their minds?" Conner asked.

His voice sounded unusually loud in the cabin.

Probably because supper had been unusually silent.

In fact, everything had been real quiet since Case and Sarah had ridden in a few hours ago. Both of them were strained and not at all talkative. Conner assumed it had something to do with the ambush by the raiders.

"Sarah?" he pressed.

"I'm sorry. Were you talking to me?"

"Hell — er, heck, no, I was talking to the rabbit stew. What do you think changed their minds?"

She blinked, obviously confused.

"Why did the raiders go after you?" her brother asked slowly. "They haven't been bothering us lately."

"I imagine it's getting damned cold of a morning in Spring Canyon," Case said.

"Is that any reason to kill a woman from ambush?" Conner asked in disbelief.

"It's a better reason than some I've heard of."

His voice was cool and clipped. It advised a change of subject. So did the look in his eyes.

Conner ignored the signals.

"Seems like Ab is having trouble with his kinfolk as well as with Moody," the boy said.

Case chewed food and didn't say a word.

"What do you mean?" Sarah asked.

"You told me you heard Ab telling Moody to raid three days' ride from Spring Canyon and no closer."

She nodded.

"The canyon you were in isn't that far away," her brother said, "and neither is this cabin, yet there was at least one Culpepper along on each of the raids."

"So?" she asked.

Conner gave his sister a disgusted look.

"So," he said clearly, "it's obvious as warts on a pickle that Ab doesn't have control of his own kin, much less Moody's bunch."

While Conner spoke, he reached past Case for the frying pan full of cornbread. The boy's chair, recently constructed of cottonwood and buckskin, creaked alarmingly.

"Ask for the bread to be passed," Sarah said sharply.

"Why? I didn't even have to lean very hard."

"It's good manners."

"Seems like it would be better manners not to bother a man who has eating on his mind," her brother retorted.

"Pass me the cornbread when you're finished with it," she said through her teeth.

"Please?"

"Please."

Case looked at the boy. "Quit baiting your sister. She's had a hard day already."

Sarah hoped her flush would pass unnoticed in the flickering light of the lamp.

Conner looked contrite.

"Sorry, sis," he said, his voice cracking in mid-word. "It's no fun spending your afternoon hugging cold stone while —"

"Pass the cornbread," Sarah interrupted. "Please."

She didn't look at Case. She hadn't looked at him even once after she realized that she had somehow disgusted him that afternoon. She didn't know what she had done.

She wasn't going to ask.

It was enough to know that he didn't want to look at her, either.

"Thank you," she said distinctly as she took the cornbread from Conner.

"You're welcome," he said. "Do you think Ab and Moody will shoot it out?"

She shrugged.

"What about you, Case?" Conner asked.

"I think Ab will haul his kin back into line by bringing in some women. Then the boys won't be so restless."

Sarah felt all the blood leave her face.

Restless, she thought. *Is that what it was all about this afternoon?*

What was it Case said? Something about how long it had been since he had been with a woman.

I suppose I should be grateful he was tender with me.

She sighed and picked at her food.

I just wish, she thought wistfully, *I*

387

could have done right whatever it is that I did wrong.

Instead of chewing on the cornbread, she gnawed on her lower lip.

"Women?" Conner asked into the growing silence. "Won't they just cause trouble?"

"It's what they're best at," Case said sardonically. "But there are times when nothing else will do."

"Huh," the boy said, and turned to his sister. "What do you think?"

"I think," she said, standing up, "that I've had enough."

Conner looked at his sister's plate.

"Enough?" he said, startled. "A bite of cornbread and a bite of stew is enough?"

"Yes."

Out of habit Sarah folded the tattered cloth that served as a napkin and put it on the table. She grabbed her jacket and headed for the door.

"Where are you going?" Conner asked.

"Out."

"When will you be back?" her brother persisted.

Her only answer was the sound of the cabin door shutting firmly.

Frowning, Conner looked at Case. The older man was watching the closed door with an impassive face and eyes that changed from gold to pale green with each shift of light.

"What's wrong with her?" Conner asked.

"She's got a lot on her mind."

"She always does, and she has never acted like this."

"Looking for silver you don't find can be wearing on a person's soul," Case said.

"Hell, she enjoys looking. I think it's just an excuse for her to go out and roam the land."

Case fiddled for a moment longer with his stew. Then he set aside his fork and pushed back his chair.

"You, too?" Conner asked.

"What?"

"No appetite. Honest, it's rabbit, not snake. I made it myself."

"I've eaten snake more than once. It's not bad, once you get past the idea of it."

Conner grimaced.

With quick motions Case slung his holster into place around his hips. He fastened the buckle and he headed out the door. As the door shut behind him, he wondered what he could say to Sarah to make her understand why they shouldn't be lovers.

It shouldn't have happened even once, he thought grimly. *My fault, all of it.*

I never should have touched her.

He still didn't understand how she had slipped past his guard. His own sexuality had never ruled him, even in his wildest days.

God, she could be carrying my baby.

The thought sent a wave of cold through him. He didn't want to feel responsible for another tiny life.

Not ever again.

"Case?"

He spun around, six-gun drawn. Even before the motion was finished, he reversed it and holstered the gun, for it was Conner who stood in the doorway.

The boy whistled admiringly. "You're fast!"

"Sorry," Case said, his voice rough. "I didn't hear you open the door behind me. I'm a little touchy after today."

"Could you teach me to do that?"

"Not with that hog-leg you're wearing.

It's damned near a two-handed rig."

"What about the guns the raiders had?"

Case looked all around. Sarah was nowhere in sight.

"She probably went off into Deer Canyon," her brother said. "That's her second favorite place."

"What's her favorite?"

"That overhang with the little seep where you first found her."

"Why does she go there?"

"She says it soothes her soul."

Case's eyelids flinched.

"But since the raiders came," Conner added, "she gets her soothing in Deer Canyon. If she's going there now, the ambush must have upset her more than she's letting on."

The ambush, or what happened after, Case thought bitterly.

Judas priest, why did I do that? I could have pleasured her from her head to her heels without risking a baby.

No answer came to him except the ache in his gut that started whenever he thought of Sarah's silky, passionate, generous response.

He had just had her, and he wanted her until he all but shook with it.

"Get one of the raiders' belt guns," Case said curtly.

His tone made Conner hesitate, but only for a moment. He had about given up ever finding Case with time to teach him how to handle a six-gun. Between hunting silver, hauling firewood and water, standing guard, repairing the cabin, and scouting for timber for the floor planks, Case was busier than three men.

"I'll be back before you know I'm gone," Conner said eagerly.

Case didn't answer. He was staring off toward Deer Canyon. In the late-afternoon light, every shrub and branch and blade of grass stood out clearly.

So did the quick, graceful shape of Sarah climbing up a rubble slope to the mouth of a nearby canyon.

He was still watching her when Conner returned.

"Don't worry," the boy said, closing the front door behind him. "There's no way into that canyon except through here. She's safe from raiders."

Though Case nodded, he didn't look away until she disappeared into the shadows on one side of the canyon. Then, reluctantly, he turned toward the boy whose quick smile reminded him all too much of Sarah.

"Which one did you choose?" Case asked.

"This one. It draws real slick."

He wasn't surprised to know that Conner had been trying out the raiders' belt guns. Neither was he surprised that the boy had chosen the quickest draw in the batch.

"It draws real slick," Case said impassively, "but it doesn't aim worth a fart in a windstorm."

Conner frowned down at the gun he was holding.

"What do you mean?" he asked.

"Have you shot it?"

"Ute would have my scalp for wasting bullets."

"Learning isn't a waste," Case said. "Follow me. No use in stirring up the chickens."

"I wouldn't mind practicing on that big orange rooster," Conner muttered.

"He's a mean son," the older man agreed. "But he sires the kind of chicks the land requires — quick and tough."

"I know. I've chewed on more than one of them. And vice versa."

The corner of Case's mouth lifted,

shifting his beard just a bit. He enjoyed Conner's sharp mind. It was like listening to a masculine echo of Sarah's quick tongue.

"Run over and warn Ute that there's going to be some shooting," he said. "I'll set up targets."

Conner ran off to the wickiup and returned at the same headlong pace.

God, to be that young again, Case thought as he walked back from the targets. *All fired up and raring to go at the thought of a little shooting.*

Hope Conner lives long enough to approach shooting cold, the way you would digging out a privy.

"Ready," Conner said, settling his hat firmly on his thick blond hair. "What do I shoot at first?"

"The little rock sitting on that big rock about a hundred feet away."

Conner drew and fired in a startlingly smooth motion.

He missed both rocks.

In fact, he came closer to shooting off his toe than he did to hitting anything made of stone.

"Holy hell!" Conner said, staring at the gun. "This trigger is as touchy as a snake's tongue."

"Has about the same range, too," Case said dryly. "That piece of iron is all sawed off, filed down, and slicked up for drawing and shooting as fast as possible."

While he talked, he drew his own gun. He reversed it and held the weapon out butt first to Conner.

"Look at the difference between the two guns," Case said.

Conner took the gun and looked from it to the raider's gun.

"Yours has a longer barrel by at least an inch," the boy said.

Case nodded. "A hair slower on the draw that way, but what I shoot at, I hit."

"The front sight is filed off the raider's gun."

"Same thing," Case said. "Speed over accuracy."

"May I shoot yours?"

"Holster it first. Then try for that little rock."

Conner's second draw looked as fast as his first, but Case knew it wasn't. Not quite.

A chunk of stone flew out from the big rock.

"Missed again," Conner said, disgusted.

"You weren't more than three inches off. Close enough to stop a man."

The boy just shook his head and holstered the gun.

"Stopping a man is almost as good as killing him," Case said matter-of-factly. "That way you can take a little more time with the second bullet, unless you're up against more than one man."

"Is that what happened in Spanish Church?"

"Partly. Mostly those Culpeppers were just too damned fast. But they shot too soon, same as you did and for the same reason. Touchy guns."

"They didn't get another chance?"

Case gave Conner a sideways look out of cool green eyes.

"If I'd given them another chance, I'd be planted out back of the bar instead of them."

"How close were they to you?"

"Nearly twenty feet," Case said. "If it had been ten, they would have killed me."

"You don't sound as if the idea bothers you," Conner muttered.

"Gamblers have a saying — scared money never wins. Same goes for shooting. The day you feel scared is the day you take off that belt gun and never put it on again."

"You mean you're never scared?"

"Not when it comes down to it. Before or after, hell yes."

Conner looked at both guns again.

"Let me try that raider's gun," Case said, holding out his hand.

The boy held his gun out butt first to Case.

"I see Ute taught you good manners," Case said dryly.

"With a gun, manners make sense," the boy retorted. "At eating time, they just get in the way."

Case holstered the gun, lowered his hands, then drew and with a speed that blurred everything into one motion. He fired three shots with a single rolling sound.

Rock exploded everywhere.

Conner whistled again. "That was really slick. Why don't you file off the sight and shorten the barrel of your own gun?"

"One out of three isn't good enough."

"What?"

"Only one bullet hit the little rock. If I'd been up against three men, I'd be looking like a sieve right now."

"Oh," Conner said.

"See that chunk of wood on the next boulder to the right?"

The boy nodded.

"Holster my gun and shoot when I say."

Conner followed instructions and then looked at Case expectantly.

"When did Ute first start teaching you how to shoot?" Case asked.

Conner blinked. "As soon as he healed up from his bullet wounds. Six of them. That's a tough hombre."

"Did you pester Ute into teaching you?"

"No, he said a man who couldn't use a gun and use it good would be a dead man right quick. And seeing as how Sarah was so fond of me, Ute thought —"

"*Draw.*"

The order was unexpected, but Conner didn't hesitate. He drew and fired.

The wood leaped up and came down as a shower of splinters.

"Good shooting," Case said.

"Slow," Conner said, disgusted.

Case shrugged. "You're big enough to soak up some lead, if it comes to that.

Better to be the last one to shoot than the first."

"I'd rather be first *and* last."

The corners of Case's eyes changed slightly.

"So would every man," he said. "But no matter how good you are, there's someone out there who's better. The best fight is the one you avoid."

"You sound like Sarah."

"She's a woman of uncommon good sense."

"She keeps treating me like a kid."

"She raised you. Takes time to grow out of that, on both sides."

Conner looked stubborn. The line of his mouth was so like Sarah's that Case could hardly bear to see it.

I never should have touched her, he realized again. *Now that I've tasted her, it will be pure bloody hell forgetting.*

I didn't know anything could be that sweet.

Or that hot.

God, I'll die remembering what it was like to feel her surprise and passion. To taste it. To slide into it and forget . . .

The sound of Conner reloading his six-gun reminded Case that he had set out to teach Sarah's beloved younger brother how to survive in the wild land.

"Ute's right," Case said. "Your sister thinks the sun rises and sets in you."

Conner lifted his head suddenly. His eyes caught the sun and turned a deep, pure green.

"I would die for her," he said matter-of-factly.

Case didn't doubt it.

"She'd rather have you alive," he pointed out.

"I'm planning on staying that way."

"Good. That means you won't argue when I tell you to go back and get the third revolver, the one that wasn't all filed down and slicked up."

For a moment the boy looked like he was going to argue. Then he smiled.

"Ute said if I got you to teach me, I should listen."

One of Case's black eyebrow lifted in silent query.

"He said you were the only man he knew ever to walk away after a Culpepper shootout," Conner explained.

"I damned near didn't. That's why I'm going to teach you more than shooting. I'm going to teach you about the Culpeppers. All their nasty tricks from ambushes to taking hostages and sell-ing them as slaves to the Comancheros."

"Have you had a lot of experience with the Culpeppers?"

"My brother and I have hunted them since the end of the war."

Conner started to ask why, saw the look in the other man's eyes, and thought better of it.

"How many have you gotten?" he asked instead.

"Not enough."

Conner didn't ask any more questions.

17

"Could you take the chow up to him?" Lola asked.

Sarah looked at the cornbread and venison stew the older woman was holding out to her. She tried to think of an excuse not to take Case's supper to him.

He was standing guard on the rim. Alone.

In the past three days, she had become very good at not being alone with him. Two days ago she had even slipped off to hunt silver by herself.

Her ears still burned when she thought of his response to that solo ride.

Being stubborn is one thing. Being a damned fool is another. The next time you go silver hunting alone, I'll track you down and bring you back tied across my saddle.

Sarah hadn't gone out looking for treasure by herself again.

Nor could she bring herself to hunt

with Case. Just the thought of what had happened the last time they were alone was enough to make waves of heat and cold go through her.

She told herself it was embarrassment.

She wasn't sure she believed it.

"I'm missing one of the goats," Lola explained. "That little black and white female with the particular fine hair."

Immediately Sarah forgot her own concerns. "How long has she been gone?"

"She wasn't with the rest of the herd when Ghost brought them in just now."

Sarah took the plate.

"I'll take Case's supper," she said. "Go look for that goat. She's the best of the bunch."

Lola gave Sarah a gap-toothed smile and hurried off.

"But if Case yells at me for going up to the rim alone, I'll sic him on you," she called after the other woman.

A laugh was Lola's answer.

Sarah didn't bother to chase down a grazing mustang for the trip to the rim. It was quicker just to walk. And that's what she wanted — to get this chore behind her as fast as possible.

When she reached the rim, the sun was sliding down the edge of late afternoon into evening. As always, the immense serenity of the land beneath the golden light called out to her. Motionless, she stood and looked out over the endless networks of shadow canyons hemmed by sun-struck pinnacles, buttes, and mesas.

The stark lines of the land were more beautiful to her than any gently rolling green hills could ever be. The richness and subtlety of the stone desert's colors, the wind tasting of cold and mystery, and the vast sweep of the land all gave a lift to her spirits.

Nearby a hawk soared on the updraft caused by the cliffs that rimmed Lost River Valley. The bird's flight was both powerful and effortless, a wild song sung in the silence of Sarah's soul.

Smiling, she half-closed her eyes and absorbed the peace of the moment.

Eyes narrowed as though in pain, Case watched from behind a screen of nearby brush. It took all the discipline he had learned in war and vengeance not to walk out and make love to her again, drinking the smiling mystery of her life.

Why did she come up here? he thought. *For the last three days she's done everything but climb the sky to avoid me.*

Maybe she knows if she's pregnant. The thought made his heart jerk.

"What are you doing up here?" he asked. His voice was harsh even to his own ears.

She spun around and eyed him as though he were a wild animal.

Or a Culpepper.

"Lola is looking for one of her goats," she said distinctly. "She asked me to bring your supper to you. Conner and Ute are both asleep."

Well, he thought sardonically, *that answers my question. She's up here because no one else could come.*

"Thank you," he said.

"You're welcome."

He grimaced.

"No need to treat me like a stranger," he said bluntly. "We're considerably more than that."

She flushed and then went pale.

"Where do you want your supper?" she asked, her voice tight.

"Not flung in my face, for starters."

Belatedly Sarah realized that she was

indeed holding the supper plate as though she planned on slinging it at him just as soon as he got within range.

"Sorry," she muttered ungraciously. "You startled me. I thought I was alone."

"Are you pregnant?"

The question was so unexpected that her jaw dropped.

"Excuse me?" she said numbly.

"You heard me."

"Of all the ill-mannered —"

"Just answer the question," he interrupted. "Save the lectures for Conner."

"I don't know."

"What?"

"I. Don't. Know." Sarah bit off each word as though tearing out hunks of his hide. "Satisfied?"

"For about ten minutes," Case said under his breath, "and that was days ago."

"If you expect me to conduct a conversation with you," she said sweetly, "quit mumbling in your beard."

"I thought you liked my beard, especially on the inside of your thighs."

She flinched as though she had been struck.

"Damn," he said savagely. "I'm sorry.

I have no right. It's just when I think how —"

Whatever he had been going to say was lost in the sound of hoofbeats approaching.

Case changed in an instant, cold and remote and utterly controlled.

"Get in here," he said. "Fast and quiet."

Before he finished talking, Sarah was sliding into the brush that screened him.

"Did you bring a gun?" he whispered.

She shook her head.

"Sorry. I didn't think I would need —" she began.

"You didn't think period," he interrupted.

She didn't bother to argue. He was right and they both knew it. No one — *no one* — was supposed to go more than ten feet from the cabin without a gun.

But she had been so upset at the prospect of being alone with him that she hadn't stopped to think about anything at all. She had simply rushed out to get the chore over with.

"Go behind me," he said softly. "About fifteen feet back there's a crack in the stone where you'll be out of sight. Stay there until I call for you."

Sarah hurried past Case. On the way, she grabbed the revolver he held out to her.

He didn't turn to watch her retreat. The small sounds of brush sliding over doeskin told him that she was doing as she had been told.

For once, he thought sardonically.

The hoofbeats stopped.

There was only one path down off the rim for several miles. Case's rifle was covering it.

He faded back into the brush just as Sarah had. While he moved, he never took his eyes off the spot where the riders would have to appear.

A horned lark called from the left. It was answered from the right.

He let out a breath of relief that was also the sweet call of a lark.

The silence that came back was like thunder.

"Whoever is in that brush," said a voice finally, "we're not looking for trouble."

"Then you came to the wrong place, Hunter," Case called. "There's nothing here *but* trouble."

An instant later a tall, strongly built

man burst out of cover, rifle in hand.

"Case?" Hunter demanded in disbelief.

"As ever was," he said, stepping into the open. "Is that Morgan out in the brush with you?"

"My God," Hunter said.

He grabbed Case and hugged him hard enough to crack the ribs of a smaller man.

Case looked startled. Then he hugged his brother just as fiercely in return.

"Thank God," Hunter said again and again. Then, "Morgan, come on out. Case is alive!"

"Of course I am," Case said. "Have you been drinking Morgan's moonshine again?"

Instead of answering, Hunter thumped his brother on the back, pushed him away to get a look at him, hugged him hard again and released him.

Morgan strode out of the brush. The wiry black rider carried a shotgun easily across his shoulder.

"Howdy, Case," Morgan said. "Mighty glad to see you this side of hell, suh. Mighty, mighty glad."

Case shook the other man's hand and

thumped him on the shoulder with masculine affection.

"You're looking pretty good yourselves," he said, "for two such ugly critters."

Morgan laughed and rubbed his hand across his tightly curled black beard.

"Who are you calling ugly, boy?" Morgan drawled. "You're as furry as I am. You hiding out as a grizzly?"

Shaking his head, Case turned back to his brother.

"What are you two doing here?" he asked.

"Word came to the Ruby Mountains that you had been killed by Culpeppers," Hunter said bluntly.

The harsh, weary lines of his face said more than his spare words.

"It was a near thing," Case admitted.

"How near?"

"Reginald and Quincy were the fastest Culpeppers I've ever drawn on."

Hunter whistled soundlessly. "What happened?"

"They each shot twice before I finished them. I took some lead."

"You look fit enough now."

"I had a good nurse." Case raised his

410

voice. "Sarah, come on out and meet some friends."

After a few moments she came out of the brush. There was no sign of the supper she had brought to Case. His six-gun, however, was very much in sight.

Her eyes were wary until she saw Hunter.

"From the size and cut of you," she said, smiling, "you must be blood kin to Case."

"Mrs. Kennedy," Case said formally, "meet my brother Hunter Maxwell and our friend Nueces Morgan."

"Ma'am," Morgan said, lifting his hat. "It's a pleasure."

Hunter took off his hat and bowed to Sarah.

"Thank you for saving my brother's life," he said. "If you ever need help, send to the Ruby Mountains. I'll come at a dead run."

"There's no debt," she said. "I've saved more useless critters than your brother."

"But not too many, I reckon," Morgan said dryly.

She laughed, liking the wiry rider.

"You're welcome to supper," she said,

smiling at Hunter and Morgan in turn. "Venison stew and cornbread, just as soon as I mix up another batch."

"That's very kind of you, Mrs. Kennedy," Hunter said.

"Thank you, ma'am," Morgan said fervently. "We've been living on hardtack and water so long my stomach thinks my throat was cut."

"Hardtack and water?" she asked.

"We were in a hurry," Hunter said simply. "A drifter told me that Case was dead."

Her eyes widened and her heart turned over at the thought of what Hunter must have been through.

"You poor man," she said. "No wonder you look so weary. I know what it's like to lose your closest kin."

Hunter was touched by the compassion in Sarah's mist-gray eyes.

"You're a fine and gentle woman, Mrs. Kennedy," he said.

"I'm sure your brother would disagree," she said tartly. "And please, call me Sarah. I've been widowed longer than I was married. I've never worn the Kennedy name comfortably."

"Sarah," he said, smiling. "Call me Hunter."

She smiled in return. The smile was like her voice — feminine, generous, and welcoming in a way that wasn't at all flirtatious.

"You can save your girlish wiles for someone else," Case said sourly. "Hunter is married to a fine woman."

Sarah gave Case a narrow, sideways look.

"I have even less girlish wiles than you have manners," she said distinctly, "and that means not enough for an ant's breakfast."

Morgan and Hunter laughed out loud.

Case said something under his breath.

She smiled at Hunter. "You're his older brother, aren't you?"

He nodded.

"Looks like you had as much luck teaching him manners as I've had with my younger brother," she said.

Hunter hid his smile by smoothing his sleek black mustache.

"We had our dust-ups," he agreed.

"I'll just bet you did," she said. "At least you were big enough to whale the tar out of your little brother. Conner is only fifteen and would make two of me."

"Closer to three," Case said. "The boy eats like a plague of locusts."

"You, of course," she retorted, "have such a dainty little appetite."

Morgan coughed.

Hunter didn't even bother to disguise his amusement at the tart-tongued widow. He simply threw back his head and laughed out loud.

"Well, I see I won't have to worry about standing guard," Case said sardonically. "All your braying will scare off the Culpepper mules."

Shaking his head, Hunter threw his arm around Case's shoulders and hugged him hard, laughing all the while.

Case didn't smile in return, but his features softened as he returned the one-armed hug.

The clear affection between the two brothers made Sarah smile even as her throat closed around a sadness she hadn't acknowledged until this moment.

Someday Conner will leave me and find his own life, she thought.

Yet even as sadness came, so did a measure of peace.

That's the way it should be. I didn't

raise him to keep me company.

But dear God, it will be lonely without him.

"Shall I get the horses, Colonel?" Morgan asked.

"I'll come with you," Hunter said. "Six is a handful."

"Six?" Sarah asked, dismayed at the thought of that many men to feed. "Are there more of you?"

"No, ma'am," Morgan said. "We didn't want to kill horses getting here, so we brought three apiece."

She looked at both men more closely.

"Did you sleep along the way?" she asked.

"In the saddle," Hunter said. "It's a soldier's trick."

"How long have you been riding?"

"I don't know," he admitted, rubbing his face wearily. "I'm just damned glad we weren't rushing to a funeral."

"We've had some shovel work here," she said, "but so far it's only been Moody's men and a Culpepper."

Hunter looked toward his brother. The sudden sharpness in Hunter's features reminded Sarah of Case.

"The Culpeppers are close by?"

Hunter demanded.

Case nodded.

"All we heard about were the two in Spanish Church," Hunter said. "Is Ab here?"

"Only until I get him in my rifle sights," Case said. "Then he's on his way to hell."

"Any more Culpeppers?"

"All of them, except for the one I killed a few weeks back."

"What happened?" Hunter asked.

"He and two of Moody's boys thought they'd flank us by coming around from behind the cabin after the moon set," Case said.

Morgan shook his head.

"I heard two tone-deaf owls hooting at each other and went out hunting," Case continued.

Sarah's mouth flattened. The terror she had felt for him that night was something she would never forget.

"Case was still hurting from his wounds," she said roughly. "The Culpepper nearly got him."

"Which one was it?" Hunter asked.

"Not Ab," Case said succinctly. "One of the man's fingers was missing. Last time I was close enough to count, Ab had all ten of his. It was probably Parnell."

Hunter settled his hat with a quick motion of his hand.

"All right," he said. "We'll worry about taking care of them after we've rested."

"Taking care of them?" she asked.

"Nothing to worry about, ma'am," Morgan said. "Just some unfinished business from down Texas way."

"There are only four of you, counting Ute," she said. "There are at least a dozen of those raiders."

"More or less," Case said. "One or two of Moody's men have just slipped out in the night. They don't like Ab."

"When did you last count the raiders?" Hunter asked, looking closely at his brother.

"Two days ago. Fresh tracks going out. None coming in."

"We'll have our work cut out for us," Hunter said.

His voice and expression said that it wouldn't be the first time.

Sarah looked at each of the men in turn, opened her mouth to ask a question, then closed it. Whatever she said wouldn't change the determination she saw in each face.

Nor could she argue with their conclusion. Having raiders for neighbors was like having a nest of rattlesnakes under the front porch. Sooner or later someone would get bitten.

Fatally.

"Eat your supper," she said to Case.

"Would you bring some up for Hunter and Morgan?" he asked. "We've got a lot of planning to do."

"It will keep," Sarah said. "They need rest more than they need a lot of talking. Both of them look like horses that were 'rode hard and put away wet,' as Ute would say."

Hunter smiled slightly.

Morgan laughed and glanced sideways at Case.

He wasn't smiling, much less laughing. He was watching Sarah with a combination of wariness and some other, indefinable emotion in his eyes.

She smiled at Case with more teeth than sweetness. The smile changed when she turned to the two weary riders.

"Just follow the trail down," she said. "I'll go ahead to warn Ute and Lola so you don't get shot."

"Lola?" Morgan said. "Would that be Big Lola?"

"Once. Now she's just plain Lola."

He smiled. "I take your meaning, ma'am. This Ute — is he a sawed-off little hombre of few words and less nonsense?"

"That's Ute," she said.

"Be damned," he said. Then, hastily, "Excuse the language, ma'am."

"Don't worry," she said in a dry voice. "I only expect parlor manners in the parlor."

"I never thought I'd see either of those two alive again," Morgan explained. "Heard Ute was killed by a posse. After that, Big — er, Lola disappeared."

"Sarah pulled Ute out of the same kind of hole I was in," Case said. "He thinks the sun rises and sets in her."

"Understandable," Hunter said. "A man thinks very kindly of a woman who saves his life."

"Your brother doesn't," she said tartly to Hunter, "so don't worry about him. His view of the world is as savagely clear as ever."

Case didn't show the irritation that surged through him at her words. Nor did he show the desire that dug spurs into him each time the wind shifted and he caught the elusive fragrance of roses and woman.

The scent of Sarah haunted him.

Don't think about it, he told himself harshly.

It would have been easier not to breathe.

Morgan looked from Sarah to Case and cleared his throat.

"How much longer are you on sentry duty?" he asked.

Case looked away from Sarah with a reluctance that he couldn't quite conceal.

"A few more hours," he said.

"I'll take the rest of your duty," Morgan said, stretching.

"You're more tired than I am."

Morgan grinned. "Hungrier, too. I figure the supper I eat up here will be bigger than whatever Hunter leaves for me down there."

"I'll stand over him with a shotgun," Sarah said. "It's share and share alike in my house."

"I'm just funning," Morgan said, chuckling. "The colonel would go without his own rations rather than have one of his men go hungry."

He turned to Case.

"Ride on down with your brother," Morgan said. "He's having a hard time believing you're still alive."

Case hesitated, then nodded. "Thanks."

"What's your danger signal?" Morgan asked.

"Same as Texas, except the all clear is a hawk's cry. Sarah is fond of them."

"Chicken-killing devils, every one of them," the rider muttered.

"Once you meet Sarah's orange rooster, you'll be cheering for the hawks," Case said. "Come on, Hunter. Let's get the horses."

"I'll get your supper out of the rocks," Sarah said to Morgan. "I'm afraid it's cold."

"Ma'am, as long as I don't have to kill it before I eat it, I won't complain."

By the time she emerged from the brush with his supper, Case and Hunter were back. They were leading six horses. All of them showed signs of having been ridden hard and long. Dried sweat stiffened the coats. Lines of white showed where the horses had sweated and dried, sweated and dried.

One of the horses was a big stallion

that had the same clean lines and deep chest as Cricket. The others were mustangs with a little hot blood mixed in.

Hunter swung up on the stallion with a catlike ease that reminded Sarah of Case.

"I'll go first and warn Ute," she said, turning abruptly toward the trail.

"No need for you to walk," Hunter said. "Bugle Boy is a gentleman. He won't mind carrying double."

"If she rides with anyone, she'll ride with me," Case said curtly. Then, hearing his own tone, he added, "Bugle Boy looks worn out."

Hunter's black eyebrows rose. It was clear that his brother felt protective of the pretty widow.

Some might even call it possessive.

Case's whistle cut the air. Cricket came trotting up from his hiding place farther down the trail. Saying nothing, he untied the reins from Cricket's neck. Then he turned around to help Sarah mount.

She was gone.

"She took off like a scalded cat," Hunter said. "Guess she doesn't cotton to the thought of riding double."

Case shrugged and told himself that

he wasn't disappointed.

But he was. He had been looking forward to the scent and feel and sweetness of having Sarah in his arms once more.

His hunger didn't surprise him.

The hurt he felt that she had run from him did.

We have to settle this, he decided. *Tonight.*

The thought sent a shaft of sensual anticipation through him.

Just talk. Nothing more.

He told himself that every step of the way down the trail.

He wasn't sure he believed it.

18

"I'm sorry," Sarah said. "Someone will have to stand. I don't have enough chairs for everyone."

"I've done enough sitting lately," Hunter said, smiling. "I'd just as soon eat standing up."

While she served supper, Conner looked from Hunter to Case and back, shaking his head.

"Talk about two peas in a pod," he said. "Hunter's eyes are gray instead of gray-green, but if you shaved Case and put a smile on his face for once . . ."

Hunter's smile was almost sad.

His brother didn't smile at all.

"Mind your manners," Sarah said.

Conner grimaced.

"Ute taught your brother good gun handling manners," Case said neutrally.

"Praise be," she muttered. "The amount of shooting that's been going on around here lately, it's a wonder I'm not wrapping him up like a puppy that's been sniffing around a beehive."

A dull red appeared on her brother's cheekbones.

"Ease up on the spurs," Case said. "Conner is doing a man's work and doing it well."

Sarah spun around and looked at Case directly for the first time since he had been in such a hurry to get her off him and fully dressed.

"Conner is my brother, not yours," she said, biting off each word. "Stay out of it."

"No."

Hunter's eyebrows shot up. He hadn't seen that stubborn look on his brother's face since before the war.

"I beg your pardon?" she asked with icy politeness.

"You heard me," he said. "Conner is man-sized and doing a man's work. He doesn't need to be tripping on your apron strings every time he tries to take a step on his own. Right now we need a man, not a boy."

She went pale. She opened her mouth, prepared to rip a strip off his hide.

"It's all right," Conner said quickly to Case. "My sister and I have been through a lot together. She's used to fussing over me and I'm used to worrying about her."

Swiftly she turned on him. When she saw the calm self-possession in her brother's eyes, her anger faded. She gave him a smile that threatened to turn upside down and went back to dishing stew.

Hunter let out a silent breath of relief.

Case changed the subject.

"How is Elyssa?" he asked.

A smile transformed Hunter's face.

"More beautiful than ever," he said. "You'll be an uncle again before autumn."

The look on Case's face was indescribable, pain and pleasure and the kind of relentless regret that wore a man's soul thin as a shadow.

"More children?" he said neutrally. "You're a braver man than I am."

"Or a bigger fool," Hunter said. "But I'm a damned happy man, either way. Being with Elyssa makes the sun shine twice as bright."

Sarah remembered what Case had told her, that a certain kind of loving between a man and a woman made the sun brighter.

He was talking about Hunter and Elyssa, she realized.

Conner looked between the two men.

"Why does a man have to be brave to have children?" he asked. "It's women who go through the birthing."

"Children die," Case said.

He didn't say any more.

Neither did Hunter.

Sarah cleared her throat.

"Eat your supper before it gets cold," she said, shoving a plate beneath Conner's nose.

He didn't have to be told twice to eat. He stood and shoveled in food with impressive speed.

Again, Hunter let out a silent breath. It was one of the few times he had ever heard his brother refer directly to the death of his niece and nephew.

Without quite looking at Case, Sarah put a plate of food in his hands. He and Hunter started to eat. They weren't as fast as Conner, but they cleaned their plates very quickly.

When Sarah refilled the plates without sitting and eating anything herself, Case looked up.

"Where's your supper?" he asked.

"I ate earlier."

He didn't believe it. With startling speed he grabbed her wrist and shoved his plate back in her hand.

"Eat," he said curtly. "If you get any thinner, you won't have to open the door to leave. You'll just slide out through the chinks in the logs."

She tried to give the plate back to him.

"I've got corn to grind," she said.

"I'll grind it."

"You've got enough to do with sentry duty and teaching Conner to shoot and making bullets and getting firewo—"

"*Eat.*"

Sarah opened her mouth to argue.

Case shoveled in a fork loaded with food.

She made odd noises and tried to talk anyway.

"It's not polite to talk with your mouth full," he said calmly. "How many times do you have to be told?"

Conner choked noisily. At breakfast he had been given a lecture on the same subject, using exactly the same words.

Case whacked the boy on his back.

"Better go to bed," he said to Conner. "You're due on the rim at midnight."

"Let him sleep," Hunter said quickly.

"Morgan and I can stand our turn."

"Thank you, but no," Conner said quickly. "You've had a hard ride. We can start dividing up guard duty tomorrow night."

During the Civil War, Hunter had learned to measure boys Conner's age and even younger. Though he had dark circles under his eyes, they were clear and alert. He was nowhere near the end of his strength.

"All right," Hunter said. "Thank you."

"You're welcome, sir." He grinned and looked slyly at his sister. "How am I doing?"

Laughing, wanting to cry instead, Sarah looked at her brother with wide, misty eyes.

"You're doing fine," she said, her voice slightly husky. "You always do. I'm just slow to notice."

"You've got better things to do than pat me on the back for acting my age," he said matter-of-factly.

A tear slid from the corner of her eye.

"You're wrong," she whispered. "There is nothing more important for me to do."

Conner made a startlingly fast move

that ended with her lifted up to his eye level.

She made a surprised sound and tried to keep the plate of food she was holding right-side up.

"Conner Lawson!"

"That's me. Your one and only little brother."

"Thank the Lord. What would I do with two of you?"

"You'd have twice as much fun."

Grinning, he hugged her close and spun around quickly.

Case rescued the plate on the way by, then steadied her when Conner put her down.

"Good night, folks," the boy said on the way out the door. "Tell Lola to wake me for my watch."

Like Case, Conner was sleeping in the brush in back of the cabin. Though neither man mentioned it, each was afraid that the Culpeppers would sneak up that way again.

"That's a good young man you've raised," Hunter said.

Sarah smiled almost sadly.

"That's more due to him than to me," she said.

"I doubt that."

"Ask Case. He thinks I'm a terrible mother."

Hunter's eyebrows shot up.

"I said no such thing," Case said evenly.

"Huh," she said. "You just keep pointing out that I'm strangling Conner on my apron strings."

He started to argue, muttered something under his breath instead, and looked to Hunter for help.

His brother smiled in open amusement and said not one word.

"Here," Case said, handing the plate of food back to Sarah. "Exercise your sharp little teeth on this."

"Are you saying my stew is tough?" she asked sweetly.

"Ju-das *priest*," he exclaimed.

She turned to Hunter.

"Short rations of sleep make your brother testy," she said. "Have you noticed? Now, if he would just trust me to stand guard, he would get more sleep."

Hunter stroked his mustache and tried very hard not to smile. He almost succeeded.

"Whose side are you on?" Case demanded of his brother.

"Whoever is holding the plate of food."

"Here," she said, handing Hunter the plate. "Eat hearty. I've got corn to grind and wool to spin."

"I said I'd grind the corn," Case said.

Hunter smiled and then began eating. Fast. He could tell when a storm was about to break.

"You need sleep," Sarah said curtly to Case.

"And you don't?"

"I'm not nearly as testy as you are."

"Says who?"

Case turned to his brother, who was heading for the door after polishing off the last morsel of stew.

"Hunter?" he said.

"Good night, children."

The cabin door closed firmly behind him.

"Where is he going to sleep?" she asked.

"Out back with the rest of us."

"Do I smell that bad?" she asked.

He blinked. "What?"

Tears stung the back of Sarah's eyes. Case's speed in getting rid of her after they had made love still stung.

Get dressed before you catch a chill.

Blindly she turned and reached for

the stew pot, which was hanging over the fire.

What's wrong with me? she raged at herself. *I never cry, but now I cry every time I turn around.*

"Lately everyone is running from me like I tangled with a skunk and lost," she muttered.

Her hand closed around what she thought was the wooden grip on the pot handle. Instead, it was part of the cast-iron trivet itself, searing hot from the fire.

"Damnation!" she said, letting go quickly.

She shook her hand and gripped it hard to ease the sting.

"What did you do that for?" Case asked.

"I'm an idiot, what else?" she snapped.

"Hell, you're no more an idiot than I am. Let me see."

Warily she flexed her hand, but she didn't hold it out for his inspection.

"It's fine," she said. "Just singed, that's all."

Case looked at the lines of strain etched around her mouth and felt helpless, which only made him more angry.

His left hand flashed out and wrapped around her wrist.

"You're so damned stubborn you wouldn't tell me if you'd burned yourself to the bone," he said, pulling her hand toward his chest. "I'll just take a look for myself."

"Who gave you the right to —"

"You did," he interrupted curtly.

"When?"

"When you invited me into your body."

She flushed scarlet and then went pale. She tried to speak.

Not one sound came out.

With a tenderness that brought more tears to her eyes, Case opened her hand. There was a faint red mark across the base of each of her fingers.

He made a sound as though he had been the one burned. Then he lifted her hand to his lips and kissed each small mark.

She shivered and made a faint sound at the back of her throat. The feel of his breath and the gentle brush of his beard against her palm brought back every intimate memory she had been trying to forget.

Especially the end, when he couldn't

even bear to look at her.

Get dressed before you catch a chill.

"Don't," she said raggedly. "Don't do this to me."

He looked up. His eyes were like green river pools, clear, yet with shadow currents moving deep within.

"Am I hurting you?" he asked.

"Not yet."

"Did I hurt you before?"

"Yes," she said starkly.

"When I was inside you?"

She closed her eyes and turned her face away.

"Honey?" he asked. "Did I hurt you?"

"Not . . . then."

He bent over her hand and breathed kisses against her skin.

"When did I hurt you?"

"Afterward. When you couldn't wait to get rid of me."

His head came up fast and hard. She wasn't looking at him. She was looking at the floor, thoroughly ashamed.

"I don't know what I did to disgust you," she whispered.

"You did—"

"No," she interrupted desperately. "Don't tell me. It doesn't matter. It won't ever happen again."

435

"It shouldn't," he agreed.

Yet even as Case spoke the words, something deep inside rebelled savagely at the thought of never again sinking into Sarah's sweet, searing fires.

A tear slid down her cheek and caught in the corner of her mouth.

He bent and stole the tear with a kiss.

"Don't," she said, trembling. "I can't take it again."

"Sarah," he whispered against her lips. "My sweet, passionate, innocent Sarah. You didn't disgust me. I would sell my soul to be inside you again."

Her breath came in hard.

"Then why . . . ?" she whispered.

"That's what it would cost me to be your lover. What little is left of my soul."

"I don't understand."

He tipped up her face with his hand. Then he kissed her with a tenderness and hunger that left both of them breathing raggedly.

"I don't know if I can explain," he said.

She simply watched him with eyes that were a mirror of his own. Hurt and hunger, passion and dark regrets.

"I went to war when I was fifteen," Case said. "I dragged Hunter with me."

She bit her lip. The self-disgust in his

voice was so strong she could almost touch it.

"My brother was married to a useless little flirt," he continued. "They had two small children. Ted and Emily."

Despite his neutral voice, she sensed how hard it was for Case to talk about his niece and nephew. She wanted to tell him to stop.

But even more she wanted to understand the darkness at the center of his soul.

"Hunter didn't want to go because of the kids, but Belinda and I talked him into it."

"Your brother doesn't strike me as the kind of man who is easily led."

"Hell, maybe he was as glad to be rid of his wife's company as she was eager to get in bed with the neighbor men."

Sarah winced at the contempt in his voice.

"I went to war all eager to save honor and civilization," Case said. "But even young fools grow up, if they survive. I figured out pretty quick that war is pure hell on good women and children, and they were all that was worth fighting for."

She stroked her cheek softly against

his chest, wanting to soothe away the tension that was making him rigid.

"I stayed sane by thinking of my niece and nephew," he said. "Especially Emily. She was bright as a new penny, full of laughter and sass. She loved everything and everyone."

He hesitated, then kept talking, his voice a monotone.

"When things were really bad during the war, I would pull out the little china cup and saucer I bought for Emily as a homecoming present. I'd just sit and look at it and remember her laughter and pray for the damned war to end."

Sarah's arms stole around Case. She held him, silently telling him that he wasn't alone with his memories.

"I beat my brother home from the war by a few weeks," he said. "I found . . . I found . . ."

A ripple of emotion went through Case, breaking his voice.

"It's all right," she said. "You don't have to tell me."

His arms went around her and he held her as though she were life itself. She didn't protest the strength of his grip, for she knew that grief was holding him much more savagely.

"Culpeppers," he said finally.

The sound of his voice made Sarah tremble.

"Southerners," he said. "Like me."

"Not like you. Never."

He didn't seem to hear. His eyes were open, unblinking, fixed on a horizon only he could see.

And what he saw was unspeakable.

"They beat me to our ranch by three days," he said hoarsely. "They killed every man in the valley, stole or slaughtered the animals, burned the houses and barns. When they finally finished off the women, they took the children and . . ."

The silence that followed was even more unbearable than his eyes.

Sarah remembered then what Lola had said about the Culpeppers.

They sold kids to the Comancheros, after doing things to the young'uns that would shame Satan.

"When I finally found Em and Ted, I didn't have a shovel," Case whispered. "I dug their grave with my fingernails. Then I went looking for Culpeppers."

She watched his eyes and wept silently, helplessly, for she knew now just what had driven Case away from laughter and hope and love.

His memories must be even worse than her own.

"Now do you understand why I pushed you away?" he asked.

Silently she looked at him, hurting for him.

"Ted and Em's death . . ." His voice died. He shrugged. "It killed something in me. I can't give you what you deserve."

"What I deserve?" she asked, not understanding.

"A husband. Children. Love. It isn't in me anymore. It's as dead as little Em."

"I don't believe it. Anyone as gentle as you hasn't lost the ability to love."

Case looked directly into Sarah's eyes.

"All I have for you is lust," he said bluntly. "When a man has seduction on his mind, he'll do whatever will get him what he wants quickest. You wanted tenderness. I gave it to you."

Sarah's smile quivered, yet it was very real.

"Did I ask for anything more?" she whispered.

"You don't have to. It's there in the way you look at me when you think I don't know."

"Like I want to put a knife in your back?" she suggested, smiling despite her tears.

The corner of his mouth lifted, making him look even sadder than before.

"You can't fool me," he said. "You're like a beehive. Once you get past the sting, there's nothing but pure sweetness beneath."

"We're both fully grown. You want something I can give you and I want it, too."

He shook his head.

"You just said you wanted me," she pointed out. "Well, I want you."

He looked at her scarlet cheeks, tear-bright eyes, and trembling lips.

"Pure wild honey," he said huskily. "Don't tempt me."

"Why not?"

"I could make a baby with you, that's why."

"A baby," she repeated softly.

Then she smiled.

Case pushed her away.

"I don't want a child," he said. "Ever."

Her arms tightened around him. She stood on tiptoe and kissed the corner of his mouth. Then she touched his lower lip with the tip of her tongue.

He jerked back as though he had been stung.

"Don't tease me into making you pregnant," he said harshly. "I would hate both of us for it. Is that what you want?"

She closed her eyes and let go of him. Without a word she went and picked up the spindle and began the endless work of spinning.

A moment later the harsh sound of corn being crushed between two rocks came from the other end of the room.

Neither Sarah nor Case spoke again.

19

"That hombre is a grinding fool," Lola said, surveying the mound of cornmeal Case had made the night before.

Sarah didn't say anything.

"You got a lot of spinning done, too," Lola noticed.

"Conner is growing faster than a weed."

"And Case is as twitchy as a long-tailed cat in a room full of rocking chairs."

"I hadn't noticed."

Lola's crack of laughter made Sarah wince.

"Don't you know by now how to take the heat out of a man's mad?" Lola asked.

"It takes two."

"You saying you don't want him?"

"No. I'm saying he doesn't want me."

"Horseshit."

"Amen," Sarah muttered.

She worked the spindle so hard it became a blur. The pile of wool beneath her fingers turned into yarn with astonishing speed.

Lola didn't take the hint and drop the subject.

"He's got a real lust for you," she said. "Gets hard as a post just lookin' at you."

The spindle jerked. The yarn stretched almost to the point of breaking.

"All right," Sarah said through her teeth. "Case wants me but he won't touch me because he doesn't want to get me pregnant. Satisfied?"

Lola snorted.

"Gal, where was your ears when I was talkin' to you about sponges and vinegar and such?"

Sarah looked up from her spinning. Whatever Lola saw in her eyes made the older woman grin. She pulled a small leather pouch out of her pants and dangled it in front of Sarah's face.

"Recollect this?" she taunted.

The spindle fell idle. Sarah looked at the leather bag with haunted eyes.

Don't tease me into making you pregnant. I would hate both of us for it. Is that what you want?

"What if it doesn't work?" she whispered.

"What if the sun don't rise tomorrow?"

"Is it certain?" Sarah asked stubbornly.

"Ain't nothin' certain except sin and death. It works better on some than on others."

"Did it work for you?"

"I never whelped no kids. I caught a few times but none took. Then I never caught again. A lot of whores don't."

With trembling fingers Sarah accepted the leather bag and tucked it into her pants pocket.

"Good," Lola said, nodding curtly. "Now we can stop walkin' on eggs around Case. You recollect how to use them sponges?"

"Yes."

"If you're too dainty to tuck it up tight, tell him. He's got nice long fingers."

"Lola!" Sarah said, flushing scarlet.

The older woman gave her a sly, gap-toothed grin.

"Well, he does," Lola said. "And don't say you ain't never noticed, neither."

Rather grimly Sarah picked up her spindle and went back to work.

Lola emptied a bag of lustrous goat hair next to the chair and laughed all the way out of the cabin.

"Cornbread is burning," she called from outside.

Sarah leaped up and rescued the cornbread. She flipped it out of the pan and onto a rag to cool. Then she added more cornbread batter to the pan, stirred up the fire, and went back to spinning and wondering how she was going to go silver hunting when Case wouldn't let her go alone and wouldn't go with her.

"Ma'am?" called a voice from outside the cabin. "It's Morgan and Hunter. If you'll just pass out some cornbread and beans, we won't bother you."

Hastily she set aside her spinning and opened the door.

Hunter and Morgan took off their hats. Both men were freshly washed and shaved.

She smiled.

"It's no bother at all," she said. "Come in and sit down. I'll get your breakfast."

"No need," Morgan said. "We're used to rustling grub for ourselves."

"Speak for yourself," Hunter said. "I've become accustomed to a high order of cooking in the past few months."

Morgan's teeth flashed in a clean white smile.

"Elyssa is spoiling you like a Christmas puppy," he said to Hunter.

The other man grinned and didn't disagree.

Rather wistfully Sarah looked at Hunter's smile.

Did Case look like that before little Emily died? she asked herself. *A smile as warm as summer.*

"I'm afraid you won't get much in the way of cooking here," she said. "Cornbread, cornmeal mush, peppers and beans, and whatever some critter hasn't eaten of the vegetables I put in the cellar."

"Sounds like heaven to me," Morgan said fervently.

Hunter winked at her.

"Don't mind Morgan," he said. "He's just practicing for the girl who's waiting for him back in Texas."

"Some might need practice," Morgan retorted. "I don't."

Smiling, Sarah set out two battered tin plates, filled two tin cups with water from a pitcher, and began ladling out beans.

"You still have some coffee in your

447

saddlebags?" Hunter asked Morgan.

"Yessuh! Excuse me, ma'am. Put a pot on to boil and I'll be back before you miss me."

"Coffee?" she asked, not sure she had heard correctly. "You brought coffee with you?"

"Yes'm," Morgan said. "We never stopped long enough to cook it on the way here."

"Better stand guard over it with a shotgun," she called as Morgan vanished. "We haven't had coffee since Ute traded some moccasins and cloth over at Spanish Church."

Hunter's mouth flattened at the name of the saloon where his brother had almost died.

"Somebody ought to clean out that den of snakes," he said.

"Waste of time," she said. "There are plenty of snakes to replace the ones you scare away."

"Some snakes are worse than others."

"Culpepper snakes?"

"You don't scare them away. You cut off their heads and bury them under a rock."

A chill went through Sarah. At that moment Hunter sounded and looked very much like Case.

It was a relief when Morgan came in with a small burlap bag of coffee beans and a hand-sized grinder. Very quickly the smell of brewing coffee filled the cabin and drifted out through the chinks in the logs.

Case and Ute appeared not long after. Case, at least, was freshly washed.

"I hope you brought your own cups," she said wryly. "I'm plumb out."

Each man held out a tin cup. She dipped out coffee for them and prodded the cornbread.

"It's ready," she said, "but you might burn your fingers."

Ute filled his plate with beans and cornbread, chose a spot near the fire, and sat on his heels. With the ease of a man who rarely used a chair or a table, he began eating, balancing everything without awkwardness.

Belatedly Case noticed that Sarah wasn't having any coffee.

"Don't you like coffee?" he asked her.

"Sure, but Conner took his cup up to the rim with him," she said.

Hunter and Morgan realized they were drinking from the only other cups Sarah owned. As one, the men stood and held their cups out to her.

"Sit down," Case said. "She can use my cup."

After a moment of hesitation, Hunter and Morgan sat down at the table again.

Sarah began piling food onto a plate. When it was full, she handed it to Case.

"I suppose Conner took his plate with him, too," Case said easily.

"Packed to the brim with food," she agreed.

"Then we'll share."

With no more warning than that, he delivered a spoonful of beans to her mouth. Startled, she took the food without protest at first. Then she realized she was eating his breakfast and started to object.

"Mind your manners," Case said. "No talking when your mouth is full, remember?"

Morgan coughed suddenly.

Hunter gave his brother a sideways, speculative look.

Case didn't notice. He was too busy feeding Sarah. Every time she opened her mouth to say something to him, she got another helping of food. Only when she kept her lips firmly shut did he begin eating himself.

"Take some coffee," he said. "Or do you want me to feed you like a baby bird, a spoonful at a time?"

Nervously she licked her lips. The sudden narrowing of his eyes as he watched her tongue made her breathless.

"I don't think," she said huskily, "that would be a good idea. I'd burn my mouth."

"Or something," he said, but his voice was too low for anyone except her to hear.

After that there was silence except for the small noises of men scraping tin plates with spoons and Sarah stirring the fire when she added more wood.

When the last of the food was gone, Hunter pushed back from the table with a contented sigh.

"I haven't had beans like that since Texas," he said.

"It's those wicked little peppers," she said. "Ute taught me to like them."

"Jalapeños?" Hunter asked.

"Sí," Ute said.

"I'll have to find some seeds for Elyssa."

"I'll send seeds with you," Ute said.

"My wife would like that. She lost most of her garden when the raiders salted it. We've been scouting seeds and cuttings and such ever since."

"We have squash, potatoes, beans, corn, and seeds for greens," Sarah said. "You're welcome to what you need. If you want flaxseed for cloth or oil, or fertile eggs, we have some to spare."

"Especially the way Conner collects eggs," Case said dryly.

"My brother hates that chore," she explained to Hunter.

"I'll take it over," Case said. "And I'll build a chicken run as soon as my own cabin is finished."

Hunter gave his brother a startled look. "I take it you're planning on settling here?"

"Yes. The land . . ." Case hesitated, then shrugged. "The land eases me. I belong here."

Hunter looked at Sarah. She was very busy scrubbing out the bean pot.

"Well, then we better take care of those Culpeppers once and for all," Hunter said calmly.

"Amen," Morgan said. "It's a durned long ride to make every time we hear rumors that you bit off more Culpepper than you could chew."

"How well are they dug in?" Hunter asked his brother.

"They're lazy," Case said. "Most of them have brush wikiups that wouldn't stop a bullet."

"Ab?" Hunter asked.

"He and two of his kin are kind of dug into the side of the canyon."

"Any good angles of fire?"

"Only one, and it's guarded."

"Any chance of burning them out?"

Case shrugged. "It could be done, but I'd hate to be the man to do it."

"Water?" Hunter asked.

"It's called Spring Canyon because water runs year round."

"Supplies and bullets?" Hunter continued calmly.

"Enough of both for a long winter or a short war."

"Weak points?"

Ute gave Hunter an approving glance.

"Lack of discipline," Case said promptly. "There have been unauthorized raids on some ranches in the high country."

"Any raiders get killed?"

Case looked at Ute.

Ute shook his head.

"Sons of bitches cow chasers can't shoot a fish in a barrel," Ute said, his voice rich with disgust.

"Any raids here?" Hunter asked.

"Case can shoot," Ute said succinctly. "We done some buryin'."

"Not enough," Case said.

"Are they watching the ranch?" Hunter asked.

Ute and Case both nodded.

Hunter looked quickly at Sarah, who was still scrubbing the pot.

"That's part of the reason they watch," Case said roughly. "The rest is Spanish silver."

"I heard some loose talk about treasure," Morgan said.

"So did the Culpeppers and Moody's bunch," Case said. "They're hunting silver."

Sarah looked up from the pot.

"They won't find it," she said.

"What makes you so sure?" Hunter asked.

"I've been thinking about it."

Case turned and looked narrowly at Sarah.

"And?" Case prompted.

"They're looking in the wrong place."

454

"What makes you say that?" he asked.

"Like I said, I've been thinking."

"About what?"

"I'm not saying one more word until I get to look for it myself," she said flatly.

"You think I'd steal it?" Case asked, his voice hard.

She looked as shocked as she was.

"Of all the fool ideas," she retorted. "Of course I don't. I don't think your brother or Morgan or Ute or Lola or the darned chickens would steal it, either."

Case lifted his left eyebrow and waited.

"I'm getting cabin fever," she said. "If I can't hunt silver, no one can."

"It's not safe for —"

"— anyone," she cut in. "But you come and go all the time. I'm tired of being a prisoner in my own house."

There was a tight silence. Then Case swore under his breath and looked at Hunter.

His brother just smiled.

Case turned back to Sarah. The look in his eyes was colder than winter.

"Where do you want to start?" he asked.

"I'll tell you when we get there."

"Of all the stubborn —"

"Looks like you're going to be busy," Hunter interrupted. "Morgan and I will divide up your watches."

Case started to object.

"As long as Sarah is with someone," Hunter said, "she'll be safer out of the cabin."

"But —" Case began.

"In fact," Hunter continued without a pause, "she might consider sneaking out after dark and sleeping in the brush with a guard. This cabin would burn like a torch."

Case went completely still.

"We've got four men to stand guard over her all the time," Hunter said to his brother. "If you can't do it, one of the rest of us will."

"Conner could —" she began.

"No," Ute and Case said as one.

"Whoever guards you will be a target," Case explained. "Conner hasn't had much practice at that."

Ute nodded. "Good boy, but he lacks seasoning."

"I don't want Conner put in danger because of me," she said tightly. "I don't want anyone put in —"

"I'll see to Sarah," Case interrupted, looking at Hunter, "except when you need me to scout Spring Canyon."

"I'm not bad on the stalk," Morgan said to no one in particular. "Particularly at night."

Ute grinned. "You almost got me over to Mexico."

"I came real close," Morgan agreed.

"You still hunting me?"

Sarah stiffened and stared at Morgan.

"I sure did love that pony you stole," Morgan said wistfully. "But no, I'm not hunting you anymore. Unless I find you near my ponies . . ."

Ute chuckled.

"Plenty horses now," he said. "Conner and Sarah sweet talk them wild ones. Mustangs take to them like flies to jam."

Hunter looked between the two men and nodded, satisfied that there would be no trouble.

"I take it you know the country best," he said to Ute.

The old outlaw grunted, swallowed the last drop of his coffee, and stood up. "I know it."

"Show me the best lookouts around the ranch," Hunter said, "the best ambush sites near Spring Canyon, which canyons are blind and which can be climbed by a man afoot."

Ute looked at Case.

"If Hunter had been a general," Case said, "the South would have won the war."

"Doubt it," Morgan said.

"So do I," Hunter muttered. "Tactics are one thing. Repeating rifles are another. Those Yankee rifles were a blazing wonder."

He stood and looked at Ute.

"Afoot or on horseback?" Hunter asked.

"Ride now. Walk later."

"When are you due on the rim?" Morgan asked Ute.

"Noon."

"I'll take noon to sundown," Morgan said, standing.

He looked at Sarah.

"Thank you for breakfast, ma'am. A man misses a woman's hand at the stove."

"You're welcome," she said. "Feeding you is the least I can do. This isn't your fight."

"Where there's a Culpepper, it's my fight."

She looked at the suddenly hard lines

of Morgan's face and wondered what the Culpeppers had done to him. Despite her curiosity, she didn't ask. After hearing about Hunter's family, she didn't really want to know anything more about the Culpeppers than where to bury them.

She turned and looked at Hunter.

"Why don't you just shoot them from ambush?" she asked bluntly. "There are 'Wanted Dead or Alive' posters out on every last one of them."

"If it were that easy, the Culpeppers would have died in Texas," he said. "They're real canny when it comes to surviving."

"I been to their camp," Ute said. "Next time I kill some."

"No," she said. "Not if Conner is with you."

"You can't protect him forever," Case said.

"I'll do whatever I have to," Sarah said coldly. "Conner has the whole world in front of him. I want him to have every bit of it."

"If it's all the same to you," Hunter said, looking at Ute, "I'd rather you didn't kick over the beehive until we've had a chance to lay some traps."

Ute shrugged. "Today. Tomorrow. Next week. Makes no never mind. Them Culpeppers is dead men walking."

"Are you riding a particular grudge?" Hunter asked.

"They shot Sarah's jacket to rags. Thought it was her. Dead men walking, every last one."

Surprised, Case looked into Ute's clear black eyes. Before the ambush in the canyon, Ute had simply played pranks on the raiders for the hell of it.

Ute was through playing.

"Ride now?" Ute asked Hunter.

"Ride now," he agreed dryly. "Walk later."

"I'll take a look around out back," Morgan said.

"Don't trip over Conner," she said. "He's sleeping near one of those clumps of big sage."

Morgan grinned and headed for the cabin door. "I'll be real fairy-footed, ma'am."

Hunter and Ute followed Morgan out. The door shut behind them.

Sarah was intensely aware of being alone with Case. Without warning she turned toward him.

He was watching her with smoky green eyes.

"Set some beans to soak," he said. "I'll saddle Cricket and Shaker."

"For what?"

"Hunting silver."

She told herself that the odd little lurch her heart gave had to do with looking for treasure, not with the veiled hunger in his eyes.

"All right, I'll set out the beans," she agreed.

"Will three packhorses be enough?"

"For all the silver?"

He made a disgusted sound.

"For all the firewood," he said. "It burns a damned sight better than foolish dreams of silver."

20

Talons of icy wind raked over the canyon country. Low, pewter-colored clouds boiled overhead. Where the clouds had stacked up against peaks or plateaus, gray became a blue-black mass concealing the land.

"Smells like snow," Sarah said.

"If it is, we'll be hunting deer instead of silver tomorrow."

Case turned up his collar against the wind.

She started to argue but thought better of it. There were extra people to feed. Animal tracks would show clearly against new snow. It was an opportunity they couldn't pass up.

"No argument?" he prodded.

"I like to eat as well as the next person."

"Wouldn't have guessed it lately. I've had to shove every bite down your throat."

She ignored him.

He was tempted to bait her. He could

handle her anger better than he could the way she avoided looking him in the eye.

Or the way she stepped aside to prevent even the possibility of brushing against him in the small cabin.

What am I so touchy about? he asked himself grimly. *I told her not to tempt me. She's doing everything she can to avoid it.*

And me.

Yet, short of vanishing, she couldn't help tempting him unmercifully.

Every moment he was awake, something reminded him of the incandescent sensuality he had discovered beneath her fear. The shine of lamplight on her hair, the scent of roses on her skin, the whispering of the spindle as she made yarn, the curve of her chin as she watched a hawk flying free across the sky . . . everything about her called to him.

And the natural sway of her body as she rode ahead of him aroused him to the point of pain.

"Come on, you stubborn beasts," he muttered, pulling on the lead rope.

Very reluctantly the first mustang speeded up. The three packhorses were tied together, and all were of the same mind. They wanted their rumps instead of their heads pointed into the winter wind.

Case looked around the rapidly narrowing canyon. From what he had seen of similar canyons so far, he guessed that the head of this one would be a wall only hawks could get over.

It wasn't a comforting thought. This was the same canyon where the raiders had shot holes in Sarah's jacket.

Another blind canyon, he thought. *Hope the damned raiders have given up on ambushes.*

Sooner or later, even dumb, bone-lazy outlaws figure out that ambushing me just isn't smart.

The back of his neck was prickling. He had a clear feeling that someone was watching them. Carefully he examined every high point for the flash of metal or glass that would give away the presence of raiders. He also watched the horses for any sign that they scented more than rock and pinon ahead.

Wonder what Sarah saw while she was dragging firewood out of here, he thought. *Nothing looks promising to me.*

Just one of hundreds of similar canyons. She would have a better chance looking for a horseshoe nail in a hay-stack the size of Texas.

Not that the silver mattered to Case. There was plenty of wood to be gathered, and that was all he cared about.

Sarah finally reined in when they were well past the place where they had been ambushed. A barrier of dead trees, boulders, and rubble lay across the canyon like jackstraws.

"I'll just be a minute," she said, dismounting.

He kicked free of the stirrups, landed running, and caught her arm before she had taken two steps away from her horse.

"Where do you think you're going?" he asked.

His voice was rough with the hunger riding him. The sound of it sent a small shiver through her.

How can I not tempt him when his need is working on my nerves like a file? she asked.

And so is mine.

Lord, I never expected to want a man inside my body, and now I can't think about anything except holding Case just as close and hard and deep as I can.

Nothing ever felt like that. I didn't even

know anything could.

A thrill of heat shot through her that made her breath catch. She wondered if she would ever again know that astonishing, almost frightening ecstasy.

"If you tell me what's on your mind," he said, "I can help you find it."

She laughed raggedly and hoped she wasn't blushing.

"I want to climb up that for a better look at the sides of the canyon up ahead," she said huskily, gesturing toward the mound of rubble.

"If you can see the canyon clearly, a man with a rifle can see *you* clearly."

"Do you really think —"

"Hell, yes, I really think," he interrupted impatiently. "You should try thinking too, or you'll end up as full of holes as your damned jacket."

She swallowed.

"Riding into the wind the way we are," Case said, "the horses can't scent anyone following us. But I'm betting someone is doing just that."

Sarah licked her suddenly dry lips.

His hand tightened on her arm as need sank its talons deeply into his body. Then he caught himself and eased his grip.

Even through gloves and heavy clothes, she felt good. Warm and sleek and female.

"What are you looking for?" he asked almost caressingly.

Her mouth went dry. She had seen his eyes like that before, green fire barely banked.

And then he had pressed into her, filling her completely.

"I'm looking for different ruins," she said huskily. "Not real rooms, but little stone caches built in cracks that are too small to stand upright in."

"Where?"

"Up canyon. On the south side. I thought I saw something when I was pulling firewood out of that mess."

Slowly he released her arm.

"I'll look," he said. "You wait here. If the horses hear something behind us, get under cover and stay there."

Case began scrambling up the mound of debris. It was a jumble of shattered logs, rock of all sizes, and dirt. The higher he climbed, the more obvious it was that a flood had cleaned out the upper reaches of the canyon sometime in the last few years.

Maybe it was the year Hal tried to

pistol whip Conner once too often, he thought.

Then he wondered if this might not be the same canyon where Hal had died.

What was it Sarah said? he asked himself. *Something about the side canyons being full of water and Lost River turning into a muddy flood.*

Using every bit of cover he found, he went to the top of the mound and flattened himself in a crevice. Carefully, thoroughly, he looked at the upper canyon through his spyglass.

Nothing moved but the wind.

He looked again, this time concentrating on the walls of the canyon, where pockets, crevices, and small overhangs had been weathered out of the solid rock.

Finally Case spotted something he thought might be ruins.

Not much to speak of, he thought. *More like a hunter's cache than a real shelter.*

No matter how carefully he scanned the narrow head of the canyon, he found nothing more impressive. He shifted his focus back to the modest ruins. When he was satisfied that he had found a route up to them, he turned toward the lower canyon again.

Methodically he quartered the middle and lower reaches of Ambush Canyon with the spyglass.

Something flashed down in the mouth of the canyon.

Spyglass, likely, he decided. *Everywhere we go, someone is watching us.*

Or trying to kill us.

Case came off the debris pile faster than he had gone up.

"Well?" she asked. "Did you see anything?"

"There's at least one man watching the mouth of the canyon."

"How close is he?"

"Out of rifle range," he said succinctly.

She lifted her head and smelled the wind like a wild creature. Then she smiled. It was a baring of teeth rather than a sign of amusement.

"They'll be real cold down there," she said. "Storms scour the canyon mouths something fierce."

"There are some ruins up along the south side of the canyon," he said. "Nothing much to speak of."

"Can we get to them from down here?"

"It won't be easy."

"But we can do it?"

He sighed. "Yes."

Eagerly she went to one of the pack animals and untied the shovel.

"What are you waiting for?" she asked.

"Are you sure you wouldn't rather —"

"Yes," she interrupted impatiently. "I'm sure."

"Hell's fire."

He went to his saddle and untied two rolled-up blankets. With a few quick slashes of his knife, he made them into thick wool ponchos.

"Put this over your jacket," he said, holding out one of the ponchos.

"But —"

"Do it without arguing. Just for the hell of it. Just once."

He jerked the poncho over her hat before she could object again. Their breath mingled when he bent and tugged the poncho in place.

It hung down below her knees.

It was warm.

"Thank you," she muttered.

"You're welcome," he said mockingly.

"How anyone can tell me to go to hell

470

and never actually say the words is amazing."

"Shouldn't be. You manage it with a look."

With that, Case yanked his own poncho over his jacket, grabbed the shovel, and set off up the jumble of debris once more.

Sarah was right on his heels.

Snow began to fall. The first flakes were soft and airy, swirling like apple blossoms on the wind. Then the wind quickened. The flakes came thicker and faster, clothing the land in a clean white silence.

"We should go back," he said as soon as he reached the top of the mound.

"What for? Only rain is dangerous in these canyons."

"What if drifts pile up?"

She shook her head. "Not here. Maybe on up in the high country."

"What about freezing to death?" he asked sarcastically.

"It's warmer now than it was before it started to snow."

"Hell," he muttered.

"At least we won't have to worry about an ambush," she said matter-of-factly. "You can't see more than twenty feet in front of your face."

"For these small things, Lord, we are grateful. I think."

Case turned on his heel and looked up the south side of the canyon again. Though falling snow blotted out most landmarks, he remembered how the wall had looked through the spyglass.

"Stay off my heels," he said. "If I fall, I don't want to knock you down."

"Does your leg hurt?" she asked anxiously.

No, but my dumb handle sure does, he thought.

He could still taste the heat of her startled breath when he had bent over her to pull the poncho in place. Like her scent, her movements, her simple presence, the knowledge of her warmth haunted him.

"Just stay clear of me," he said through his teeth.

Twenty minutes later he levered himself up over a chest-high lip of stone. The ledge he found beyond was less than six feet deep. The overhang barely gave a man room to sit upright.

More a crevice than an alcove, the ledge ran for about thirty feet before tapering away into a nose of rock. At one time the nose had been a tall red finger of stone, but frost and water had eaten through the softer rock at the base and tumbled the pillar into the canyon. It was impossible to say whether the pillar had tumbled yesterday or a thousand years ago.

A low wall and several storage compartments were built into the crevice with native rock. At first glance, and even at second, it was hard for Case to be certain that the remains of the walls weren't just random debris. The native stone naturally broke into roughly rectangular shapes that required little finishing by man to become small building blocks.

"Are we there yet?" Sarah called up from just below him.

"Such as it is."

Kneeling, he set the shovel aside, turned, and reached down to help her up onto the ledge. As he did, he spotted what looked like a twisted piece of wood poking out from behind one of the low walls. Turning his head, he looked more closely.

The remains of a buckle were attached to the oddly shaped scrap.

He gave a soft, soundless whistle.

"Grab hold," he said. "It's warmer up here out of the wind."

"Are they really ruins?" Sarah asked impatiently. "Sometimes it's hard to tell at a distance."

"Judge for yourself."

Saying nothing more, he lifted her onto the ledge.

She crouched on the cold rock and looked around eagerly.

"Watch your head," he cautioned.

The first thing she saw was something poking out from behind a crumbling wall. She reached for it so quickly that she banged her head on the low ceiling despite his warning.

She hardly noticed. Her fingers were curled around an ancient leather strap. It had been dried to the consistency of wood by the alternating fire and ice of the stone desert.

"Is it as old as I think?" she asked, her voice awed.

"I don't know. I do know that no Indian left it here. They didn't have metal."

She turned and looked at him with wide, radiant eyes.

"The Spanish did," she whispered.

"So did a lot of others since them,"

Case said. "It's a long way from a scrap of harness to three hundred pounds of silver."

But the heightened gleam of his eyes told Sarah that he was excited, too.

She started forward to see what else might be behind the low, crumbling wall. Then she hesitated.

Be there, she prayed silently. *For Conner. He deserves better than life has given him.*

"Sarah?" Case asked, touching her arm. "Is something wrong?"

"So many hopes," she said simply.

Pain twisted through him.

"Don't let hope get to you," he said. "All it will do is hurt you."

"No," she said. "Memory hurts. Hope heals. Without it, we would spend our life in pain."

Saying nothing, Case let go of her arm.

Sarah crawled around the low wall and peered into the darkness beyond.

Darkness looked back at her.

She dug beneath her poncho and carefully pulled out a tin of matches. After a moment, flame leaped at the end of a tiny wooden stick.

There was nothing behind the ruined

wall but more rectangular chunks of rubble.

Disappointment went through her like black lightning. The match burned down, flickered, and died, scorching her glove. She didn't notice.

For a long time she didn't move. Then she sensed Case crouched in the gloom just behind her.

She turned toward him.

"There are other canyons," he said quietly.

Though she nodded, she made no move to turn and go. Her hand was clenched so tightly around the fragment of harness that even her glove couldn't soften the bite of metal against flesh.

"Were there any other ruins in this canyon?" she asked.

"I didn't see any."

"Then there aren't any."

He didn't disagree.

"It was a long shot," she said after a time. "There isn't a red finger nearby. I thought maybe it came down in the last big flood a few years back."

"When your husband died?"

"Yes," she whispered. "Hal told Conner that he would never find the silver until the old ones came back and opened their hiding places, and the red finger would point the way."

"Did Hal talk much about his treasure hunting with Conner?"

"He only talked about it once," she said, "when he was dying. He was always tormenting Conner."

Hal baited him once too often, Case thought.

But he didn't say it aloud, for he had promised Conner.

"Is this the canyon where it happened?" he asked after a moment.

"I think so. From what I saw when I was gathering wood . . ." Her voice died.

Case looked at Sarah sharply. She didn't realize it. She was staring out at the snow with eyes that saw only the past.

Suddenly she shuddered.

"Dead man's silver," she whispered. "Just like you said. I'd never touch it but for my brother."

For the space of several breaths he looked out at the snow, thinking about the huge mound of flood debris they had climbed to get to the insignificant ruins. The fingers of red stone that stuck up all over the wild land looked permanent, but he had seen proof in more than one canyon that even stone gave way over time.

"How far back do the ruins go?" he asked, looking into the darkness.

"I don't know. There's a lot of rubble about five feet in front of me."

"May I see?"

Wordlessly she crowded against the solid stone that formed the back side of the crevice.

There was just enough room for him to squeeze by her. He set aside the shovel and eased forward. As he moved, his poncho scraped and snagged on the ragged ruins, dislodging a rectangular stone.

The rock tumbled out of the crevice and vanished into the thickly falling snow. From the sounds that came back, the stone struck the steep side of the canyon a few times, then hit the top of the flood debris and stopped moving.

Snow muffled all echoes with silence.

He struck a match and looked into the darkness just beyond the fitful flame. Once the floor had been smoothed by hands long dead. Now it was buried by broken stone once more.

Silently he measured the height of the ruins, the depth of the crevice, and the

size of the pile blocking his way. Something wasn't quite right, but he couldn't
decide what it was.

The match died.

He pushed forward until the natural
wall of stone crowded him on one side,
the man-made wall pushed him on the
other side, and the rubble made a solid
barrier in front of him.

Too much debris, Case realized, understanding what seemed wrong.

The ruined wall wasn't high enough
or wide enough to account for the heap
of stone. Even if his eye had been mis-
led by the uncertain light of the match,
most of the stones that fell out of the
ruins would have dropped into the canyon and vanished, as had the one he
accidentally knocked loose.

*It could have been like a little stone
crib for storing things,* he thought. *If the
structure fell in on itself, that would
explain a lot of the stones.*

He lit another match and studied the
mound. It didn't quite reach to the low
ceiling. There might be enough room at
the top for a man to look over and see
what was on the other side.

The second match went out.

"See anything?" Sarah asked, but

there was no real hope in her voice.

"Rocks."

She didn't ask any more.

Case took off his hat and levered himself to the top of the rubble pile. Awkwardly he struck a match and peered into the inky black at the far side.

He didn't see anything. There just wasn't enough room for him to look over.

He blew out the match.

"Get as far back as you can," he said to her. "I'm going to shift the top of this mess so I can look over on the other side."

"Be careful. Some of these ruins are dangerous."

"Are you just figuring that out?" he muttered.

"I've known since I looked at the first one," she said indifferently.

"But you kept at it."

Whatever she said was lost in the sounds of stone grumbling and scraping when he started shoving debris away from the top of the mound. As much as possible he pushed the stone away from him, into the darkness ahead.

The rattle and bounce of debris told Case that the area beyond the barrier was open. He pushed faster. A cascade of stone ran down the far side, clunking and scraping with dull sounds.

Then came a sound that wasn't stone striking stone.

"Was that your shovel?" Sarah asked.

"I left it behind you."

"But something sounded like metal."

"Stay back," was all he said.

He shoved more stone away from the top, pulled off one glove, and began running his fingers over the newly uncovered debris.

Stone met his touch. Then more stone, rough and cold. Then something very cold.

And smooth.

He struck a match and stared at the rubble that was only inches from his face.

All he saw was pale rectangles of rock and a few stones so dark they seemed to absorb light.

Black rectangles? Case thought. *I've never seen black rock in these canyons, except for veins of coal.*

Is this a stash of coal?

Abruptly he plunged his hand into

the rubble. His fingers closed around a black rectangle.

Cold. Smooth. Heavy.

Much too heavy for coal.

"Case? Are you all right?"

Distantly he realized that Sarah had called to him more than once.

"I'm fine," he said.

"What are you doing?"

"Sorting through debris."

"It got so quiet all of a sudden."

"I'm just catching my breath."

The match flickered out.

Case hardly noticed. He didn't need light to remember what the heavy black rectangle looked like.

There was a cross carved into it.

With an effort he managed to free his knife from its belt sheath. Working by feel in the dark, he gouged at the bar with the sharp tip of the steel.

He lit another match.

A teardrop of pure silver gleamed out of the black rock.

"I will be damned," he said.

"What?"

"It's here. The silver is here."

Sarah made a startled sound and clawed her way toward him.

"Move over," she said.

He couldn't, but he could roll onto one side.

"I can't see anything at all," she said, frustrated. "Are you sure there's silver?"

She struggled to dig a match out of her jacket. Crowded next to him as she was, it was nearly impossible.

"Don't bother," he said.

"But —"

"Take off a glove," he said over her objections.

With an impatient jerk, she stripped off a glove.

"Brace yourself with the other hand," he said.

A cold, smooth weight settled onto her palm. Like Case, she knew instantly that no stone was that heavy.

Nor was a handful of *reales.*

"Bullion," she breathed. "Dear God. It's a bar of silver bullion!"

Disbelief and excitement raced through her. Her fingers clenched around the precious silver bar.

"There are more," he said.

"More," she repeated in a daze, afraid that she wasn't understanding him. "I can't believe it."

"Give me room to dig. You'll believe it."

"I'll help you."

"Honey, there's not enough room for us to light a match wedged in like we are, much less dig together."

"But — oh, blazes, you're right."

Dragging the heavy silver bar, she eased back through the tight passage. Then she crouched a step away from the base of the rubble, balancing the bullion in both hands.

"I'll pass the bars back to you as I find them," he said.

"How many are there?"

"I don't know." He grunted and pushed a bar into her hand. "Start counting."

"Oof."

"Oof?" he said dryly. "I make it two bars so far. Here comes number three."

"Wait!"

There was a muted, almost musical clatter as Sarah dumped the first two bars against the back of the crevice. She pulled on her glove and reached forward again into the gloom.

"Ready," she said.

Another heavy, tarnished silver bar smacked against her palm.

"Three," she said.

Without pausing she chucked the third bar off to the side.

"Ready," she said.

By the fifth bar Case and Sarah established a rhythm that varied only when the silver was difficult to drag out of the rubble. Then she would rest while he muttered under his breath and lit a match and shoved rock aside until he freed more bars.

Shivering, cold without realizing it, she waited for silver wealth to be shoved into her hands so that she could toss it aside and hold out her hands for more.

Rock shifted, grumbled, and filled up the hole where Case had been digging.

"How many?" he asked.

"Forty."

"That's more than we can take in our saddlebags. Especially with this added on."

He backed out of the hole and turned. Black coins spilled from his hands. The tarnish didn't change the sweet chiming of silver against silver when the coins tumbled to the ground.

"Enough to fill my saddlebags, and yours in the bargain," Case said. "We'll have to leave the bars for later."

"What about the packhorses?"

"No time," he said.

"We can't just leave the bullion here."

"Why not?"

"Someone might find it," she said impatiently.

"Nobody has up to now."

"I'll guard it. You go back for —"

"No," he interrupted. "Anywhere I go, you go."

"We can't both stay here."

"Uh huh. That means we're both going."

"But the rest of the silver —"

"Better hustle," Case said, turning back to the leather sacks of *reales* that lay within the rubble. "It's going to be a hell of a scramble carrying saddlebags of silver down those snow-slicked rocks."

Sarah's teeth clicked as she shut her mouth. Some of her excitement ebbed when she eyed the pile of bars and the crumbling leather bags that he was gently easing from the rubble.

Silver was unreasonably heavy.

Like lead.

"What are you waiting for?" he said.

"Wings."

"You'll freeze to death first. Get moving, honey. You're already shivering like a sick hound."

Clumsily at first, then more easily, she helped him get some of the bars down the steep side of the canyon, and then carry the empty saddlebags back up.

Case wanted to stop with the saddlebags.

Sarah refused.

She wasn't leaving until every last bar they had found was loaded on. She had hunted too long and too hard to leave anything behind.

The snow had almost stopped falling by the time Case finally heaved heavy saddlebags onto Cricket's back and buckled them in place. Sarah's little mare was carrying her share as well.

The packhorses had their ears laid back. The dead weight of metal was the hardest kind of load to carry.

Cold settled over the land like a second kind of silence. Veils of snow drifted and vanished, revealing the land one second and concealing it the next. Gradually the snow stopped. The moon rose clean and bright enough to throw shadows. The tracks of the horses stood out starkly against the glittering white land.

There was no sign of raiders at the

mouth of the canyon.

Sarah sighed and began to relax. As the excitement of finding treasure slowly faded, her elation became a bittersweet kind of acceptance.

Conner's future was assured.

Her half of Lost River ranch belonged to Case Maxwell.

"Are you sure you don't want to change your mind about taking half the silver instead of half the ranch?" she asked after a while. "The silver is worth a lot more."

"Not to me."

She didn't ask again.

In silence Sarah rode back toward the home that was no longer hers. Her eyes roved the land, memorizing its stark beauty, engraving it on her mind.

Soon memories would be all that was left to her of the ranch she loved.

21

Run! The flood is coming and he's drunk and mean and looking for you!

Faster, Conner! You're too big now for me to carry you!

Sarah awoke in a heart-pounding rush. Cold sweat chilled her skin.

Oh God, Hal will catch me this time for sure.

Frantically she looked around.

Though she was outside, no floodwater frothed around her. There were no walls, no doors, nothing to keep her from fleeing her husband.

She took a broken breath and tried to orient herself.

No moon dimmed the wild, cascading glory of the stars overhead. Snow lay silver upon the land. What wasn't covered by snow was a strangely luminous ebony as deep as night itself.

Abruptly she remembered where she was, and why. At Hunter's suggestion — order, actually — she had decided not to sleep inside the cabin as was her custom. After it was too dark for any spy to see her, she had taken her bedroll outside.

A steep canyon wall was at her back. Brush flanked her. Horses were hobbled randomly throughout the area. Their senses would pick up intruders long before human ones would.

And Case was sleeping somewhere nearby, invisible in the darkness, guarding her and the Spanish treasure.

Sarah took another breath, a deeper one. The air was cold and sweet and free.

Just a nightmare, she kept telling herself. *Nothing to get in a lather about.*

Hal is dead.

Conner is safe.

I'm safe.

Yet even as the thoughts came, anxiety shivered through her, a fear that no reassurances could touch. She hadn't felt this way since she had realized that her parents were dead, her brothers and sisters were dead, and she was responsible for Conner's sheer survival.

The silver means that Conner never will want for food, and neither will I.

I never will have to marry or turn to

whoring simply to survive.

So why do I feel so frightened?

Then she remembered that the price of Spanish treasure had been very high — Lost River ranch.

I've lived through worse losses.

I'll live through this.

Somehow.

"Sarah?"

Case's voice was so low that it carried no farther than a few feet.

"I'm awake," she said softly. "Is something wrong?"

He condensed out of the night beside her.

"That's what I was going to ask you," he said. "You were thrashing around like a fish on a hook."

His shoulders blocked out a wide patch of stars. The makeshift poncho he wore swirled around his knees like night itself.

She took a quick, ragged breath. The air was still cold and clean, but now it smelled of leather, wool, and man.

"Just a bad dream," she said.

"The flood or your husband?"

"Both, I think. I don't remember much except the fear."

Though Sarah's words were matter-of-fact, her voice still trembled with echoes of terror.

Saying nothing, Case sat on the foot of her bedroll. Gently he lifted her into his lap, wrapped a blanket from her bedroll around her, and held her against his chest.

"Sometimes it takes a while for the nightmares to fade," he said.

Giving up Lost River ranch, like the death of her family, wouldn't fade. But she didn't refuse the comfort he offered. She gave a jerky sigh and leaned against him.

Silence and the soft whispering of their mingled breath filtered through the night.

"Look around you," he murmured after a time. "The land is as beautiful as a meadowlark's song."

She didn't have to look. The land filled her eyes, her heart, her soul.

"The snow will melt tomorrow," she said quietly. "But until then, everything will be like a Christmas angel, all sparkling with light."

His breathing hesitated, then continued evenly despite the memories running like razors through his heart.

"Did your family have an angel at the

top of their Christmas tree?" he asked.

She nodded. "Of all the decorations, it was my favorite."

"Emily loved the angel best, too."

The echoes of pain in his voice made Sarah ache. Saying nothing, she shifted until she could put her arms around him. His arms tightened around her in return.

Snow shimmered like the wings of angels, white and glistening, feathery veils of innocence that both softened and emphasized the stark beauty of the land.

How can I leave this? she thought.

Breath squeezed raggedly from her lungs.

"Still afraid?" Case asked quietly.

"I know the difference between nightmare and night," was all she said.

He pulled her closer and tucked her head beneath his chin. With each breath he inhaled the clean scent of her hair.

Tenderness and desire fought within him.

Both won.

"What are you thinking about?" he asked after a time.

"Land and silver and Conner."

"He was so excited he was dancing in place."

"Until I started talking about sending him back East to school," Sarah said.

"Conner was thinking of spending that silver on good cattle and digging wells and such."

"He can do that after he has a university education. If he still wants to."

Case opened his mouth to point out that Conner's future was her brother's decision, not hers.

Yet in the end he said nothing.

"Hunter wasn't very excited about the silver," she said.

"It means trouble."

"We were poor and had trouble. Now we're rich and have trouble. I'd rather have the silver as well as the misery."

Again, Case held his tongue.

Then he thought better of it. If Sarah understood just how great the risk had become after the Spanish treasure was found, maybe she would grab Conner and get the hell out while the rest of them took care of the Culpeppers.

"We were followed once we left that side canyon," Case said flatly.

"We've been followed before."

"We were carrying firewood then."

"So?"

"We come out of that canyon with no firewood in sight, yet our animals all cut deeper tracks than they did on the way into the canyon."

Sarah stiffened.

"Ab Culpepper is a good tracker," he said. "So are most of his kin. They know you were hunting for Spanish treasure."

"And now they know we've found it," she finished bleakly.

"That's what I would think, if I had been the one watching and tracking."

"Nobody knows where the silver is hidden now but the two of us," she said fiercely.

"You wouldn't last long once Ab started questioning you. Neither would I. He's a man of rare cruelty."

"Then you'll just have to keep me out of his hands until I get that silver to a bank."

"I have a better idea. Take Conner, four bars of silver, and six horses. Run without stopping for Santa Fe. Ute will go with you as a guard. You can come back once the raiders are taken care of."

"Conner won't go," she said.

"How do you know?"

"I'm not a complete fool. I want my brother out of here in one piece. But he won't leave. When I told him I wouldn't give him any silver if he stayed, he just shrugged."

"Damnation," Case said through his teeth.

"Amen."

She sighed jerkily.

It's all coming apart, all my plans for the future. Why did Conner have to grow up so stubborn?

Starlight glittered across snow like frozen tears.

Sarah closed her eyes, shutting out everything but the comfort of Case's body so solid against hers and his arms strong around her. A shiver that was both sadness and pleasure went through her.

"Don't think about the nightmare," he said softly.

"I wasn't."

"You trembled."

"I was thinking about how fine it would be just to stay here in the night with you and let the rest of it slide away, all of it, all the bad memories and the fear . . ."

His eyes closed. The longing in her voice was echoed in his own heartbeat, his own soul.

"Just live here and now?" he asked.

"Yes. Like a good dream, the kind you wake up from smiling instead of sweating."

"Like a dream," he said. "Nothing before and nothing after. Just a sweet dream . . ."

His lips whispered softly over her hairline, her eyebrows, her cheekbones, the corner of her mouth.

"Case?" she whispered.

"Just a dream," he said. "That's all. Just a dream."

The tip of his tongue traced her upper lip, then her lower one, leaving a delicate fire in its wake. Her breath caught and her heart turned over at the tender caress.

Then she remembered his blunt warning.

Don't tease me into making you pregnant. I would hate both of us for it.

The leather poke that Lola had given Sarah was back in the cabin. She knew if she went to get it, Case would withdraw again behind his carefully built walls.

Only now, this instant, was he vulnerable.

Like her.

It doesn't matter, she thought. *I'll be gone from Lost River ranch before either one of us knows if I'm pregnant.*

And maybe, just maybe, I can get so far inside those walls of his that he can't shut me out ever again.

She didn't really believe it, but she hoped . . .

Her teeth nipped his lower lip. The startled breath he took was the opening she wanted. Her tongue slid into his mouth and began exploring.

Without knowing it, she shivered and made a throaty sound of pleasure when she tasted him.

"I love your taste," she whispered. "I love the way your teeth feel so slick and hard and your tongue is all velvet and warm."

Case made a low sound. His arms tightened until he held Sarah in a powerful, warm vise.

"You shouldn't say things like that," he whispered.

"Why?"

"You'll make me lose my head."

"Just for a while. Just a dream. That's

498

all," she whispered. "A dream."

Before he could pull away, she shifted in his lap, trying to get even closer to him. As she moved, her hip rubbed over his aroused flesh.

He was full, hard, ready.

She made another low sound and moved again, frankly caressing him, knowing at some deeply feminine level that this was the way to reach past his barriers, if only for a time.

Just a dream.

He tried to speak. All that came out was a throttled groan when her mouth slanted over his. The taste of her as she met and matched his hungry tongue, the feel of her moving in his lap, and the ragged catch in her breathing told him that she wanted him as much as he wanted her.

The knowledge was like raw whiskey in his brain, stripping away his control. He fought against himself even as his tongue stabbed into Sarah's mouth again and again, seeking her as deeply as she was seeking him.

Yet no matter how fully their mouths joined, it wasn't enough. He needed more, much more. He needed all of her.

Her name was a husky question on his lips.

Her answer was a hungry movement of her body that inflamed him.

Case stopped fighting against what he needed more than the blood in his veins. Beneath the blanket he had wrapped around her, his hands sought and found the feminine weight of her breasts.

He stroked her urgently, but it was skin he hungered for, not clothing. Quickly he unbuttoned her flannel shirt and undid the ties of her chemise.

His fingers were cool from the night. Sarah gasped when they plucked at her nipples. When he hesitated, she put her hands over his and held them to her breasts.

"Don't stop," she whispered.

"My hands are cold."

"Cold?" she laughed raggedly. "They're fire. Pure, wonderful fire. I want them all over me. But most of all, I want to have you inside me again."

He made a deep, broken sound and pushed her back onto the bedroll. Together they fought their way through clothing until she felt him opening her naked thighs.

The scent of her arousal pushed him over the edge. He caressed her once, deeply, and felt liquid fire spill over his hand. He tried to say her name but couldn't. She had taken his breath.

Long legs wrapped around his hips. He yanked at his pants until they were open, then barely managed to throttle a groan when her hips lifted to him, touching him with fire.

He rubbed against her slick heat. She shivered with pleasure and returned the caress, sliding over his hungry flesh. He guided himself to her, testing her readiness. As he stretched her, more of her intimate heat spilled over him.

It was like setting fire to a torch.

His body corded. He sank into her as far as he could go. He drank the startled, sensual cry she made before it went any further than her lips. His hips moved, then moved again, driving him faster, harder, deeper into her sultry, clinging center.

Sarah's legs tightened and her hips moved in return, urging him, arousing him until he knew nothing but the sensation of her living fire surrounding him. He wanted to slow down, to regain his self-control, but he could no more do that than he could resist the satin heat of her passion in the first place.

Her nails sank into his thighs as she twisted up to meet him. The night came apart around him in a series of deep, wrenching pulses that left him shaken and light-headed, fighting for breath.

Uncertainly Sarah held Case, stroked him, gently kissed his forehead and eyelids and lips.

After a long time he lifted his head and looked down at her with glittering eyes.

"Did I hurt you?" he asked.

"I thought I was hurting *you*," she said unhappily. "You sounded like you were dying. Did I — did I disgust you again?"

"Disgust me? What are you talking about? You've never disgusted me."

"Not even the first time we did this?"

"You couldn't disgust me if you tried," he said flatly.

She let out a long breath of relief.

"But I'm disgusted with myself," he said roughly. "I've never lost control like that. I'm sorry."

He gathered himself to get off her.

Her legs locked around his hips.

"You said I didn't disgust you," she whispered.

Case caught Sarah's face between his hard hands.

"You don't disgust me," he said distinctly. "You excite me as no other woman has, ever."

"Then why are you going away?"

"Because I'm crushing you."

Smiling, she rocked her hips against him. The hot, delicious sensations that went through her at each movement made her want to hold him even closer, deeper.

"You're not crushing me," she murmured. "You're keeping me warm from the inside out. That's a handy thing on a cold winter night. Would you like a job as my blanket?"

He made an odd sound and lowered his face next to hers on the bedroll.

"Case? Are you all right?"

"No. You make me want to . . ."

His voice unraveled. He couldn't explain the complex emotions seething just beneath his control.

". . . to laugh," he said finally. "I don't want to laugh, to feel, to love. Never again. *I can't.*"

Sarah was glad that the night concealed what his words did to her; pain and denial, anger and a savage kind of grief.

And above all, acceptance.

She understood what drove Case away from her, and why. She could not fault him for his choices.

She loved him.

"It's all right," she whispered fiercely. "Laugh or cry or do nothing at all. This is just a dream, remember? Dreams don't count."

As she spoke, her hips moved with a sensuous need that was unmistakable to Case.

She still wanted him.

A hot shudder racked him from head to heels. His heartbeat doubled. Blood raced through him and gathered in a storm, transforming him. His whole body tightened against her. He filled her until she overflowed.

"Oh, my," she whispered dreamily. "That feels wonderful."

Her hips moved in counterpart to her words, stroking Case and pleasuring both of them.

"Sarah."

"Mmm?"

"You're burning me alive," he said roughly.

"Is that good or bad?"

"Ask me again in a few minutes."

"What?"

His answer was a kiss that filled her mouth as thoroughly as he was filling her body. He didn't stop until she was breathless and twisting against him hungrily, seeking the ecstasy she sensed just beyond her reach.

Only then did he roll away from her. Hastily he began stripping off the clothes he had merely unfastened before.

"Wait," Sarah said urgently, reaching blindly for him. "Where are you going?"

"Nowhere. I'm as hungry as you are."

Belatedly she understood that he was simply taking off his clothes. Starlight ran in pale streamers over his skin as he lay on his back and twisted out of his pants. Still slick with her passion, his hard, aroused flesh glistened against the night.

He looked huge.

"Dear God," she whispered, stunned. "Was all that inside me?"

Case made another odd sound, laughter or pain or both at once.

"Every bit of it," he said in a low voice.

Even darkness couldn't conceal the widening of Sarah's eyes.

"I don't believe it," she said.

"I do. You liked it, honey. You twisted up against me like a cat, wanting more, but I lost control before I could give you what you need."

She reached toward his hard, intimidating arousal. Then she stopped short.

"May I . . . touch you?" she asked uncertainly.

Something very close to a smile gleamed in the moonlight as he looked at her.

"Anywhere you like," he said. "Anyway you like. But would you mind sharing those blankets first? It's cold out here alone."

Trembling with sensations that were neither entirely fear nor wholly pleasure, Sarah lifted the blankets in silent invitation.

She still couldn't believe that she had held all of him inside her body without being torn apart.

There was a rush of cold air and then Case was beneath the blankets with her. She lay on her side, facing him. At first his skin was cool against hers.

Then it became deliciously warm.

Slowly, thoroughly, he gathered her close, putting the naked length of their bodies together for the first time. His blunt arousal lay against her stomach like a length of warm rock.

"Dear Lord," she breathed. "There is an awful lot of you."

Though he made no sound, his shoulders moved in what might have been silent laughter.

"No more than there was before," he finally whispered against her lips.

"It's hard to believe."

"It's hard, period."

"I noticed."

"That's why women are so soft," he murmured.

"As in the head?" she whispered tartly. "So that we'll let men put that great hard thing inside us?"

Again his shoulders moved.

Again Case made no sound.

"Your head is harder than mine," he whispered after a moment.

"Ha!"

"If you don't believe me . . ."

His fingers closed around hers. He pulled away just enough to guide her hand down his body.

Sarah's breath came in with a startled sound as he stroked her fingers from the smooth, blunt head of his erect flesh to the hot thatch of hair at the base.

"See?" he asked huskily. "Not so hard after all."

"It's as hard as stone."

"Stone doesn't have a heartbeat." He wrapped her fingers around him. "I do. Feel it."

The pulse of his life's blood beat unmistakably against her palm.

The wonder of it took her breath.

Curiously she explored with her fingertips the strange flesh that was both rigid and alive.

"Sleek satin here," she murmured, caressing his tip, "and so different down here. Not rough. Just . . . different."

As she combed gently through his dense hair, she discovered another way that men were different from women. She curled her fingers around the tightly drawn spheres and at the same time smoothed her palm over the heartbeat hidden within stone.

His breath came in on a husky curse and a ragged prayer.

"Are you sure I'm not disgusting

you?" Sarah asked anxiously.

"Damned sure."

Still, she hesitated.

"Does this disgust you?" Case asked.

His hand slid down between her legs. He threaded through the hot nest of hair and found the slick, aroused flesh beneath. Deliberately he circled the sultry opening.

Her breath broke.

"Does this disgust you?" he asked again.

"You must be joking," she said, trembling. "Don't you know how good it feels to me?"

"Does it?"

"Dear God, yes."

"That's how it feels to me," he said. "Good. So good. And this is even better."

He parted sleek folds of skin and teased her until she made a broken sound. Silky heat licked over his hand.

"Pure fire," he breathed. "God, I love feeling your response. How could something so generous disgust me?"

Sarah didn't answer. She couldn't. His thumb was rubbing against the coiled knot of her passion.

"Put your leg over my hips," he whispered.

As she moved, she realized that she was opening herself to him. She remembered the gleaming, fearful length of him against the stars.

"Case, I —"

Her voice broke.

His fingers were teasing her deliciously, unbearably, plucking, caressing, probing the depths of her response. Without knowing it, she began to moan.

"Give me your mouth," he whispered.

Blindly she lifted her face to him.

"Now," he said, against her lips, "give it all to me."

His tongue slid into her mouth as his fingers probed the secrets of her body.

Sarah shivered and would have cried out, but her mouth was ruled by Case as surely as her body was. The knowledge sent a shudder of raw emotion through her.

It wasn't fear.

It was a wild freedom that came from a woman's certainty about her man. She knew he would protect her while she was helpless in his arms, just as she had protected him when he lay shivering and spent against her breasts.

Pleasure stabbed through her, arching her like a drawn bow. At the peak of it, Case stroked deeply, increasing the delicious pressure. Then his thumb moved and pleasure shimmered, smoldered, and burst into a fire that ravished her.

He drank her broken cries, muffling them so that none went beyond the blankets they shared. Slowly, reluctantly, he released her silky, sultry core.

She protested in the only way she could, arching her hips toward him.

With a throttled sound he gave her what she was asking for, whether she understood it or not. He pushed his rigid, hungry flesh into her. When he couldn't get enough of her that way, he rolled her onto her back and drew her legs up around him beneath the blankets.

He sank into her completely.

The feel of her all tight and hot around him made his whole body clench with pleasure and an elemental hunger that shocked him. He wanted her more than he ever had before.

Distantly Case knew that he should have been afraid of the fiery, living need consuming him; but as it had been for Sarah, at that moment the lure of ecstasy within their interlocked bodies was greater than any fear.

"I wish I had a big feather bed to lay you on," he said in a low voice. "Are you cold?"

"All I can feel is you."

He looked down at her. Her eyes were closed and her face was taut with what could have been pleasure or pain.

"How do I feel to you?" he whispered.

"Wonderful."

He let out a long breath and reined in the savage urgency of his body.

"Now, so there's no confusion about it," he said, "put your hand between us."

Her eyes opened. Starlight made them a gleaming mystery.

"Go ahead," he whispered. "Do it."

"Like this?" she asked, pushing her hand between their chests.

"Lower."

Her hand moved down to her belly.

"Lower," he urged.

Her hand moved down again. Her eyes widened suddenly, pure silver in the night.

"Yes," he said against her lips. "Every bit of me is inside you. Still scared?"

"Astonished."

She moved experimentally.

Delicious sensations spread up from where he was so deeply lodged inside her.

"We fit," she breathed. "We really fit."

"God, yes."

He bit her lips delicately and was surprised by the quick, broken rush of her breathing. He knew she had found release just moments before. He hadn't expected her to want any more sensual play.

Yet there was no mistaking the instinctive tightening of her body around him.

"I'm going to start moving again if you keep doing that," he whispered.

"Doing what?"

"Stroking me all over, deep inside."

Again Sarah caressed him without moving her hips at all. She shivered at the delicious sensations that cascaded through her with each hidden clenching of her body.

"Like that?" she whispered.

"Just like that."

"But it feels so good to me. I don't want to stop."

"How about this?" he asked.

Case moved his hips sinuously

against her. He barely covered her mouth with his own in time to muffle her surprised, sensual cry. He twisted against her again and again, exciting her even more with each powerful movement of his body.

Her nails scored heedlessly down his back and dug into his flexed hips. It set fire to him more than any tender caress could have, for he was too completely aroused to feel a gentle touch. He had to have something as primitive as the urgency cording his body until sweat glistened over every bit of his skin.

She gave him what he needed, all but fighting him for the embrace, demanding that he give her everything he had in turn.

She had to have it or die.

She would have screamed her need if she could have, but his mouth was joined to hers, enforcing silence. Sweat slicked her body as she fought to get closer and closer to him and to the ecstasy that shimmered just out of reach.

And then it wasn't out of reach. It was all around her, inside her, light and darkness shattering into endless colors.

Yet still he moved against her, driving

into her, feeding the ecstasy until she shivered and wept and gave herself to the blinding, pulsing colors that knew no darkness, only joy.

With a hoarse cry, he gave himself in turn, repeatedly, blindly, knowing only the golden fires of ecstasy burning him all the way to his soul.

It was a long time before either Case or Sarah could speak. They simply held each other hot and close, gentle and fierce, hungry and sated, stripped naked and basking in the searing, tender fires of completion.

"Dear Lord," she whispered finally.

"Amen," he breathed.

He brushed her lips with his own, tasted her, felt her sweet tasting of him in turn.

"You're incredible," he murmured against her mouth. "So damned *alive*."

"It's you, not me."

"No, it's you," he insisted.

She laughed softly.

"We've got the rest of the night to argue about who is burning whom alive," she said.

White flashed briefly against the black of his beard.

"There are certain kinds of, uh, arguments that a man can't do more than once or twice a night," he said.

"Really?"

"God's truth."

She smiled and stretched deliciously against his naked male strength.

"Does that mean I can pet you now and have you fall asleep peacefully in my arms?" she asked.

He nuzzled against her neck, yawned, and rolled onto his side, taking her with him.

"If you like," he said very softly. "For a while."

Just a dream. Just for a while.

A dream, that's all.

Just a dream.

Despite the tears burning against her eyes, Sarah kissed Case's neck, his shoulder, the hard hand that was cradling her cheek. She tasted the salty sleekness of his skin, tested the muscular resilience of his biceps with her teeth, caught the hair on his chest between her lips and pulled.

There was no teasing in her caresses, no seduction, no demand. She simply was experiencing his textures in every way she could. Slowly she worked her way down his big body, turning her face from side to side, smoothing her cheeks over his chest and belly, inhaling the elemental scents of man and woman and completion.

The line of hair that arrowed down from his navel to his groin intrigued her. It tickled her lips in a way that made her smile. She was still smiling when her mouth brushed against firm male flesh that was becoming increasingly familiar.

It was increasing, period.

Her head lifted until she could look at his face. He was watching her with a smoldering intensity that even night couldn't conceal.

"Is this a permanent state with you?" she asked softly, perplexed.

"Never was before."

"Before what?"

"You."

"Oh. Is that . . . good?" she asked.

"I don't know. It's never happened before. But I'm looking forward to finding out."

Sarah put her cheek against him. Her breath sighed out over his swelling arousal.

She kissed him.

Rather distantly Case wondered if he

had died and gone to heaven instead of to the hell he had always assumed awaited him.

The tip of her tongue drew a line of fire over the pulse that beat so heavily in his rigid flesh.

"It's good," he whispered roughly. "It's so damned good I can't believe I'm not dreaming."

"You are, remember?" she asked, tasting him. "Just a dream."

"For a while. Until dawn."

Sarah closed her eyes.

Dawn, when all dreams ended. But until then she could dream a lifetime of dreams, enough to last her until she died.

"Until dawn," she said. Then, so softly that she hoped he couldn't hear, she whispered, "I love you, Case."

Despite her care, he heard the fragile confession. He wanted to protest the pain he knew loving him would cause her.

Yet he couldn't speak.

He couldn't even breathe for the hot, sensuous pressure of her mouth around him.

He stopped trying to speak, to think, to breathe. He simply reached for the golden flame of Sarah the way a dying man reaches for life.

And like life itself she came to him, hot and sweet and generous.

22

Sarah awoke with the warmth of Case surrounding her and his heart beating beneath her cheek. She murmured lazily, snuggled closer, and fell back asleep.

When Case felt the small movements, he was torn between pain and peace.

Pain because he never should have been in her bed.

Peace because he was.

What if she's pregnant?

The question had haunted him throughout the night, keeping him from sleep.

I can't let it happen again.

Even Case didn't know whether he meant making love to Sarah, or feeling responsible for a child's life, or losing that child to death. He knew only that a chilling fear had settled in his gut. It was unlike anything he had ever experienced before, even during the bloodiest of the war.

Concealed by darkness, he had smiled.

Hidden in silence, he had laughed.

Last night he had lost himself in Sarah's generous passion.

Never again, he thought bleakly. *I can't go through it again, the laughter and the loss.*

Sighing, Sarah burrowed closer to him. Her trust kept breaking over Case in waves that were hot and cold, exhilarating and chilling, threatening every certainty he had.

She loves me.

I can't love her.

I'll hurt her.

I can't hurt her.

She loves me.

I can't!

Thoughts circled and swooped, raking Case with a pain that should have made him bleed, but was all the more agonizing because it didn't.

"Sis?" Conner called quietly. "Are you feeling all right?"

Case felt the change that went over Sarah when she heard her brother's voice. The tension of being fully awake shot through her, stiffening her.

"What's wrong?" she called softly.

"The sun is up and you aren't," her brother said. "I thought you might be sick."

"Never felt better."

She yawned, stretched . . . and fully realized for the first time that she was naked beneath the covers.

The look on her face almost made Case smile.

Almost, but not quite. The price of laughter was simply too high.

"Hunter said to let you be, you'd probably had a hard time out here last night," Conner said, "but I was worried."

Case felt the heat of Sarah's blush as clearly as she did.

"Uh, yes, a hard time," she muttered.

When she heard her own words, she blushed even more hotly.

A smile tugged at the corners of his mouth. He fought it to a flat line, but couldn't deny the tenderness that shivered through him when she hid her scarlet face against his chest.

"What was that?" Conner asked. "You sound funny."

She cleared her throat with unnecessary force.

Case opened his mouth, only to have

her small hand clamp right over it.

"I'm just fine," she said distinctly. "Hunter is right. Sleeping out here wasn't as restful as being inside, that's all."

"You'll get used to it," her brother said cheerfully.

She doubted she would ever get used to anything as elemental as Case in her bed, in her body, in her very soul. Heaven at midnight in the full flight of dreaming. Hell at dawn, when all dreams ended.

The eyes of her lover said that dawn had come.

"Go on into the cabin," she said quietly to her brother. "I'll be along in a few minutes to make breakfast."

"Morgan is doing it. Have you seen Case?"

One black eyebrow rose in silent query as he looked at her over her hand. His eyes were shadowed with ghosts and vivid with the life he refused to accept.

"Blazes," Sarah muttered, lifting her hand.

"What?" Conner asked.

"Yes, I've seen Case," she said.

All of him, she thought. *Every bit.*

I tasted him, too.

Lord, I didn't know how bittersweet life could be, heaven and hell and everything in between.

"Where is he?" her brother asked. "I have an idea about spying on the Culpeppers that —"

"Case is right here," she interrupted.

There was a short silence.

"Oh," Conner said. "Uh . . ."

"Yes. Uh . . ." Sarah repeated sardonically. "Now, would you mind letting us wake up in peace?"

"Well, shoot, how was I supposed to know?"

"By using your head for more than a hatrack," she shot back.

"Are you, uh, all right?"

When she heard the combination of love and protectiveness and embarrassment in her brother's voice, her irritation evaporated into affectionate laughter.

"I've never been better," she said.

"Aren't you going to ask after me?" Case said blandly. "Your sister is a mighty fierce woman."

"Case Maxwell, if you weren't too big to paddle, I'd —" she began.

"But I am," he said across her words.

"So you won't. Go on in, Conner. We'll be along shortly."

The boy's laughter came back through the thicket like a second dawn. He was still laughing when the cabin door finally closed behind him.

There was no laughter in Case's eyes.

"Sarah," he began.

"No," she interrupted.

"What?"

"No. Just plain no. Don't ruin it by telling me how you don't love me. I know you don't. I don't need to hear the words."

He closed his eyes, trying to shut out the pain in hers.

And in his own.

"We can't do this again," he said, his voice tight.

"Can't?" She laughed raggedly. "You're as hard and full of life as ever. Don't talk to me about can't."

He could hardly argue the point. He was pulsing against her hip as though he hadn't had a woman in years.

"All right," he said through his teeth. "We must not do this again."

"Why?"

"I could make you pregnant!"

She shivered and shifted her hips

slightly, measuring his readiness.

"No doubt about it," she agreed.

"Then I would have to marry you, and —"

"Why?" she interrupted.

He stared at her as though she had gone mad.

"I'm a rich widow, not a poor virgin," she said matter-of-factly. "Besides, next time I'll use what Lola gave me."

"There won't be a next time."

"Then it's not pregnancy you're really worried about, is it? What's wrong? Didn't you enjoy what we did?"

Case's mouth shut with an audible clicking of teeth.

Even beneath his beard Sarah could see that his jaw muscles were clenched.

"You know damned good and well I liked it," he said through his teeth. "Hell, I more than liked it. It's the best I ever had."

Or ever will have, he acknowledged bitterly to himself.

"Then there's no problem." She smiled brightly at him. "Come on, lazy man. Let's go see what kind of cook Morgan is. Unless you'd rather see if we get better with practice . . . ?"

With a muttered curse Case shot out

of bed. He dressed quickly in the cold air. His speed was helped by the fact that admiring gray eyes were memorizing every inch of him.

"Get dressed," he said.

"I can't find my drawers or chemise. What did you do with them?"

He looked around with something close to desperation. Her chemise peeked out from the foot of the bedroll. Her drawers were dangling from a low branch of sage, flung there by a hand that had had better things to do than worry about tomorrow.

While he gathered her underwear, he remembered peeling off soft, warm muslin and finding ever softer, hotter flesh beneath. Hastily he tossed the garments in the general direction of the top of the bedroll.

A naked, elegantly feminine arm came out from under the covers and dragged the underwear beneath, where it was warm.

Warm, hell, Case thought. *She's a fire in winter. I'll die remembering what it was like to sink into her.*

Salt and sweet, all woman, hot honey on my tongue, on my body. Winter fire burning just for me.

A shudder of raw hunger went through Case. It was all he could do to stuff his unruly flesh into his pants.

"Need some help?" Sarah asked.

Humor and admiration and memories ran through her husky voice like heat through flames.

"I've been dressing myself for some years now," he said roughly.

"How about helping me? I'm just a beginner."

The sensual teasing in her voice made his blood run even hotter.

"So was Eve," he muttered, "but she learned quick enough."

Case looked up in time to see his words quench the laughter in her eyes.

"Sarah," he began.

This time she didn't interrupt. She simply disappeared. The blankets seethed and rippled as she dressed beneath them. Very quickly she emerged fully dressed but for her boots.

"In the interests of keeping Conner from knowing how much you dislike me," she said evenly, "could you try to be civil to me in front of him?"

"I don't dislike you."

"Fine." She yanked on her right boot.

"Then being civil to me shouldn't be a problem."

Her tone of voice told Case that she didn't believe a word he had said about not disliking her.

"Men don't spend nights like that with women they dislike," he said tightly.

"Of course."

She jammed her left foot into the other boot and stood up quickly.

"Damnation, listen to me!" he snarled.

Cool gray eyes cut over to him.

"I'm not only listening to you, I'm agreeing with you," she pointed out.

"But you don't mean it."

Cinnamon eyebrows arched in two elegant, disbelieving curves.

"If you say so," she murmured.

"What?"

"I'm being agreeable. You should try it. Just for the practice, of course. I won't expect it when Conner isn't around."

Case took a grip on his temper. Then he took a deep breath and another, tighter grip.

She was like nettles under his skin.

Rather distantly he wondered where

his usual discipline had gone.

Memories of taking Sarah and being taken in turn went through him like hot black lightning, telling him just what had happened to his self-control.

I never should have done it.

But he had. Now he would spend the rest of his life regretting it. Winter seemed so much colder when he knew that there was a fire burning just for him.

Just beyond reach.

It must stay that way.

Beyond reach.

"Have you seen Conner?" Ute asked.

Surprised, Sarah turned from the pot of beans that was bubbling over the fire. She had just finished slicing one of her hoarded onions into the pot, along with several of Ute's lethal green chilies.

She hoped they would burn Case's mouth.

What am I complaining about? she asked herself wryly. *This morning I asked him to be civil to me, and by God, he has been.*

He's been so civil he makes my back teeth ache.

And so distant.

She sighed and resumed stirring the beans.

Ute cleared his throat.

Sarah jumped. She had forgotten that he was there, waiting for an answer.

"I haven't seen Conner since breakfast," she said, hoping her blush would pass unnoticed. "Why?"

At least Conner didn't tease me about Case. Other than a grin that split his smug face, of course.

Saying nothing, Ute looked at the pattern of sunlight cast across the dirt floor by random holes in the chinking. The light was a rich, buttery yellow.

Late-afternoon light.

"Breakfast, huh?" he asked.

"What's wrong?" she asked sharply.

He shrugged, but she wasn't fooled. She had become very good at reading the older man's weathered, falsely angelic face.

"Ute," she said.

She didn't have to say any more.

"He was due up on the rim two hours ago. When I didn't come in, Lola come along to see what's what. She's up there now, taking Conner's turn so I can rest and eat."

Frowning, Sarah gave the beans a

531

final stir and added a stick of wood to the fire.

"Maybe he's with Case," she said. "They've been doing a lot of six-gun work together."

"I looked. Ain't there."

Uneasiness rippled through her.

"It's not like Conner to miss his watch," she said.

"Yep. That's what I'm thinking."

"Where is Case?"

"With his brother, planning ways to bury Culpeppers."

"What about Morgan?"

"Spying on Culpeppers."

Silently she added another piece of wood to the fire and watched the flames bite into the branch. She wiped her hands on her flour-sack apron.

"I'll look for him," she said.

"Figured you would."

"Is someone watching Lola's goats?"

"Ghost."

"Hope he doesn't lose that black and white one again," she muttered.

Ute paused on his way out the door.

"Weren't the dog's doing," he said. "That she-goat is plumb contrary. Minute Ghost chases one herd quitter, she high-tails it in the other direction."

"You always stand up for that dog."

"Been a stray myself. Hard life."

The door shut behind him.

Instantly Sarah's expression changed, showing every bit of the fear she felt. She had just remembered what her brother had said that morning.

I have an idea about spying on the Culpeppers.

"Conner," she whispered. "You weren't foolish enough to go alone, were you?"

With a tight movement she yanked off her apron and hung it on a nail.

"Morgan is watching the Culpeppers," she told herself aloud. "He won't let Conner do anything foolish."

The words seemed to echo in the room.

Conner.

Foolish.

She ran outside. The door banged behind her. She didn't notice the bite of the wind or the sting of tiny snowflakes whipping across her face.

"Conner?" Sarah called. "Where are you?"

Blindly she ran toward the clump of tall sage where her brother had set up his camp.

"Conner? Conner!"

The wind brought her cries back to her, mocking her as she had been mocked once before, when she called out to the darkness and flood for her younger brother.

I found him then.

I'll find him now.

His camp was empty, but his saddle was still there, still waiting to be used as a pillow.

"Conner! Answer me!"

Nothing answered but the wind.

Strands of hair ripped loose by the wind lashed across her face. She caught the hair and hung on to it, twisting it through her fingers like a lifeline.

"Not now," she said. "Not when I've finally found the silver for you! Where are you? Conner! *Conner!*"

She was still calling her brother's name when Case spun her around and wrapped her in his arms. Hard.

"Easy, honey. Easy. Get hold of yourself and tell me what's wrong."

Only when his gentle, velvet voice penetrated her fear did Sarah realize that she was screaming her brother's name again and again.

"Is Conner with you?" she asked hoarsely.

"He's up on the rim."

"Are you certain? Did you see him up there?"

"No, but he knows when it's his turn to stand watch."

"He didn't go."

"What?"

"Lola is on watch. Conner never showed up."

Case turned and looked over his shoulder.

"Hunter?" he asked.

"Haven't seen him," Hunter said.

"Morgan, what about you?" Case asked.

"No, suh. Nary hide nor hair."

"Morgan!" Sarah said.

She jerked herself free of Case's arms and turned to face the black gunfighter.

"Why aren't you spying on the Culpeppers?" she accused. "You're supposed to be there!"

Warily Morgan glanced at Case.

He was looking at Sarah as though she were a stranger.

"Take it easy, honey," he said. "Morgan is following Hunter's orders."

She closed her eyes as though to shut out everyone, especially Case.

"Did he talk with you about spying

on the Culpeppers?" she asked tightly.

"Conner?" Case asked.

It took every bit of her self-control not to scream at him that of course she was talking about her brother.

"Yes," she said in an unnaturally calm voice. "He's the only one missing, correct?"

Case looked at her as warily as Morgan had.

"If you say so," he said carefully, "then Conner is missing."

"I say so."

The bleakness in her eyes made him want to hold her again.

"This morning . . ." she said. Her voice went from hoarse to silent. "This morning, Conner said he had an idea about spying on the Culpeppers."

Morgan said something scalding under his breath.

Hunter's mouth flattened into a grim line.

"Go on," Case said.

"There's nowhere to go," she said. "Conner had an idea and now he's gone."

"Morgan," Hunter began.

"I'm on my way."

"I'll go with you," Case said.

"So will I," Sarah said.

Both men turned to argue.

Three quick shots from the rim cut off whatever the men were going to say. There was a pause, then a fourth shot.

"Company," Case said tersely.

"Just one," she said.

"Just one showing," Hunter countered. "Case, stay with her. Morgan, come with me."

"Ute will take the cottonwoods," Sarah said. "He always does when Conner is gone."

Hunter nodded. He and Morgan left for the brush behind the house at a trot, weapons in hand.

"Don't worry," Case said. "Hunter won't let us be outflanked."

"I hope Lola doesn't shoot them by mistake."

"She'll never even see them."

Shivering, Sarah said nothing.

"Where's your jacket?" Case asked.

"In the house."

"Of all the fool places for it to be," he muttered, peeling off his own jacket and holding it out to her.

She was already heading for the cabin at a run.

He suspected it wasn't the jacket she

was worried about, but her shotgun.

He was right.

When she reappeared a moment later, there was a shotgun in her hands. She was wearing her jacket more as a means of carrying extra cartridges than for warmth. The pockets bulged with ammunition.

"Don't show yourself," Case said.

"But —"

Sarah's words were cut off as he dragged her into the cover provided by brush and boulders.

"You won't do Conner any good dead," he said curtly.

Case pulled out his spyglass and began watching the trail down from the rim. In tense silence she waited.

"It's Ab," he said.

"Alone?"

"As far as I can see."

A prickle of unease went over Sarah's spine. There was something in Case's voice that made her cold. She searched his face, but saw nothing.

Then he lowered the spyglass and turned toward her. His eyes were as empty as death.

"He has Conner's hat."

All color left her face. She swayed as

though she had been struck.

He reached for her, only to have her push his hand away sharply.

"I'm all right," she said.

Her voice was as empty as his eyes.

"Likely your brother is still alive," Case said neutrally, "or else Ab wouldn't parade in here alone with his hat."

A shuddering, sawing breath was her only answer.

"Let me talk to Ab," he said.

She hesitated, then nodded.

"Stay out of sight," he added. "Ab can be . . . unreasonable . . . when women or kids are around."

Sarah made a harsh sound that could have been a laugh.

"Unreasonable," she said bitterly. "That's like describing hell as a passably warm place."

"I'll stand where you can cover Ab without shooting through me."

"Stay close enough that I can hear."

It wasn't a request. He knew he could stay close or she would follow him and to hell with her own safety.

He didn't blame her. If it had been Hunter whose hat was in Ab's hands, Case would have done the same.

Swiftly he made a diagonal path through the brush to a place where Ab would pass close by on his way to the cabin. He loaded both barrels of the shotgun, cocked it, and waited with the patience of death.

Ab made no attempt to hide himself. He rode brazenly down the trail, holding Conner's hat like a shield in front of him.

And it was.

No one would touch Ab until Conner's fate was known.

Nothing has changed, Case thought bleakly. *Peace or war, vultures still follow the Culpeppers.*

Conner isn't their first hostage.

But by God he will be their last.

"That's far enough," Case said. "State your business."

Ab took his time about stopping the mule. His pale blue eyes searched every bit of cover. He couldn't see the man behind the voice.

"You ain't very neighborly," Ab said.

"Keep it in mind."

With deliberate movements, Ab pulled a plug of tobacco from his pocket, gnawed off a hunk, and began chewing.

Case waited.

By the time Ab was halfway through his chaw, it was clear that Case wasn't going to start any conversations or make any foolish moves.

"All right," Ab said. "I got her brother. I want her silver. We'll swap even up."

"What makes you think Mrs. Kennedy has any silver?"

"Been following you. Dug every hole you dug. Empty." Ab spat into the dirt. "The last time I backtracked you, your horses' hooves cut deep. Been searching real hard, but you musta got it all. Them holes is as empty as a grave waiting for a burying."

Case wasn't surprised by Ab's words. He had guessed what the raider wanted from the moment he saw Conner's hat.

"We give you the silver, we get Conner back alive, and every last one of you sons of bitches hits the trail for California," Case said neutrally. "Deal?"

Wind combed through the brush, rattling dry branches. It was the only sound for a time.

"She brings the silver," Ab said finally.

"No."

Silence and wind moved through the brush.

"Guess that boy's a goner," Ab said indifferently.

"He dies, you die."

"No!" Sarah called from the brush. "I'll bring the silver to you!"

Case hissed something savage.

"I'll bring the silver or there's no deal," he said to Ab.

"What makes you think I'd cotton to you more than to a lively little gal?" Ab mocked.

"I'm one of those Texicans you worry about."

Ab went real still.

"Any particular part of Texas?" he asked.

"Heaven Valley."

Ab grunted and his lean face flattened even more.

"Thought so," he said. "Mind showin' yourself? Your voice is kinda familiar like."

"It should be. You thought I worked for you in the Ruby Mountains."

The lean mule jumped as though it had been stuck with a needle.

"You murdered my kin," Ab said savagely.

"I killed them," Case said. "There's a difference."

"Dead is dead."

"Your kin were men and they were armed. They had a choice. That's more than you ever gave our children or women."

Ab looked to the place in the brush where Sarah's voice had come.

"He can carry the silver for you," Ab said to her. "Bring it at dawn to our camp."

"She stays here," Case said flatly.

"Her choice." Ab grinned and spat again. "But I think the gal wants to see her brother alive."

"I'll go," Sarah called.

Case didn't think so, but he kept his mouth shut.

"Dawn," Ab said.

With a sharp movement, he reined his mule around.

"Ab?" Case said softly.

The quality of his voice froze the other man in place. Mule and man looked warily back at the brush.

"If Conner is hurt," Case said, "everything you did to him will be done to you. And then we'll hang you."

23

"Damnation, woman, will you listen to reason?" Case asked loudly.

"Say something reasonable and I'll listen," Sarah retorted.

"Stay home."

"And get Conner killed? If that's your idea of reason, it's a wonder even your horse listens to you!"

Ute, Morgan, and Hunter were outside the cabin, but that didn't mean they couldn't hear every word. They shifted their feet uncomfortably and tried not to listen to the man and woman who were standing nose to nose inside the cabin and hollering as though they were across the yard from each other.

Lola just grinned and kept on carding the wool she had gathered from the black and white goat.

"A sawbuck says she goes," Lola said to no one in particular.

Ute grunted and shook his head, refusing the bet.

"Boys?" Lola invited.

Morgan and Hunter looked at each other. Neither one accepted her offer to wager ten dollars on the outcome of the argument.

Lola spit an arc of tobacco juice, chuckled, shifted her legs on the cold ground, and kept on carding wool for Sarah to spin as soon as she quit arguing. The basket in Lola's lap was rapidly filling with a mound of clean, combed wool.

"That boy done met his match," she said after a time. "He just don't know it yet. But he'll settle to it."

"Don't bet any money on the long run," Hunter said quietly. "The war changed Case. Cold where he was hot. Silence instead of laughter. Have you ever seen him smile?"

Lola looked thoughtful, then shook her head.

"Some men don't have no sense of fun," she said, shrugging.

Hunter smiled sadly. "Case had enough play in him for a sack full of puppies. The war burned that out of him, too."

"She's going to Spring Canyon," Lola said.

"Ute could keep her here," Morgan said.

The old outlaw's smile was even sadder than Hunter's had been. He shook his head.

"Man that keeps her here better never turn his back on her again," Ute said simply.

"All right. I'll do it," Morgan said.

For a moment Ute looked thoughtful. Then he shook his head.

"I'll fight you," he said.

"For the love of God," Hunter muttered. "Why?"

"She wants something. I fetch it for her."

"Well," drawled Morgan, "that explains the blooded bull mixed in with the range cows."

The old outlaw grinned. "Followed me home, he did."

"I'll bet," Hunter said dryly. "Same for the better bred horses, too."

"And half the supplies and the tools and every other thing around here that needs cash on the barrelhead," Lola said. "Sarah cottoned onto the rustling and made Ute stop, but she ain't figured out the supplies yet."

Lola stopped carding wool and looked

up at Hunter with clear black eyes.

"Don't waste no time trying to talk sense into Ute about that girl," she said evenly. "He's plumb loco on the subject. Better bend your mind as to how best to use him to keep her alive."

"I've got an idea about that," Hunter said. "If Ab thinks Sarah is bringing the silver, that's as good as having her go."

Morgan looked at Hunter, glanced over at the short, wiry old outlaw, and smiled widely.

It took Ute a few moments longer. His eyes widened. Then he laughed.

Lola spat a dark brown arc.

"Wondered how long it would take you men to get around to seeing what's plain as the nose on your face," she said.

"Will you do it?" Hunter asked Ute bluntly. "Or will you fight us?"

"I'll do it, if'n she'll let me."

Hunter cocked his head toward the suddenly silent cabin.

"Do you suppose my brother has worn her down enough to listen to common sense?" he asked.

Lola snorted. "Men. Ain't a lick of common sense in the lot of you. That gal in there is one hell of a lot tougher than she looks."

Hunter's smile warmed his slate-gray eyes. He gave Lola an amused look and tipped his hat in acknowledgment.

"I've discovered that some women are indeed stronger than they look," he said.

"His wife taught him," Morgan added slyly.

"It wasn't an easy lesson, for either of us," Hunter admitted.

Lola spat another arc of tobacco juice and gathered up the wool she had just carded.

"Easy ain't worth a tinker's damn," she said, standing up. "Easy folds when you need it most. Ain't one bit of easy in Sarah."

"Or in Case," Hunter said.

"Like I said. Good match. Mettlesome, mind you, but good."

Silence continued to radiate from the cabin.

"Which one of you brave boys wants to take this here wool in to her?" Lola asked blandly.

"No, ma'am," Morgan muttered.

Ute grunted and kept his thumbs firmly hooked on his belt.

Hunter held out his hand.

Chuckling, Lola gave him the basket of wool.

"She don't bite," the old woman said. "Leastwise, not hard enough to leave scars."

He tipped his hat again, then turned to Morgan.

"Find out if Conner is still alive," Hunter said. "Ab has a reputation for killing prisoners."

"If he's alive, I'll try to get him out."

"Not unless you're sure of doing it without getting either one of you killed. We stand a better chance together than apart."

Morgan hesitated, then nodded.

"Slow and easy," he agreed. "I'll be quiet as a shadow."

"Be back two hours before dawn."

"What if Conner is dead?" Morgan asked.

"Get back on the run."

"Mind if I cut some throats on the way?" he asked.

"Just get back in one piece."

"Burn them out," Ute said. "Only two ways out of Spring Canyon. Two men on the rim at each end. Easy as shooting tin cans."

Morgan nodded, liking the idea.

"The Culpeppers burned out a lot of folks," he said. "Tried it on us up in the Rubys. Live by the sword and die the same way. It's about time those boys did their dying."

"Two hours before dawn," Hunter said. "Get moving."

Without another word he turned away, strode to the cabin and knocked on the door.

"It's Hunter," he said. "I've got some wool for Sarah."

"The door is open. Do come in."

He sighed. Her voice had an edge that could slice bacon thin enough to read newsprint through. He opened the door, ducked to accommodate his tall frame to the low doorway, and went into the cabin.

Sarah was stirring beans as though life itself depended on keeping the bottom of the pan scraped.

Case was watching her.

The look in his eyes surprised Hunter. He hadn't seen that kind of seething, unsettled emotion in his brother for years.

"Where do you want the wool?" Hunter asked.

"Away from the fire," she said tersely. Then, belatedly, "Thank you."

He set the basket in a corner of the cabin and turned to look at the man and woman whose frustration and anger were thick enough to touch.

He cleared his throat.

"We have a plan," he said.

"It damned well better include me," she said flatly.

"It damned well better not," Case snarled.

"You both get your wish."

As one, Sarah and Case turned toward Hunter. The wary hope and fierce determination in her eyes reminded Hunter of the woman he loved.

"You've never met my wife," he said to Sarah. "I hope you do someday. You're both cut from the same honest, stubborn cloth."

She smiled wearily. "Someday. If we all survive tomorrow's dawn."

"You will," Case said, "if it's the last thing I do."

"I'm going."

"You're stay—"

"Excuse me," Hunter interrupted. "Time is wasting and we have a lot of planning to do."

"You better plan on her staying here," Case said.

"Think," his brother said. "The instant Ab knows that she isn't along, Conner dies."

Case looked at Sarah, plainly wishing she weren't listening. But she was, and she wasn't going to leave.

"Conner may already be dead," he said flatly.

Her breath came in hard and stayed, threatening to strangle her. She didn't want to think about Conner's death.

Yet it was impossible for her to think about anything else. That was why she had lashed out at Case and everything else within reach.

"I sent Morgan to find out," Hunter said.

"I should have gone," Case said.

"Why? He's as good as you on the stalk."

"I could have lowered the odds while I was looking around."

"So will Morgan, if Conner is dead."

Sarah made a low sound of protest.

"Ab won't kill Conner until he has the silver," she said.

"Likely not," Hunter said.

"But once he has the silver," Case

said, "he'll kill everything he can, burn the rest, and run."

"It's what the Culpeppers are best at, raping and killing and running," Hunter agreed.

"I'm afraid for my brother," she said starkly.

"You have reason. But he's too big and too strong to bring out the worst in Ab," Hunter said simply. "Conner is much more a man than a child."

Sarah closed her eyes and tried to breathe. When Case gathered her in his arms, she didn't fight him. She simply held on to him and prayed that her brother was alive.

Case stroked her hair and held her in return, wishing all the way to his soul that he could give her back her brother.

"If Conner is dead . . ." he said to Hunter.

His brother nodded grimly.

"Otherwise, this is what we're planning," Hunter said.

Sarah lifted her head.

"It better include me," she said.

Hunter started talking before Case could start arguing.

Sarah watched the fire in the hearth

with eyes turned gold by the flames. She had moved back into the cabin, for the need to hide herself and the silver was gone.

It was long past her normal bedtime, but she knew that sleep wouldn't come to her tonight.

The whisper of flames and her spinning were the only sounds in the cabin.

Firelight ran in streaks of brightness over the moving spindle and the motionless barrels of the shotgun that lay within reach on the table. Her jacket hung on the other chair, its pockets bulging with cartridges.

She tried not to think about anything at all but keeping the fire burning throughout the night.

So little heat. So much cold.

"Sarah?"

The soft voice made her jump, but she didn't reach for the shotgun.

"Come in," she said quietly.

The door opened and closed. Case loomed out of the darkness. As he walked toward the fire, light and shadow slid across his body like a lover's hands.

"I smelled smoke," he said, "so I knew you were awake."

"The fire . . . comforts me."

"Morgan just came back."

Sarah's heart turned over. She looked at Case as though will alone could bring the answer she wanted.

"Your brother is alive," Case said quickly. "Chewed up some, but otherwise fine."

The relief was so great that she slumped toward the fire.

With a swift motion he lifted her and carried her to her bed. Gently he put her on the pallet and began rubbing her cold hands.

"I'm all right," she said.

"Uh huh," he said, not convinced.

"Truly."

She gave a deep, shuddering sigh. Color slowly returned to her face.

"Stop worrying about dawn," he said.

A fragmented laugh was her only answer.

He whispered her name and pulled her into his arms again. He held her, comforting both of them.

"Conner will come back to you alive," Case said. "I swear it."

"B-but —"

"Hush," he whispered. "Morgan is already headed back to Spring Canyon. He thinks he can get in close enough to protect Conner."

Or try to, Case thought grimly, but it wasn't something he wanted to say aloud.

From what Morgan had said, Conner was staked out like a goat waiting for a hungry tiger.

Sarah took a broken breath, then another.

"They won't expect us to be up on the rim with the sun behind us," he said calmly. "Lola and Ute are working on the *reales* like you asked, though I'm damned if I know why you want them polished."

She nodded, but she didn't look directly at Case.

"If you don't sleep, you won't be any good to us tomorrow," he said. "We're counting on you and Lola to cover our retreat."

At least, that's what we want you to think, he added silently. *What we really care about is having you out of the line of fire.*

Again, Sarah nodded.

Again, she didn't meet his eyes.

"Say something," Case coaxed. "Lord

knows you were talkative enough earlier."

"What is there to say?" she whispered.

He looked at her pale lips and knew she was right. Talking about tomorrow would only make the wait longer.

"If you get pregnant, go to the Ruby Mountains," he said. "Hunter will see that you and the baby have a good home."

She didn't answer. She couldn't. Before she even absorbed the fact that he didn't expect to survive past dawn, his mouth was over hers, sealing in any words or arguments she might have.

After the first taste of him, she didn't fight the sensual oblivion he was offering. She reached for him with an urgency that equaled his. Even as he struggled with her clothes, she was removing his.

For every kiss she gave, she received two. For every caress, a greater intimacy. When his fingers probed between her thighs, he found her hot, soft, honeyed with passion. He entered her in a single thrust that made her cry out with a pleasure so great it was nearly pain.

"Sarah?"

"Don't stop." Her nails dug into his hips. "Don't ever stop."

He groaned and began measuring the depths of their mutual passion with each thrust of his body. Hunger consumed his control with a thousand licking fires.

"Next time," he said huskily, thrusting into her. "Next time — I'll be slow. So damned — *slow.*"

A sound clawed free from her throat. Her back arched and her hands clenched on his hips as she convulsed beneath him. He swallowed her cry and his own husky shout as he poured himself into her, giving himself to her in the only way he could.

It wasn't enough. He didn't know if anything could ever be enough.

He had to have her.

He had to *become* her.

"Sarah?" he whispered.

And then he moved deeply.

"Yes," she whispered brokenly.

Each time he moved she called his name. He answered with all the hunger in him until she was shivering again, burning again, consumed again.

He drank her ecstasy and kept rocking against her, driving her higher and higher, going with her, holding back winter's dawn until there were no more words, no more questions, nothing but the elemental union of woman and man.

She came to him like fire, and like fire she burned, consuming the winter that surrounded them.

Whipped by a cold wind, Sarah watched Ute and Case ride away into the seamless darkness. Hunter had already gone ahead into the night. He would take up a position that would let him cover Case's retreat.

If there is one, Sarah thought. Then, quickly, *He's still alive. Don't think any other away. He's alive!*

A thin sheet of wind-packed snow crunched beneath the feet of two pack horses. Their hooves bit through snow and cut deeply into the dry soil beneath.

Rocks, she thought, looking at the bulging packs. *Only rocks, except for one of the bags.*

Just like a salted mine.

Her own saddlebags were fat with silver. The newly polished *reales* would shine like pieces of heaven in the dawn.

Along with provisions for a hard ride, the remaining bars of silver bullion were divided among six mustangs. The women would ride two other horses.

Sarah didn't want to think about why they were setting off into the darkest part of the night, carrying everything that they needed to survive and build a new life; but Case's last words to her kept echoing in her mind.

If we don't come back, you two run for the Ruby Mountains. Elyssa and the baby will need some of that silver.

In the end, Sarah had agreed even as she refused to accept the underlying meaning of his words.

She couldn't imagine a world without Conner.

Without Case.

Shivering, she wrapped Ute's jacket around herself. The smell of stale tobacco, sweat, goats, and years of campfires surrounded her.

Case smelled of apples that night, she thought. *My God, it seems like a thousand years ago.*

"You awake, gal?"

Sarah turned to Lola. "I'm awake."

"You looked like you was dreaming."

"Just remembering . . . Case smelled

of apples the first time I met him."

The other woman laughed.

"Ute smelled like gunsmoke, whiskey, and horseshit," Lola said. "He was sitting in a pile of road apples, skunk-drunk and shooting at flies. Lordy, lordy, that was a long time ago."

Despite her fears, Sarah smiled.

"Lot of years I been with that man," Lola said. "Lot of years. Too many to let him go and get killed by hisself."

Starlight turned the older woman's eyes into glittering black stone.

"You take them four ponies and run for Nevada right now," she said to Sarah. "If there's need, someone can catch up to you quick enough and bring you back."

"No."

"Listen, gal, you —"

"No," Sarah interrupted calmly.

Lola sighed and bit off a chunk of tobacco.

"Any chance of changing your mind?" she asked.

"No."

For a time Lola chewed reflectively on the wad of tobacco. Then she spat through a gap in her teeth.

"I suppose you got a plan," she said.

"I know Spring Canyon better than anyone."

Lola grunted.

"Ab Culpepper might be mean as a snake, but he isn't blind," Sarah said. "He won't be fooled by Ute for long."

"Don't have to be. Bullets ain't slow."

"Flesh is," she retorted. "Come on. We don't have much time."

Quickly Sarah mounted Shaker.

Swearing through her mouthful of tobacco, Lola climbed aboard her mount. The chunky mustang looked like it was part plow horse.

"What about them pack animals?" Lola asked.

"Bring them. I have a plan for that bullion."

"That's what I feared. Fool things, plans."

It was Lola's last complaint. Without another word she followed the trail through cold darkness and even colder moonlight.

Sarah didn't feel much like talking herself. The closer she got to Spring Canyon, the more foolish her plan seemed. The only part she was certain of was that her destination was nearer than the east rim of the canyon, where the men were going.

No matter how foolish, anything is better than wringing my hands and waiting to see if Conner and Case are alive, she told herself firmly.

Besides, they need me. No one else can reach that part of the canyon. From there I can shoot right down into the camp.

I can make the difference between living and dying for Conner.

For Case.

It's not a foolish plan. Not really. Not when you think about it from all directions.

She kept telling herself that as Shaker began the climb out of the canyon up onto the large, windswept plateau. Lost River had eaten through the plateau's solid stone to create the valley where grass and willows and cottonwoods thrived. Lost River Valley was the biggest canyon that water had gouged from the body of the plateau, but not the only one. There were hundreds of other, smaller side canyons.

Spring Canyon was one of them.

Before the raiders came, the canyon had been Sarah's refuge, a place of mystery and peace and dreams. She had gone to it many, many times. Along the canyon's south-facing wall there were ruins in a large alcove fifteen feet below the lip of the sheer stone cliff. The ancient rooms were slowly, silently dissolving back into time and dust. Only a few handmade stone walls stood as crumbling ramparts against an enemy long dead.

Twenty feet farther down the sheer cliff were the springs that had allowed the ancient tribe to build their fortress. Ten feet below the mossy crack where stone wept cool, sweet water, the outlaws had set up their camp.

Sarah never hesitated on the way to the ruins. Many times she and Conner had hidden among the ancient rooms when Hal had gone on a drunken frenzy, lashing out at everything in sight.

No matter how hard her husband hunted her, he had never found her. Though slender for a man, he still had been too thick to squeeze through the hidden passage she had discovered leading from the plateau top down to the ruins.

Conner is too big now, she thought. *I'm the only one who can fit in that crack.*

There was no other way into the ruins except to climb down on a rope from the top. Hal had done that once, looking for silver. He found nothing but dust and broken pottery.

Without hesitation Sarah reined her mustang onto a trail she hadn't used since Hal's death. This particular route up the plateau was too steep, too dangerous, to take under normal circumstances.

Especially at night.

But night was when Hal went crazy. Night was when the fastest way to get to a safe place was worth any risk.

"Gal, where'n hell you going?" Lola asked.

"Up on the plateau, then over to the rim of Spring Canyon."

"You're plumb loco."

Sarah didn't disagree. "Stay here, then."

"Like fiery hell I will."

The mustangs were blowing hard by the time they scrambled up the last steep pitch that led to the top of the plateau. No ranch-raised horse could have made the climb. Only an animal that had grown up running wild through the steep canyons had the uncanny sense of balance and hard hooves to stay with the trail.

The wind whipped and snarled around them like a living thing, howling its strength.

"Lola? You still here?" Sarah called.

"I ain't never speaking to you again, gal."

"Promise?"

"Shee-it."

"Can you see that notch?" Sarah asked.

Her arm made a solid black pointer against the stars and moonlight.

Lola grunted.

"That's the start of an old foot trail to the springs," Sarah said. "It's not wide enough for a horse."

A stream of tobacco juice landed on the wind-scoured rock. It was Lola's only comment.

"You don't have to go," Sarah said.

The old woman hissed a word and waited.

"About a quarter-mile down," Sarah said, "there's a place where a man can look out over the canyon. If I were Ab or Moody, I'd have a guard there."

Lola grunted.

"Take a pocket full of silver," Sarah

continued. "If you find a guard, tell him you've stolen the rest and want his help."

"Lead is cheaper."

"Noisier, too."

"Long as it's done quiet like, you care what happens to that son of a bitch, supposing he's there?" Lola asked.

"No. I just don't want anyone firing across the canyon at Case and Ute."

"I'll be quiet as a knife."

Sarah reined her horse closer, gave the other woman a hug, and said, "Thank you."

"Hell, gal. No need. My man's tail is stuck in the same crack as yours."

But Lola hugged her hard in turn before she dismounted and set off for the notch.

After an anxious look at the eastern sky, Sarah sent her mustang at a trot toward the hidden trail down to the ruins.

The land dipped where runoff water collected before it raced down and over the cliff in a seasonal waterfall. Now only a ragged veil of snow lay in the dip. Wind had peeled the land down to bare rock bones.

The same wind went through Sarah's

jacket as though the wool was little more than muslin. Shivering without realizing it, she dismounted and unfastened the saddlebags. They hit the ground with a thump and jingle.

Wind overwhelmed the sound and swept it behind her, away from the canyon, burying everything in a howling kind of silence. The wind would do the same for any noise short of that made by gunfire.

She glanced at the sky again. Her stomach clenched.

The eastern horizon was a lighter shade of black.

Hurry!

Teeth set against the cold, she half-carried and half-dragged the saddle-bags down the runoff channel. Moving in the dark over rough land with the heavy saddlebags took so long that she wanted to scream with frustration.

Then the land dipped steeply beneath her feet. She gave up trying to control the bags and simply let them bump and tumble in her wake. More quickly than she had expected, less quickly than she had hoped, she found herself in a narrow crevice that rapidly deepened until it rose over her head, all but shutting out the stars.

Without the wind, the sound of her own panting seemed loud enough to raise the dead. She looked up only once, just long enough to tell her that time was running out for her. The faintest of the stars directly overhead were already fading.

The men will be on the other rim soon. Hurry!

Panting, yanking at the stubborn saddlebags, trying to keep her shotgun and rifle from banging against the stone that was closing in on either side, Sarah fought for every inch of progress she made. None would have been possible but for the long dead hands that had chiseled parts of the passage from solid stone, and the footsteps that had worn sharp edges into smooth ripples.

Just a few more feet.

Sweat ran down between her breasts as she jerked and heaved, yanking the saddlebags of silver closer and closer to the entrance of the ruins.

Forerunners of daybreak spread across the sky in shades of pale yellow and faint peach. Night began to slide down the sides of the plateau and gather in the canyon bottom.

But there was no place to hide from the sun. Even the canyon floor would know the weightless caress of light.

Tumbled by the wind, voices drifted up from the canyon floor forty feet below the east rim.

Angry voices.

"Dammit, it's dawn and I don't see no silver, dammit. Don't see no woman, neither, dammit."

Moody's complaint was echoed by several other men.

"No sun," Kester said.

"Dammit, Ab told me dawn, not daybreak, dammit! I say kill the kid and go after the silver."

A ragged chorus of agreement came from Moody's men.

"No sun, no dawn," Kester said.

"Dam—"

"No dawn," Kester interrupted.

The fact that he was holding a shotgun meant more than any logic. Moody and his men subsided into curses that grew louder as the sky grew brighter.

Case and Ute merged their outlines with the piñon growing near the east rim of the canyon. Behind them, dawn was spreading tongues of red and gold over the wild, windswept land at the top of the plateau.

"Them boys is getting short of patience," Ute muttered.

Case glanced to the east. The sun wasn't above the edge of the plateau yet.

"They'll have to wait," he said.

"Is Ab still in them willows with Conner, just beneath the spring?"

Case nodded.

"You see Morgan?" Ute asked after a time.

"No. But he's down there. Somewhere."

"Hunter?"

"He's on the south rim, at that lookout you told him about."

Ute grunted. "Probably a guard there."

"Probably was. Now Hunter is there."

The old outlaw chuckled.

Silently, inevitably, the burning arc of the sun ate through darkness at the eastern rim of the canyon. As the arc swelled into a half-circle, Case stepped out of the shadows into the shaft of light. The heavy saddlebags hanging from his shoulders transformed his long shadow into that of a black angel sweeping across the canyon.

"Look!" called one of the men below. "Up on the east rim!"

"Ab!" Kester called.

"I see him!"

Another, smaller shadow appeared beside Case. The hat and jacket belonged to Sarah. The rest, including the badly braided hair jammed beneath the hat, belonged to Ute.

"We're here," Case called. "Let the boy go."

Weapons lifted to cover the two people on the canyon rim.

"We've got men with rifles along the rim," Case said. "You start shooting and there won't be anyone left to bury the dead."

Kester melted back into the brush. So did another long, lean Culpepper.

"Them Culpeppers is real coyotes," Ute muttered.

Moody's men didn't even notice that they were now alone, exposed to rifle fire. Their eyes saw only the saddlebags hanging over Case's shoulders.

"Lower your rifles, boys," Ab called. "Time enough to sort things out later."

A curt order from Moody sent the rifle barrels pointing slightly away from the east rim.

"Let's see that silver," Ab yelled from the willows.

"Not until I'm sure Conner is walking and talking," Case said. *"Let him go."*

After a few moments Conner stumbled forward out of the willows. He was moving his arms and legs as though they were stiff. Loops of recently cut rope dangled from his ankles and wrists. His face was bruised. Yet with each step he took, strength visibly returned to him.

"There he be," Ab called. "Show me that silver!"

Case shrugged off the saddlebags that were slung over each shoulder. They hit the ground at his feet.

The clang and clatter of silver bars knocking against one another went through the men gathered below like a swig of raw whiskey. If any man noticed that only one of the saddlebags gave off the sweet sound of metal wealth, he didn't show it.

"It's here," Case called. "As soon as Conner walks out of the canyon, we'll throw the saddlebags down to you."

Silence answered him.

"Hope Conner is looking for a hole,"

Ute said calmly. "Sure as sin, it'll be a turkey shoot."

Conner kept walking, ducking and weaving through the gathered raiders. The closest cover was thirty feet away, in the piles of rubble at the base of the east side of the canyon.

"Ain't her," Kester called to Ab.

"What?" Ab demanded.

"Ain't her."

"What are you yammering about?"

"You dumb egg-sucking son of a bitch," Kester yelled distinctly. "It ain't her up there!"

The willows thrashed as Ab made his way closer to the edge of the thicket.

Conner's movements quickened.

Rifle barrels gleamed and shifted like mercury in the shadows.

"Gonna get lively right soon," Ute muttered.

"We have to give Conner every second we can."

"What if Ab has a spyglass?"

"It will give Morgan a dandy target."

Apparently Ab thought so, too. The willow thicket shifted again, but there was no flash of glass lens throwing back the light of the sun.

"You up there," Ab yelled. "Take off

574

your hat and let down your hair!"

"On three," Case murmured.

Slowly he lifted his hat.

"Shee-it!" Ab snarled.

"One," Case said softly.

"Not you!" Ab yelled.

"Two."

"The other one!"

"Over here," Sarah yelled. "Is this what you're looking for?"

The raiders spun around and looked up toward the south wall of the canyon. Sarah's hair burned like a second sunrise among the ancient ruins.

But even more compelling were the polished *reales* pouring like a musical silver waterfall into the canyon from her upended saddlebags.

Moody's raiders ran toward the coins.

Case and Ute hit the ground, grabbing for their rifles as they fell.

Conner jumped the nearest raider, grabbed his six-gun, and started firing.

The Culpeppers began shooting from cover.

Rifle fire exploded from all directions in the canyon. The first to die were Moody's men, shot in the back by Culpeppers before they even reached the dazzling waterfall of silver that had blinded them to danger.

Bullets whined wildly off the east rim as Culpeppers turned their fire on Case and Ute. Chips of rock and grit stung both men while they snaked along on their bellies, trying to find both cover and a good place to fire back at the raiders.

"Damn," Ute said, spitting out rock dust. "Them boys is good shooters."

Another rifle opened up. The shots were spaced, methodical, as cold as the wind.

"Hunter," Case said. "Probably covering Conner."

Counting shots, Case eased up to the canyon rim. When he knew his brother had only a few rounds left, he started shooting. As Hunter had, Case swept the valley with systematic fire, pinning Culpeppers down while Conner retreated.

A shotgun boomed once, then again, shredding the willows where Ab and the other Culpeppers had taken cover. Moments later, the shotgun boomed twice more.

Conner didn't wait for a better opportunity. He ran for the brush and vanished like the hunter he was.

The shotgun fired again, keeping the Culpeppers hugging the ground.

"That's my gal," Ute said, grinning over his rifle barrel. "Taught her how to reload quick as a flea jumping."

"Lola?"

"Sarah. Bet them Culpeppers is praying for deliverance right now."

"One way or another, they'll get it."

Ute laughed, then leveled his rifle at a piece of brush that moved when it shouldn't have.

"Hell is gonna be a busy place tonight," the old outlaw said, sighting down the barrel.

Case had seen the same movement Ute had. Both men shot into the brush.

Nothing moved there again.

The sun soared above the edge of the plateau, spilling golden light throughout the canyon floor below. Gunsmoke turned blue and then gray as it rose toward the rim.

Gradually the shooting died into silence. Case put his hat on his rifle barrel and poked it out over the canyon.

Shots from the willows sent the hat spinning away.

Rifles and shotguns answered in a deadly hail that lasted until everyone was forced to reload.

No answering fire came from the willows.

Silence expanded, filling the canyon with an almost unbearable pressure.

A horned lark called from below. Case answered. So did Morgan.

Nothing moved in the willows.

Ute gave a hawk's piercing cry. An answer came from the canyon floor where Conner had taken cover. Another answer came from the ancient trail down to the springs where Lola was.

No answer came from the ruins.

"Sarah!" Case called.

"*Sarah!*" Conner yelled.

He came out of cover at a run, yelling his sister's name.

A shot rang out from the willows.

Conner stumbled and fell out of sight again in the brush. From the ruins came a scream that was Conner's name.

Sarah, Case thought. *Thank God!*

He was the first one to fire into the willows where the shot had come from, but he wasn't the last. Unnatural thunder rolled through the canyon until Hunter's shrill whistle cut the air.

The shooting stopped.

Case uncocked his rifle and began shoving cartridges into the magazine.

Reluctantly, Ute lowered his rifle.

"You sure they're done for?" the outlaw asked.

"Hunter and Morgan are going through the brush right now. If it isn't over, it will be soon."

"Hope Conner ain't hurt bad. Sarah sure sets store by that boy."

"I know."

Grimly Case shoved another bullet into the magazine, filling it against a need he hoped wouldn't come.

It seemed a very long time before the call of a horned lark lifted above the valley once more.

Hunter walked out into an opening in the brush and looked up at the east rim toward his brother.

"It's over," Hunter called to Case.

"All of them?"

"Every last one."

Slowly Case stood. He pulled a worn "Wanted Dead or Alive" poster from his jacket. Only a few Culpepper names remained.

He tore the poster into scraps the size of *reales* and flung them over the cliff. They turned in the rich light and floated as slowly as ashes onto the canyon floor.

I hope you rest easier now, Ted and Emily. God knows the living will.

24

With a startled cry, Sarah grabbed her brother's shoulders to balance herself as he lifted her off her feet.

"Conner Lawson, no sooner do I bandage you than you do something to start the bleeding all over again," she said. "I should have left you for the Culpeppers!"

"But you didn't leave me," he said, grinning. "You rescued me because I'm your one and only brother and you love me more than a fortune in silver."

Laughing, he lifted her even higher and whirled her around the cabin, barely avoiding upsetting the two chairs and small table. If the ache of bandaged wounds in his left leg and arm bothered him, he certainly didn't show it.

For Conner the exuberance of being alive hadn't worn off in the hours since he and Sarah had ridden into the ranch yard leading mustangs laden with silver. Despite the circles under his eyes, the colorful bruises on his forehead, and two chunks taken out of his hide by bullets, he was overflowing with energy.

Smiling, Sarah put her hands on either side of her brother's face. Beneath her palms she felt the subtle roughening of his skin that spoke of the man he was becoming. Bittersweet pleasure twisted through her. She looked into clear, deep green eyes that reminded her so much of their father that her heart ached.

"Listen to me, Conner. Please. Take your half of the silver and go East. With an education, you can travel anywhere, do anything, *be* anything."

The smile left her brother's face. Gently he lowered Sarah to the floor and returned her searching look.

"I know," he said. "And in a few years, I might. But first I want to get the ranch to a stage where it will feed and shelter you no matter what."

"My half of the silver will do that."

Conner gave her an odd look, as though he had been expecting a different answer. His next words told her what that answer was.

"What about Case?" he asked bluntly. "You love him, don't you?"

Sarah wanted to tell Conner that it

was none of his business. Unfortunately, it was. He and Case had more in common than her brother guessed.

They both owned half of Lost River ranch.

Somehow she had to make her brother understand why the man she loved didn't love her. She didn't want Conner and Case to become enemies over her.

"Yes, I love him," she said. "But my love alone isn't enough."

"Hell, he must love you or he wouldn't, uh, well, *hell.*"

The smile she gave her brother was as painful as her thoughts.

"It's not like that for a man," she said simply.

"What kind of man would —" Conner began angrily.

"A good man," she interrupted. "A gentle man. A man who healed the wounds left by my past. A man whose own past left him afraid to love."

"Case isn't afraid of anything."

"Unwilling, then. Or unable. It doesn't matter. All that matters is that Case doesn't love me."

"How can anyone not love you?"

Softly, helplessly, Sarah laughed

when she would rather have cried. Then she hugged her brother very hard.

"It's all right," she said. "Truly, Conner. Don't be angry with Case. He has given me more than any other man, more than I ever believed a man had to give to a woman."

Conner's arms closed around her, surprising her with their strength and fierce protectiveness.

"Money doesn't last," he said finally. "The land does. Once I build up the ranch, you'll never want for anything. You'll be as free as those hawks you love."

"That's the same thing I want for you."

"For me freedom is here, not in some Eastern school."

If Sarah had seen the least hesitation in her brother's eyes, she would have argued.

But there was none.

The time for argument and persuasion was over. Whatever had been left of the child in her younger brother had died during his night of captivity and the gunfight that followed.

Conner was no longer a boy. He was a man and he had made up his mind.

With a long, shivering sigh of acceptance, Sarah stood on tiptoe to kiss her brother's cheek.

"All right," she said. "It's your choice to make, not mine."

He returned the kiss as gently as it had been given.

"Thank you," he said.

"So quiet?" she asked huskily. "No throwing your hat in the air and crowing your victory?"

"Yesterday I might have. But not today. Today it's enough just to be alive. After the Culpeppers jumped me, I didn't expect to see another dawn."

A grim look settled on Conner's face. Up to this moment, neither he nor his sister had talked about the long night or the battle that followed. They had simply taken the silver bullion back to the ranch and buried it even as Case and his brother were burying Culpeppers in Spring Canyon.

Despite a bullet wound in his arm, Morgan had insisted on staying to help with the grim work, declaring it a task he had long looked forward to. Even Lola had insisted on staying. She said she wouldn't believe Ab was dead until she put pebbles on his eyelids and shoveled dirt into his grave.

"What ever possessed you to go to that overlook in the first place?" Sarah asked.

"Same thing that possessed Hunter when he went there, and you when you sent Lola there. Next to the ruins, that overlook is the best place to spy on Spring Canyon. Or to shoot into it."

"You shouldn't have gone alone."

"It's a mistake I won't make twice." Conner grinned unexpectedly. "But I would like to have been there when Lola found Hunter."

"She didn't. Not exactly. She found a dead Culpepper and figured that whoever was on the overlook now was either Morgan or Hunter."

"I never even saw Morgan until he shot that one-armed outlaw who was fixing to shoot me in the back," Conner said, shaking his head. "Fastest draw I ever saw."

"Morgan was in the canyon all night, watching out for you."

"I owe him," Conner said simply.

"I told him to take all the *reales* I poured into the canyon."

"Good."

Sarah gave another shivering sigh

and touched her brother's face as though she still had difficulty believing he was alive.

It was worth it, she thought, *all of it. Even what is yet to come.*

"Hey, are you all right?" Conner asked, catching hold of his sister's shoulders.

"Just . . . tired." She smiled despite her pale lips. "All of a sudden. Tired."

"You should sleep. You look worn out."

From what I remember about Mother, being pregnant does that to a woman, Sarah thought ruefully. *In the first few months, she used to fall asleep every time she stopped moving.*

She said nothing aloud about her growing belief that she was carrying Case's child. She told herself it was too soon to be certain, but that was only part of the truth. The last thing she wanted was to set her brother against the very man who now owned the other half of Lost River ranch.

Conner wouldn't understand why Case didn't marry her, no matter what scars the past had left on his soul.

Sarah understood.

She had known yesterday, when she saw his eyes after they made love.

Fear, regret, anger. A raging kind of distance.

The eyes of a trapped hawk.

Her love didn't bring comfort to Case. It brought only greater turmoil.

He had healed the fears left by her past.

She hadn't been able to heal his.

Perhaps burying Emily's murderers will give Case some measure of peace.

Sarah didn't know. She knew only that her time on Lost River ranch was nearly over. Even if she had still owned half the ranch, she couldn't stay.

Don't tease me into making you pregnant. I would hate both of us for it.

She could endure anything but that. Being hated by the man she loved would be more than she could bear.

"Sis?" Conner asked, troubled. "Maybe you better lie down."

Forcing herself to smile, she looked up at her brother.

"Later," she said. "Right now I think I'll just put a pot of beans on to cook. Then maybe I'll go to Deer Canyon and watch the hawks fly."

And I'll wish all the way to my soul that I could fly with them again, in Case's arms.

But instead of going to her hawks, Sarah waited until Conner was asleep. Then she quietly began packing her clothes. When she was finished, there was plenty of room left in the two saddlebags for a few bars of silver.

As she strapped up the bags, her glance fell on the unusual joined mugs that Case had found in the ancient ruins. She picked up the tiny bit of pottery and remembered the miniature teacup and saucer Lola had found among Case's belongings.

Ah, Case, Sarah thought sadly. *If we had met before Emily died, would you have loved me?*

All that answered her was the echo of her own silent question.

She put the cup back in its little niche, caressed the ancient pottery with her fingertip once, and turned away.

It was late afternoon before everyone returned from Spring Canyon. Lola went straight to tend to her goats. The men washed up and headed for the huge pot of beans and pans of hot cornbread they knew would be waiting.

Sarah greeted each man with a smile

589

and a heaping plate of food.

"I'm really going to have to make some more chairs," Case said, holding a plate of beans as he stood near the fire. "But first I'm going to cut planks for that floor I promised Sarah."

She almost dropped the plate of beans she was handing to Morgan.

"Watch it," Morgan said, rescuing the food.

"Sorry. I'm not usually so clumsy."

"You have a right. You've been through a lot lately."

She looked into Morgan's dark, compassionate eyes and smiled wearily.

"Not as much as you or Hunter or . . ." Her voice frayed. "I don't know how to thank you."

"None needed."

"Please take those *reales*."

Morgan started to refuse as he had the other times the subject came up, but Case cut him off.

"I'd do it if I were you," he said. "That pretty girl you left behind would look more kindly on the man who set off on a cattle drive and didn't come back for nearly a year, if that selfsame man had some silver in his pockets."

Morgan's grin flashed whitely. "It's not

money my woman is looking for coming down that dusty trail back to her."

"You saying that a gold ring and a little ranch of her own wouldn't make her smile?" Case asked.

"There are other ways of making Letty smile."

Ute snorted and stood up stiffly, setting aside his already empty plate. Favoring his right knee where a ricochet had left a bruise the size of a fist, he turned to Morgan.

"Nueces," the old outlaw said, "don't you make me ride all the way to Texas just cuz you're a stiff-necked son of a bitch."

Morgan blinked and look rather warily at Ute.

"Meaning?" he drawled mildly.

"Meaning," Ute said, "that what Sarah wants, I get for her. You either take that damned silver with you or have me hunt you down in Texas with a bad temper, a loaded gun, and two saddlebags full of *reales*."

"Take the silver," Hunter advised, standing up.

"Would you?" Morgan retorted.

"If the choice is silver or Ute camping on my tail, I'll take the silver."

Morgan grinned. "Colonel, you've got yourself a deal. You take half and I take half."

"Wait, I didn't —"

"Or would you rather have me camping on *your* tail," Morgan continued, talking over Hunter.

"He's got you," Case said to his brother.

Hunter muttered something under his breath and then turned to Sarah.

"Ma'am, you have better things to do with that silver than give it away."

She shook her head.

"Conner?" Hunter asked a bit desperately.

"I always do what my sister says," he said with a wide-eyed innocence that made Ute snicker. "Just ask her."

"Hell," Hunter said.

He shot Case a glittering look, then forgot whatever he was going to say.

Case was fighting a losing battle against a smile. The sight of it amazed his brother.

"Divide up the silver," Hunter said absently to Morgan. "I'm hitting the trail at first light tomorrow. Elyssa will be wanting to know that Case is alive."

"She'll be a lot more relieved to know

that your sorry hide is whole," his brother retorted.

Hunter just grinned.

"Would it be too much trouble for you to see me to the nearest stage or rail-head?" Sarah asked.

The silence that followed her words was thick enough to sit on.

"Conner could do it, but he won't be comfortable riding a horse for a few days," she continued calmly. "Neither will Ute."

"What are you talking about?" Case demanded.

"Taking a trip."

"If it's getting the silver to a bank you're worried about, I'll haul it myself."

"Thank you. It saves me worrying about it." She turned back to Hunter. "If you want to get back to Nevada as fast as you came here, I can sleep in the saddle. I won't slow you down."

Hunter looked toward Case. Though there was no expression on his brother's face, his eyes were narrowed as though in anger or pain.

"Talk it over with Case," Hunter said. "Afterward, if you still want to ride out with me, I'll see you safely to any place you like."

"That won't be necessary," she said. "Just as far as the nearest —"

"Anywhere," Hunter interrupted. "It's the least I can do for the woman who saved my brother's life."

"I've been amply repaid for that."

"Ute, Conner, come with me," Hunter said. "We're only in the way here."

Sarah started to object, then shrugged.

"Sis?"

"Go with Ute and Hunter," she said to Conner. "I won't be far behind you."

"I'll put your saddle on one of the mules," Hunter said. "But if you need it, my brother is a fool."

She watched the three men file out, leaving her alone with the man she loved.

A man who didn't love her.

"What in hell are you thinking about?" Case asked bluntly.

"I'm going to buy land and raise horses. In California, I think. Perhaps Oregon."

"You're not making sense."

"It makes perfect sense to me. I like ranching."

He made an impatient, chopping gesture.

"You know what I mean," he said. "You have the start of a good ranch here. If you want to raise horses, Cricket is as fine a stud as you'll find west of the Mississippi."

Sarah took a hidden breath and confronted what she had hoped to avoid.

Damn Hunter anyway, she thought wearily. *What business is it of his whether Case and I have a shouting match before we part?*

"Lost River ranch isn't mine," she said.

"Half of it —"

"— belongs to you," she interrupted. "The other half belongs to Conner."

"What!"

Under other circumstances, the look of shock on Case's often expressionless face would have amused Sarah. Now it simply was painful.

"I gave Conner half the ranch after he — after Hal died," she said.

"You knew he killed your husband?"

Sarah's eyelids flinched.

"I knew only one of them came back," she said. "I thank God every day that it was Conner who survived."

"Hal was trying to pistol whip him. Conner fought back. The gun went off.

It was an accident."

She swayed and took a broken breath.

"Thank you," she whispered. "I always hoped my brother didn't kill for me. But, God help me, I was so grateful . . ."

Case stepped forward and gripped Sarah's shoulders, holding her as though he was afraid she would fall.

"Forget this nonsense about leaving," he said roughly. "Conner and I will settle for a third of the ranch each."

"No."

He blinked, then looked at her through narrowed, gray-green eyes.

The eyes that met his were the color of storm clouds. If she had looked weak a moment before, she no longer did.

"Why not?" he asked. "Conner would be the first to offer."

"Just what kind of future did you have in mind?" she asked sharply. "All the, uh, *comforts* of home and none of the responsibility?"

A dull red appeared on Case's cheekbones above his beard. He let go of her and stepped away as though he had been burned.

"I didn't mean it that way," he said.

"What did you mean?"

He raked his fingers through his hair in a gesture of frustration that made Sarah's heart turn over with a bitter-sweet combination of love and loss.

But nothing of her feelings showed on her face.

"I don't want you to leave," he said.

"Put what you want in one hand and spit in the other and see which fills up first," she suggested ironically.

"*Damnation.* You aren't listening to me!"

"That's because you aren't thinking very clearly."

"And you are?" he retorted.

"Yes. You don't want marriage, be-cause marriage means children."

His breath came in hard.

"You don't want an affair," she con-tinued, "because sooner or later I'll get pregnant."

Case went still.

"We can't just pretend we were never lovers," she said. "At least I can't. What you give to me is . . . the flight of a hawk. I couldn't bear being so close to that kind of ecstasy and yet having it always beyond my reach."

"Sarah," he whispered.

Hoping against hope, she waited.

He said no more.

Nor did he need to. The words he had once said were burned in her memory: *I don't have love left in me. I don't want it. I'll never again love anything that can die.*

"Now you understand why I can't stay," she said, turning away. "I can live with not being loved by you, but I couldn't bear your hatred. Tell Hunter I'm ready to leave right now."

"To hell with Hunter," he said curtly. "What about Conner?"

"You were right about him. He doesn't want to go back East to school."

Case hissed a bitter word between his teeth. "That's not what I meant."

"My brother won't be surprised," Sarah said. "He knows you don't love me."

"I was talking about the fact that Conner is still a boy," he said tightly. "He needs you."

"He isn't a boy. You know that better than I do. You were the one to point it out to me. What he needs is less apron strings, not more. Which you also pointed out to me, as I recall."

"You're trying to trap me," he said savagely.

"No. I'm letting you go."

Sarah turned back and opened her hands as though to show Case that there was nothing to hold him.

Yet his eyes were wild.

The eyes of a captive hawk.

"Fly away," she whispered. "You're free."

There was another harsh word, another raking of fingers through thick black hair.

Then he spun around and yanked open the cabin door.

"Do what you like," he said. "It doesn't matter to me."

The door slammed shut behind him.

Hunter, Ute, and Conner were standing about a hundred feet away. The sky on the western horizon was the pale yellow of winter butter.

Overhead it was a dark, dark blue that was as cold and empty as Case felt.

Conner started to say something as Case stalked by.

"Later," Hunter said clearly. "Right now my brother is looking for a fight. Let him take it out on himself. He's the one who has it coming."

Case spun toward Hunter. "Just what does that mean?"

"I'll tell you the same thing you told me a few months back. Go talk to your horse's butt. It has more sense than you do."

"That's more sense than all of you put together have," Case snarled.

Hunter smiled.

Case took an eager, gliding step toward his brother, then stopped.

"That's right," Hunter said, nodding. "Hammering on me won't change anything. Hell's fire, if I thought a good thumping would change you, we'd be rolling around in the dirt right now. But it won't."

The only answer Case gave was a whistle whose shrill edge sliced the night. A few moments later Cricket trotted up.

He didn't bother with a saddle or a bridle. He simply swung up on the horse and rode off into the descending night.

Around him cottonwoods lifted their bare branches, embracing the icy grip of winter. The pattern of pure black traced against the darkening sky was as beautiful as a hawk soaring.

The air was cold, clean, infused with time and distance and silence. Beyond the river, cliffs rose in ebony ranks, shouldering the increasing night with massive ease.

Half of this is mine, Case thought.

He waited, but no pleasure came from the knowledge that he owned half of the wild land. The cost of possessing it was higher than he had guessed.

Sarah loved the land as much as he did. Her words kept echoing through his mind.

Lost River ranch is all I want of the world. Being here suits me all the way to my soul.

Yet she was leaving it.

Because of him.

Blindly Case rode farther into the night. Time lost all meaning. Only he was alive. He and the night.

He and the night and a torment he could neither endure nor ignore.

Moonlight slid along the surface of Lost River in silver swirls that reminded him of Sarah's eyes, mystery and light combined. The liquid murmur of the water was like her hushed laughter when they lay together in the warm, tangled aftermath of passion.

He would die remembering her soft confession whispered against the very flesh she had once feared.

I love you, Case.

Emotion splintered through him, shaking him.

No, he thought harshly. *I can't go through it again, the love and the loss. That's what pain is for, to teach you how to avoid more pain in the future.*

But not for Sarah. Pain, like pleasure, was for her simply part of being alive.

Sarah, who was a fire in the center of his icy life. Without her there would be no fire.

Only winter.

Anguish twisted inside Case, a pain so deep that he couldn't breathe. It was like being pulled apart.

No!

This can't be. It simply can't be!

Yet it was.

The agony was a living thing inside him, devouring him. He hadn't felt such torment since he rocked his dead niece in his arms and knew that nothing within his power could change what had happened.

He hadn't wept then.

He wept now.

* * *

Sarah didn't want to wake up. Being awake meant that it was morning, and morning meant that she would be on the trail, riding away from everything she loved.

She whimpered and moved restlessly, trying to evade the dawn that even in her sleep she knew must come.

Tender kisses soothed her struggles. Strong arms held her, gentling her. Warmth radiated through her as though from a nearby fire.

Sighing, she reached out for the dream she needed more than her own heartbeat. She wrapped the heat around her like a blanket against the approaching chill of dawn.

The tip of a warm tongue traced her lips. She smiled and savored the sensual dream.

Just a dream.

A dream of sunlight caressing me. Sunlight and —

"Case!"

Sarah sat bolt upright. The oil lamp was still burning on the table, but the fire had gone out.

She was naked, which only added to her confusion.

"I fell asleep sitting at the table," she said, dazed.

A long arm snaked out of the blankets and pulled her back into the warmth.

"I carried you to bed," he whispered.

He pulled her against his body. Skin smoothed over skin. Pleasure was a sweet fire shivering through her.

"I was dressed," she said, still trying to understand.

"I undressed you."

Teeth nibbled delicately at her earlobe. Her breath caught and her thoughts scattered.

"I'm still dreaming," she whispered.

It explained everything.

He laughed and kissed the pulse beating in her neck. The caresses continued down her neck to her breasts. So did the soft laughter.

"Now I know I'm dreaming," she said sleepily.

"Why?"

"You only laugh in my dreams."

"You'll get used to it."

He kissed the tip of first one breast, then the other. Smiling, he watched her change with each brushing caress of his beard.

Eyes closed, she stretched languidly,

lifting herself against his smile. Then she sighed and gave herself completely to the wonderful dream.

"Sarah?"

"Don't wake me up. I don't ever want to wake up."

Long, strong fingers slid down her belly and traced the soft skin between her thighs.

"Some things are better when you're awake," he said.

Her only answer was a movement that opened her to his touch. He caressed her hot, sleek flesh. Her answering passion licked over him like molten silver.

His breath stopped. Then he lowered himself between her legs and took her with deep certainty, giving himself in turn. He moved unhurriedly, thoroughly. With dreamlike slowness the silky contractions began in her and spread to him, undoing him completely.

It was a long time before Case had enough breath to speak.

"We keep this up," he whispered, "and you're going to get pregnant for sure."

Eyes closed, Sarah shook her head languidly, clinging to the wonderful dream.

"Can't," she murmured.

"Why not?"

"Already am."

"What?"

Her eyes flew open. "Oh, God. It really wasn't a dream, was it?"

He stared at her.

"Are you sure?" he demanded.

"Almost. I'm so darned sleepy all the time, just like my mother was."

A long shudder racked Case's strong body. Slowly he lowered his face to her breasts.

Her heart turned over when she felt the heat of his tears and his laughter combined.

"You make me whole," he said huskily.

She went still. Suddenly she slid her fingers into his hair and lifted his head until she could see his eyes.

"What did you say?" she whispered.

He smiled.

Sudden tears starred her long eyelashes and made her eyes a silver mystery.

"I thought it was just the land calling to me, sinking into me," he said. "But it was you. It was always you. A fire in winter burning just for me."

"Case," she whispered.

He bent and brushed his lips over hers.

"I love you, Sarah. And the only place you're going tomorrow is to the nearest preacher."

She kissed him.

"No arguments?" he asked.

"Why would I argue with the man I love? Especially when he's making sense for once."

Smiling, Case drew Sarah close and felt her love in the warmth of her lips against his chest.

That was the way he fell asleep.

Smiling.

Epilogue

Emily Jane Maxwell was born in autumn, when cottonwood leaves turned the color of candle flames against the windswept sky. Case fashioned her cradle from the same golden wood he had cut to build a new house for his growing family. Emily's first memory was of her father's laughter as he lifted her toward the ceiling and spun her gently around.

In the years that followed, more children came to Case and Sarah. Two more girls with deft hands and sharp tongues. Three tall boys who took endless delight in alternately teasing and protecting their sisters.

Conner left his nieces and nephews long enough to get the education that Sarah had wanted for him. He returned to Lost River ranch with a bride. In time the valley was filled with the quick arguments and ringing laughter of more children.

Through all the natural sorrows and

joys of living, Case and Sarah's love increased. Their union was a fire in all seasons, gentle and fierce, intense and serene, a radiance that warmed and gave life to everything it touched.